Five
Talents

Yennaedo Y. Balloo

FOR MY UNCLE BUGGY

Thank you for showing me the humor in wisdom, the wisdom in humor, and most of all that the Creator of the universe has a better sense of humor any of us, so we may as well have a laugh or two while we're here.

ACKNOWLEDGMENTS

I'd like to thank my parents for their continued support- you both go above and beyond what parenthood requires in your love and confidence in me.

Thanks as well to the friends, readers, and editors who make sitting at my desk joyful work. In particular, my gratitude goes out to:

My editorial friend, Alana
My collegiate friend, Graves
My bossy friend, Gerard
My sassy friend, Alexandra
My motherly friend, Sarah
My lawyerly friend, Andrew
My newphewly friend, Cris
My readerly friends, Catrina and Beverly
&
My friend of serendipity, Nathalie

Once more, and always, thanks go to the Author of all creation for the inspiration to tell this story.

There is no reason why good cannot triumph as often as evil. The triumph of anything is a matter of organization. If there are such things as angels, I hope that are organized along the lines of the Mafia.

-Kurt Vonnegut, Jr. *The Sirens of Titan*

GAST

Men of lofty ambition aspire to offices that loom high over the masses below. Gast liked his office to be on the second story so he could look closely upon the humanity he needed to know for his work.

Gast slid his hands down the silk-lined pockets of his tailored trousers, pinning the fans of his open charcoal jacket to his side with his forearms. He grinned, listening to the voice in the headset on one ear while his other ear twitched at the susurrus coming from the street below.

Gast was in a modern mood, so today his office was an open layout with his computer and phone set on a sliding shelf at chest height to his right. Minimalist white leather chairs formed a loose circle behind him, and a sleek mini bar was the only other furnishing under the silver-plated chandelier looming over his head.

When he knew he was closing a big deal, Gast liked the focus this layout inspired. When he was doing more ground work such as cold calling potential souls looking to make a deal and planting the seeds of temptation, he went more art deco with bolder lines and colors.

He took a deep breath. She was asking the question every meat sack asked just before they took a deal for with a Devil for their soul.[1] "You're sure you can make me a famous rapper?"

---

[1] Humans are regarded by Hell as being the dour and odious spirits occupying the fleshy goodness of a physical body. The souls being of little consequence except as a squatter on the corporeal real estate, Demons refer to humans by the epithet of meat sack.

Gast grinned toothily and relaxed. Poor girl, he thought to himself. Classic case of being careful what you wish for. Gast relished that she'd asked to be a famous rapper but not to be famous for rapping. "Miss Banks, a charlatan wizard would hesitate to answer as he weighs his doubts in his mind."

Gast paused. The palpable awe he felt in the hushed silence was not lost on him. "But I am no man. I am Gast. Devil of the House of Wrath. Not only can I deliver you the fame you desire. I shall."

Gast turned on the heel of his Italian leather shoes and faced the Manet portrait he had hung on his far wall for the day. "All you have to do is say the word."

The woman agreed. They always did at this point. No one picked up the phone to review a contract he'd offered if they weren't already planning to accept. He was at his computer, logging the sale as the words of acceptance left her mouth.

Gast clapped his hands together. "Great! We'll get started immediately! Your deal comes with full management of your social media, plus you get the enticing looks enchantment so you'll always be well dressed wherever you go." Gast confirmed the soul acquisition internally with accounts receivable, then started on a delivery request with an Imp in the courier services department.

"Some extra things to keep in mind: TMZ is ours, so if you see any of those guys, just know they're part of the package."

"Right, I'll be sure to say hello."

Gast tutted. "Oh, no, no, no. Tell them to fuck off, eat shit, or whatever. We want them to keep you in the tabloids. No one famous gets airtime for being polite. Well, except Tom Hanks." Gast glared at the sky out the expansive window. "That pristine-mannered prick."

The woman's laugh tumbled out and snapped him from his reverie. "Okay, Ms. Banks, your studio sessions and other appearances will be loaded on the phone one of my Imps will be running over." Gast heard a doorbell through his headset. The Imps that ran deliveries were much better ever since they'd re-organized to have deliveries managed by Wrath and Pride rather than by Sloth.

Whoever's brilliant idea it was back in the nineteenth century to have Imps from Sloth handling deliveries were single-handedly responsible for the age of romanticism being able to burst onto the scene. Some crafty work, a steady nurturing of nationalist xenophobia, and a few wars, and Hell had turned things back on course by the twentieth century. Ever since that fiasco, Sloth's Imps had been relegated entirely to catering.[2]

"That phone has your calendar, which for the first month you need to follow to a T. It should be easy thanks to the enticing looks bonus. You don't ever need to shower or change. You'll always arrive as fresh and well-dressed as you need to be to turn heads. Your social media will be run by us, and after that who cares whether you're on time or not? You'll be famous. Do what you want."

Gast confirmed that her Instagram was already up to a hundred thousand followers and increasing by the

---

[2] Gluttony might seem a more natural fit for this, however they could never be trusted to leave behind any of the food they prepared for the events. While Sloth's quality of cuisine generally left much to be desired, at the very least you could always count on hastily warmed Hot Pockets to be waiting on a platter.

second. The feed had been updated with an almost nude selfie from the woman's cloud that the Imp had just delivered. Gast told himself to give whichever Imp that was a commendation for their initiative.

Gast was interrupted by another question he was used to receiving. "No, the looks enchantment is only applied to clothing. We don't change appearances. We used to do that more back in the '80s, but ever since Michael Jackson, if you change your looks too much, too fast, you become a sideshow. These days, everyone's getting plastic surgery, so do it if you want, but in my professional experience? Being well dressed is enough.

"Justin Timberlake, Steve Buscemi, Taylor Swift? Meh in the looks department, but they can dress—" He paused, listened to her inquiry, and rolled his eyes. "No, we don't have deals with them, but that's precisely my point."

Gast kicked himself. It was the one thing that could flub a deal, and he huffed a breath of relief that her contract was already locked in. Reminding people, especially desperate people, that fame and everything they wanted was possible without the shortcut Hell offered was usually a surefire way to get the door slammed in your face—especially if the target had actual talent. Gast's real trophies were the ones who very well could accomplish what they wanted but were too lazy, selfish, and arrogant to try it without his guarantee.

The consideration made him scribble a quick note to confirm a certain pop star's latest mug shot had reached his boys at the TMZ office and that there would be corresponding tweets to rile the fanbase.

The woman squealed with joy at having seen the effect of the looks enchantment for the first time. She'd walked from her apartment in jeans and a white t-shirt and emerged onto Venice Boulevard in a leather jacket, halter top, designer jeans, and Manolo Blahniks. She squealed the details gleefully in Gast's ear.

Gast hollowly echoed her zeal and reminded her to keep the Hell phone handy. "It's how you can reach me, and it's how I'll reach you."

When he finally got off the phone, Gast collapsed into a chair he manifested just as he fell into it, and his office took on a more traditional executive appearance of mahogany desk and leather furnishings amid walls lined with floor to ceiling bookshelves. "Another sale closed," he murmured to himself and sat back, staring blankly at his monitor.

Gast reviewed his sales record; at least a soul a day for the past ten years. Five times better than the closest competing Devil in his or the other six orders. He regarded the numbers and the robotic consistency of them. They didn't say anything to him or offer any congratulations. An email came in from Hell's Muse on retainer, drawing his attention back to the screen.

With a resolute intake of breath, he sat up and set to work on his management of another deal he'd launched just the week before. He'd promised a young intern at the *LA Weekly* fame as a writer. Gast shook his head and snorted. Who wants to be a writer these days?

He had tried selling something glitzier at first: "How about a book of photographs? Like one of those Tumblr collection things?" Gast loved the "Hungover Owls." On the rare occasion he allowed a hangover to take him even briefly, he really identified with those round-eyed little buggers. But no, Matt Reade wanted to be a writer—an essayist and novelist in particular.

The kid had talent. He could probably do half of the writing he wanted Hell to do for him were it not for the limitations on the meat sacks needing sleep, food, and to die- not to mention all the other stuff they let get in the way. Gast skimmed the article the Muse, Eurydice had written up.[3]

Matt's deal had been planned by Gast for him to climb the ranks of the *LA Weekly*, get a following of the hipster savant that elevated Matt's kind to fame in this town, and then have him jump into an independent career.

Gast used his powers to replace another intern's article with the article he had just received from Eurydice, then did a quick check. Matt wasn't anywhere near the *LA Weekly* office. He had stopped going in altogether after signing his contract with Gast a month ago. Matt was lounging by the pool on the rooftop of the Standard Hotel, drinking a Bloody Mary.

Gast scanned the copy that would go to the printers that day, trying to find the article he was using Hell's powers to replace. It was a theater preview of Wicked, which was premiering that coming weekend at the Pantages Theater, written by the other intern, Calvin Graves. Gast did the replacement and put in the command for memory wipes on the editors. Closing off the command prompt, he refreshed the *LA Weekly* website. The Wicked review was on the front page, Matt

---

[3] Following the Renaissance, the Muses of the Greek pantheon found little enjoyment of freelancing and began looking for more gainful career paths. While her sisters had all chosen different paths, Hell had managed to sign a multi-century contract with one, Eurydice, as their permanent Muse to deliver on contracts that were artistic nature. As with most jobs, Hell had added social media management, press releases, speech writing for executives, and editing Lucifer's various screenplay specs to her exhaustive list of responsibilities.

Reade's name was now in the byline.

A thought tugged at Gast as he was leaning back satisfactorily at his work. He brought up his sent messages and noticed that he had left the intern, Calvin, off the memory wipe request he had just sent. Gast thought about adding a second request, but the Imps who handled these things were testy about getting corrections.

Gast shrugged and laced his hands behind his head. So the kid realizes his article was supposed to be printed and no one but him remembers it? Worst case is he tries to prove his article ever existed and goes insane in the process. Best case? He tries to murder Matt in raving lunatic vengeance, making Matt famous for his writing, per the contract.

"Check and mate," Gast muttered to himself.

HELL'S CORPORATE STRUCTURE

Unlike Heaven, which has been perfect from its very conception, Hell evolves alongside the evils of man and society. Over the ages, Hell has gone from chaotic myriad of barbaric brutes to a loose union of feudal clans, caste orders of nobility and lesser aristocracies, and that greatest of evils among the wicked and ignorant: a populist democracy.

Since the turn of the twentieth century, Hell has maintained the hierarchy of a private corporation. Gast, Devil of the order of Wrath, liked the most recent order. Even though many Devils had fooled themselves by saying so of previous structures, he felt this one would stick around for the long haul even if, unlike most of the rest of Hell, he was sure that there was only one ending they were barreling towards in futility.

Through whatever structural changes and fluctuations of CEO strategy, Hell has always been concerned with its one-upmanship of Heaven in claiming souls. At the base level of operations, formless demons work ethereally through whispers to distract, tempt, and sway human beings away from the Creator. In the modern hellish corporation, they are R&D, marketing, and customer service.

Imps are demons inhabiting lesser bodies who can interact with the physical world. Their bodies, having been crafted by Lucifer, are grotesqueries. While many may have forms that are functional, logical, or even (to some human perceptions) pretty, their curse and truth is that none of them are what Lucifer actually intended them to be, despite what he may claim.

Much like your friend that one time when he was smashed at the party and made that wicked beer pong shot off the wall, a person's hat, and into a cup, neither he nor Lucifer "totally meant to do that." As such, Imps are relegated to working primarily as couriers and handling catering for Hell's employee events. Think of your first internship out of college.

From Directors up to Executive Management, Devils are those Demons who have proven their ambition, cunning, and personification of the order of their calling: Greed, Lust, Wrath, Sloth, Gluttony, Pride, or Envy. They have been granted the empty husk of a human being whose soul has vacated the vessel. These bodies are those claimed along with the souls of people who had made a deal with Hell once they inevitably died. Devils given these bodies are also privy to a host of other powers to sway humans in the performance of their primary function: Soul Acquisitions.

Since the turn of the twentieth century, Gast has been

the highest producing Devil in soul claiming deals of his or any other order.

According to Aba Don, Executive Director of Wrath and lead guitarist of Hell's House Band (and Gast's boss), Gast is the worst at his job of any Devil in his or any other order.

SALLY

Salvatore "Sally" Degneri rolled a pinch of herbs to release their flavor and scent, then sprinkled them into his gravy, still lightly steaming from the stove. He lowered the heat, stirred it slowly a pair of times, and lifted the sauce pot to pour the gravy over his fresh biscuits.

He smiled at the biscuits and its companion dishes before he set them on the bussing tray to carry the whole order for the table. He considered taking a photo of them for a new menu image but shook the thought despondently from his head. What's the point of updating the damned menu?

He admonished himself for slipping into that kind of thinking before he walked out of the kitchen with the tray balanced on his shoulder into the crook of his neck. His free hand opened the swinging kitchen door that he smoothly spun around.

He set the tray on the corner of the largest table in the dining room, which was the only one that was ever used. Sally restrained himself from looking sullen to see, once more, that today he was only serving four. Yet another day he'd been kept from opening the restaurant because Benjamin "Benny" O'Houlihan had "business" to conduct.

Sally gave the slightest of nods to Benny and his

cohorts, Maury O'Brien and Claudio Donaghy. The fourth player at the table was new, and Sally got the barest of croaks out to try to introduce himself before Benny spoke up. "Food's here! Eat up, you piece of shit, and by the time you finish eating, you'd better have an explanation for how the product we asked you to hold got so stepped on."

Sally set the dishes on the table then slunk aside to sit at one of the nearby tables. He knew they wouldn't need anything else, but he couldn't help but stay in the hopes he'd hear how the meal was. Benny slammed a fist on the table. "Well? Eat up! Sally went to all this trouble. Enjoy the meal, and we'll talk about what happened to the— Claudio, how much did we leave him with?"

"Forty kilos of pure boss." Sally winced at Claudio's raspy voice. Sally's skin crawled at how much Claudio's tone, sharp nose, and skulky posture reminded him of a rat. It was the natural response of the chef in him, he supposed, and also because Claudio was a sleaze who regularly hit on Sally's wait staff. Well, waiter. I'd have to have more than one for it to be a staff, and of course she isn't even here for the one service we'll have today.

"Forty kilos and pure. Pure, Toddy." Benny looked across the table at Maury, the bulky muscle of the group, even though the muscle was packed for shipping under a hundred pounds of marshmallow fluff. "And how pure was it today?"

"Fifty percent, boss." Maury answered in his thick Bronx accent while eyeing the food Toddy was now timidly serving himself.

"Fifty." Benny looked up theatrically, running his hand over his fiery beard. "So that means twenty kilos disappeared."

Toddy shoveled a biscuit clumsily onto the plate

before him and began to stammer protest. "Now wait, it was all—"

Benny slapped Toddy so hard on the back of his head that when Toddy raised his face he had a beige speck of the gravy on the tip of his nose. Sally almost laughed but was on the edge of the seat waiting for Toddy to pick up the fork.

"Let's say the coke we checked was the right purity, instead of the fifty percent Claudio tested." Benny grabbed Toddy by the chest of his shirt and roared while shaking the lithe hipster. "There was still ten kilos missing!"

Claudio shook his head in disbelief. "What dumbass steals that much coke but also forgets to cut it back to the amount he originally got left with?" Claudio put a finger to his nose and made a quick sniffing noise at Maury. The pair snickered.

"Hey, I'm an organic-prolacto vegan! I was totally going to pay you guys back!"

Benny clenched his eyes and pinched the bridge of his nose. "Toddy, you understand how much a pound of pure costs?"

"Yeah! I've got a brew of my vanilla lavender milk stout wrapping up and two more batches on back order. That'll cover the ten kilos I owe you!"

Benny looked around the table, then over at Sally, who did not meet his eyes. "You believe this guy? He steals twenty-five kilos of pure and tries to tell me he only owes me what he forgot to add back in the cut?"

Benny wheeled on Toddy again, grabbing him by the V-neck of his shirt. "Listen here, you little hipster shit. You owe me for forty because my buyer is only interested in uncut product."

Drops of sweat beaded from Toddy's brow down his

nose and through his patchily bearded cheeks. "Well listen, it's not gone. That's what I'm trying to explain." Toddy stammered while straightening his turquoise thick-framed glasses as Benny released him.

Benny settled back and growled quietly before he urged, "Go on. Where do we get it?"

"I told you, I'm an organic prolacto vegan. Me and my boys don't touch that kind of processed stuff. But we knew where it would sell." Benny looked across the table and raised his eyebrows slightly, crossing his arms and sitting back interestedly. He nodded for Toddy to continue. "Like I said, the brew I've got? The brew that's back ordered for the next, like, three batches?"

Toddy held his hands out as if it were obvious, but he was met by blank stares, even from Sally. "Guys, I used it in the brew." A terse silence awaited, and Toddy sought desperately for understanding. "Guys, think about it. Why's Coca Cola so popular? You know they're allowed to put coca leaf into their soda? Think how addictive it is!"

"You put pure Colombian cocaine into your craft beer to get people hooked on it like Coca Cola? Here I thought it was all that refined sugar!"

"Well, you're right, that high fructose corn syrup is its own kind of crack." Toddy forced a nervous chuckle at his own quip, trying to enjoy the fraternity he was fostering with the mafioso.

To Toddy's visible relief, Benny laughed hoarsely and slapped his knee, then cuffed Toddy genially on the shoulder. "Holy shit, Toddy, here I thought you were a junkie I'd have to make an example of. Turns out you've got brains and balls. Eat up, kid!" Benny took one of the dishes and shoveled some food onto the plate for himself. Maury and Claudio finally made similar motions for the other plates.

Sally was perplexed at Benny's reaction but didn't dwell on the turn of events. Toddy pressed his fork into the biscuit to cut a portion of it and speared the morsel over his lips. Toddy chewed, and Sally watched in rapt attention as Toddy rolled Sally's food over his taste buds. Toddy's eyes went wide and bright, then suddenly dimmed behind a splash of red.

Benny had waited until Toddy was chewing the food to whip a switchblade from his pocket and cut the boy's throat. Sally was on his feet in such sudden shock that the large brown tray clattered to the tiled floor from his lap as he screamed, "What the shit!"

Toddy's eyes rolled back. He gurgled amid the blood spilling from his throat, the mouthful of barely chewed biscuit tumbling out and down his chest before his head slumped and he fell from the chair, lifeless. Benny grimaced at the dying hipster beneath him. "You had to know he had it coming."

"What the shit!" Sally looked in wide eyed terror at Claudio, who regarded his blood stained shirt with revulsion. Claudio's clothes and all the plates on the table were splattered with blood. "Artisinal vanilla flower beer? Come on, Sally, we should have killed him just for that. Far less the coke thing."

Maury shuffled to stand over Toddy's blood spattered body. "I dunno, the beer sounds pretty tasty."

"Guys." Sally paused a moment panting, while forcefully shaking an arm at Toddy's now-pallored corpse. "What. The. Shit!"

Benny misread the intent of the inquiry. "We'll handle the body, Sally. Claudio, run down to Ralph's and get some Clorox and help Sally mop up." Benny peeled a bill from the wad he produced from his slacks.

Claudio nodded dutifully as Maury came back from the kitchen with a fistful of garbage bags. Sally watched as they wrapped up Toddy's body, then Benny and Maury carried it toward the kitchen. He repeated once more in horror, "What the shit!"

Maury backed through the doorway first and Benny stopped to intone threateningly, "Don't mention it to the health inspector, or anyone else. Cool it or we'll have another problem to clean up." Benny followed Maury through the kitchen to the car out back in the alley.

Sally slumped back into the chair and stared at the smeared streaks and puddles of blood on his white floor and muttered again, "What the shit?" before he groaned, "What the hell am I supposed to do with the beignets I made?"

FROM HELL'S CORPORATE HANDBOOK: ON SEXUAL HARASSMENT

Sexual harassment is looked down upon when it gets in the way of Hell getting souls. If it happens on your own time and between assignments, keep it to yourself. No one like a tattle tale and snitches get stitches. Hell's official policies on sexual harassment are broken down in the following categories of demonic order and house of sin.

Please refer to the following guide before completing form UWHR-WC13 to ensure that your complaint will not just be tossed in the rubbish and instead end up in the appropriate unending quagmire of bureaucratic distribution, review, and inaction.

If your complaint is against a....

Demon: What are they sexually harassing you *with*? They don't have physical forms. If you're being possessed by one and they're making your physical form do things, technically they're not sexually harassing *you*. Possession makes it *their* body. If anything, they're just masturbating while you watch from the backseat of the body's mind space.

Imp: Poor little guys, they try so hard.

...a **Devil** from the order of...

Sloth: You actually got them to move enough to do what might be considered harassing?

Envy: If they're sexually harassing you, just harass someone else, and they'll want that person more and leave you alone.

Avarice: Keep something shiny in your pockets at all times to use as a distraction.

Gluttony: Your limbs must look like a turkey leg. Stop tanning so much.

Lechery: Well, duh.

Pride: Honestly, you should probably take this one as a compliment.

Wrath: First aid kits are available in bathrooms on every level.

KAREN & THE NATS

Karen arrived to work at the *LA Weekly* before nine and claimed the free office for whichever intern or writer happened to be there early. The only other intern who consistently arrived as early as she did was Calvin, but he generally allowed her to have the office even on days he arrived before her. She knew it was because Calvin liked being able to move around and collaborate as well as help other writers with their projects. He barely spent any time at whatever desk he was occupying any given day.

Karen always hoped that Calvin would claim one of the two cubicles outside of the office she occupied, but he had done so only once. The cubicles in question were usually occupied by Natalee and Natalie, or "the Nats," as Karen and Calvin called them. They were a pair of near-identical blonde interns who had been hired to compete with Karen for the permanent Fashion Staff Writer position four months earlier.

Karen considered texting Calvin to see where he was posted for the day, but her idea was sidetracked by the shrill giggles Karen instantly knew belonged to the Nats.

The girls were both wearing black dresses that looked painted on. Natalie wore a knee-length cardigan over hers, and Natalee a black leather jacket. Both girls wore dark shades and were clutching venti Starbucks drinks. Karen saw them toss their bags onto the cubicle desks outside and smoothly turn into her office. Karen did little to mask her ire at their presence and focused intently on her computer to try to hide from them behind work.

The girls tumbled in, their steps trudging tiredly in their high strappy heels to settle into the chairs on the other side of the desk from her. They wore matching coquettish grins and sipped from their blended drinks as Natalie said, "You missed such a fun night."

Natalee seconded, "Seriously, so much fun."

Karen had ignored their text messages inviting her out to Hyde Lounge. Aside from not being her kind of night out, "It was a Sunday night."

"Sunday Fundaaaaaaaay," the girls chimed together before sliding into deep slouches and nursing their drinks.

"Well, glad it was fun. Seems like it only just ended." Karen nodded delicately at their dresses.

"Yeah. We hooked up with guys who happened to live in the area, so we figured, let's just come in and see what the early morning is all about," Natalee said proudly.

"You like them so much," Natalie added.

Karen rolled her eyes while opening the email with the week's issue. "It's crazy fun, you know, working, and helping each other with work."

Natalie rolled her eyes back at Karen. "Geez, we get it. At least have some fun with it. What's the point of working here if you don't use the fact that you're a fashion writer for the *LA Weekly* to have fun?"

Karen opened the attachment to begin her proofread of the copy but shot a confused look at both the Nats in turn. "We're not fashion writers, we're interns. We're working to earn the position of writer." Karen was baffled that she had to spell it out. After four months of this ongoing frivolity in the Nats, it was their first time appearing on a Monday morning before Karen had finished her first cup of coffee that had found her ready to unload on them. "Do you two not get that? We're competing for a job. Against each other. I'm not saying we can't be friends, but coming in late and just loafing around isn't going to get either of you the job."

The Nats managed to look equal parts offended by and pitying of Karen. "You really think they'll fire us? Geez, grow up Karen. It's just a motivation tactic."

"Yeah, like telling someone they'll get cake if they do well at school," Natalee said.

"And you get the cake anyway."

"Yeah, because who lets cake go to waste?"

"There's no cake!" Karen said incredulously.

"Well, of course not, it's a metaphor," Natalee said.

"Analogy," Karen corrected.

"What?" Natalie asked.

"Never mind."

"Besides, the print journalism industry is going down the pipe, they can't afford to fire us."

Karen was stunned to silence as the Nats stood. Natalie offered a final rebuke. "It's cute that you think everything the big bad editor says is true, but come on, Karen. They're not going to fire any of us. It's the Fashion section. Look at us." Natalie posed proudly. "Seriously. Relax just once in awhile, and enjoy the life you're working so hard for."

Karen squinted in confusion and looked back the computer. "You know, Calvin actually told me something like that the other day?"

"The dorky intern?"

"The less dorky one," Natalie clarified.

Karen ignored them. "He said the work is what he's working for. You've gotta love the job, not the pay."

The Nats groaned together. "Ugh, calm down, Warren Buffett," Natalee said.

Karen put her face in her hands. "Warren Buffett isn't—" Her lament was interrupted by the singsong voice of Maggie Pitman, the Fashion Editor the three girls reported to, poking her head into the office.

Maggie was a mother of three and, as a result, dressed very pragmatically despite her position as the Fashion Editor. Jeans, T-shirt, knit button-up sweater. "Good morning, girls!"

All three looked up at her, and Karen couldn't be more glad for the editor's arrival. The Nats, despite their prior creed on hard work not being necessary, were both upright and beaming. "Good morning, Maggie!"

Maggie smiled, and Karen saw a knowing look behind her regard of the Nats as she asked sweetly, "Getting to work on anything exciting today?"

"Oh, yes!"

Maggie and Karen both waited for more details. Neither girl had showed up to an assignment meeting since their first week and had never turned in drafts of the assignments they had taken that week (which Karen had written for them the week after, and she doubted they had noticed). Maggie stood, patiently expecting the girls to give some mention of what they might be working on, but the Nats turned and left without another word.

Maggie waved for Karen to follow her but then caught herself. "Unless you're in the middle of something."

Karen gave a grateful look. "No, you just saved me from something."

Maggie led Karen into her office down the hall, and as Karen was following her in, she spotted the "less dorky" intern, Calvin Graves, coming up the row. She waved briefly at him and took the seat opposite Maggie. There were a couple stacks of pages clipped together on Maggie's desk, and she smiled at them. "I'm glad Harry got these together so quickly. I requested them last night with Sam's approval."

Karen didn't pretend to know what the Director of Human Resources might have put together or what the Editor-in-Chief had approved that would please Maggie, but Maggie held the stacks of pages out to Karen. "You're being offered the position of Staff Fashion Writer."

Karen looked at the contract and laughed in joy. Thanks tumbled out as she ran around the desk to hug Maggie. Maggie gave some basic instructions on filling out the forms, the salary and benefits package, and who to submit the forms to.

"So what's the first order of business for my new staff writer?" Maggie asked when Karen stood to leave.

"I dunno. I'm going to proofread this week's copy, but do you want any help with the team?" she asked, referring to the Nats.

Maggie giggled and clasped her hands officiously over her desk. "I don't think there's much need to have them, with the position filled." Maggie leaned forward in conspiratory fashion. "You've done more work this morning than they've done in four months. Might as well cut them loose."

Karen nodded before turning to the door. She opened it part way and looked back at Maggie with a fire stirring in her gut. "Can I tell them?"

CALVIN

Calvin timidly poked his head around the corner from the elevator bay into the foyer with the receptionist's desk to see who was there before he straightened up and walked to the curved desk. It was a bad habit- he told himself that repeatedly- one he should have gotten over after having worked at the *LA Weekly* for a month—far less than the three months he now had under his belt. Today, at least, his anxiety was a survival tactic until he got the job at the publication. *If you get the job*, he worried.

Lily Clark was on the phone and nodded only slightly as he approached, which made him freeze on the spot in case she had nodded to get his attention in order to tell him something. Lily was focused on her computer monitor at the desk, so Calvin made a motion to resume his entrance to the editors' pool, but his pause made Lily look up at him urgently with her hand over the receiver of her phone. "You need something?"

Calvin froze and felt abashed at interrupting her with his hesitation, and was paralyzed under the gaze of her wide green eyes. He fretted that he was distracting her again with his hesitation even more. He shook his head and pointed at the offices. "No, I'm good, thanks."

Lily nodded patiently and hurriedly returned to whoever she had been helping on the call. Calvin felt the hot tingle of embarrassment and told himself that Lily couldn't be that mad at him for the misstep. He immediately refuted his own claim that she very well could be and very likely was that mad at him for the misstep.[4]

Lily was busier than most people in an already frenetic office, and by his awkwardness, Calvin had just cost her precious time on what sounded like an important call. He glanced over his shoulder, and was concerned that her next call might be to an editor about how the dumb intern needed to waste less of her time.

"You're already on the ropes as it is," he muttered as he rounded the corner into the rows of cubicles and offices for writers and editors. Calvin adjusted his messenger bag and gripped the strap, pulling it against his shoulder as he slowly tread over the carpet in his Chuck Taylors, peeking into the offices as he went past each one.

It was mid-morning, so while some editors were already studiously working through this week's copy of the paper at their desks, some were already out on

---

[4] Psychologists refer to this immediate oscillation from self-assurance to self-doubt as playing mental chess blindfolded against oneself where the stakes are one's own self-esteem.

assignments. The office Karen usually claimed was suspiciously empty even though the lights were on, but Calvin caught sight of her heading into Maggie Pitman's office.

Calvin made mental note to check with Karen about how his article had been cut for Matt's at the very last minute. Especially when Matt hadn't announced any intention of writing a competing article in the assignment meeting. He assured himself Karen would see eye to eye with him on it being an injustice—unless she didn't and took the Darwinist, survival of the fittest position.[5] He was bracing himself for the editor of the Theater and Arts section to take that very position against him just now.

Calvin reached Errol Tipp's door and took a deep breath. He ran over the speech he had rehearsed for his entire drive in from Los Feliz about understanding that Matt's article was good but there having been wasted time on his rewriting and editing and how there should be some principle to these kinds of decisions and the values of full transparency.

The door to the office opened as he was retooling a bit of his planned phraseology regarding disclosure and Errol almost collided with Calvin. Despite the lack of contact, Calvin flopped to the floor in fright like a World Cup soccer player looking for a Yellow Card call.

Errol chuckled and bent over to help Calvin up. "Geez, Cal, didn't expect anyone to be waiting to jump me." He grunted at the effort to hoist Calvin up. "Or that I had the moves to turn the tables like that."

Calvin forced a weak laugh and murmured an apology, to which Errol patted his shoulder with a friendly

---

[5] There's that mental chess again. Should be easy to guess which side is winning.

glimmer in his eyes behind his horn-rimmed glasses. Errol made the gesture of turning to leave but paused. "Were you waiting for me?"

"Yeah, I have a question about my article? Can we?" Calvin gestured politely but stiffly into Errol's office. The editor looked perplexed but motioned for Calvin to follow him back in. Errol walked around his desk and smoothed his maroon cardigan as he sat and offered Calvin a seat.

Calvin spun his bag from his shoulder and set it on the floor beside his seat, which he immediately regretted. Errol probably didn't expect this to take more than a minute, and here he was putting on airs that he was settling in for tea. Calvin considered his bag and felt his neck burning but told himself it was all just nerves about the conversation, so he forced himself to dive right in. "Errol, when did the decision to replace my article take place?"

Errol was taken aback and sat straighter, clasping his hands and looking sideways in consideration. Calvin continued, "Especially after all the work we did on it? I don't mind it being bumped for something better, but it would have been nice to have things be a little more transparent. Maybe if I'd known Matt was writing the same article we could have worked together, or I could have done something else."

Errol pursed his lips for a moment and glanced inquiringly at Calvin. "The *Wicked* article?"

"I know things move super fast here, but how close to copy did he get it in? And when did he get the time for those interviews?"

"Matt submitted the article last week. You're saying you wrote it?" Errol regarded Calvin with officious wariness at the gravity of the claim he thought Calvin was lodging.

"Yeah." Calvin reconsidered the question and shook his head frantically. "Wait, what? No, I wrote one, he wrote one too."

"Like paragraphs?"

"No, it was about three thousand words. I didn't count paragraphs—"

"So, you wrote the whole thing?"

"The article going to print?"

"What other article is there?"

"The one I wrote?"

"So you wrote it with Matt?"

"No, I'm saying I wrote it myself."

"So Matt lied?"

Calvin put his hands up in exasperation and stopped the volleying. He took a deep breath, and Errol did the same, albeit less theatrically. "I wrote an article on *Wicked*. Matt wrote one too. It is a *completely* different article than the one I wrote."

Errol looked flummoxed and turned to his monitor to try to sort out his own thoughts. "Well, if you were writing one, why didn't you check with Matt to contribute to his?"

"Contribute? How was I supposed to know he was writing the same thing?"

"I dunno, maybe pay attention in the assignment meeting?"

"Yeah, I paid attention when that assignment went up for grabs—"

"And when Matt took the assignment?"

Calvin was the one taken aback now, albeit far more pronouncedly than Errol had been. He had expected a rigmarole about the subjective quality of their writing styles, tones, or structure, but to have to argue objective fact of who had taken the assignment had not even made it anywhere onto the sizable list of things he had worried over in mentally preparing himself.

"Errol, I took the assignment. Matt wasn't even there." Of the first claim, Calvin was certain. Of the second, less so. He hadn't noticed the mousy boy anywhere in the conference room used for assignment distributions, but that didn't mean the milquetoast intern hadn't simply melted into the scenery.

Calvin recalled Matt had actually worn a shirt the exact same off-white color of the office walls their first day together. The HR Director, Harry Martin, had accidentally brought only one set of employment forms because he simply hadn't noticed Matt blending into the walls.

Harry had filed a workplace incident report on himself for the misstep lest there be a formal complaint lodged against him of preferential treatment, discrimination, or prejudice.

"Nope, that was Matt." Errol typed through to the shared office document of assignments, then spun the monitor. "See? Matt." Calvin read the document. Matt's name was under the Theater section next to *Wicked*. Calvin considered asking to see the history of the document but recalled it was read-only except for editors who had the password to make changes.[6]

"What about the work we did on it last Thursday?" Calvin asked Errol in disbelief that their late night together in the office had meant and amounted to

---

[6] If Calvin had asked to see the document history, Eurydice's access of the document would have been plain as day. However, both Errol and Calvin would have assumed it to be the username of an editor with a penchant for Greek mythology.

nothing. Errol had called his husband and told him he was staying late, and Calvin had ordered pizza for them while they plugged away on their articles, trading drafts and offering each other feedback.

Errol looked blankly at Calvin for some indication of what work he was referring to. "Calvin, my husband and I went to see a dumb Marvel movie last Thursday. I remember because it was our first date night in months."

Now, not only his professional claim but also the bonding moments they had shared were being called into question? Calvin felt what he could swear was heartbreak because he knew the feeling entirely too well and kicked himself for admitting as much. Worse, besides his familiarity with heartbreak, was to feel it over a late night in the office with his favorite editor.

Calvin could at least jog Errol's memory in one way. Lines of prose are like a signature to a writer. The swoop and curve of it feel uniquely their own, and Calvin was sure Errol rereading some passages they had worked on together would settle the claim. "Okay, Matt claimed the *Wicked* article, and I messed up there." Calvin unzipped his bag and retrieved his laptop. "You don't remember working on..." he drawled out the word as his screen lit up. Calvin scanned his desktop, showing only his recycle bin and his command bar.

Errol raised his eyebrows. Calvin mouthed an apology, having expected the file to be on his desktop where he had been working on it until that Saturday evening. He went into his documents archive, but it was missing from the folders he kept meticulously organized.

"Hang on." Calvin panicked, then recalled he had emailed the article to Errol that weekend after he'd finished work on it. "Wi-Fi," Calvin muttered.

"*LA Weekly* two four seven. It's Guest access."

"Two four seven? It's asking a password."

"It's Guest."

"You said two four seven."

"No, try Guest."

Calvin began singing hymns of praise in his head when it connected and his email loaded. Going into his sent folder, he checked his list from Saturday. Some emails back and forth with Karen, his parents, then nothing until this morning when he'd emailed Karen just thirty minutes earlier to let her know he was rescheduling an interview for his next assignment and coming in.

Calvin tried searching for emails sent to Errol, but even though a list of some sixty emails were found, none of them had been sent since the last assignment meeting. Errol's eyes were pained in concern, seeing the puzzlement Calvin's face was stricken with. "Cal?"

"Sorry, Errol, you know what? I got the assignments mixed up. I was thinking *Wicked* was something else I was already spit balling around." Calvin's mouth flapped helplessly as he struggled to craft a deflection. It was a weak escape route, but with every wisp of evidence evaporating, his mind was screaming to mitigate the damage and try not to look psychotic as much as possible. Like *Back to the Future II*, Calvin was the only one who remembered what 1985 had been like before Biff went back in time with the Sport Almanac.

"But you said we worked on it?"

"Yeah, remember that idea I had for an article on E3?"

"The video games expo?"

"Yeah, that one."

"Cal, you specifically said *Wicked*, though."

"Yeah, I did," Calvin tried using bravado to play off the miscommunication, a tactic favored heavily by politicians and celebrities alike.

"So did you mean the play or not?"

"*Wicked*'s a play?" Calvin played confused, and slapped his forehead. "Aw, no, I'm sorry. I didn't realize that." Errol crossed his arms, and Calvin ventured a good-natured clarification as if Errol had been the slow one. "I was talking about the wicked article, as in the theme being what's wicked and what's lame at E3 this year." Calvin pressed on confidently, despite his brain screaming at him being a complete moron. "*Call of Duty* trailer? Wicked. Another *Super Mario* game? Lame. And maybe a sliding scale of wicked to lame based on what I see and how the presentations are."

Errol bobbed his head. "Well, the press badge is up for grabs if you really want to attend. Go for it. That was gonna come up in the next assignment meeting, but seeing as you have such a solid, sorry, such a *wicked* idea for it, take it as a freebie."

Calvin admired his good luck. He mused proudly how, despite his anxieties, he did have fantastic luck. Even though stammering and stumbling, he found himself through most messes better than he'd gotten into them. "Thanks, sir!"

"Anything else?"

Calvin knew to quit while he was ahead and said his farewells but paused at the door. "While you have the assignment doc up..."

Errol gave a sardonic thumbs up. "Already put your name on it."

Calvin bit his bottom lip and jostled his phone in the pocket of his denim jacket. After a moment, he darted back into the room, took a quick photo of Errol's monitor, and dashed back out, returning the thumbs up before he rushed into Karen's office. Natalie and Natalee were both wearing similar black fitted dresses and heels, throwing their things into their handbags with dejected pouts.

"You ladies done for the day or on your way out for hangover remedies?" Calvin smiled amicably, having heard them announce their departures numerous times for that exact pursuit.

Despite his good nature, both the Nats flipped him their middle fingers and told him where he could fuck off to as they stormed away. He was surprised, mostly because the location they had directed might have been enticing to some, but he knew better, and opted to ask Karen about it.

TO HELL WITH YOU!
[AN EXCERPT FROM HELL'S EMPLOYEE TRAINING VIDEO]

Welcome to Hell! The number one employer of demons worldwide and the second highest employer of emo hipsters and Wiccan. We're right on your heels, Peet's Coffee! To get started with your work, we're here to help you with what that work is. Here's how you can contribute to Hell's mission!

Most, if not all of you watching this, are probably demons. Don't worry! Everyone starts somewhere, and no doubt you're eager to get to work and earn yourself a body to climb the ranks to Imp and then up to Devil!

But you may be saying, golly, how am I supposed to help Hell without a body to do work in? Why, by working on the spiritual plane with those lousy meat sacks, you silly demon, you! As demons, you're given free run of the spiritual plane that surrounds those numbskull humans to guide them here. Look at the humans as our cattle because that's what they are. You're the rugged cowboy rustling them up back to the ranch to get slaughtered, skinned, and tanned for their sweet soul leather.

So what's your job as a demon, and how do you set yourself apart? Well, Hell is constantly tracking the results of your work: souls that come our way, acts of sin and atrocity committed by a human who's lost touch with the world—all of it. All you need to do is use the tools and techniques at your disposal to guide them in.

Of course, haunting is the first and easiest way to do it. Hang around them and try to nudge and ply them with your words from the outside. Pushing them to sin is the work of a truly artful demon. Remember, though, that when you're haunting and trying to whisper at them from outside, you're trying to be heard over everything else around them, so let's talk about some ways to cut through that noise.

Indwelling is the safer way to get your point across. Indwelling is having opened the door through physical or emotional pain and finding your way into their minds. From here, your voice is the first thing they hear right beside their own, and if you're really careful about how you find your way in, they'll even think it's their *own* voice. However, remember that indwelling is just being along for the ride in the vehicle, but the human is still the one at the wheel.

So, what if you need to run the shit off a cliff? That's what possession is for! There are a number of ways to get full control of a human. Some may actually *ask* for it, others may let go of control in exhaustion and pain without realizing it. Some can have it wrested from them if you're strong enough.

Possessions are usually great for numbers and

productivity; just be warned that they can throw up certain red flags all but the most oblivious meat sacks will notice.

GAST & ABA DON

Gast's idle time was short-lived. A call from the executive floor had summoned him to his boss, Aba Don's, office. Outside his office, Hell's Director level was a cubicle farm as far as the eye could see in every direction. Each pod only took the form of an office to the perspective of those within them. These paradoxes were par for the course and made Hell's building codes and worker's safety guidelines a pointless nuisance to give the blobs of mouth breathers that called themselves Devils of Sloth something to do.[7]

The elevator took Gast down two floors to Aba's executive level, just one removed from the CEO himself. The foyer to Aba's office was linoleum-tiled and fluorescent lit with worn chairs and a sleepy receptionist Imp. Gast knew the decor. It was the same oeuvre Hell

---

[7] Many places, things and beings in this universe have a depth of characteristics and facets that reveal themselves as a matter of perspective and understanding. Oftentimes, this is a matter of conscious decision of what to perceive and what to be present to others to be perceived. Hell is, in its truest base aspect, a dark pit in which all demons and souls suffer. However, much like that ex you chastise yourself for not realizing was a loser sooner, the Devils of Hell present the collective aspect of it being a functioning corporate office to themselves and each other. It's a facade all involved agree upon, given the alternative.

had pushed on every meat sack responsible for designing a DMV. It matched right down to the screen mounted on the wall, frozen for centuries on "Now Serving: 776." Dozens of meat sacks were waiting hopelessly for a meeting with the Executive Director to try to contest some term of their agreement, argue some loophole, or request some form of mercy to get just a little more time up there to make good on what they thought they had bargained for.

Gast recognized some from as far back as the Dark Ages, still staring hopelessly at the screen and the little paper slips with their numbers in their hands, waiting even though the screen hadn't advanced since the year 35 AD. They hoped against the very natures of Hell and the universe that they could argue their own case out of the underworld.

This was Aba's spiritual filibuster.

Most humans who died with their deals fulfilled were sent downstairs. Their bodies were claimed in fulfillment of their contracts. As for the souls, they became a part of the writhing and suffering mass of Demons, joining eventually in the work of Demons and attempting to climb the ranks to Imps and Devils once they had forgotten their own humanity under their jealousy and hatred of what they'd lost.

Gast ignored the receptionist and walked smoothly to the wooden door that would have been locked if any of the human souls tried the handle. Sure enough, having seen Gast proceed unimpeded through it, a few of the less despairing souls rushed the door to try it. He heard door shaking violently after it closed behind him as the dead tried to force their way in.

Inside, he was only aware of the door in a section of his mind—the paradox once more. Where he stood now was a long hall of stone columns lit by red braziers along either wall hung with crimson tapestries from the towering ceilings. Though plain at first glance in the dim firelight, Gast knew the finery of the tapestries shifted depicting scenes of war, violence and fury of man throughout history in red on crimson—fury on blood.

Gast found it all boring and cliché. He knew better than to let his expression betray his opinion of it because for the entirety of the trek, Aba's eyes were fixed on Gast over his steepled fingers from the alabaster throne he occupied atop the dais under the black banner emblazoned with Hell's pitchfork logo.

Gast refused to quicken his pace, and when he noticed Aba's eye twitch just slightly at the rhythm of his stride, he made a point of clicking the heels of his shoes on the stones underfoot to echo around him. Gast wondered how Aba got any work done without a desk in such dim lighting but knew the answer was probably that Aba's work these days consisted mostly of being four centuries behind the times and grousing at any Devil who dared to peek at what changes had taken place on Earth since the 1600s.

When Gast finally reached the steps, Aba narrowed his gaze down at him. Gast knew Aba expected the outdated modes of pomp and deference. Aba was the last Devil who had opposed the latest reorganization of Hell's structure. All others who failed to adapt had been demoted. Gast ignored Aba's clear expectation for him to kneel and instead manifested a comfortable armchair that he flopped onto and crossed his legs.

Aba's nose twitched, and Gast regarded the pale countenance blankly. Gast also knew that Aba's tact was to never speak first when he was seeking the upper hand, and Gast was blithely pivoting the tactic by toeing the line of the Executive Director's sensibilities.

Aba parted his hands to snap his fingers, at which the office morphed to match the form Gast had left his own office.

Gast wondered how Aba had known. Aba spread his serpentine fingers over the keyboard, spinning the monitor to face Gast. Only then did Gast realize they were truly in his own office, and he was now seated in the stiff wooden guest chair facing his own desk, Aba in the high-backed executive leather chair.

Aba still looked ridiculous. His resistance to the times was even more offensively stark in contrast to Gast's office design. Gast snapped forward and looked at the screen. It was the contract he had just finalized for delivery with the rapper from that morning.

"Is something wrong, Aba?" Gast asked before kicking himself for speaking first, but psychological displacements were what Aba had a deft hand at. Through the wordless moves of changing setting, and an unforeseen invasion of Gast's private space, he had goaded Gast into it.

Aba settled back into the chair, his black robes blending with the dark leather so that Aba appeared to be a pallored visage floating against the back of the chair.

"This deal, Gast." Aba tapped his slender finger on the bottom edge of the monitor screen. "Tell me, what are you offering her?"

Gast crossed his arms and legs in a play of ease with the situation to stay ahead of his boss. "Standard wealth and fame deal."

Aba bowed his head graciously. "Ah, I see, and there's a twist of some sort on it? A 'be careful what you wish for' of a sort?"

Gast cocked an eyebrow smugly. "Yeah, we're going

to make her a famous rapper for reasons other than her music. We have the Imps all over her social media, and our partners at Gawker are keeping an eye out."

Aba made an expression of being mildly impressed. "Such sharp efficiency."

"Humans are just cattle, after all," Gast said, repeating the company line. "Nothing else about it."

Aba offered a hungry grin, which flashed his sharp incisors. "And how will she feel about all this?"

Gast pursed his lips while wondering when Aba got the degree in emotional therapy, and if he'd ever heard the executive talk that way about humans in the epochs they'd worked in Hell together. "Who cares what the meat sack feels?" Gast's voice betrayed his trepidation with the barest scratch on the final word that tilted it into an octave of inquiry.

Aba, for his part, did not betray his pleasure at having lured Gast into the snare. "I care, and you *should* care, as a Devil of Wrath." Aba's voice and eyes smoldered. "You've been missing this facet in all your work for the past half century." Aba glowered over his once more steepled fingers.

"What? She'll be torn to shreds, and she'll be a laughingstock, famous for all the wrong reasons, just like Tila—"

"Tequila." Aba's nose curled. "A dunderhead who can't catch the irony of her own infamy? Yes, that little trophy of yours. Where is her wrath? Where is her anger and spite at the world's mockery? It does not do to simply outwit them. That is merely half the battle, Gast."

"Well, Tila isn't angry per se, no." Gast scrambled mentally for some ground to hold against Aba, "but she is *inciting* anger with her wild claims and conspiracy theories."

Aba rolled his eyes, an uncommon gesture that looked uncomfortable for his gaunt face. "They *laugh*, Gast, and she's a *cautionary* tale. You might as well take credit for taxes, the weather, or spoiled milk ruining their moods!"

"Well, it all adds up and spreads—"

"This is the argument not even the least and most grotesque of Imps would stand upon!" Aba's eyes ignited to hot crimson. The room swam into pitch darkness so that his flaming eyes and chalk visage were all Gast could see. "You are so concerned with closing your deals and your mechanical movements that you have lost all sight of what a Devil of Wrath is to be!"

Gast was stricken stiff in terror. Aba's voice did not travel as sound, but his message cut right through Gast to his core being. The light slowly returned to the room. Aba's eyes flickered and melted back to inky black. Aba leaned forward so that his fingertips lightly swept over the polished surface. "You are hereby placed under probationary evaluation. Should the evaluation be found unsatisfactory, you will be removed from your physical body and demoted to Demon until a suitable reassignment to a different Order of Hell can be determined."

"Evaluation? You can't-"

"I will not be the evaluator, since I am the one filing for the evaluation." Aba raised a hand, snapping his fingers. The door to the office opened and a gigantic figure with a frame so wide it had to turn sideways to enter came in to stand behind Gast. Towering over him, the giant in a double-breasted suit leered down at Gast, who did his best to appear obsequious.

"I understand you and Tie have had your *encounters* in the past." Aba sneered, relishing the truths and mayhem behind the euphemism. "He'll be an objective enough third party."

Gast snapped to his feet. "Now, hang on. You know very well those encounters more often than not involve pranks, mayhem, and destruction of property and body of a commonly non-consensual nature."

Aba looked facetiously surprised. "Oh? Is that so? Then be glad I chose your evaluator to be a threat you're already aware of. Believe me, Gast, there are plenty of other sharks in the deep waiting to taste your blood in the water."

Aba gave an eager look at Tie and only nodded his head before he proceeded from the office. Gast took a deep breath and turned to Tie.

As Gast had noted, their encounters always ended in something or someone being destroyed or maimed. Gast and Tie still hadn't determined who was responsible for the Berlin Wall, but they had managed to keep that one a secret from their colleagues as it was one of the bigger mistakes made in the eighties.[8]

Tie's body had belonged a Mongol who had served under Genghis Khan. The warrior had made a deal to climb the ranks of the Mongolian army. Once requisitioned in the late twelfth century, the body had sat in storage for four centuries because no other Devil had wanted to use a body so large and conspicuous to try to deal with humans. Tie, on the other hand, had chosen it right away after asking the Avarice Devils running the warehouse for "the biggest body and dick" they had.

Four hundred years later, he kept the hulking frame clothed in finely-tailored suits, just as Gast kept his own.

---

[8] The rise of Richard Simmons and his body image positivity was argued Gluttony to have been far worse as it devastated their numbers for several years.

Tie kept his body's hair coiffed and perfectly parted, just as Gast did his own. Tie cracked his knuckles with a voracious glint in his eye. "School is now in session."

CALVIN & KAREN

Calvin walked into Karen's office after the Nats stormed off and was surprised to find Karen clapping and grinning at him.

"Ask me if I'm thirsty!"

Calvin was confused and checked his watch. Nine thirty, so it was likely she had some trick in mind for him to buy her a coffee. He predicted that she might know he would repeat the question dutifully. He would say, "Are you thirsty?" She would chime it at the same time, then shout, "Jinx! Buy me a coke!"

It was morning still, so he felt coffee might be more appropriate. Could she be planning to shout, "Buy me a coffee?" He wondered whether or not he might use her own trick against her and be the one to shout jinx instead. He came back to the coffee versus Coca Cola question, though. He wasn't sure that would necessarily be fair since custom was to buy a Coke, but he wouldn't bother to argue the point against her—she'd win, after all.

He screwed his face slightly to ponder why he'd fight her at all. Aside from being his only friend in the office, Karen was objectively gorgeous, even and especially by the scales in as impossibly superficial a town as Los Angeles.

More dangerously for Calvin's focus and affections, she was entirely unconcerned with it because she was driven to write about fashion rather than to model it, and she was an almost impossibly quick and clever writer. If a girl like Karen wanted him to buy her coffee, that's money well spent, he told himself. If she would accompany him on that trip to the Coffee Bean at the corner, then he'd buy out the pastry section also.

Calvin, having thoroughly weighed his options at so simple a request for exactly as long as the above explication might lead you to think, was relieved to find her still smiling expectantly and patiently at him. He surmised she must have guessed all of the preceding internal monologue because he saw in her smile a warmth of knowing. If nothing else this morning, that smile sent a rush of pride from his chest up as heat through his neck and face. "Are you thirsty?"

"Parched!" She immediately stood and grabbed her handbag.

His surprise at her retort was doubled when he felt her arm lace around his to guide him out of the office. He puzzled for a moment at the fact that he was apparently buying her a coffee or Coke without the traditional flim flammery of a well played jinx, then he wondered why he was worrying about needing the prank anyway. He was still winning, after all. "Wait, coffee or Coke?"

Karen looked offended. "Who celebrates with coffee or Coca Cola? I didn't get a gold star in kindergarten, Cal." They stood by the cubicles the Nats had just vacated, and Karen beamed electric once more. "I got the job!"

Calvin looked at the cubicles beside them and finally deduced the Nats' foul moods. Before he could properly congratulate Karen, her arms were around his neck, forcibly choking the congratulations out in unintelligible sputters. When she pulled back, she held his hands in hers lightly. "Let's go treat ourselves to a Mimosa brunch!"

Calvin allowed himself to be dragged by Karen to the

elevators. Perhaps this was more than fine consolation after his article and byline had been thefted and his sanity made dubious since there may never have been an article in the first place despite his memories.

Karen squeezed his arm emphatically. "Plus, we're celebrating your cover story!"

Calvin stopped abruptly and planted himself with such uncommon resolve that Karen regarded him with equal parts surprise and admiration. "*My* cover feature?" Calvin sought to verify.

"The *Wicked* piece? I saw it made the front page. Very cool for a theater piece."

"*My* piece?"

Karen huffed. "I wasn't going to ask for a shared byline if that's what you're afraid of. I read it over a couple times for you, same as you do for my—"

Calvin shushed her anxiously and shuffled her from the end of the cubicle row into the hallway that connected the editorial pool to the marketing and advertising sections on the opposite side of the floor. Calvin dug his phone out of his pocket while stammering, "Karen, I just had the weirdest convo with Errol." He held the phone up to her. "Not only did my piece magically turn into a piece by Matt Reade, but Errol has *no* memory of my article."

Karen squinted at the screen. "What? You two were working on it when I tried luring you out for Happy Hour last Thursday."

Calvin snapped his fingers. "There you go! I *knew* it! *He* says he was home with his husband, but I know we were here working on it!"

"After all that work you get your article bumped by that mousy slice of milquetoast?"

"No! That's the thing, the article doesn't exist!"

"Doesn't exist?"

"Poof! Not in Errol's memory, not in my emails, not on my laptop, gone. *Back to the Future*'d out of existence except for your memory and mine," Calvin said frantically.

"So, what's Matt's place in all this? Doesn't matter what we remember, it's the byline that matters."

Calvin proceeded down the hall, speaking over his shoulder at Karen. "You're right! I need to see what he remembers." Calvin corrected himself in a murmur, "or what he *claims* to remember, and get to the bottom of this."

He strode briskly to a message board where photos and contact information for the staff was posted. Calvin was hunting Matt on the wall with such focus that he did not notice Karen had slunk away to the elevators without him.

Calvin worried at the poor boy in the photo: emaciated, pale, his sweater blending him in perfectly against the cubicle, his pallor making his black hair look damp and matted against his forehead. "Where the hell did you find a sweater the same color as the cubicle partition?"

The answer to his question came from his right. "TJ Maxx."

Calvin jumped and yelped.

"No need to yelp," Matt said in a cool baritone.

Calvin gave an affronted look and tried to straighten his posture. By his recollection, he was at least a couple inches taller than Matt. The Matt Reade before him now was of a good summery athletic build, the kind of body that looks right at home on lakes or casually playing sports in fields with varsity athletes.

Calvin tried not to worry over Matt's drastically

different physicality, but it was difficult with the man before him. It was clearly the same person he had met that first day, but it was also clearly not. The best Calvin could utter in retort was, "I didn't yelp."

"You did. The narrator said so." Calvin could barely register before Matt looked wistfully at the photo on the wall and plucked it out from under its thumb tack. "Yes, I bought it because it was on sale. Fifty percent off." He flipped the photo for Calvin to look at once more. "Should've known if something's marked off, it's because no one wants it."

Calvin looked over his shoulder for Karen. He was wary about making claims regarding fashion without her counsel, and Matt no longer seemed to be one to argue with. His black leather shoes, dark jeans, sport jacket and shirt all reeked of high fashion designer labels. He looked right off a page of a GQ men's style guide. Calvin glanced one more time at the photo and back at Matt himself, trying to understand what had taken place in the last month. Had Matt gone on some high school teen comedy romp to break into a party at the Playboy Mansion that had matured his style and panache overnight? Was it a girl? Was it some LA chic mentor?

Matt flicked the picture away, and it spun in a smooth arc into a small trash bin twenty feet away. Matt clapped his hands. "I came by to apologize." Matt swung a consolatory cuff at Calvin's shoulder.

Calvin looked aghast at the spot on his shoulder Matt had jabbed while Matt continued speaking. "You see, I have a deal with a Devil, and it seems he removed your article from existence to honor it."

Calvin looked away, trying to weigh the insanity now being posed to him. Perhaps it was the well-attuned sense of style, or perhaps it was the deep, collected tone, but

Calvin actually took the statement in hand.

Here was the very thief he had been planning to investigate admitting that he, Calvin, was not insane. However, Calvin was now facing his sanity being proven valid by a thoroughly insane twist of reality itself.

A deal with a Devil? Calvin weighed the possibility. He was agnostic and wouldn't deny the possibility that the Devil *could* exist.

"I'm sorry, but I was hoping to get going. There's a Happy Hour at Hotel Irwin I wanted to catch." Matt put a hand on Calvin's shoulder and smirked. "We're good, then? No hard feelings."

Calvin's mouth flapped, and he finally managed to sputter, "Is the *Devil* sorry?"

Matt chuckled and glanced at the ceiling in earnest consideration. "I'd call it pity, but sure. I don't think that'll stop him from doing it again if that's what you're asking."

Calvin tried to process the possibility, and his head began to grow hot. He held his breath trying to comprehend the new world paradigm that included unfair supernatural assistance to competing writers. "Fuck me," he muttered.

Matt scrunched his nose and shook his head sharply. "I'll pass."

UNDERWORLD INCIDENT REPORT
UW-PR1001 / CASE #W091-DD89

This is a formal incident report regarding the two Devils, both of Order Wrath under Executive Director, Aba Don, for their proximity to, and speculated involvement with the fall of the Berlin Wall and the overall political trend thereafter which ended the Cold War. At this time, no formal accusation of malfeasance has been entered against either the Senior Director Gast or Senior Director Tie. This report is logged to Hell's Human Resources Database as acknowledgement of witness accounts should a formal complaint be lodged to which these are material.

Both Senior Directors were reported as leaving the offices four months preceding the fall. Witness designated as Lechery - 001 reported the two devils as being "three sheets to the wind in full tilt" at the time of their departure and commented regarding the "handsy-ness" of Senior Director Tie. This was not documented in a workplace harassment report as Lechery - 001 was grateful for Tie's attentions.

Various Imps reported providing deliveries of alcohol and other recreational substances (Nutella, deep fried Oreos, and vats of cocoa butter) to the Devils. While the Directors' presence in Europe can be verified during the months in question, there are no eye witness accounts linking them to any pertinent incidents or specific persons of interests involved in the turning of the tide.

Both Devils have had their gross and unholy uses of the cocoa butter reviewed and have received commendations for Mayhem, Sexual Misconduct, and Sexual Mayhem in the First Order.

TIE & GAST

"School is now in session?" Gast asked.

Tie blinked. "What?"

Gast strode to his mini bar and grabbed two glasses. He filled one with vodka and paused before pouring a second. Gast looked at Tie, who gave a look of impatience before Gast tossed the entire bottle at the giant. Tie threw back a quarter of the bottle in a single swig as he flopped onto and filled the three-seater leather couch with his bulk.

Gast tossed back half of the first glass and grimaced. "It's an evaluation, not an exam. Come on." Gast surveyed his bar and grabbed one of the bottles of scotch. Returning to the couches, he hopped gracefully over the arm of the chair near Tie and landed sideways on the seat. Gast unbuttoned his suit jacket and finished the second glass of vodka he had poured, then threw the glass at the wall.

"I'm not gonna ask what you'd say because you've had this whole time to come up with something better." Tie took another loud gulp of vodka. "Spree descaley."

"It's *esprit d'escalier*, you fat pleb." Gast scrutinized the label, thinking he'd grabbed something at least five years older than what he was holding. "I won't bother trying. We've got better things to discuss."

"Like how I managed to get the gig as your evaluator?" Tie asked with a sly grin.

"I saw this coming since before Berlin."

"Did you now?"

"Yeah, it's why I had us posing as face-pissing rivals the past thirty years."

"Sure, *that's* why."

"And now that Aba thinks you're on his side. I've got a man on the inside."

"You're a little off from what you told me back in Berlin." Tie tried to read Gast over the bottle he was draining.

"Oh, please." Gast took a long swig of the whiskey. "I could never forget anything that happened while we were

45

swimming in all that cocoa butter."

Tie got to his feet and swaggered around the armchair to the bar from which he snatched a bottle of cognac and wove back to the couch. He plucked the cork with a loud pop and wagged the bottle at Gast. "You told me you were going after Aba."

Gast emptied his bottle and pitched it away. "And?"

"Looks more like you were waiting for Aba to come after *you*," Tie clarified. "You've had me acting like a dick to you for three decades, and now we're on the defensive."

Gast got another bottle of scotch and flopped back into the chair. Gast squinted out the window at Vine Avenue. "You don't think that'll make him cocky? He'll think he's a step ahead of us and slips into the trap I have for him?"

"If you had a trap, sure." Tie stopped himself from taking another swig to interject. "I think you had a plan when we got back *thirty* years ago, but it got sidelined."

"I've been biding my time," Gast retorted weakly before taking another sip and settling deeper into his chair.

"Yeah? Because it sounded pretty damn imminent until we got back and Lilith was gone."

"She had nothing to do with it."

"And when I asked about her, you told me we needed to act like we weren't friends for the plan."

"So, what makes you think there's any point to asking about her now?"

"Is there?" Tie pelted the empty cognac bottle against the wall behind Gast's head, raining shards and splinters of the glass all over Gast.

Gast remained largely unresponsive to the exploded bottle but scowled and drained the remainder of his whiskey. Gast pointed the empty bottle at Tie while he spoke. "I haven't seen her since she left and went rogue. Haven't even heard from her. Whatever she's doing, she didn't want me involved, so I don't need her in *my* plan."

"Yeah? So why'd the plan really get delayed?" Tie challenged.

Gast pouted sleepily, the whiskey starting to make his vision swim. He wouldn't recall his answer to Tie, but when his head slipped against the back of the chair and the office went black, he slurred, "It fell off."

Tie huffed at Gast's reticence. Whether his friend would admit it or not, Tie had spent thirty years soundly convinced that his friend's depression at Lilith's departure had taken the wind out of his sails. Gast's chest had no fire in it and that had Gast playing prey rather than predator.

Losing Lilith had made ambition pointless to Gast, and Tie worried his friend had something of a death wish. In the eternities all Devils experience and suffer through, they lack any of the love the rest of creation can find if they only seek it. It makes even the flawed affections they might somehow find that much more impactful.

THE BAR

There are myths of a bar where killers drink and dine.

You may think I'm telling you about a specific bar in a specific city, but you're wrong.

In every city, once there are enough crowds for the faceless and nameless to disappear into, the bar puts up shop for those wanderers to find their refuge.

It is in every true city, where you may see a particular face once and never again. In every true city, where you

47

may see a particular face every day of your life and never realize you've seen it before among the masses of strangers, the bar is there.

The bar is where these faceless killers have their truce, their honor among killers. No weapons are drawn and no contracts are executed, only negotiated. It is where those looking to hire these faceless men and women find them, and where they take the jobs only the faceless can deliver.

You know this bar, even if you've never entered it.

It could be that dive bar that's worn and musty, that never has a crowd except the grizzled regulars who barely register your presence. It could be the lounge where the staff are quick but the chairs stiff enough that you can't get comfortable enough to stay more than an hour. Perhaps it's the brick building marked only by a neon sign reading "BAR" that you doubt is actually open because the sign is never lit.

The Bar does open, you could just check Yelp for its hours and reviews. It's closed on Sundays and Mondays and it has 4.5 Stars from 783 reviews. You are welcome to pass through, but you'd likely notice nothing unusual about any of the denizens in this bar.

The Bar has an owner, and that owner is an intermediary for the faceless and those looking to hire them. The owner of The Bar is a father, and his daughter helped as a bartender, until she was hired by Benny.

TESSA

As with many mornings arriving for a lunch service that would serve no one, Tessa considered calling and asking her father for her old job back at The Bar. A stubborn resolve not to admit defeat in her vow to find her own calling and independence in the city of angels kept her from making any more than chit chat when she checked in with her father. Least of all, she didn't want to her father to think it was a matter of squeamishness at the prospect of her first hit.

Her father had tried to bail her out and replace her on the contract she'd taken months earlier. Defensively, if only to prove she could handle herself, she'd walked out on The Bar just to prove a point. Almost daily, once she rounded the corner and saw the restaurant sign from down the block, Tessa reminded herself that having (accidentally) taken up a contract wasn't bad pay at least.

Her deal with Benny had been for her to lie in wait until Benny designated the time was right. Until then, he was paying her a handsome salary to work undercover. Being kept on call for the hit paid well enough that she could afford a charming one-bedroom flat in Los Feliz, and on top of it, Sally paid her very well for a waitress, especially one who never had to wait a table.

She entered through the front door and could tell someone had been whacked by Benny and the others. The long table was out of the middle of the room against the booths. Its chairs were scattered around the space. The floor was pristine, and the smell of bleach stung her nose.

Tessa was an ignorant waitress as far as Sally knew. Some distant cousin of a friend of Benny's that the mob boss had recommended Sally hire when the restaurant was first opening two months prior. It still hadn't opened. Benny's intent had only ever been to satisfy his theatricality of having an Italian restaurant he could use as his stage to play mafia don.

Tessa pretended not to know Benny's side of things and instead played the role of waitress disinterestedly collecting a paycheck and spending six hour shifts reading and learning to cook whenever Sally managed to be upright. She walked through the swinging door to the kitchen and found that she'd likely get through a good amount of the Grisham novel she'd packed.

Sally was sprawled in the uncomfortable-looking position of being seated on a high stool and doubled over onto the steel countertop under his seat. It looked improbable because the counter was slightly lower than the seat, and even more so because Sally had a bottle of cooking sherry clutched in one hand and a bottle of his homemade spice blend in the other.

Tessa had expected Sally to be in this state or on her way there. Not being able to open the restaurant made the odds of Sally drinking himself stupid increasingly high the longer he went without opening. It was a guarantee that he'd be hammered if his job was to serve to a meal to someone who had been brought over just to be whacked before they could enjoy it.

Tessa had once tried cheering Sally up by posting a five-star review of the restaurant on Yelp after having tried his shrimp scampi for the first time. It had driven Sally into a bender so bad that her only work for the next three days had been rolling him onto his side and filling water glasses for him.

Today, though, there was a rising groan of acknowledgement from the heap of chef on the counter, so she might not need the book after all. Sally managed to right himself with another groan of effort. Tessa glanced at the bottle of sherry, only half empty.

She took a seat on the stool beside Sally. "Not opening today either, boss?"

Sally clutched both bottles, slumping his shoulders. "Nope."

Tessa didn't like seeing him look so drawn. He was a young man in his late twenties, not much older than she, but when he drank and was miserable, it aged him far beyond his years. She worried that this was how people died too young, so she resolved to lighten him up even a little. "Can I get a lesson today, at least?"

Sally's face drew a line of consideration, and he managed a grin with his chocolate eyes even giving a twinkle at her. "Sure can." He lifted a bottle to his mouth for a quick swig, but it was the spice bottle, which made him sputter and spit the dried leaves into a cloud between them.

Tessa laughed as he scampered to the sink at the end of the counter to wash off the leaves sticking to his lips and swished water in his mouth. He took a couple mouthfuls and stood upright, wiping his chin with his striped apron, then he waved for her to follow him to the freezer.

She couldn't help but smirk as he marched past the shelves in the walk-in like a general surveying his platoon. He theatrically waved his hand as he commented on each of the meats he was choosing from. "Beef? Too heavy for today's lesson. Chicken? It is Monday, but let's not go with boring just because it's a boring day. Shrimp? I'll spare you the smell since I already reek of sherry."

When he reached the lamb and held the shank up before her, she was excited that he was going to break routine and show her a Greek fusion recipe he'd been workshopping for lamb shank and accompanying dishes.

The Via Fresca was an Italian restaurant. However, Sally's skills as a chef went well beyond just any single cuisine, and he'd demonstrated dishes and techniques ranging from Cajun to Chinese and many in between. Tessa had wondered how Sally hadn't sold Benny on actually opening the restaurant but found out that Benny had never tried a morsel of Sally's cooking, nor did he want to.

She watched Sally preparing the rub and bringing out wine for the shank's preparation. She loved seeing the joy with which he approached cooking and how electric his voice became whenever he described each little decision to her. Tessa knew Benny didn't want to try Sally's cooking on the outside chance it made ordering the hit on Sally more difficult.

Every time she tried more of Sally's cooking she wondered if it hadn't been a mistake since she had accepted the contract to pull the trigger.

LILITH – A HISTORY

Myths and legends tell of Lilith, but her inclusion in biblical mythos is apocryphal at best. She would explain that her inclusion in existence itself is similarly apocryphal and smartly change the subject to something even further out of your depth before you could properly understand how little you really understood about her response.

You see, Lilith, like all beings, was made by the Creator. Like some we have encountered, she is among the immortal beings. Unlike the others, she was not created in Heaven and banished to Hell. She was created on Earth in Eden and wandered off from the Garden on her own before that whole fiasco with the fruit.

As such, Lilith retains her immortal and perfect nature as the direct and superb product of the Creator- unmarred by original sin, but still human in a host of other ways despite dodging that particular bullet.

Because of her marginalia existence, she has come to

resemble something neither human nor spirit as we know it. Lilith has the privilege of picking and choosing the facets of existence and life that suit her moods. Boredom, she would say, is her greatest enemy. Time passes slowly for her. With eternity behind and before her, she would say the only real fear she has is drudgery.

Given this, Lilith has occasionally stopped into Hell when the fancy took her. This made it clear to Tie that she was the inspiration for Gast's plot to overtake Aba as the head of Wrath which he had shared when they were on vacation in Berlin.

This made it seem clear to Gast why she had left: he was just another part of the drudgery she despised so much. In the face of that rejection and her disappearance, he had thrown himself headlong into being that cog for the past half century with the kind of joyless gusto reserved for accountants in tax season.

ABOUT THAT DEAL

Calvin held the door open for Matt to enter the Coffee Bean on the corner from their office, his phone buzzed in his pocket. Matt ordered a complex latte while Calvin read Karen's text message: "At Paulie's, meet me when convenient."

Calvin worried that she might be offended he had ditched her in pursuit of Matt but tried (unsuccessfully) to assure himself that Karen would understand. He was in the process of returning his phone to his pocket when it buzzed again in his hand with another message: "If inconvenient, come anyway."

Calvin ordered himself a vanilla latte and was irked to find that Matt, who had already moved to sit at a table in the corner, had left Calvin to pay for both their drinks. Calvin paid and joined Matt with the drinks. "There you go." Matt was busy reading his phone as Calvin sat, so his delivery had little, if any, noticeable impact.

Matt looked ponderous over something on his phone screen, seemed mentally to make a decision about whatever it was, and then put the phone away. Whatever it had been, Matt was in a much more officious rush now. Matt spoke quickly. "This will be faster if you let me explain, and then you'll have time to ask a couple questions."

Calvin was nonplussed and remained quiet for Matt to proceed. "After our first week, when we were at our Happy Hour..." Matt paused, showing a brief moment of anxiety at whatever he was recalling. "I found myself drinking when he found me. We started talking, and he offered me a deal. He said that he was a Devil and that Hell loves making deals with people to give them the leg up they need.

"I did ask him: so there's more than one Devil? He said to me that Devil is a title for Demons who are high up enough on the ladder to have earned a physical body to roam in. See, Hell's a business, and their economy is based on souls. He said it isn't as nefarious as folklore would have us believe. Hell is a business, and a business has to a sell a product, and an inferior product simply won't do. So he offered me a deal, and I took it."

Matt sat back with a proud smile, and Calvin looked him up and down again with fresh eyes. "And the deal was for... a discount at the Marc Ecko store?"

Matt gave a droll roll of his eyes. "No, it was to be a famous writer. The clothes are a perk. He makes it standard with all his deals. Magically makes it so that I'm always expertly dressed for whatever occasion I arrive for."

Matt checked his watch anxiously while Calvin asked, "How does he make you a famous writer?"

Matt stood. "You saw it already: he's helping me top competition like you and climb the ranks here at the *LA Weekly* first."

"But—"

"And then I'll break into TV journalism, maybe write a memoir or commentary on my youthful success, and that'll be that."

"Yeah, but—"

"Calvin, I need to get going." Matt dug into his pocket. "Here, you wanna keep talking? Let's meet for dinner." Matt tossed a business card onto the table. "Let's say dinner and drinks at six. I'll text you."

Matt hurried out the door. Calvin looked at the card. It was a simple white with a crimson frame around Matt's information. Calvin noticed Matt's untouched coffee and fumed for a moment that Matt had ordered the drink purely to establish some sort of alpha control in the conversation. He berated himself further that it had worked.

Calvin didn't dwell for long as his phone buzzed again from Karen now grousing that she was starting on round three without him.

A DEVIL & HIS WARD

Gast awoke, not in his armchair but hanging by his ankle from the ceiling. Tie had, in their usual tradition, left him passed out in some unlikely position. This time he was tethered to the plated chandelier in the center of his office. Gast was relieved to find he was still fully clothed. Other times he had not been so lucky.

With a snap of his fingers, Gast burned through the rope tying him and fell with a painful crash onto the glass coffee table underneath. Gast picked, pulled, and yanked the shards of glass from his back, shoulders, and arms and tossed the bloody pieces aside. He was sure Tie had chosen to hang him in that particular spot for the follow-up crash landing on the table and would have to devise a comeuppance for the giant later.

For now, he got his phone and contacted Matt. He told his ward to meet him as soon as possible. Gast surveyed himself, his suit disheveled from Tie's hanging him up. With another snap of his fingers, he summoned a new suit, this one a heather gray, two-piece Hugo Boss. His hair was once more immaculate. His phone buzzed in his breast pocket with the notice of the suit requisition from the Avarice Demons in Accounting tracking his expenses.

Gast had long ago stopped worrying over why an Accounting department was necessary if Hell's resources were limitless as they claimed. The true answer was that they were *practically* limitless but confined to the material constraints of the world within which they work. Hell is finite as are its resources. Only one being can command infinity in this universe. Cosmic omnipotence notwithstanding, Gast still didn't see the point of bean counters monitoring how many suits he wore, except for the sake of having something to do.[9]

Well dressed and ready, Gast sat in his office chair and spun it slowly. As the chair turned towards the wall

---

[9] This is also regarded as the raison d'etre for most of Hell and any position in government where the word "oversight" fits into the job description.

behind his desk, he instead turned to face the table in a secluded booth in the bar. The bar was, as usual, sparsely populated. A few scattered individuals were reading newspapers or their phones. One was eating an early lunch. Gast had come into being unnoticed, and even if any had known he hadn't been there a moment before, none would bother him. The Bar is home to faceless men, the perfect place for Gast and his kind to meet their wards.

Gast checked his watch. Matt was being held up by something. Gast surveyed the room, it having been a very long time since his last visit here. Tie was a regular to the bar. Ingratiating himself among assassins, whispering in the ears of the desperate to lead them here, it was a favorite pastime of Tie's in any city where the bar existed. Tie had brought Gast here years ago before they'd begun their ruse of being face-spitting enemies.

Gast admitted to himself that it would have had to serve some legitimate purpose for that to be the case. Tie was the second best Devil in Wrath, the only one who kept in some kind of step with Gast's numbers, although his were far less consistent. This was why Gast had formed an alliance with him so naturally once Tie had been promoted centuries earlier.

Gast's rumination was short-lived once his ward appeared. Matt was wearing all black: jacket, linen Henley shirt, and slacks. Even his hair seemed to have darkened a shade for the environment. A bartender came over automatically with Gast's usual drink, bourbon with a flick of cigar ash in it. Matt ordered a milk stout the bar kept on tap.

The bartender nodded and left them alone. Gast grinned at the irony that he was the one wearing the relatively bright suit. "I need to talk to you about the progress on your deal."

"Good, because I had something come up too." Gast was taken aback, but motioned for Matt to continue. "I need to know what the terms of confidentiality are on my contract."

Gast's words caught in his throat, and he was further flummoxed. In all his centuries of working this gig, a ward had never asked about confidentiality. He assumed terms of non-disclosure had to be somewhere in the agreement, but worried why Matt might think Gast had told anyone about the deal. Then it occurred to him: by letting Calvin see and remember the article replacement, he might have violated those very terms.

"I may have slipped and told someone about the deal," Matt confessed.

Gast masked his relief expertly and turned his expression to rebuke. "You told someone about your deal with a Devil? Do you want people to think you're crazy?" Gast scolded confidently. In these situations, he knew the best defense was a good offense, and he could easily cover his slip by making Matt's flub the core issue.

"You're at liberty to tell whoever you want, but it makes my job all the more difficult. If it flat out impedes my work, the contract is null and void." Gast was standing on firm contractual ground. In the event that a human should take action to directly impede their Devil's work at delivering the terms of their agreement, the whole agreement was nixed, and their soul would be surrendered to Hell as a penalty. These terms had been standard ever since Faust had led Hell on a goose chase for decades trying to escape the terms of his deal and gotten away with a divine loophole.

"I'm not trying to get in your way, I just- I don't know. It's the other intern. He looked really bummed, and I wanted to give him an explanation, and it just came out. What's the worst that could happen?"

Gast shook his head. Here was the stammering milquetoast he'd signed the deal with. Matt's bravado had blossomed in facing other humans, but around Gast, who held the keys to those glamours, the facade crumbled easily.

The beer arrived at the table, and Matt thanked the bartender before taking a sip. When the glass was set back on the table, Gast instructed Matt. "I think there may be potential here for us to fast track your progress." Matt's eyebrows raised, and Gast leaned forward. "We need to chase him off. Sure, we can go head to head with him, but that would take months. You want the job this week? Tell him *everything*. He'll either think you're crazy, or he'll see what happened today and be scared off.

"Do it one on one. That way if he does try to rat you out, everyone in your office will think he's nuts. He'll ruin his credibility and future if he tries to take you on."

"I told him we'd do dinner tonight! I'll tell him then!"

Gast fought not to roll his eyes at Matt's geeky energy with only moderate success. "Fine, tell him on your date tonight. In fact," Gast reached into his breast pocket and produced a slim black business card with only his name written in white on it. "Give him this and tell him if he's smart and sees how the situation really is going to play out, he'll give me a call." Gast slid the card across the table and looked at Matt. Matt only sipped his beer, thinking over Gast's instructions. "You have the phone. Call me when it's done if he doesn't call me first."

Gast stood from the table and walked across his office back to his desk. Matt was left alone pondering why Gast would want to work with Calvin when *he* was the one with talent. Matt was dancing around considering the corollary of why he needed the deal with Gast since he was the one with talent, but this quandary was easily overshadowed by the more pleasant choice of what he could do until six that night since he didn't have any work to get done.

CALL YOUR PARENTS 1 - CALVIN

As he walked down Olympic Boulevard, Calvin gave his mother a call. On Central time, she would likely be having her lunch break.

Mom: Hi, Cal, how's the day going?

Calvin: Good so far, I guess.

Mom: Are you okay? You sound stressed.

Calvin: I'm good, just, listen, my article got bumped.

Mom: Oh, no, honey, so they're delaying it?

Calvin: I guess. Yeah. I'll have an article in the next issue.

Mom: Okay, well, just work hard and you'll be everyone's favorite writer in no time.

Calvin: Thanks, Mom. How are you doing?

Mom: I'm good, busy at work. Linda next door asked about you, I told her to check online for some of your writing you already got on the website.

Calvin: Yeah, still trying to crack into the print copy, but yeah—

Mom: Linda said your food review was *very* good. She wants you to take her to that taco-ria if she visits sometime. Is that the one we went to?

Calvin: No, Mom, that was a different place.

Mom: Different?

Calvin: Yeah, there's more than one restaurant that sells tacos and margaritas in LA.

Mom: Maybe you should do a book on them, an encyclopedia of tacos.

Calvin: I think people already have Yelp for that.

Mom: Well, sure, if they like their smartphones, but sometimes people want books.

Calvin: Sure, Mom, I'll look into it.

THE EDITORS

Felicia Swanson-Thomas strode into the *LA Weekly* office every workday at exactly five-past ten in the morning. This was after she'd stopped for a delicious fruit smoothie made by the delicious undergrad barista at the organic café en route from her mansion in Brentwood.

Felicia dressed smartly, typically in skirts that hugged her body, shirts and blouses that proudly displayed the work her alimony had allowed her to have done, and heels that streamlined her calf muscles just so. Her stride was a slinky traipse past the offices and cubicles to her own at the end of the hall.

She usually enjoyed seeing the Nats fighting back their awe at the woman who, allegedly, was twice their age but could turn heads twice as effectively. They were nowhere to be seen, which only mildly disappointed her. They weren't her favorites to pass by anyway. Next, she crossed Karen, who kept her focus diligently on her computer, then past Errol, who she assured herself she could turn away from his husband even if women weren't his cup of tea.

Finally, there was the lottery she really enjoyed. She was never sure where he would be, always in motion working on an article or pitching an idea. She would spot him and will his gaze to her, then lock eyes and make him drink her in as she slinked past.

Calvin was nowhere to be seen this morning, though, nor was Karen or either of the Nats, and Errol was alone in his office with a flustered look. Maggie was the only person in the offices that looked to be working at a regular clip, and the staff writers were already out on assignments for the day.

Felicia swung her Dolce bag onto her desk and sat down at her computer. Being Food Editor was a good way to kill time for her. It kept from getting too bored since she didn't really need the paycheck. Her late husbands had all left her comfortably seen to with the accommodations of their estates left to her. All told, on the right day in the market for the portfolios she had inherited, Felicia generally hovered at the cusp of being a billionaire, even in spite of her generous bites out of her holdings for her entertainment and upkeep.

The *LA Weekly* was a good outlet for her time and energy for the while. She knew the routine was useful for her sanity, and it afforded access to other frivolities. She opened this week's copy in her email for proofreading with the excitement of her new pursuit titillating her. She wanted to read Calvin's feature and offer him thorough congratulations, but to also lure him into her office for notes and—

She squinted in confusion. The front page had the article on the *Wicked* show, but the byline read "Matt Reade."

"Who the flying fuck is Matt Reade?" She scanned her memory. The image of a mousy boy simpering nervously behind Calvin during his orientation tour came to mind. Felicia hadn't cared enough to catch the boy's name then. She had been too focused on introducing herself to Calvin and leaning forward at just the right angle in offering a handshake to put her generously-unbuttoned blouse right in his line of sight.

Sam Dority, the Editor-in-Chief, was rushing by, and she called out to him, making the laconic man jump. He looked at her with some surprise and poked his head through her partway-open door. "You need me?"

She motioned for him to come in. He looked over his shoulder warily before he sauntered in. He had a hard copy of the week's issue in his hands he was poring over with a red pen clenched between his teeth so she looked at the copy on her monitor. "I thought Calvin had the *Wicked* article?"

Sam pursed his lips and flipped back to the front page of his copy. "No, it's the other intern, Matt Reade." He flipped it over to where his finger had kept his place on his proofread.

"I remember Calvin being assigned that one. Did it get reassigned?"

Sam checked his phone distractedly. "Nope, assignment page says it was Matt."

Felicia looked blankly at the screen and weighed her options. Perhaps she had mixed up Calvin's excitement, but she knew he had been eager to finally make the print copy this issue. It was no bother if he had been bumped since that presented her an opportunity nonetheless. "Well, since the other intern got into print this week, I'll talk to Calvin about some stories I have on queue that can get him in my section."

Sam quoted the company line: "We don't *give* print articles. We choose them from the pool of stories we have available by merit and quality. Have you read Matt's? It's really good."

"It's about a musical."

"A really good musical."

"That's an oxymoron."

Sam gave Felicia a look of mild impatience and waved off the exchange. "You can work with Calvin, but you can't just 'give him' priority to get into print. It's got to be based on quality."

Felicia harrumphed and crossed her arms. "He's already online, and his articles have great view counts. Plus, the people who comment on them really like his voice. I don't get why print copy still has this prestige when he can get more views online in an hour than the print copy gets all week before it ends up being used by hobos for a blankets."

Sam finally put the papers down on his thigh, and looked wearily at the Food Editor. "Felicia, I know the reality of the industry as well as you. I'm trying not to be the dinosaur staring up at the meteor, but print *still* has prestige. For a writer to be so good that they get put into print, not just online, is evidence of *real* talent. Online is definitely dominant in terms of reach, speed, and cost, but there's still that tradition, and I think it's one we can all stand behind."

"It's all about the numbers game for me. In *ev*erything."

Sam wasn't sure what he should make of that comment, so he regarded Felicia only momentarily to see if she had more to say. She had already turned back to her monitor, so he stood to leave. He paused at the door to ask if she had more to discuss but thought better of it and proceeded to his office where another awkward conversation awaited him.

KAREN & CALVIN – DINNER PLANS

When Calvin reached the café, he was surprised to find a waiter occupying the other side of the booth from Karen. Before Calvin could approach them, his phone buzzed and another text from Karen read: "Please bring Manager to table."

He went dutifully to the host podium by the door and sought the assistance politely. "Is the manager around?"

The portly man clad in all black pointed a thumb at his own chest. "That's me."

Calvin was surprised at the automatic challenge in the manager's poise but proceeded nonetheless. "My friend just asked me to bring you to her table."

Calvin pointed at the booth. When the manager looked over, his brow furrowed in ire at seeing a young waiter sitting in the booth. Without another word, the manager took off with Calvin in his wake. The manager was quickly berating the employee for having the gall to sit with and hit on a patron while on shift.

The waiter, for his part, looked contrite and apologetic, but didn't help matters much by looking confused about the fact that he had "found himself" sitting and stammered that he didn't know what had come over him.

By the time the waiter had shuffled away, red in the face with his head hanging low, the manager had promised to comp the meal and drinks to make up for the affront. Karen graciously accepted and told the manager not to be too hard on the boy.

Calvin sat down and blinked a few times in amazement at Karen. "Did you?"

"No." She waved off the inference he was trying to find the words for while taking a sip of her mimosa. "The waiter *did* sit down uninvited and didn't take any of my hints that I was waiting on someone and that I'd prefer to wait alone."

"Tough being a single lady in this city," Calvin empathized as the manager rushed a Mimosa onto the table before him. Calvin raised his eyebrows and looked inquiringly at Karen, who confirmed with a nod that she had ordered it for him.

"Tough having a boyfriend too, which I told him at least once." Calvin didn't dwell much on the comment. Karen had joked about being single and too busy for any of the dimwits the Nats tried to push on her, but perhaps the situation had changed recently. He'd only known her for a couple of months, after all. "Speaking of boyfriends, what did Matt have to say?"

Calvin almost choked on the sip of Mimosa he was taking at the time. He looked gravely at her while sputtering and considered how to confess he was seriously considering the story Matt had woven for him as a distinct possibility. He ran over the logic in his head and decided to start from the top. "Okay, so my article?"

"The one you had me read and lost?"

"Yeah, the one you and I both know exists that I was assigned last week." When Karen nodded, he proceeded. "Okay, that article doesn't exist. Never did. It got wiped from history. According to Errol, I was never assigned that article. According to my computer and email account, the article doesn't exist, and I never wrote or sent it." Karen pulled out her own phone and began typing, presumably to check her own email archive while Calvin continued. "According to Errol, Matt was assigned the article, and it was always the one that was going to print."

Karen raised an eyebrow at her phone. Calvin assumed

it was her finding her inbox bereft of any evidence of the article. "So, what did Matt say about it?"

"He says he has a deal with a Devil to be a famous writer."

Karen didn't scoff or betray any kind of skepticism. "That's the deal? And he's doing it through the *LA Weekly* of all things?"

Calvin was caught off guard by the ease with which Karen had accepted that revelation, but he shook his head and went with her line of questioning. "He said it was a stepping stone to other things."

"And you're the competition he has to steamroll to get what he wants?"

Calvin gulped the last of his Mimosa down. "Looks like it. They can alter reality and memories to do it. So I'm what most experts would call: fucked."

Karen seemed to be weighing her words carefully. Her gaze was serious, and she appeared to make a decision on which tact to employ. "You're not flattered, though?"

"Flattered? Karen, I lost a cover page byline because of someone using a spiritual cheat code. Also, since when are you superstitious?"

"Four years at a Lutheran high school and lingering welts on my cheeks make me ironically open minded."

"Welts? Your cheeks are perfect."

"I didn't say my face, genius." Calvin choked on a sip of his drink once more. "Like you said, I remember the article, and I see what you see. It'd be foolish to rule out what seems impossible as an explanation for a situation that seems equally impossible."

Calvin had it on the edge of his tongue to ask how whatever had wiped Errol's memory hadn't affected them, but she continued before he could. "At any rate, don't you think if they're pulling this stuff it's because you're actually competition?"

"Obviously, we're interns for the same Staff Writer position."

"Yes, but think about it: they not only have to push Matt *up* with the dark powers of the the underworld, they need to actively push you *down*." Karen reached over the table to put her hand on Calvin's consolingly.

Calvin felt like a vice had locked around his throat and tried to determine whether it was pure nervousness or if some excitement might be mingled in at the soft touch of Karen's hand. For a brief moment, that cocktail of emotion made everything else melt away and took a deft shake of his head and sharp intake of breath to bring it all back.

"Well, thanks for finding the glass half full." He meant it gratefully, but even as he was saying the words, he knew finding the silver lining in being cheated by supernatural forces didn't change the fact that he was being cheated by supernatural forces.

"Well? Are you going to push back?"

Calvin was puzzled; he'd never seen this expression on her before. It was a hungry look, dark in its focus, fiery in its intensity. "Push back?"

"Haven't you ever read *The Devil and Daniel Webster?*"

"I've seen the *Simpson's* episode parodying it."

"Good enough. You get the principle then. There's always a loophole. No contract is perfect."

"I don't think I can afford a lawyer."

"You don't need one! You're a journalist, do the research. Get him to go into details and find the loophole yourself."

"Like love?"

"Or *maybe* it's something the Devil is supposed to include you can block Matt from getting? If not bylines, then maybe something else?"

"He *was* willing to have dinner tonight."

Karen clapped her hands boisterously, making Calvin start slightly in his seat, but the conversation had thrown his mind into a frenzy of planning. He dug his wallet out from his jeans while Karen continued. "There you go! Get him liquored up and act like you're interested in taking one of those deals yourself. Tell him you want to get a feel for negotiating terms and all that!"

Calvin nodded and thanked Karen quickly, taking a crisp twenty from his wallet and putting it on the table. He apologized profusely and said, "I have until six, but I need to run back to Highland Park and get ready before meeting him."

Karen's face suddenly took on a pallor, and he worried he'd offended her with his rushed departure. Before he could apologize, she began to look worried, a little meek even and apologized to him in a soft but high-pitched fervor. "Oh, no, you're right! I'm *so* sorry I kept rambling! Get going! If you need anything, just call me? Or text if it's easier. I'll be around," Karen looked confused and distracted, but Calvin nodded and thanked her. He hesitated and bent over to hug her, and felt his heart jump when she squeezed him tightly back.

With a wave, he was off to get his car from the *Weekly* parking lot and head home to watch *The Simpson's* Halloween episode he'd mentioned as research.

The manager returned and asked if Karen wanted anything else. She apologized to the manager for no reason at all, left another twenty on top of Calvin's for an eight dollar tab, and scurried anxiously back to the office, worried she might get in trouble for the mid-morning excursion.

CALL YOUR PARENTS 2 - KAREN

Karen called home while walking back to the office. Her father answered. "Hey, honey. How's it going?"

She instantly felt the unique comfort of speaking with her father. "It's good."

"Uh oh, what's up, Kare-bear?"

She walked into the lobby and spun on her heel, not wanting to enter the elevator while continuing on the phone. She lingered by the doors for a moment, realized with embarrassment that it was even more rude to block the lobby doors, and shimmied to the corner of the lobby by the window facing Olympic Boulevard. "Nothing. Everything's all good with me. It's a friend of mine from the office, got some uh, bad news on an article of his."

"Uh oh, what happened?"

She leaned against the window with one arm crossed over her chest curled up in herself and sighed before she began. "He wrote this really great article and it, um, it got bumped for another article by a guy who didn't sign up for the assignment."

"Sounds underhanded."

"Yeah, kind of an uncool move."

"But was the article they went with better?"

Karen paused and considered the question while looking distractedly at the single elm tree on the lawn outside. Los Angeles seemed oddly satisfied with itself to only have a tree every quarter mile or so, and she never understood why. In her opinion, lone trees looked sadder than none at all. "I don't know." As she admitted this, she knew how her father would retort.

"Well, honey, I know it sounds unfair, but maybe the editors were being fair to give the better article the spot? Maybe they did review and considered them both. Their job is to make the paper as good as they can."

"Yeah." Karen bit her lip nervously, unsure how much more detail to go into. "But they could have, you know, been more transparent about it. Calvin put a lot of work into his article."

Her father ah'ed. "*Cal*vin. You know, your mom and I wanted to visit this weekend. Do you think we could do din—"

"No!" Karen immediately threw her hand over her mouth. Karen could swear she heard her father muffling the receiver with his hand and his laughter still leaking through it. "No. Sorry, Dad. He's just really busy and— Listen, we're really good friends, and I don't want him getting the wrong idea."

"Because you want it to be the right idea at the right time?"

"I don't know, maybe. No, what? Dad, I—"

"I'm sorry, hon. I didn't mean to fluster you. Just teasing. Your mom and I are coming for dinner, and you can invite whoever you want as a friend or otherwise."

"Thanks, Dad. Sorry. Just a crazy day."

"Sounds like it, but you're okay?"

"Yeah, I should get back to work. I'll call you and Mom later?"

"Sure thing, hon. I'll tell Mom you called when she gets home."

It wasn't until Karen returned to her office and looked at the stack of paperwork for her new job that she realized she hadn't told her dad the good news. She buried her face in her hands at how anxious Calvin's dilemma suddenly had her but was thankful that the Nats were no longer hovering around outside her office.

"At least that's the last we'll see of them," she consoled herself.

TIE

Unlike Gast, Tie loved ditching his physical body once in awhile to do work as a Demon. Oftentimes, the nudges and whispers he let drift over a meat sack were just the influence needed to push them into his waiting tree trunk arms for a deal. Tie delighted in the little ways he plied their influence and was enthralled whenever he found a human broken or weak enough to indwell or fully possess. In the cases he managed a full possession, he was rarely kind to the bodies.

Tie was very proudly responsible for every incident of a teenaged individual falling into an animal enclosure in a zoo in the contiguous United States. Humans are rarely so mentally weak and susceptible to demonic possession than on overlong sightseeing vacations with family. Let that be a lesson to you.[10]

Tie was well within his rights given his role as evaluator of Gast's work to seek out Gast's latest target and see what he might bestir in the situation. Finding Gast's little ward was easy enough, but Tie had an alternate plan in mind. He had reviewed the dossier Aba had offered and saw Gast's note about leaving off a memory wipe on the ward's competition. Driving someone mad in this instance was always a surefire bet for some good old fashioned mayhem. All Tie had to do was to find the meat sack.

He was in luck. Finding the ward in the *LA Weekly* offices, the competition made himself apparent

---

[10] Among his other Demonic achievements, Tie is also responsible for most of the menu items added to Taco Bell in the past five years. For this, he is much beloved in Sloth, Gluttony, and most US college campuses.

immediately, but Tie couldn't get in. His mind was a steel trap of anxieties woven over and around more fear and nervousness. He was focused too intently on Matt's words and story to be penetrated by Tie's whisperings. Tie hung back, knowing there would be a slackening of Calvin's focus soon enough, where he'd soon be overwhelmed by the futility of the scenario Matt was describing and make an opening for Tie.

To Tie's displeasure, no such opening appeared. Not even when Matt finished his explanation minutes later down at the coffee shop. Tie wondered how Gast would feel about the ward divulging so much information and also how Gast had felt waking up tied to the chandelier. Tie lamented that his dedication to work got in the way of his seeing Gast cut to bits from falling onto that ostentatious glass table.

It was an old trick, and Tie had last pulled it on Gast the night they'd both gotten smashed at the premiere of Beethoven's "Ninth." Existential self-centric artistic movements were incredible for business, and the age of Romanticism had been Hell's best in centuries until modernity blew even that away.

With Matt gone, Tie snapped his focus back to Calvin, but Calvin's mind was too tightly wound, even in conversation with his mother. Tie followed along and found the mind was not hitting the note of despair he was hoping for. Calvin's mind resolutely gathered information and facts, and held onto them firmly. Calvin was not trying to force them into a preconceived architecture as so many meat sacks depend on for their comfort and confidence. To Calvin, these were simply experiences which he held simply among objective experiences where they couldn't cause more calamity to his nerves than everything else already would.

It was interesting, at least. Tie was tired of dealing with people who opened the doors so easily or left the doors open perpetually. Finding someone with such a balanced mind that could hold ideas without truly entertaining them was a welcome challenge. Arriving at a restaurant, Tie reminded himself that this was no mere side project. He had a job to do, and raising quick mayhem for Gast was his aim.

Calvin eventually sat down with a girl so pretty that Tie thought for a moment that Calvin had accidentally sat at the wrong table, but then they began talking, and it became clear she was a co-worker. Somewhat puzzling was that Gast's dossier had only mentioned Calvin as being left off the memory wipe, but this girl shared Calvin's true memories as well. Perhaps there was a loophole through her position as a fellow intern, that or the Imps downstairs had messed it up.

Tie listened to Calvin relate what he had just been told. Surprisingly, the girl also accepted them with aplomb.

Then he saw his route laid bare before him. She reached for his hand as a gesture of consolation. Tie shifted over to the girl's shadow, and he felt it. However baffling, it was clear that she loved him, and if there is any emotion that can be corrupted in the name of the best intentions to the worst of things, it's love. This wouldn't take much. She just needed to use that love to encourage him in the wrong direction.

"He is talented," Tie whispered in concordance of the feelings he could feel radiating from her so plainly. "*So* talented that a Devil has to bend reality to fight him. It's not fair. He shouldn't take that lying down." He waited. Karen took his words into consideration and asked Calvin if he was going to push back or not.

Pleased with himself, Tie pressed on. "It's a deal, like

any other. There must be a way around it, a loophole to exploit." She came up with her own example and argument of Tie's point echoing him.

It was perfect. Now all that was needed was to tell Gast he had a rabbit wandering into a snare. The girl was already running away with the seed he had planted as if it had been her very own. That was what many younger Demons on the grind missed, and it was something Gast did perfectly in his Sales work as a Devil: you plant the seed, but you let the mark bring it to blossom.

No one wants to hold onto an idea they can't feel is their own, but if they do feel that ownership, then they'll fight tooth and nail for it. Even if reality stares them in the face and tells them the sky is blue, they'll cry the sky is pink while cutting out their opponent's tongue.

Tie was ready to find Gast. They could discuss next steps and how to use this situation as the foil for Aba. As Tie was readying himself to turn back into Hell's offices, a familiar voice called over his shoulder, the bright happy tone of a woman greeting him. "Hey, babe!"

His last thought was pure terror.

"UNDERWORLD CORPORATE" FEATURE STORY – HELL'S MOST AWESOME C.E.O.

Demons, Imps, and Devils all want to be him. They also all want to kill him, but "to kill is to become," Lucifer tells me as he guns down the last Tasmanian tiger in the wild. It's a fascinating *raison d'etre* for Hell's most successful [ed. note: only] CEO.

Lucifer laughs from his belly and gallops forward with enthusiasm to the corpse of the tiger before I can ask anything about this aphorism. He's holding the dead tiger up to me with his fingers at either corner of the mouth, pulling the furry skin into a grin.

"Luce," as he asks me several times over the course of our day together to call him, is keen to laugh. You might expect him to be more glower, cloak, and dagger, but by his own words not long after the tiger's corpse is left on the doorstep of a conservatory, he explains to me: "Laughter makes that dark stuff cut deeper."

At his behest, we're hiding in the bushes nearby, waiting for one of the animal conservationists to come outside and find the corpse. Lucifer has bet me a plague that one of the scientists cries. He wins the bet. I don't have a plague to give him and only remember now while writing this that I never took the bet in the first place. "You can bet I'll come round for that plague," he assured me after we set off, all the same.

We started the interview in Western Europe where some political machinations and technological developments had drawn Lucifer's attentions, then rode the wind out to Australia.

You might expect me to have answers to some of the most penetrating questions you could ask Hell's eternity-long CEO, especially when it's widely public knowledge that this interview was requested by him personally. Unfortunately, Lucifer is difficult to pin down. No sooner does a question occur to you than you find yourself swept along to some new locale, shown some new wonder, laughing along unwittingly at some joke, prank, or mayhem he's telling, causing, or inflicting.

He doesn't allow time to stand still or coalesce in any meaningful way. He's off before your laughter can even chortle in your throat and showing you the next travesty or spectacle. For those of you wondering about Hell's restructures over the ages, pay attention. This is the mind behind it. Lucifer does not sit still. Satisfaction in a given moment is not his style. As soon as the payoff has been seized, he's already hungry for the next and pursuing it.

Some Devils reading this may be waiting for me to reveal some inclination of our leader's favorite sin, his primary vice, and I'm sorry to tell you there seem to be none. Since the Fall, he's a constant embodiment of pursuing them all, moment to moment, unrelentingly.

"We've all heard humanity's take on your existence, but how do you turn that into the successful business Hell has become when PR is king?" I finally ask him this question after we leave the weeping scientist in Australia. Eighteen hours, and it's the first question I've managed to finally ask him. He looks almost dissatisfied with himself that I managed to fire this one off, but he's actually more disappointed in the question I chose to ask rather than my asking one at all.

"That's it, eh?" We're atop a mountain, and I consider asking if this is the one from that story in the Bible, but then reconsider because I'm only averaging a question every eighteen hours so I need to choose carefully.

"I've been showing you this whole time."

He finally sits still.

It's eerie, because when he sits still, everything does. It's as if the wind itself somehow died. I look around and think over the past eighteen hours. It makes sense to me, and if doesn't make sense to you, then Lucifer wants you right where you are until you figure it out.

I have the opening for another question, so I dig right in: "What about cocoa butter, though?"

He grins, the kind of wide, toothy grin human beings must picture him having—it's a little sinister but still full of guile. "Well, look who's a clever girl." He appreciates the irony (and that's the last hint you get, dear reader).

Lucifer's role as CEO affords him all the free time he wants, and he admits to me that while he's been less than fully committed to the career, he lives for the craft.

For those who think Hell's captain is a tireless workaholic, he respects Sloth just as much as any other sin. He has found that when you embody what you live for properly, even distractions serve their purpose in your path forward, even if that path is a flat circle.

"I know I'm stuck in Hell." He admits this with a casual shrug when we find ourselves in Paris to conclude the interview. It has the tone of an observation he feels not many others around him are aware of or admit to themselves. We're standing at the observation deck of the Eiffel Tower, and he's just talked a man out of jumping off the upper deck (to my puzzlement) [ed. note: the man in question would be the father of the inventor of company hold music].

It's a strange thing for him to say because he has not confined himself to Hell at all. Lucifer has, unbeknownst to many of his followers, abandoned his post for entire epochs to, among other things, compose music, run jazz lounges, captain ships for the British West Indies, and serve on the board of directors of a startup named Monsanto.

"Doesn't mean I can't grow." He says this to me atop that tower under the starry firmament, to which he outstretched his hands.

I'd find out later that he is truly the prince of lies. If you've counted on hearing which sin is his worst and biggest, it's that one: that he lies to himself that he might still grow and truly evolve and his carrying about in running Hell as if this were true. [ed. note: redacted due to personal history causing this inference.]

-Lilith, Senior Staff Writer

H.R. HARRY

Harry Anderson paused just before he crossed in front of Felicia's office. As a rule, he moved past her office as quickly as he could. Deniability was a valuable thing for a Human Resources Director, and the less he saw of her attire, behavior, and posture, the less he would be predisposed to forming presumptive opinions about her in the event that a complaint was lodged against her. Complaints regarding Felicia's conduct were less a possibility and more a seasonal guarantee for Harry, so the ability to remain a disinterested party was invaluable to him.

The first time Felicia had received a complaint from a fellow editor, Harry was pleased to have come into the mediation with Felicia having not the slightest clue who he was. He was even more pleased that during the mediation for her second complaint when she was surprised to find out that he was a full-time employee at the office and not an ad hoc contractor for these conflict resolutions.

Harry's goal was to be as completely unnoticed and unaffecting to the office population as possible, and he had drawn a sense of pride from mediations three, four, and five wherein she had consistently forgotten or misspoken his name (Henry, Halibut, and Hagrid, respectively).

Harry could herewith muse for you on the nature of those complaints and their resolutions. However, as they had been settled and the files sealed as confidential, Harry will not since it is his duty to keep them private from us all, dear reader. What he will note, as he shuffles along down the hall towards Sam Dority's office, is the regularity with which those who lodge complaints against

Felicia agree to sealing the outcomes and complaints themselves, and the clockwork nature by which such persons subsequently resign from the *LA Weekly* in pursuit of other ventures.

Harry's position was not undermined by his well wishes for those individuals and happiness at their ambitions. He hoped they had noticed the extra happy lilt of his stamping and initialing on their employment termination documents as he bid them all farewell.

Harry hustled to the open door of Sam's office and knocked. Sam did not look up from his computer but lifted a hand and waved for Harry to enter. Harry made a point not to glance at the monitor lest he see anything of conflict. Sam was a good work friend in his care for shielding Harry from any potentially compromising workplace exposures or conflicts of interest.

When Harry had started helping in Human Resources nearly a decade prior, and Sam was a Staff Writer. Sam had regularly refused Harry's invitations to grab drinks after long days. Harry surmised this was merely a friend's respect for his station and not wanting each other's ambitions in the office to be undermined by frivolous socializing that may impede either man's ascent. Harry had taken the job in Human Resources at Sam's encouragement. Sam had told him to cover those duties until such time that Sam could bring him back to the writing side from Human Resources.

For a decade now, either it had been the lack of an opening in the editorial pool (Sam had recently assured Harry that the Staff Writer positions the interns were competing for would be too far beneath him) or a lack of alternative personnel to handle Harry's H.R. duties in his wake, but Harry trusted Sam.

Harry, never said so openly (again, wanting to preclude

any possible conflict of interest), but he hoped Felicia would find her way from the *LA Weekly* so that an editorial position might open up. Eight years later, Harry had an two drawers dedicated to her records alone, but Harry remained ever hopeful.

Sam had climbed up to Editor-in-Chief, and Harry now reigned as the Director of Human Resources. It was a dubious title for Harry since he was the only employee in the department, thus leaving him no one to direct. He considered Sam a brother in arms, and they were two knights bound by honor and shared conquest of keeping the paper and its staff running smoothly.

Harry had taken the seat facing Sam across the editor's desk, and Sam gave an impatient raise of his eyebrow. "Did you want to discuss something?" Harry shook his head from the prior reverie and stammered a chuckling apology while Sam rolled his eyes. "No, please, don't let me interrupt."

Harry pried a pair of green processed checks from his leather folio and set them flat on the table before he slid them over to Sam. "Small issue this week, Sam. Seems we cut the wrong checks for the interns."

"We pay the interns?"

"No."

"Then why the checks?"

"Because it's payroll week."

"And you just said—"

"I said we do not *pay* interns, which we don't." Harry puffed his broad chest with pride. "We pay *writers* for *articles*. The interns remain unpaid workers. Were we to compensate them as workers, we'd incur the additional burden of having to pay health bene—"

"Okay, okay, Harry. Thanks for the red tape." Sam leaned forward and flipped open his reading glasses to read the checks. "So we're paying the interns *for writing?*"

"Yes, the writers' stipend." Harry tugged at his argyle sweater vest to get it more completely over his ponderous belly since it had slid up with his taking the seat.

"What's the issue?"

Harry chuckled. "Well, darnedest thing. I was double checking the stipends against this week's copy, and for some reason, Calvin seems to have gotten Matt Reade's check made out to him." Harry leaned forward and pointed. "See? He only has one article published online, which should be fifty, but his check is for one-fifty, which is what Matt should get since he has an online article *and* a print article."

"So, you mixed them up?" Sam snorted and shook his head in sardonic disappointment. "Not like you, Harry. We may want to get an auditor in here to spot check your docs, or get you some help if you're finally cracking."

Harry's tone went flat, and his eyes leveled darkly from under his bushy brows. "Sam, I'd like to remind you that the process for check allocations starts with *your* editors confirming story publications, *your* review and confirmation of those publication numbers, then *your* notification to me of those numbers." At this point, Harry leaned further forward over his generous paunch and firmly tapped his index finger on the one check's signature line. "It ends with *your* signing the checks I cut against all those directions."

Harry did not move for a few seconds. It wasn't long before Sam realized he had frozen in fear under the menace of the Director's tone. Sam swallowed hard and apologized. "Sorry, Harry. I just forward the emails I get from the—"

"Well!" Harry's grin immediately flashed on as he sat back in the chair in evident satisfaction. "I checked the emails, and it seems the assignments in the *emails* are all correct."

Sam furrowed his brow. "So, what do you need? Should I tell the interns you need a few extra days to recut their checks?"

Harry shook his head. "Oh no, I have them already." He pulled two more checks out and slid the unsigned ones for the correct amounts to Sam. Sam uncapped his pen and signed them with quick swishes of his signature while Harry continued. "I only managed to catch this since I decided to check the print copy that got emailed around today."

Sam paused and eyed Harry carefully. He could sense the suggestion coming, and he held his breath for it. "Thanks, Harry. That was a great catch."

"Hey, it's no problem. I know an extra set of eyes can't hurt on the copy. We're all in it together."

"You did a great job." Sam hoped his tone had the right amount of polite finality to it and tried returning his hands to the keyboard to emphasize the full stop, but he was too slow.

"Well, Sam, it seems to me maybe that could be a more official part of the copy process. You know? Me checking it along with you all."

"Oh, Harry, I don't want to give you more than you already—"

"Not at all. If anything, reading the copy with the editors and catching this *saved* me a bunch of work. You know how hard recovering a cashed check would have been?" Harry blew impressively as he mentally rattled off the four separate documents he'd have to file with Sam, Calvin, the bank, and Accounting.

"So, just for double checking assignment stipends?" Sam asked cautiously.

Harry beamed. "Yeah! And if I catch anything glaring in the copy, I can point it out too."

Sam winced at Harry's enthusiasm. Harry had started as a writer with Sam a lifetime ago, but Sam had convinced Harry to "increase his market value" by helping out with Human Resources, then eventually being transitioned fully into it once Sam had the clout to grant him the "honor" of being the Director. Sam scrambled mentally to try and block Harry from finding his way back into the editorial pool Sam had successfully relocated him from years ago. "Harry, if you get taken up with proofreading, you're the only H.R. person."

"Like you said, we can bring in a consultant to help. Like *I* said, this helps me do my job." Sam's throat croaked while he sought words for another retort, but Harry was quicker once more. "Or we could have a procedure mapping meeting? Review the official procedure documents for payroll requisition and management, confirm we understand proper processes through training tests, and then have a process revision discussion, followed by actual revision to the documentation, associated reviews, implementations, and training on the updated procedures?"

Sam froze at the threat and saw the glint in Harry's eye. He was in checkmate and knew it. "Fine, Harry. Mondays I'll start including you on proof review with the rest of us." Harry hopped to his feet and walked with a surprising bounce to the door. Sam urgently called after him. "But you're included purely for payroll verification! Proofreading and copy edits are *not* required, nor will we wait for your approval on content before finalizing for print!"

Harry stopped at the door and shrugged. "Good enough."

"Wait, Harry. How did you get this week's copy for proofing, anyway?"

"Felicia sent it to me. Something about an article you allowed to be switched and wanting to check against my list of article publications for the payroll." Harry waited a moment for Sam to ask a follow up, but the Editor-in-Chief only nodded to indicate he was finished.

Harry gave a small salute from his brow with two fingers. "Fear not, oh captain my captain. The proper report for concerns regarding misallocation of funds had been filed before I did the research, and the report for confirmation of misallocated funds has been logged, as well as the forms confirming the correct reallocation of the originally misallocated funds. I'll have them on your desk before I leave for your signatures."

Sam waved Harry off while fighting with all his might not to groan. The Editor-in-Chief checked his email but nothing had come in from Felicia all day. Not even her usual open invitation to lunch for the bullpen. It was getting close to one, and he wondered what Felicia was up to with this noise about Calvin's article.

Sam buried his face in his hands and cursed that Harry was at all aware of whatever she had going on with Calvin. "Not another damned mediation meeting."

THE AUDIT

Gast scowled at the coffers of the Avarice Devils beside each desk: overflowing, yet never full—the paradox of greed. Each Devil hunched over their desk, constantly tabulating accruals, interest, gains, thefts, acquisitions, desires, targets, wants, and needs. Occasionally, they fit the small work of bean counting souls and other tangible resources for Hell in the process.

Gast hoped this part of the evaluation might have been skipped, or at least ignored, but the summons for the audit had been sent by Aba himself. He couldn't afford to lose ground by such a formality, so he was there on time looking every bit the furious Devil for having to visit the Greed Devils for it.

Some of the coffers overflowed with gold and money, others had collectible items Devils worked at encouraging humans to hoard. There was a section of the floor dedicated entirely to Devils managing human obsessions with Pokémon memorabilia, and another shrinking but still busy section focused on Beanie Babies. Adjacent to Avarice was the IRS—not merely for Hell, but for the United States itself.

Gast strode purposefully up the rows, occasionally having to turn against a desk as an Envy Imp or Devil raced past him, almost bowling him over. Envy and Greed worked closely together, as did Envy with Lust, Pride, and Gluttony, as Gast considered it.

Partnerships between Envy and Wrath were a subtle art, and only the most artful of demons knew how to let the envy of peace or justice be twisted to lead humans to the sins of Wrath. Very few Devils seemed aware of the nuance. Gast mused that the only truly isolated sin was Sloth, as its perpetrators and Devils only wanted to binge watch *Orange is the New Black*, so could you please get out of the way, the theme song is starting and that's the best part.

There is but one Devil in Avarice whose coffer always runs empty, and it was his desk for which Gast searched. Pitch had earned himself the stout body of a fiery-haired French infantryman who had traded his soul to climb the ranks of the military. Aba's message demanding the audit had mandated Gast submit to it today; however, it had not assigned a Devil to perform the evaluation, which meant Gast could choose for himself.

Gast chose Pitch.

Gast eyed the coffer beside Pitch's desk. His was a seven-foot-tall, reinforced steel monster of a safe, and the wide open door was facing Pitch along with its bare shelves. For many centuries, Gast had maintained that Pitch was better suited to just about any other order of sin than Avarice. It was Lilith, sometime in the 1960s, who had seen what Gast hadn't about Pitch and why he was actually superlative among the Devils of Greed with his empty shelves.

Gast shook his head to dismiss the memory of her and knocked his knuckles on the corner of Pitch's desk. Pitch looked up, and a smile curled over his freckled countenance before he sat back and knowingly twirled his ginger moustache. "I take it you're here for the audit?"

Pitch was the only Devil other than Tie who knew of Gast's ambition. Gast was extremely cautious in picking his allies. However, it had to be clear Gast had machinations since the question among Devils (except Sloth) was never whether or not they had ambition: it was what that ambition was and if you were along the way of it or in the way of it.

"I thought the Beggar Devil would suffice." Gast sneered while using the nickname that other Devils derided Pitch with. Gast knew that Pitch secretly prided himself on the moniker. He said any Devil who thought it was a barb was only proving their simplicity to him. Once again, Gast shook his head at the resurfacing memory of Lilith and took the chair Pitch had summoned for him beside the safe.

Pitch began typing on the computer, and within

moments was cocking an eyebrow. "Steady soul acquisitions. Reasonable resource management and applications." Pitch pointed at one section of the screen, then scanned elsewhere and made an ah'ing motion. "Efficient uses here and here, I see what you did. Very efficient, indeed." Pitch murmured to himself as he analyzed the expenses and numbers. "Can't fault you having good taste in suits." Glasses manifested and perched on Pitch's round red nose as he leaned in to read more closely. "Yes, two birds with one stone, that's artful stuff."

Gast crossed his legs and smirked with pride. He could feel the other Devils' eyes on him. They knew he was down here for an audit and were clearly impressed at the impossible sight of someone with such a pristine record of expense and resource management.

He was relishing the smug feeling of showing them what a masterful Devil was capable of, but the feeling was quickly overridden by shock as walls manifested. He found himself alone in an office with Pitch, shielded from the eyes and ears of the other Devils.

"Gast, this is *too* good."

"You're not laughing, though." Gast tried a weak chuckle, but it didn't catch on with Pitch and wilted quickly in Gast's throat. The red-haired Devil stared stonily at him. "Come on, too good? What in Hell does that possibly mean? I'm the best. So sign off on a memo saying I'm doing my job well and efficiently, and be on with it."

"I sure could. It's about the only thing I can do."

"Damned right."

"Except how many other Devils get audited with that kind of result?"

Gast was momentarily confused, since it seemed

obvious to him. "I imagine it's rare."

"You imagine wrong. This is Hell, not state government work. No Devil in this day and age even goes a week without a gross mismanagement of resources and improper expenses on their accounts."

"In this day and age?" Gast snorted dubiously. "I'd have said it never happens in any age."

"That's even more accurate."

"Well, how about that?" Gast grinned proudly.

"You don't get it, do you? It's *too* clean. This record reeks of a Devil who wants to be the best but has been trying his damnedest to keep his head down and not draw *any* attention to himself so he can strike at the right moment."

"Not draw attention? I'm the *best*, Pitch. That's what I'm trying to draw attention to."

"Yeah, but the best at *what?* Getting souls efficiently, sure, but being a Devil?"

"If that's not being a Devil, then what's wrong with that attention?" Gast asked in disbelief.

Pitch rolled his eyes. "Because it's the wrong kind of attention. It's a Devil who claims he had nothing to do with the collapse of communism thirty years ago that hamstrung his boss suddenly changing his act and performance *com*pletely. You went from spending the GDPs of small nations on cocoa butter alone to suddenly being a robot?" Pitch pointed at a specific line in Gast's expenses. It was a line where the amounts went from being seven or more figures to no more than five or six.

Gast desperately tried to reassure both Pitch and himself by proxy. "So? At least I haven't given Aba ammunition."

"You don't think this is ammunition?" Pitch's fiery brows arched almost to his hairline. "Then why was Aba down here last week? You don't think this audit is part of a case he already knows he can win?"

"Aba wasn't—"

"I can guarantee you he was already pulling your numbers. This audit is just a fugazi. He wants to see what you pull."

Gast huffed and crossed his arms. "I can't change my numbers. That'd give away that I know they look too clean, or that I know he's gunning for me as more than just a performance exercise."

Pitch tutted at the monitor. "And if you *don't* change them, you're playing right into whatever he knows they represent."

Gast chewed the inside of his cheek in a moment of deep thought and felt an uncommon chill creep up his spine. Lilith had managed to make plenty of friends in her time in Hell. The problem was that popularity naturally meant enemies[11] and she'd made an enemy of Gast's own boss, Aba.[12] Now Lilith was gone, and her old allies were apparently stuck in her mess.

Gast, Pitch, and Tie had all known their association with Lilith as drinking buddies had drawn a line between them and others. Gast stood on one side of that line facing Aba. Gast had seen enmity boiling up following

---

[11] Lilith also clarified that this was not a problem unique to her, but universal of all intelligent, beautiful, talented women, such as the author's girlfriend, and of yours, dear reader.

[12] It's wise to be careful about agreeing to blind dates, especially when the matchmaker is a Devil, or, in this case, Lucifer himself. It's also wise rather than to have to dodge, evade, ignore, and refuse seventy three calls, emails, text messages, and even a candy-gram seeking a second date, not to date a Devil in the first place.

Aba's failed dalliance with Lilith, and cemented by Gast's own feelings for her. What Gast hadn't expected with that line having been drawn, was Lilith leaving him there with nary a word before her flight.

"Fuck it. File the report. I can at least play dumb so he thinks I'm a step further behind than I really am."

Pitch glowered while typing up the report. "Still leaves you at least two steps behind him, then."

Gast slouched with his arms crossed. "Go suck a Beanie Baby."

CONFESSION

"Tell me your sins, my child."

"Only if you promise me you've got your pants on," Benny replied. There was some cursing from the priest's side of the confessional accompanied by the shuffling of cloth and the clinking of a belt buckle. Father Llewyn McFadden fought his trousers back up in the cramped space. "Perv," Benny grunted.

"It's flippin' hot today, Ben," Llewyn complained while fastening his pants.

"Oh sure, like confessions of infidelity and lust don't factor in."

Llewyn leaned toward to the grating. "Those ladies come through on Saturdays. Mondays are always pain in the ass retirees confessing to stealing grapes from the produce section." Llewyn groaned. "It doesn't help that it's a hundred degrees and this box has no ventilation."

Benny grew serious. "Llewyn, I need your help."

"In the religious sense?"

"In the business sense."

"Oh boy, what happened now?"

"What happened is your little hippy dippy holder idea backfired."

"What?"

"The kid you told us to let hold the product? He ended up blowing half of it then cutting the rest to shit. We're out forty kilos." Benny slammed a fist into the paneled wood between them.

"Flynn? He knows better than that. He's about the cut when he returns the product."

"Flynn? You said Toddy."

"Yeah, Flynn is the guy you met at *Toddy's* party. He brought those delightful ginger snaps."

"You said the guy I met, Toddy," Benny ventured unsurely but realized his error and felt fire under his skin.

"The guy you met at Toddy's *party*." Llewyn snickered at Benny a moment then asked, "He stole the product?"

"Used it in some hipster beer he's brewing then cut what was left down to *fifty* percent. You know this wouldn't have happened if you'd just let us use the church."

"No can do. Whatever comes in is property of the Catholic church."

"I'm talking about drugs, not money for laundering."

"Did I stutter?" There was a sound of more movement, and Llewyn instructed Benny to follow. Benny followed Llewyn down the rows of pews, where Benny noticed Llewyn walked straighter until they reached Llewyn's office down a hall, at which point the lithe man's slouch and swagger returned as he swept into the leather chair behind the desk.

"So, you're out forty kilos?" Llewyn confirmed while Benny was gently closing the door to the office behind him.

Benny fumed. "The Greek gave us two weeks to turn

the product, and Franco won't buy anything cut. I don't know if thirty cut kilos can make do anywhere in this town."

"Nah. LA's got more fresh powder than the Alps in January. Anything you can siphon off the restaurant?"

"We already siphoned off what was left of the startup capital for the forty in the first place."

"So, you're thinking..."

"I've gotta turn Franco's property into the capital."

Benny had impersonated Sally in the reading of their former boss, Franco Degneri's will earlier that year. Since then, Benny had kept Sally's inheritance of the storefront property being used as the Via Fresca in Los Feliz a secret. Franco had planned to reveal it to Sally as a gift for his thirtieth birthday to open his own restaurant, but had passed away before the day had arrived.

Benny lied and told Sally the ownership had been shared by both he and Franco, and was transferred fully to him in Franco's passing. Benny had magnanimously offered a job as chef in the restaurant. This allowed Benny to use the property for his business, but also kept his thumb on Sally in case he needed the property as collateral.

Sally's agreement to this arrangement was first one of wide eyed fervor of being offered the chance to open and run his own restaurant. When that fervor had quickly met the reality of Benny's intent, Sally's continued complacency was a matter of blackmail and threats. Benny routinely assured Sally that ratting him out would expose Franco's shady past, and ruin Sally as well- if Claudio and Maury didn't get to Sally first.

Llewyn leaned back in the chair so that he faced his ceiling. "First you need to make sure you can get your hands on the money."

"I found a lawyer, gonna meet with him tomorrow." Benny counted off on his thumb, waiting for Llewyn to add to the list of items to get done. Llewyn's attention to detail was the main reason why Benny still visited for counsel despite Llewyn's retirement several years prior.

"And the kid." Llewyn paused and pursed his lips, unable to bring himself to continue with the planning.

"I can't have him around after the papers go through. He could split with the money."

Llewyn regarded Benny's resolve impassively. Llewyn couldn't maintain Benny's gaze and averted his eyes from it. "Shame. He sounds like a good kid."

"Good, bad, everyone dies." Benny dismissed the sentimentality coldly.

"Benny, you can't be anywhere near this one." Llewyn sat forward looking grave at the turn the conversation had taken. "This isn't some street kid no one knows about, he's a chef at your restaurant. You're talking about going to a bank about *his* property, and you even had him sign papers before this, for Christ's sake."

"For tax purposes! And you took Lord's name in vain!" Benny brandished a reprimanding finger at Llewyn.

"I'll say five Our Fathers when you leave. Point is, if the kid disappears or turns up dead and leaves money from a loan he just *happened* to take out against his property to you? Guess who the cops look at first." Llewyn looked overwhelmed by the notion and sat back in astonishment at the risk, waving his hands in refusal. "It's big. You can't be *anywhere* near it. Not even Maury and Claudio should be within a hundred feet of it."

Llewyn looked hopeless, if not a little relieved for some reason, but Benny had a glimmer in his eyes. "I've got a professional. A *real* pro." Benny leaned forward so his chin was just inches over the surface of the desk. "I found it. The *Bar*."

Llewyn perked up, suddenly fascinated. "Here I thought that was a tall tale. How did you—"

Benny betrayed a wince of shame. "Toddy. Kid said it was a decent bar. Four stars on Yelp."

Llewyn snickered while he sat back and laced his hands behind his head. "Almost as good as the Fresca. It's got five, last I checked."

SPLITTING THE BILL

The whole way to the Santa Monica, Calvin wondered if people who had deals with Devils might have access to some underworld mass transit that let them get around LA traffic. Matt had texted him at four that they had a reservation at a neat little sushi spot in Santa Monica for six. In order to make the dinner reservation, Calvin had to leave his home within minutes of receiving the message. By the time he'd crawled down the 10 freeway, found the restaurant and parking, he'd walked in to find Matt sitting alone by a window, idly stirring a Gimlet with a swizzle stick.

Calvin didn't know why, but he was strangely impressed by, and jealous of Matt's astute choice of drink given the late spring heat. He told himself to find calm and focus on building his case the way he knew best: gathering his facts and reporting.

He set his messenger bag down and pulled out his digital recorder, pen, and pad. Matt offered a tired smile in greeting before Calvin began. "I hope you don't mind if I treat this like an interview?"

Matt held his palms open. "Why not?"

Calvin turned the recorder on and opened his pad. He

pressed his pen to the page to jot ideas and follow-up questions as they occurred to him. "You could probably have your Devil wipe the tape if you didn't like it, anyway. Is that one of his powers?"

Matt bobbed his head. "I guess if he didn't like what you were going to do with it. Yes, I think he could."

Calvin made a shorthand note of Matt's use of the third person. Calvin saw it as Matt disassociating himself from the decision process and the Devil's strategy to keep in mind. "If I were to pitch this as a story to the *LA Weekly*?"

Matt gave a wary look. "Would you?"

Calvin blew away the notion and did his best to look at ease- just an interviewer entertaining a hypothetical to his subject. "Let's just say I would. Humor me."

Matt seemed to grasp the exercise and suspiciously eyed Calvin's demeanor for only a moment before he relaxed again. Calvin saw Matt conclude there was nothing this conversation could do to harm his chances. "I guess he might let you do it under current circumstances. You'd be damaging your own credibility and helping me along as a result."

"What if I pitch it after you've moved onto the bigger, better things?"

"You're welcome to damage your credibility however you like after I've gone on to greener pastures."

Calvin turned the hypothetical around in his mind with a dreamy look at the ceiling. "So then what if *I* went to another publication with it?"

"What publication—"

"What if I pitched it not as journalism but as a creative piece?"

"I don't—"

"Wouldn't that ruin your Devil's work?"

Matt breathed heavily and gave it a serious moment's rumination. Calvin could see on his face that he once more reached the conclusion that he was secure in his Devil's power. "I think someone would have to take the whole thing seriously for my Devil to care. Even if they did, what could they do to stop us?"

"Maybe call you out on your work not being yours? Even if people didn't take it literally, a story about your work not being yours could raise eyebrows and make things difficult."

"I think since I'm working in the realm of journalism, there's less of a concern about that sort of thing. So long as I'm not copying other peoples' work, I'll be okay."

"But if you're put under scrutiny to prove the work is yours..."

Matt smirked. "You say that like I'm stealing or plagiarizing. Hell has a Muse, a spritely little lady who I'm told was hired after the Renaissance. She does this for them. Loves it, apparently. She writes articles, songs, poetry—everything. I get articles from her as part of my deal. No theft. Simple transaction."

"So she's in Hell? A Muse?"

"Just like my Devil is."

"Why not just have the Muse write a book for you instead? Why the *LA Weekly*? Seems like writing some pulp hit is a quick ticket to fame." Calvin thought of any number of viral young-adult hits.[13]

"I thought so too, but it turns out the Muse can only *tell* stories, not make them up. That's a purely human thing."

---

[13] We would be remiss, dear reader, if we did not advise that this tale falls into the more Adult category rather than Young Adult. This should, however, be apparent by this point, if not by the end of this chapter.

"A novel is a—"

"*True* stories. She can embellish or inflate with artistic flourishes, but she can't come up with something completely original. If I have an idea, she can produce a draft for me. Until I have that idea, though, using her to tell news stories in news is the safest bet."

Calvin recalled a bit of his college literature courses. "So in *The Odyssey* when Homer asks the Muse to sing in him?"

"Homer's asking the Muse to help him tell a true story."

Calvin sat back with the air of being mildly impressed and enjoying the conversation while his mind raced to pick his next tact. "You're saying Hell and its Muse was responsible for the most famous story ever told?"

"She was hired *after* the Renaissance, which is quite a while after Homer." Matt drained his gimlet, and the waiter appeared almost out of thin air to take Matt's order for two more without so much as glancing at Calvin.

Calvin tried not to betray his dislike for gimlets and asked, "So *The Odyssey* is all true?"

"In a fashion. I don't know the specifics." Matt accepted the fresh drink from the waiter, who seemed only to have taken a single step away from the table to refill it.

"And they only tell *true* stories?"

Matt gave a tired look again, returning to the dour visage he had been wearing when Calvin arrived. "Hence the journalism track," he drawled before tossing back his gimlet in a single pull then holding the glass up. The waiter was back again, taking the empty glass and placing a full one in Matt's hand without him having to move.

Calvin considered what else he might ask, but Matt became even more curious to him when his other hand raised and wagged two fingers as if calling another waiter over. From the same shadowy area outside his periphery, two girls appeared and took seats on either side of Matt. Calvin wondered if they were friends of his, but the girls giggled and spoke with each other as if Calvin and Matt weren't there.

Calvin took a sip and found that his love for gin had not manifested in the last ten minutes to supersede all his prior years of distaste for it. "So, even if I were to somehow draw eyes on you by telling a story about you as a *creative* endeavor, you would *not* be worried about being associated with the Devil? And your Devil wouldn't care about being so public?"

Matt glanced at the gorgeous girl in a snug blue dress on his right. "Actually, he's kind of hoping to be more public. Kind of a modern Devil from the looks of it."

"Modern?" Calvin was flustered by Matt reaching to caress the girl's chin. As he did, the chestnut-haired girl to his left pouted and leaned from the edge of her chair to drape herself over Matt's shoulder so that she could whisper right into Matt's ear.

Matt's eyes were closed from the girl's breath on his ear, and he spoke as if in a trance. "No such thing as bad PR. He likes working with people in media like us."

"Us?" Calvin stiffened in his seat as the two girls began competing more and more for Matt's arms and attention.

"My Devil wants to offer you the same deal." Matt's eyes fluttered as the girls licked and nibbled at his ears and neck respectively.

"To be famous?" Calvin asked in surprise, momentarily distracted by the offer from gratuitous displays before him.

"A famous writer." Calvin noticed one of the girl's

arms was sliding up and down what Calvin hoped was just Matt's thigh. Calvin darted his gaze around the restaurant, but none of the other patrons were taking any kind of notice.

"I actually like writing, though," Calvin muttered.

All three looked at Calvin from across the table. "But why not enjoy it without all the late nights? The ten drafts just to get a hundred words approved by one editor and then ten more drafts to get the next editor's approval? Who wants that when you can just take the bricks out of the briefcase? When you can be guaranteed to reach the peak instead of getting stuck on some plateau in a shit publication or some dead end editorial section?"

"The payoff isn't just in what I get rewarded *with*. The payoff is getting to *do* the work I love."

Matt blinked a couple times. The girls looked from Calvin to Matt in confusion. Matt's head snapped back, and he belted laughter. Calvin waited for it to cease, looking fitfully around the restaurant for someone else's ire at Matt's obnoxious volume, but still no one seemed to acknowledge Matt's antics.

Matt didn't stop laughing even when Calvin had scanned the whole bustling room. Matt continued to guffaw throatily even after Calvin shut off his recorder and slid it into his bag along with his pad and pen. Even as Calvin stood and flipped the bag over his shoulder, Matt was still wheezing giggles while the girls went back to trying to vie for his attention.

"Good luck with that work, slugger. Wait and see how many bylines it gets you!" Matt cackled after him as Calvin raced to the door.

The hostess halted Calvin at the entryway. She had a slip of paper in hand and held it to his chest to stop him. "You have five gimlets you need to close out for, *sir.*"

"Five?" Calvin looked back at the table. Matt and the two girls raised glasses at him. "Oh, no. I only had one."

"Did you water the plants with them? Because I saw you alone scribbling in your little book," the hostess snarled at him.

Calvin looked back at the window. The table was empty. He dug into his pocket for his wallet. "Fuck me."

"Just need the tab closed. With money. Thanks."

FREELANCING CAN BE HELL

Muses, to be technical, are demigods, or rather, immortal beings. They are not beings of any kind of cosmic power over material creation or manipulation, nor do they seek worship. They do command a fantastic power of artistic creation. When movements of art and philosophy were largely concerned with the human form, objective nature of existence and the spirit, as well as history and myths derived from the inspiration of cultural forebears, the Muses were doing great business.

That section of the museum with all the angry-looking plaster and marble faces and slinky bodies? Each and every one of them has a Muse's invisible signature on it.

However, modernity, as it began rumbling up from the march of industrialization and scientific progress, was not very palatable to them. While one of the Muses had inspired Nietzsche to write of the void and the abyss; those were factual enough things you can point to in every human,[14] they were none too keen on everything

---

[14] For biological point of reference: in females, the void can be found in the tummy. In males, the void is within the area of the frontal lobe responsible for accountability and higher conceptual and sympathetic thought.

that came next.

The Muses read the signs and knew they were going to be able to take the next few epochs off. If ever there might be another cultural movement to invigorate their work, the age of social media proved such a reinvigoration unlikely, if not a long ways off.

There were three Muses, all sharing their own inclinations and preferences in artistic medium and style, but all skilled across the various arts of man in music, prose, poetry, sculpture, cooking, and even golf.

Two of the three, seeing the direction the wind was blowing, decided to head off among other civilizations in existence.[15] The third, however, was not quite so keen to leave the nest. Eurydice, being the Muse inclined more to stories of homecomings, of native lands and pastoral scenes of comfort and belonging, could not bear to depart our world. So when she was offered a job as Hell's Muse on retainer, she was happy for the work since it helped her maintain a lifestyle in a neighborhood she'd grown to love.

THE VIA FRESCA

Tessa was flipping through the copy of *GQ* she'd found in the bathroom after Sally had finished the cooking lesson, gone back to drinking, and gone down for what she kindly called a nap in one of the booths out

---

[15] While these are technically aliens, do not presuppose, dear reader, that they don't exist on this planet. Instead, wonder if they necessarily exist along this particular assortment of the dimensions or within your current plane of perception. This is to say that you may not be looking hard enough. Try squinting with one eye.

front. She was scanning an interview with Seth Rogen when the swinging door opened slowly and Sally peaked his head in with a look of mild surprise to find her there.

"Thought you'd have gone home." Sally checked his watch as he slunk into the kitchen. "Figured you'd know we're clearly not opening tonight." He shook his head. "Again."

Tessa shut the magazine smartly. "Didn't want you waking up alone and scared." She offered a teasing smirk and puzzled inwardly at the warmth she felt seeing Sally return the smile.

"Thanks for that."

"No problem. Gotta earn my paycheck somehow. Besides, I got caught up reading and lost track of time. Didn't expect you to have *GQ* lying around."

Sally peered at the magazine. "I feel like there's an unintended insult in that, but I'll try to ignore it."

Tessa laughed and cooed apologetically. "No! It's just that I only ever see you in chef mode, so I don't know." She shrugged, assessing him anew. "I never pegged you for a fashion type of dude."

She glanced at the cover with Rogen in a suit wearing an afro wig, and Sally crossed the kitchen to look at it. "Not really, but believe it or not, I own more than this one pair of pants." He pointed at the black slacks he wore to the kitchen every day. "I do like keeping on that sort of thing. I made more money when I was a sous chef for that."

"A sous chef?"

"Yeah, the number two chef in a full kitchen."

"I know what a sous chef is, dummy. I meant, where was that?"

"Upper West out in Santa Monica first. Then I got the chance to run my own restaurant and I—" He chortled the recollection off for fear of having to tell her about Benny. "Anyway, ancient history.

"Ancient history? It was three months ago."

Sally bobbed his hands sheepishly as if juggling balloons. "That's like a third of a new baby." He looked at the shining, mostly unused kitchen around him. "Besides, it's just a matter of time before Benny closes up shop on me. He's gotta be losing so much money not charging rent. Even if—" Sally cut himself off on talking about Benny's other business ventures for which the restaurant served as a front.

Tessa sat up and looked at him in shock, catching on the other detail Sally had let slip. "He doesn't charge *you* rent?"

Sally cleared his throat and felt his neck grow hot enough to be feverish. "He and my dad went way back. He offered me the restaurant as a, uh, favor to me when my folks passed away." Sally stared dumbly at his feet for a couple moments. His throat was tight thinking about that grief again. "So I run it the way Benny wants in, uh, honor of that memory." Sally knocked his fist on the stainless steel counter. "Hopefully this place doesn't sink me too low in debt that I can't bounce back from it."

"You're still young. You can bounce back," she tried, immediately regretting it.

"You know, funny thing about being twenty-nine, you don't feel young even though everyone tells you that you are."

"Tell me about it."

"Go figure, I'd have pegged you for twenty-five." Tessa panicked, trying to recall if she had ever told Sally a different age as part of her cover, but he continued not noticing the worry on her face, or more likely politely pretending not to. "You definitely look young. Then again, I guess everyone out here does."

"Out here? You're not from LA?"

"Well, originally, yeah, but my family moved to Chicago when I was ten. I came back out here for a cooking gig after graduating culinary school. My dad helped me. Really wanted me following my own calling."

"Wow, culinary school. So there's an actual degree behind all that raw talent?"

"Pun intended?"

Tessa blushed. "Sure."

"I don't want to keep you. Can I walk you out? I'll lock up and head out too."

Tessa checked her phone. Usually Benny would text her by this time in the evening if he had any updates to discuss, but he had been quiet all afternoon. She typically turned down Sally's polite offer to walk her out because to his knowledge, even with her generous paycheck as a waitress, she couldn't afford a car. In reality, with his paycheck and Benny's fees, she owned a Benz.

She glanced uneasily at the door that led to the avenue where her car was parked. "Oh, no, really. I don't want you inconvenienced—"

Sally waved her off. "Honestly, I'd be more bothered worrying about you waiting alone for a bus with some weirdo next to you."

"It's out of your way," she flailed.

"I'm planning on just wandering the neighborhood anyway, possibly grabbing a drink somewhere. You'd be helping me do something other than drinking."

Tessa stood and reached for her bag in surrender. "Sure. Guilt me into it."

"You're my hero, Tess." She smiled as he held the door to the alley open for her. Tessa tried to break the silence after Sally clicked the lock shut with his keys and began walking alongside her. "So, culinary school and then out to LA?"

"Yeah. There's always some new restaurant or fusion idea popping up around here. Half the time it's a passable chef with a great idea, and the rest are great chefs with boring ideas. Either way, I figured LA is a great town for a chef who has a footprint of his own he wants to make."

"So which one are you?" Tessa challenged as they reached the end of the alley and turned onto the boulevard. Tessa stole a longing glance at her car in the opposite direction up the street while Sally grimaced up at the tomato on the sign to his restaurant as he weighed Tessa's inquiry.

"I know I'm a damn good chef, but I haven't gotten the chance to see how my ideas are." Tessa was taken mildly aback by the forthrightness of his statement, which he noticed. "You don't think so?"

"I just didn't expect you to be so blunt about it."

"Gotta be. If I didn't think I was a good chef, I wouldn't have gone to culinary school, or applied for the jobs I got, or gone to places where I learned what I've learned that made me better."

Tessa followed Sally down the road away from the restaurant. "Wow, when you put it like that."

"That's how my mom taught me. You find something you love and get good at it, and you apply how good you are to getting better. Then reapply and reapply."

"Like math in school?"

"Sure, I guess that works the same, right?"

"Do they have math in culinary school?" She hit the button on the corner lamppost for the pedestrian cross light.

"Trig and calculus? Not at all. We learn real math, like budgeting and staff management and such. Not that nonsense people don't actually use."

"Except to go into space, but you're right. Useless." The pair laughed together and Sally conceded she was right. "So this restaurant? You said you had ideas for the menu other than Italian?"

"Not sure how good the ideas are, but I know the skill behind them."

"So that's why you took the chance on a backer who didn't see eye to eye with you?" They continued down the next sidewalk past a cafe and used bookstore.

"Better than no chance at all, right?" Despite the statement, he hung his head and stuffed his hands in his pockets. "I guess this *is* pretty much no chance if I'm never allowed to open."

Sally pointed at the sky while an idea roiled in Tessa's mind. It took a moment for her to realize he was pointing to a bus stop to confirm it was her bus. She hesitated but quickly agreed that it was hers despite having no idea where the bus was going.

Sally checked the sign and gave a thumbs up. "Great. This one passes through Downtown. I'll just ride with you and hop off." Sally leaned into the road to peer up the boulevard for signs of an approaching bus.

Tessa winced at how poorly this was going. "Downtown? Don't you live right in Glendale?"

"I know a couple really good bars in Downtown."

"You don't want to stay closer to home?"

"Normally, yes. But I figure this gives me the ride into Downtown to convince you to stop off and have a drink with me." Sally smiled impishly. She darted her glance away, partly to avoid the charm and partly in fear since her plan had been to board the bus, hop off a stop or two away, then double back for her car. Sally was proposing taking her four miles away on the notion that, per her cover, she lived five miles beyond even that.

Tessa smiled up at Sally while it finally occurred to her that Sally might actually be equal parts naïve and sweet to think a waitress would commute ten miles by bus for a job, even one that paid as well as his did. She saw the bus approaching a couple blocks away, held by a red light, and she blurted out the idea she had still only acknowledged but not fully considered: "Only if you let me talk you into opening just once."

Sally was stricken, and he suddenly looked fearful. "I don't know if—"

"Oh, come on. The freezer is full of food that's gone bad, been thrown out and replaced, and gone bad again. Is it really because of Benny?"

"Yeah, I've got to wait for Benny. My dad—"

"Your *dad* would want you to open the damn place, at least once. What's Benny really gonna do if you open and he doesn't like it?" Sally considered the possibility and her advice on what his father would really want. Tessa grinned as the bus pulled up and opened right before her. "See? Might as well give it a go. We'll figure it out in the morning." She patted his shoulder encouragingly as she climbed on.

To her dismay, Sally followed her on. "Tomorrow? We've got an opening day menu to plan out. You're definitely having those drinks with me now."

Sally dug in his pockets for bus fare, and Tessa felt her phone buzz. Benny had texted her to tell her: "Meeting with lawyer tomorrow. Deal gets sealed soon." Followed immediately by a text from Maury: "Gonna cook the goose soon," and Claudio's that was entirely emojis of a gun, an emoticon with x's for eyes, and a boy and girl holding hands.

While Tessa cringed at Claudio's choice of emojis,

Sally followed her to the back of the bus where they shared the rearmost seats, and he looked at her in concern. "You okay?"

Tessa bit her lip. "Sally, you sure you want to open *tomorrow*? Maybe we can hold off a bit?"

Sally crossed his arms and thought a moment, then shook his head resolutely. "Nope. You're right. We're doing this. The sooner we do, the less time there is to talk ourselves out of it."

"But your deal with Benny, maybe there's a term in your contract—"

"I don't care what Benny does. I'm dying sitting around not living up to what my dad wanted from me. You're right, I needed that wake up call." Sally's eyes were welling with gratitude she found difficult to meet but was entranced by all the same. "Who knows? Maybe if we have a good opening, it'll keep him from killing me over it. Better yet, maybe he'll let us keep serving or at least keep us alive."

Tessa's eyes went wide, and she averted her gaze to a spot of peppermint gum mashed onto the floor of the bus. "Hope so." She glanced at her phone, wondering how much of everything she'd said in the past ten minutes she'd actually meant.

DRINKS ON CALVIN

"So after all that, he stuck you with the tab?"

Calvin admitted the fact, and Karen bubbled with laughter into the back of her hand, looking at him through tipsy eyes. "You're not going to like how this chapter ends."

Calvin ignored her and flipped open the notebook.

"Can you take a look at this for me?"

Karen tried peering over the rim of her beer stein while she tilted it back for a long chug to drain the mug. When the glass was emptied, she held it aloft and smiled at the bartender, who practically sprinted at her beckon and nodded emphatically when she called for another round, then looked confused when she clarified she needed one more for "my boyfriend."

Calvin ignored the moniker and tapped his finger at the page. "See, he said the Muse Hell employs can only write two kinds of stories: creative ideas the person dictates to them *or* true stories. Hence the journalism job."

Karen nodded while thirstily eyeing the bartender refilling the mugs. "That would be why he took a theater *pre*view and not a *re*view." Calvin blinked in response, and Karen explained tiredly, "The Muse can report on the objective fact of what the show is shaping up to be and what the cast has to say about it. She couldn't offer an opinion unless *Matt* had one of his own, which it sounds like Matt doesn't have in ample supply."

"She?" Karen gave a curious look, so Calvin clarified his question. "You're assuming the Muse is a woman?"

Karen smirked. "You think a man is getting that much work done?"

"I take that as a challenge." He reviewed his notes and glanced up. "I guess I'd just thought of the Muse as its own thing without gender. But you're right, the Muse would need Matt to give an opinion or a story idea to write out. He's got *plenty* of opinions about deals with Devils and the whole nine yards." Calvin bobbed his eyebrows in sustained disbelief at the repast he'd shared with Matt earlier.

Karen harrumphed. "Fine, he has plenty of opinions,

like a little unique snowflake whose mommy told him he would be a famous writer someday but didn't tell him it'd take hard work. I'm sure they're shit opinions, though."

"Thank you, first amendment. So I realized, the Muse he has working for him will only replace a *true* article."

"So you're going to start writing more reviews? You could make a following in the music or theater write ups."

"Yeah, except I started thinking, if all Matt needs to do is give the Muses *an* opinion, why can't he just steal mine and then do the magic mind wipe thing again?"

"True. He has you there."

The bartender set both mugs in front of Karen and watched, with a mix of concern and surprise, when she slid one of them to Calvin's hand. Calvin often reminded himself that it wasn't that he was some troll, it was that Karen was just that pretty. Calvin accepted the drink and took a sip while she watched him patiently and nodded at his thanks.

"This is where you tell me your brilliant idea around how screwed you are by supernatural forces of evil." Calvin began to speak but she warned, "If you say exorcism, I empty this beer on your head."

Calvin paused with facetious caution. "Okay, plan B then," he joked but proceeded to cross out the note he'd written to himself about researching exorcism. She laughed with him before draining half her beer in a single pull. "I got this email from Felicia earlier. She said she was bummed my article got pulled and is open to helping me work my way into a print byline in her section if it's something I want."

"*Helping* you?"

Calvin couldn't hide how flummoxed he was by the incisiveness of Karen's inquiry. Playing dumb never worked as a defense with Karen, and playing dumb was becoming a decreasingly effective defense against Felicia's wiles also. Still, he had very few moves in his playbook, so he went with the tried and true. "Yeah, she's immune to whatever hit Errol and everyone else. Go figure, right?"

"You don't think that's suspicious?"

"Well, you're immune to whatever it is too."

"I think you may be barking up the wrong tree. What good does her being immune to the memory thing do, anyway?" Karen retorted before she inhaled the remainder of her stein.

"Because if the article gets wiped from her section, she'll remember it and put mine back into her section."

"So, why can't you write for fashion? I could help you. I'm not an editor but—"

"You just got hired, I don't want you risking that for me." Calvin's expression as he cautioned her was both urgent and earnest. Karen set the mug down and tilted her head in sweet appreciation. "Better Felicia. Even if it is playing with fire, at least I'm keeping you a safe distance from the voodoo and professional liability."

"You know, you could actually work this in your favor. Felicia could get fired for whatever leg up she gives you, and that opens up the field: there'd be an editorial *and* staff writing position open. *That* could get Matt to leave you alone."

Calvin took a sip of his beer and grimaced. Karen had ordered him a red ale, which was his least favorite. "The thought did occur to me."

"And?"

"I saw her file on my first day when Harry was logging some other report. It's two inches thick. She's already had a dozen complaints against her." Karen was impressed by Calvin's adeptness at professional espionage. "If she still has her job, then she's got Devil magic all her own, or a really good lawyer."

"They're pretty much the same thing." Karen checked her phone. "Uber's here." She hopped off the bar stool to leave.

Calvin automatically stood to follow but a gruff, "Hey!" made him spin on his heels. He turned to face the scowling bartender who was sliding the black leather book with the tab to Calvin over the bar. "You need to close out, lover boy."

WHAT HAPPENED IN VEGAS? – PART 1

Tie knew the seasons of man. He knew the turnings of human longing and desires. He was aghast to see his knowledge and understanding completely turned on its head.

"I thought the Puppy Bowl happened in March!?"

Tie was on the edge of the casino floor at the Aria in Las Vegas near one of the convention halls where a large poster was advertising the Puppy Bowl.

Memory resurfaced for a moment like a rolling fog. He had been doing his job of prodding that girl, Karen, and heard a voice—"Sir, do you have your tickets?"

"Tickets?"

"Or are you on the list?"

"List?" Tie asked stupidly, looking around at the milling crowds taking long ways around his bulky frame to reach the casino floor or wherever they were heading.

The memory of another voice came to him—"What's your name?"

"Tie."

"Thai, thai, thai," the man muttered while scanning the list on his clipboard.

"Tie like a knot, not the nationality."

The man blinked hard. "Isn't that what I said?"

Tie looked away as the man resumed scanning the list and tried to go back to the memory and fill in the blank of how he'd arrived in Vegas. The man's voice jarred him once more. "Got you right here on the list! VIP!"

Tie turned back to the small man, plump, middle-aged, wearing a tan suit and blue shirt with a pink tie. A nametag identified him as Paul, but Tie knew his last name also. "You know what, Clemson, I'm good." Something about entering the Puppy Bowl had him uneasy despite the potential havoc he could wreak.

As he turned away amid Clemson's protests, he saw a line of chorus girls running across the casino floor in ostentatious feathered costumes from a cabaret. That wasn't what had drawn his attention; it was the adulation and awe as they were followed by a black-caped magician riding atop a white horse to the auditorium on the opposite side of the resort.

"What's that for?" Tie asked.

"That's the cabaret magic revue. It's sold out. If you'll just come this way, your seat for the Puppy Bowl—"

"You can shove that seat right up your ass. I wanna see that magician trample them floozies!"

Clemson called desperately after Tie, pleading for him not to waste the seat to the Puppy Bowl. Tie shouted back at Clemson, "Oh, don't worry! Those puppies won't waste!"

Tie was barreling through the gambling pit, jostling, knocking. and shoving people aside as he gave chase like a lineman looking for the sack. Clemson did his best to waddle after Tie, trying to maintain order in the casino and to lure Tie back to the Puppy Bowl lest the front row VIP seats he'd gotten for the high roller went to waste.

HELL'S COMPANY WEBSITE: EXECUTIVE LEADERSHIP BIOS

Hell's executive team is committed to driving Hell's corporate machine to excellence and constantly innovating the means and methods of temptation, damnation, and rock & roll. Hell's executive team is made up of:

Lucifer - President, CEO, & Chairman of the Board of Directors. Lucifer was here before any of us and will be here after we have all been collapsed within the crunch of time itself coming to an end. Hell's welfare is the sole purpose of his existence, and he has led us from the dark fury of the fall from grace to the current golden age of damnation disguised amidst the trappings of modernity. He is a tremendous fan of Duran Duran and lists the glam rock craze and Hulk Hogan's career as his crowning achievements.

Lucinda Crabbe - CFO & Vice President of Avarice. While we were all dusting off the brimstone of the impact from the fall from grace, Lucinda was already collecting the shards and hoarding them away. Her coffer is wide, deep, and hungry. It gapes for men to fill it with their desires and even taking as much as she has, it still gapes and aches for more. Aside from Avarice, she has a strong penchant for cross functional work with Lechery and is a writer of some of Hell's best-selling erotica, including the preceding sentences of this bio.

Screwtape Linton - General Counsel & Vice President of Pride. Despite controversy in his literary past, Screwtape is Hell's chief litigator, silver tongue, and twister of words. As the head of Pride, he has utilized his position and skills at wordcraft to motivate some of the greatest evils of recent history through men's pride, including the Trump 2016 presidential campaign.

Leslie Snatch - COO & Vice President of Lechery. Leslie wants me to write here that you should picture a challenging cock of his eyebrow when you read her name, and that if you ask him if she chose that last name himself, you should imagine a lilting laugh while she presses himself against you and leans her lips right to your ear while his hand slides down your stomach and—Leslie enjoys wind surfing.

Kraven Plunk - CIO & Vice President of Envy. "What Pride said."

Bob - Chief Communications Officer & Vice President of Sloth. TBD.

Aba Don - Executive Director of Wrath and Lead Guitarist/Vocalist of Hell's House Band. Aba Don was among the first of Lucifer's officers to distinguish himself after the fall. While the dust had barely settled in the pit, Aba's fury put all of Hell into the regiments and orders that would guide us through all permutations since. Aba plays the sickest lick of "Shoot to Thrill" that you will ever hear, which almost makes being sent to Hell worth it for the souls of the damned...almost.

HELL'S QUARTERLY BUSINESS REVIEW

Gast squirmed in his seat. Leslie Snatch had finished her division update nearly an hour ago, and her hordes of lecher Devils were still fornicating in the auditorium aisles, over the chairs, and from the chandeliers as Kraven finished his update on the work Envy was doing in social media. "Hashtags were great. What an easy route to tempt someone to look at more of what they lack and want, and to see more and more of it to envy. It was the great cross-divisional success of the year."

Kraven had a narrow face that came to an almost needle point of his long protruding chin, which he stroked smugly despite it being completely hairless. It made reading his expressions difficult since he did not have eyebrows. With the conclusion of his remarks, Kraven thanked the Devils assembled and moved off the stage. His circle, Envy, sat in the dark terrace wing of the convention hall. From there, they could look down on every other circle and stew everything they saw the other circles had that they wanted for themselves. They had been fixated for the last hour on all the sex they weren't having that the Lechery section had been embroiled in since Leslie had given his speech.

The lights went down. Gast could smell the stale sweetness of dry ice for light effects and felt terror sweat dampening his brow. Aba Don had not done this in decades. Rumors swirled that Aba worried of his reputation since the fall being perverted from fearsome eviscerator to show pony. In refute to this rumor, laser lights fired up at the wing of the stage and filled the auditorium with a web of neon lights that swept from the ceiling down over the crowd as other flush lights swung through the mist. The guitar roared its opening lick.

"Shoot to Thrill."

Gast had heard it incessantly in the early days until it had been sent up as part of the last deal Aba had signed to make a band famous.[16]

Aba materialized on the stage with his gun-metal

---

[16] The right music, after all, can and does inspire humans to reckless and terrible behavior. Rock music can make careless daredevils of us, or Sarah McLachlan can make you call that ex you really need to get over already.

Fender and began tearing through the song with the rest of the Hell house band. Gast recalled with a chill the last time he had heard Aba play it. Aba had sold the song as part of what had seemed like a mid-eternal life crisis. That he was bringing it back out only stirred mounting terror in Gast that Pitch had been right: Aba was coming for him. The drums shook the room with their beat, the bass set the sparks to tinder, and Aba set it to an inferno with his skills on the axe and screaming out the lyrics of the song.

"I'm gonna shoot you down!" This song was no mere showcase of skills on the guitar. This was the return of that warrior who had long ago rent the abyss and demons in it into the order they had been in since the Fall.

As Gast sat, arms crossed in the midst the rioting audience of Wrath, he wondered how he had ever managed to be lumped with them. He questioned Aba's wiles and methods all the more. Except for Coldplay, all Wrath Devils love a five-piece set that knows how to tear the roof off.

Gast was more of an indie rock and hip hop kind of guy. "Shoot to Thrill" just sounded like a bunch of cheap noise to him. As Aba carved out the final riff, the Wrath Devils were frenzied. The chairs and other furnishings had been thrown, broken, and set afire in the mosh pit that had formed. Only Gast sat firmly planted on his chair in the center of the carnage with a resolute scowl on his face.

Tie would love and gobble this all up, but the greater concern now was that Tie had fallen completely off the map. Gast didn't have to make a far leap to think about his conversation with Pitch, about how Aba may be two or even three steps ahead of him. Whether or not Aba knew Tie was Gast's compatriot was only the difference between bad and worse. Making Tie disappear when he was supposed to be Gast's reviewer had Gast in hot water regardless of their alliance.

The song wrapped, and Aba chucked his guitar into the crowd at the Lechery circle. Gast followed the guitar's arc through the air and was unsurprised that the Lechery orgy had not slowed during the song. If anything, it had taken on a more furious and violent temperature. One Lechery devil caught the guitar out of the air but didn't keep it as a souvenir. Aba's instrument found its way as a gift to where the sun really didn't shine in another Devil.

Gast held his breath. The stage trappings dematerialized, and Aba was left standing alone at center stage. The only lights left were the spotlights above Aba and the floor lights from back stage, giving him the same aura Avarice had designed for Steve Jobs to present the iPhone.

Aba did not move except to calmly turn his gaze around the auditorium, from the roiling sweaty mass of Lechery devils, to the seething hordes of the Envious, over the fiery pit of Wrath, and beyond.

"Brothers, we sit here today for another of our eternal checkpoints in a battle which seems never ending. Our battle from darkness against the light, our crusade to claim the glory for ourselves. However, once in an age, we come to witness the onset of a new era, an evolution of the nature of how we wage this war. Some may denigrate and tell you that we are fighting the same war, unending, never changing, and futile.

"They are small minds! They are stuck in the pit! They landed too hard when they fell from above!" The room stopped dead. Even the roiling fuckery of the Lechers had slowed to a barely perceptible writhing. Gast had forgotten Aba commanded this kind of power among them. For so many of these reviews, Aba had gotten up and run down a perfunctory list of figures and stats. This time, by sheer force of will, he had them all rapt.

Gast felt the uncommon pang of true fear watching it unfold. Gast's mind simmered with the horrifying thought of Aba being able to command every Devil in the room against him and his being torn asunder by their gnashing teeth and claws.

"Do not believe those who might convince you that the war itself has changed because of the sheen of our tools and the age. They are traitors who should be driven from our midst for such treasonous outlooks! The war is simple: darkness and light. That accursed lie of purity and our truth: the reality which that light fears to illuminate! We are the very essence of the world that light espouses to own. The light is subject to us and will bow to *our* will!"

Aba breathed deep as the armies of Hell broke into cacophonous cries of voraciousness. This was Hell. This was the mass of raw hunger, fear, anger, and impulse riled up by the base binary of us versus them. Gast knew the dangers of this whooping fervor, but he couldn't budge. He doubted Aba could really see him, close as he was to the stage.

"While our tools have changed, our aim remains the same. You have heard before me—" Aba gestured magnanimously to the VPs of the other divisions, "the testament to mastery of this age and its technology. It is ready to be wielded now as a weapon in the battle which will win us the war. The war's end is before us! Do not believe any who tell you it is eternal! Victory is in our reach! The light shall bow and bend to our wills!"

The crowd was deafening. Gast could not move. Aba basked in the dark adulation of the hordes. The other

Vice Presidents of Hell, Aba's supposed peers who had higher titles than he but had been sorted by Aba himself into their very order remained silent in the dim-lit wings of the stage.

Within moments, Gast was racing back to his office. First on his mind was finding Tie. Whatever Aba had planned, the furor Gast had just witnessed would be a difficult upper hand to out maneuver.

Gast cursed loudly when his call to Tie went to voicemail for the third time that day. He flung the phone against the wall and fumed. Gast was certain Aba had a hand in Tie's disappearance. It was too convenient. He was between a rock and hard place, and the only safe place to be was anywhere but the offices. He decided getting out and checking on Matt Reade would be a useful way to spend the night.

LATE NIGHT EMAILS

Back at his house, Calvin was reading over the article he had typed up while he dialed Karen. He was hoping she hadn't gone right to bed, and was pleased when she answered.

"Cal! You're awake!"

"I'm surprised you are." He grinned at his clock; it was after one. "I have the article ready if you want to take a look at it for me before I send it to Felicia?"

There was a hum of hesitation, and Calvin was sure Karen would try talking him out of it. "Sure… can you let me in?"

"Let you in?"

"Yeah… I'm at your door. An Uber just dropped me off."

Calvin heard a knock at the front door and nearly fell out of his desk chair. His dog, Cordy, who had been asleep on his bed next to the desk, sat up startled. When Calvin got back to his feet breathing quickly in panic, the dog flopped back to sleep with a slight groan.

Calvin's mind raced in confusion that Karen was there so late after they had already been out drinking. Was it purely out of concern for his ethics or was there more to it? Surely a woman showing up like this said certain things beyond point of contention, but that was for other guys he told himself.

When he finally answered the door, he was surprised that the girl who had gotten into an Uber and come all the way to his house was standing there as if she had just been considering calling another Uber to flee. Karen practically jumped when the door opened, and she even had her phone in her hand, which she stuffed away frantically while managing to look terrifically red in the face even in the dim of his porch.

Calvin looked at her and she at him. They each murmured hellos, but there was no move by either from the doorway. Finally, Karen's face flushed even deeper, and she spun to leave. "I'm sorry, I don't know why I'm here—"

Calvin ran out after her. "Hey! Don't worry! It's okay." He put his hands gently on her shoulders. "It's all right. I wanted your help, anyway. It's far from a bad thing that you're here to give it."

Karen met his eyes for a few moments in the darkness of his stoop. Her blue eyes caught the warm light from just inside his doorway. She took a deep breath in and smiled. Calvin realized she hadn't been breathing the whole time he'd had his hands on her shoulders and pulled them away nervously.

"What can I help with?"

"The article?" Calvin beckoned her in and led her through the living room to his bedroom. He didn't notice the mild awe and reverence with which she took in his modest flat, but he did notice the way her eyes went wide when he motioned for her to take his seat at the desk. He sat on the bed beside his dog, who only opened her eyes slightly in acknowledgement of him and his gentle petting.

Karen looked from the seat to Calvin and seemed to ask with a slight tilt of her head if he was sure it was okay. He looked confused but beckoned with his hand confirmation. She sat and began reading. "So, this is the article about a fake restaurant?"

"Well, not fake. Just already out of business. It's an Italian place here in Los Feliz. I passed by again last week, and it hasn't opened once in three months."

Karen returned to the article. He remained silent, ready to answer any other questions she might have. He was mildly surprised that she didn't have a speech for him on why he shouldn't be writing the article, but she sat with perfect posture. One hand held her index finger lightly on her lips, the other on the mouse to scrolled slowly down the document as she read. His surprise at her focus was thoroughly overshadowed by his admiration of her features in the cool light of his laptop monitor.

Minutes later, Karen turned back to him. "Well, it's good writing, not that Felicia will care."

Calvin swallowed hard at Karen's reference to Felicia. "I just need it to be good enough that Felicia doesn't check it or else it could start to unravel."

Karen pursed her lips. "I'm really not sure you—" She paused, seeming to weigh her words. A wind rushed into the room. Calvin wondered if the front door had been left open and got up to check it. As he did, he noticed Karen had sat back, much more relaxed in the chair. He was only mildly puzzled by the change in posture, but more so that he saw her clicking open a new window and typing.

"What are you—" He saw it was a new email, and she was dragging the article file from the desktop into it.

"I'm sending it to Felicia." Karen clicked open his browser.

"Whoa, hang on. Shouldn't we—"

"Shouldn't we what?" Karen had coy tone of challenge in her retort while her fingers continued to fly over the keyboard, typing out the message to Felicia.

Calvin watched as she smoothly finished typing and clicked the send button. "What did you—"

He was terrified, but Karen was up and had her hands on his shoulders, shushing him and rubbing him consolingly. "I told her you had been struck with a bolt of inspiration while eating dinner in desultory fashion, and that writing an article for her had been the first and best idea you'd had all night, and that you needed to get this to her even with the later hour for her to consider for the online section."

"You didn't—"

"Phrase it like that?" Karen asked, acknowledging his concern. "I think there was even more innuendo in it than I just managed."

"Karen!"

"Oh, who *cares* what she thinks reading your email in Beverly Hills at this time of night or tomorrow morning," Karen began gently pulling him towards his bed, "when I'm here with you?"

The dog jumped off the bed just before Karen pulled

hard on Calvin's arms and waltzed with him to spin down on top of him. He gulped as he looked into her eyes. "You don't have anything you want me to read?"

Another breeze, not unlike the one before, passed through the room in response to Calvin's inquiry. What followed was Calvin feeling gently and enjoyably led under Karen's tutelage, instruction, and guidance. Karen rolled off of him and bit her lip, asking him if he could turn off the lights. Calvin obliged and climbed back into bed beside her and she nuzzled against him. He wasn't sure how or if to resume and continue their lovemaking until she snuggled closer against him and he felt her warm breath on his neck and how her legs rubbed against his.

They continued until the dark became light.

WHAT HAPPENED IN VEGAS? – PART 2

Tie was pushing a rolling cart of chips. Having started with a hundred bucks earlier in the evening after the show, he had run enough blackjack, craps, and roulette tables to almost bankrupt the casino and dozens of high rollers alike. At each game, Fatty Clemson had ushered him away in ever increasing panic seeing how his hundred dollars was turning into millions more at each table.

Since the cabaret, Tie had torn a bloody path of impossible luck through the gambling pit, infuriating the croupiers while ingratiating himself to the waitresses and the other gamblers who were trying to amass their own fortunes betting on the high roller who finished his cigars in a handful of drags and finished bottles in just a pair of pulls. Finally, Tie was just about tired of causing the same joy turn to misery among his betting companions when they bet too heavily on him, so he was about ready to cash in and set the whole nut ablaze when Fatty Clemson came waddling once more from the corner of his eye.

"Mr. Tie, sir!" Fatty squeaked.

"Whatcha want, squeaker?" Tie growled through his cigar-clenching teeth.

Fatty yelped slightly at Tie's smoky acknowledgement and forced himself to proceed despite the quaver in his voice. "Mis-mister Tie, I was hoping you'd be open to some more, ah, light entertainment?"

Tie wheeled the cart around to the cash cage and sniggered through the cigar before taking an unhealthy drag of the stogie. It was as thick as one of the casino manager's fingers, and Tie continued his menacing chuckle as he exhaled a veil of tarry smoke around the manager. "I've played everything you've got to play, Fatty. I've seen every show you've got to see. Not like there's any more tables I can clean out or destroy."

Clemson stammered in terror and blanched at the memory of the carnage. "Mr. Tie, I have no idea how the puppies from the Puppy Bowl got loose, or why they went after the magician and his retinue like that, but I assure you, they're all in stable condition at Vegas Memorial—"

Tie slapped Clemson's back to stop him. With a tilt of his head, Tie signaled to Clemson he should know better than to bore with him details of people's wellbeing. Before Tie could elaborate, the cash cage manager had sidled to the gate and croaked, "Can I help you, sir?"

Tie guffawed. The manager was required to oversee all exchanges of over a hundred thousand dollars in chips. Tie easily had as much in the first rack of the cart he was pushing. The manager, Marge Lipinski, was a squat octogenarian stooped forward by age and a spine that had long ago given up on the effort for erect posture. Marge was a lifer in the Vegas casino scene. Starting work at sixteen, she had gone around the clubs and hotels on the strip as a waitress, dancer, escort, dancer again, stripper, hotel manager, stripper, hotel stripper manager, waitress, stripper hotel manager, croupier, pit manager, croupier, stripper, and now cash exchange manager.

She had been cash exchange manager for the past ten years.

Tie hungrily leaned towards the bars guarding the pit. "What do they call you, sweetness?"

"They call me the lady who's counting your money. Cut the shit, lummox." Marge nodded at his cart, and Tie hooted as he began to slide the racks of chips to her through the opening.

She began rearranging the chips to matching colors per rack as much as possible, and Tie continued leering at her while Clemson wrung his hands together. With the amount of sweat slicking them, his hands slid over one another easily. Tie hoped Clemson had the decency to generously tip whatever dry cleaner would handle the suit he was wearing. He was sure it was a sopping swampy mess under the double-breasted jacket, likely three shades darker now than it had been that morning thanks to Fatty's nerves.

Tie couldn't fault Clemson for his fervor. Tie had turned a hundred dollars into millions. Clemson would be up shit's creek if Tie walked out the door with it. Tie mused that, worse yet, his plan wasn't to walk out the door with it at all. He was going to set fire to it right there on the casino floor and walk out empty-handed, laughing at them all as the fire alarms and sprinklers went off.

"Mr. Tie, while Marge is checking your chips, which will take a while, we're hoping we can offer up some entertainment. Free of charge, of course." Clemson grinned sickly through his sweat-streaked cheeks.

Tie guffawed. "You've got nothing I want to see." He turned back to admiring the old woman's slow rearrangement of the chips in her arthritis-gnarled hands.

"Yes, I'm aware you saw the magic cabaret, and the puppies are no longer available—"

"I saw the puppies already, Fatty." Tie chuckled devilishly because, well, you know why.

Fatty's face blanched further to the complexion of freezer-preserved birthday cake. He coughed, not because of a dry throat or any illness, but purely because it was the only sound he could manage before he finally found words. "We're willing to put on a VIP show, just for you. Whatever you'd like to see."

"Well, the magician—"

"Is recovering in the hospital."

"Can he come back?"

"No." Fatty drew the word out, unsure why he'd need to answer.

"I'd get a kick out of seeing him try to do magic in a hospital bed with his stitches." Tie sniggered and took another drag of the cigar, shortening it by a full inch in the single pull. Clouds of smoke billowed from his mouth and nostrils as he spoke. "Guess you've got nothing I want to see or play." Tie turned back to Marge hungrily. "Unless this hot rod comes out of that cage for Daddy to give her a spin?"

Marge looked over her red horn-rimmed glasses wearily. "Fats, get Lydia down here to finish this up." She turned and began her slow waddling walk over the linoleum tiles to the exit from the cage. Her sneakers squeaked on every step the whole way, and Tie's eyes widened in disbelief.

"I, uh..." Fatty was dumbstruck. "I suppose Ms.

Lipinski will be performing a, uh, private dance for you, sir."

Tie looked at Clemson and expertly swung the cigar from one corner of his mouth to the other with just his tongue and lips, then spoke through his teeth again. "She called you Fats."

Clemson surrendered. "Everyone does since you got here."

Tie belted laughter and wrapped an arm around Clemson, unsurprised but still disgusted at the heat and rank moisture he could feel on Fatty's shoulders. "Well, looks like the place is that much better for havin' me! Lead the way!"

A half hour later, Tie was occupying a booth in the hotel's Mexican restaurant with five bottles of liquor he was enthusiastically pouring down his throat and various mixers he was generously ignoring. The tables had been pushed aside and a makeshift set of risers erected by his booth to serve as the stage. Tie had demanded a wad of dollar bills. Clemson obliged with a roll of twenty thousand dollars in hundreds he hoped Tie would return to them over the course of the show.

Tie had demanded Clemson make change for it and bring it back in ones.

The twenty thousand singles was piled on the soft cushioned seat of the booth beside Tie in neat stacks. Tie finished the fourth bottle of rum and the waitress returned, clearly terrified that Tie hadn't simply dropped dead by that point. She still offered to bring him whatever he wanted, or to give him a warm up dance with the rap music that was now being blasted at deafening volume from the restaurant PA system.

Tie shouted over the music that she was a trollop and demanded she bring more liquor and hurry Marge onto the stage. Within minutes, he was obliged. The lights lowered and a mobile spotlight they had brought to the restaurant shone on the risers where Marge had been hoisted up by a pit enforcer. Marge was already down to her undergarments.

To call it underwear would be a disservice, dear reader, to what you are likely wearing. Marge wore a brassiere the color of long-curdled milk (when a woman of her seniority wears that particular garment, it is always a brassiere), immediately under which an eggshell-colored girdle covered the span of belly from ribs to lower waist, followed by a billowy ghost white pair of underwear that went a third of the way down her thighs. Her white socks were pulled up to knee height.

Tie howled and applauded, wondering who was going to help the lady get the garments off. Only Marge's arms and lower thighs were exposed. She waddled down the riser in short, jerky steps. Tie mused cruelly about how she ever got undressed at all. Maybe, he thought, the clothes were simply permanent fixtures.

Since she had agreed to do the show for him, he felt no remorse—not that he would have otherwise. He began hooting and wolf calling. He slapped wads of money against his table before unwrapping them and flinging them into a fluttering cloud of green paper around Marge, calling for her to take it all off. Marge had been shaking her arms and trying to slowly turn in a circle amid the falling dollar bills. It had taken her a full minute to make a single turn, and she faced Tie exhaustedly, waving a hand for him to settle down like a school marm.

She had managed to finally reach the end of the stage, and Jay-Z's third verse was already starting. Tie was leaning over the table, watching as Marge slowly worked her arms back to find the clasp of her brassiere. They found their way, inch by inch, until her fingers were able to take hold of it and twiddle with it. Tie stifled his laughter, wondering if there was a Mr. Lipinski (answer: there is) who undid all her clothes for her (he does) and how he reacted to seeing the old woman naked (with a Viagra-assisted erection, usually).

The old lady's face screwed in frustration, and she gave the clasp a mighty jerk. The force of her pull shook her grip loose and pulled her off balance from the stage. Marge Lupinski tumbled right off the riser over the table and into Tie's waiting arms and lap.

Tie's head was foggy with alcohol-clouded pain from the impact, and he was surprised that amid the smell of all the booze he had been sucking down, it was not the smell of mothballs, Bengay, and Gold Bond that greeted him. It was the smell of sandalwood and lavender, of an icy vanilla breeze, and a cloud-dripped sunset.

When Tie opened his eyes, it was to round, smooth breasts in a buttermilk-colored bra (when breasts looked like this, it's a bra, not a brassiere). A flat latte-colored stomach led his eyes down to a snug snow white pair of panties then to slender legs beyond. He was tense and could not move, swallow, or even breathe, but his eyes reversed their path and followed the frame back up past the slender, gently-curved shoulders and arms that were alighted around his neck but might as well have been a boa constrictor's vice grip.

He met her green eyes and finally managed a horrorstruck gulp of abject terror. The blaring music was drowned out behind the pounding of his body's heart in his ears.

"Hi, babe! How have you been, Tie?" Tie could feel sweat pouring from everywhere his meat sack could perspire. He acknowledged a mounting sympathy with

Fatty Clemson while she pouted a pomegranate lip. "You haven't forgotten me, have you?"

"Lilith." Tie stated the fact as simply and bravely as he would acknowledging Clay Aiken's singing voice, Gary Oldman's superlative acting ability, or any of the other immutable laws of the universe he and every Devil found terrifying.

The pout snapped like lightning into a brilliant smile. Lilith hugged him. "I missed you!"

Tie's eyes went wide with her head nestled in the crook of his neck, and he scanned desperately for an escape route or, barring that, a weapon. A bottle was a tempting option, but he realized even with a gun she'd overpower him if she wanted. More likely, she'd convince him to use the gun on himself, and he'd do it with a smile if that's what she wanted.

That was Lilith.

She pulled back and kept one arm around his neck and guided her other hand to her chin in a demurely thoughtful manner. "We need to talk. I believe we're running over one another unnecessarily between your little game with Gast and my current ward." She tapped Tie's nose lightly with her index finger. "I didn't ask for much when I left, so this is *quite* the impasse."

"Impasse." Tie repeated the word flatly, trying to spur himself to manage more in his terror.

Fatty Clemson came rushing in, blathering in a panic, demanding to know what had happened to Marge and who this was on Tie's lap. Clemson assumed it was an ambitious waitress trying to milk tips from Tie and ruin Fatty's chances to use Marge to get the boatload back.

Lilith set her chin on her hand in the fashion of a student fed up with her trig lesson. Despite drawling laconically, she was clearly heard over the Soulja Boy that was now playing. "You're going to wire the money to an account we'll designate, and you just had a *great* idea for recovering the casino's losses you need to go tell your bosses."

Fatty looked up and made an ah'ing expression with the realization Lilith had just told him he had possessed and rushed back out. Lilith sneered wickedly. "Whoops! Gave him the feeling of having an idea without an actual idea! It's never too hard to convince a man he has a great idea when there's not a single thing in his head at all. Like Hollywood execs, am I right?"

Tie tried to nod or even smile appreciatively but was still unable to move. Lilith turned her attention back to their business. "So, about our pickle. Because this *is* a pickle. So much of one that I'm showing my face here now—lucky you." She now spoke in a grave tone with an icy gaze locked on Tie's wide-open eyes.

Tie finally exhaled and muttered, "Fuck me."

Lilith climbed off and groaned. "I'll pass. We need to get back to LA."

BLIND DATES ARE AWKWARD EVERYWHERE

"You know that line he has that everyone's always quoting? A man's greatest pleasure is to defeat his enemies?" Aba pointed his thumb proudly at his chest with a smirk. "This guy."

"Who, exactly?"

"Khan. Genghis Khan said that. Well, I said it originally, but now all the meat sacks attribute it to him." Aba drained his grog and snapped his fingers for the Gluttony Imp waiter to refill his mug.

Lilith sighed and continued bobbing her crossed leg

like a bored cat lolls its tail. "Yes, but who's the everyone you said quotes it?"

Aba looked confused for a moment as he recalled what he'd said, then snapped his fingers before accepting the refilled mug. "The meat sacks. They wrote it down. In hundreds of books." He took another long drink and smacked his lips. "Thousands, maybe. They'll be saying it for ages, and those are *my* words. He was one of my wards, you know."

Lilith mockingly raised her eyebrows. "Wow."

"Yeah, tore a path through Asia. I took him all the way to the door of Western civilization." Aba sneered with revulsion. "Even a meat sack can be something with the right tutelage."

Lilith pursed her lips and crossed her arms with her leg bobbing once more while looking around the room for the waiter with their food so she'd have something else to focus her attention on. "It's quite the story."

Aba froze and harrumphed. "For a human, sure. Matter of scale, though. Nothing compared to what I did down here."

Lilith cocked an eyebrow, which Aba mistook as a prompt to elaborate, which in turn forced her to fight to restrain her sigh at his sustained boasting. "Thousands, no, *millions* of denizens banished to Hell after the Fall. Lord Lucifer reeling from the debasement of his exile, all at the mercy of the chaos in the pit. I tore through the chaos and darkness to make order of this mass of brutes."

"That was your first act as *Director*?" Lilith smirked as the food arrived. She looked at the tilapia to redirect the mischievous glint in her eye.

Aba cleared his throat. "*Executive* Director. Another line Khan took from me? Conquering is easy. Getting off the horse to govern is difficult."

"Right, that's good. It's nice of Lucifer to spare you the stress of a VP title." Lilith dug the knife in a bit deeper and focused on cutting into her tilapia.

"I've always been a boots on the ground sort."

"Clearly. I mean, you were the one tearing everyone this way and that to make sense of this pit ages ago. How could anyone forget?" She moaned appreciatively at the first bite of the fish, rolling her eyes in ecstasy.

Lilith, at this point, had only made occasional visits to the underworld. She had quickly caught Lucifer's eye who had first asked her to write a CEO profile on him he could frame in his office, and he had subsequently cajoled her into taking his "main bro" Aba out to dinner to try to "loosen him up." Despite her distaste for the scenery, and most Devils, she had to admit the foods- especially the desserts- were incredible.

"Of course. They can't possibly forget." Aba straightened himself and smoothed his robes self-assuredly.

"Oh, they can forget," Lilith corrected him. "After all, it's Genghis' name in all those books, not Aba Don's."

Aba's face was stone set, and he grimaced at his food, all appetite stricken from his pallet. "They don't know what it was like, but I'll show them again. The age is coming. We ascended from chaos, and we're always just a few steps away."

"So you think the universe tends towards entropy?" Lilith checked while spearing asparagus on her fork. She made the difficult decision to pass on dessert so dinner need not last even a minute longer than finishing her entree.

"Not at all. You seem to think chaos is a pit. Chaos isn't a pit, it's a ladder. Only the ladder matters. Climbing it is all there is." Aba regarded her stonily, completely forgetting his meal.

Lilith bobbed her fork at Aba. "Something tells me that someday that line'll make it up there too." She pointed her fork at the roof of the underworld cavern in which they were dining.

To her credit, George R. R. Martin had been born earlier that year in the human world, and Aba would eventually sign a deal with him to help him spread some of the bloodiest and most engrossing fantasy literature in ages (and Aba also oversaw the subsequent deal to make it an even more addictive and rage inducing TV show).

Whether it was an admirable guess or just further jabbing, the timing of her remark was—as Lilith was prone to being—wonderfully astute.

SUBMISSION

Felicia finished her nights the same way regardless of the hour or whether or not she was alone or had brought one or several men home with her. She had her home computer displaying several different websites: her stock portfolio, her bank account, and bookmarked news articles of the legal troubles and convictions of her ex-husbands following her divorces from each of them.

The first was convicted of pedophilia, the second corporate embezzlement, the third murdered his assistant in a fit of drug-fueled rage, and the fourth had been caught for tax evasion after an improbable sequence of events beginning with an unpaid parking ticket.

Felicia looked at all of this and touched herself before she slept. It was the only way she could sleep. More than any men she ever brought home, it was the only way she achieved release. It was almost three in the morning when she noticed the little number one on her email icon. She gasped and stifled the noise with a hand even though she was alone in her palatial Brentwood manor.

The email from Calvin had an attachment and a succinct message that he'd decided to take her up on her offer of a "closer, working relationship," which she reread several times to appreciate the subtlety of his comma placement, even if she'd enjoy correcting him on the relationship word choice.

Felicia dropped her legs from where she'd propped them on her desk to lean forward and read Calvin's article. Lust aside, she admitted to herself easily that he was a damn fine writer. The article was ideal for the website: a brief review of a little Italian place in Los Feliz.

She noted that he'd cranked out the article on the closest neighborhood spot he could find to have the excuse to email it to her at this hour of the night. Perhaps, she considered, he was hoping for a response in the vein of: "My, my, up late? Staying up much longer?"

Felicia grinned and felt her cheeks and more burning. This wasn't going to end satisfactorily through a sloppy late night booty call, even if he sprung for an UberX. No, no. This was the NBA finals; it had to go the distance, seven games to the buzzer.

At any rate, she liked the article. Calvin's writing was impeccable, and the website didn't fall under the kind of copy edit scrutiny as the print edition. She opened the website publisher and scheduled the article to post to the front page of her section at eight that morning, then updated the e-newsletter scheduled to go out to the subscriber list in the morning.

She sat back and grinned at the saved updates to the website and the draft. She was sure Calvin would be pleased. He'd likely come into her office giddy at the place he'd been afforded. She wouldn't have the heart to tell him that the only people who subscribed to her food section newsletter were Instagram-posting hipsters claiming to be "foodies" and old gay couples.

Or maybe she would tell him since despair could be a delicious ball of yarn for her to cloy and unravel. For now, the game was afoot. She stared at his name in the byline of the update going live in just a few hours. She fixated on the C of his name and lifted her legs back up.

For the first time in years, she finished herself and her night staring at something other than money and misery.

SING IN ME, O MUSE- BUT FIRST,

As Hell's Director of Social Media and Contract Muse, Eurydice told herself having work in this day and age was a lucky thing. The kids didn't want Muses, they wanted new Instagram and Snapchat filters. Inspirational prose was limited to a hundred and forty characters and hashtags. The art of sculpture for most people began and ended with ordering a ten-by-ten from In-N-Out Burger.

Eurydice was working several deadlines at once. An architect in China needed her to finish a scale model of a suspension bridge by that evening his time. All across America, students had essays on English Literature she was on the hook for by first period. Eurydice was, as usual, eating over her work. She had been holding the sandwich in her mouth for so long while pounding at her keyboard that the contents of her sandwich slid out and landed with a wet slapping thud all over her keyboard.

She swore loudly and checked the clock. She was barely going to hit her deadlines as it was; she couldn't afford the time to clean up what should have been her lunch that she had only started eating in time for dinner and was now tossing aside while assuring herself she'd treat herself to a nice breakfast in the morning.

Her tracker flashed with an urgent flag. Gast, the smarmy Devil from Wrath, had asked her to monitor this deal he had with a writer Matt Reade and ensure any articles written by a Calvin Graves were instantly replaced with Matt's legitimate version of the same article.

Eurydice squinted at the screen and read the article that was now being included in the pending e-mail update from the *LA Weekly*. She bobbed her head admiringly. It was good writing. She opened a new document file and prepared to start writing, but her hands didn't move with their usual lightning speed. She hesitated and went back to Calvin's article.

"Ah," she realized the dilemma and closed the article to return to her original train of work that she was now two more minutes behind on. She assured herself that Gast had only wanted her replacing *legitimate* articles. Calvin had written about a restaurant that wasn't actually in business, so she should let that fly. She considered sending Gast a message to let him know, but she had a couple hundred deadlines to get to by morning, and hundreds more after those.

Weighing the options, she knew slowing herself to send a superfluous email to Gast meant skipping the breakfast she had only just resolved to treat to herself.

"I *can* have it all," she promised.

FANCY MEETING YOU HERE

Sam didn't need to turn around. The elbow jabbed into his rib cage with such painful over-eagerness that he knew who it belonged to. "Mornin', Harry." Harry always walked in just after Sam settled into line and began scanning the menu.

Harry never scanned the menu for two reasons, both of which made Sam groan inwardly. First was that Harry generally rambled at Sam with an intensity unbefitting of the daylight hours before work in Sam's opinion. Second was that Harry had the same thing every morning.

Harry was beside Sam doing his usual uninvited rundown about his morning commute and how glad he was that he was sticking with the cycling he'd taken up for a New Year's resolution. When they reached the front of the line Sam motioned for Harry to order first, and Harry ordered "the usual." After ordering, Harry pivoted to chatting with the clerk he somehow knew by name until an inquiry snapped Sam from his assessment of the smoothie menu.

Sam looked blankly at the clerk then Harry in turn.

"The usual?" the clerk repeated.

Sam looked in confusion at Harry, who he was sure he'd heard already confirm wanted his "usual."

The clerk looked concerned and clarified, "Onion bagel and a latte?"

Sam wondered how the clerk knew when Harry explained with off-putting ease, "It's *your* usual."

Harry paid the clerk, saying they were both together. "You can get me tomorrow." He slapped Sam's shoulder genially before he marched out.

Sam stared in disbelief at the coffee cup and bagel in the brown paper bag in turn.

"You okay?" the clerk asked.

Sam felt his forehead burn. Not only did he have no idea how many mornings he'd made the same order without realizing it, but he didn't even know the clerk's name who had noticed it, or when Harry had apparently become his close friend.

"I'm surprised you know my order."

The clerk leaned forward in a conspiratory whisper. "It's okay. I know you only stare at the menu to avoid talking." Searing heat flooded Sam's cheeks and neck. "Not everyone's a morning person. You've got a good friend, though."

Someone cleared their throat loudly behind him. It was Lily Clark, who met Sam's stupefied expression with a bulldog's resolve that clearly communicated he needed to get out of her way since he was holding up the line.

He took his usual and walked out to the street where Harry was waiting for him. When he bid Harry farewell at his office door, he slumped down at his desk and muttered, "Fuck me."

"I'll pass." Felicia said passively. Sam jumped in surprise, spilling a quarter of his coffee onto his shirt. Felicia had been sitting on the small couch in the corner, and he'd walked right by her when entering.

Felicia had business to discuss, and her eagerness to talk was disconcerting if only because it had gotten her into the office before ten for the first time in years. More so even that she insisted on following Sam into men's room while he cleaned up the spill in order to have the conversation that much sooner.

GOOD FOOD AND QUESTIONABLE PEOPLE

Sally remembered he and Tessa finishing their night drunkenly back in the restaurant kitchen. They wanted to revise the menu based on their conversation after their seventh set of drinks and had taken a Lyft back to the Via

Fresca. Sally would have sworn they had passed out scribbling ideas into a little notebook in the kitchen.

When he woke up, he was curled up in one of the booths in the dining area, clutching a ladle and jar of allspice. More surprising than his location was that he had never bought allspice for his kitchen before.

It was a knocking at the door that had roused him, and he groaned to think he'd have to deal with a hangover and Benny hand in hand. When he managed to climb out of the cushy booth seat, he was taken aback to see it wasn't Benny at the door, nor was it Maury or Claudio. A young man, twenty-something, with wet-looking blonde hair swept sideways long over his brow and bald on the left side of his head was at the door.

Despite the summer heat, he was wearing a scarf balled around his neck over a purple Henley t-shirt and black vest. Sally groaned loudly before he opened the door.

The guy held a hand up in a casual wave, and Sally tried to appear as gracious as he could despite the hangover making the entire enterprise agony. He cracked the door only halfway and tried to smile, which he knew looked simpering with how he was cringing against the morning light. He wasn't sure what time it was, but it was already warm enough that the hipster's scarf and vest looked ridiculous.

"Can I help you?"

"Uh, yeah." The hipster pulled his cell phone out of his back pocket and began navigating on it with his thumb, speaking to the phone rather than to Sally. "Are you open for breakfast?"

Sally grimaced. Foot traffic like this wasn't totally uncommon, though it had slowed more and more the longer the restaurant had gone without opening. He checked the sign on the door past his shoulder. It was flipped to displaying the "Sorry, We're Closed" side of the sign, so he pointed. "Sorry bud."

"Okay, wasn't sure. The hours online just say 'whatever' so I thought that meant you were like an early morning, late night kind of deal."

"Hours online?"

The hipster flipped his phone for Sally to see the screen. He was on the Fresca's Yelp page, and the hours did indeed say, "Whenever."

Sally recalled drunkenly creating the page when he'd been told by Benny that the restaurant was a front that would never open, and Sally had started typing, "Whenever my big bad mafia boss realizes a cover business needs to do business to be a cover." Yelp had saved only the first word of it.

The blonde man examined his phone in droll surprise. "I didn't know you could do that."

"Me either," Sally croaked.

"So you're not open for breakfast?"

Sally looked at the sign in the window again and shook his head. "No, we're an Italian restaurant."

"Italians don't eat breakfast?"

Sally blinked a few times and felt the acrid taste of the hangover in his mouth. Being around and preparing food over a hot stove when he was discombobulated, dehydrated, and mentally deflated sounded like agony.

"No, they do, but—" The hipster looked up from typing out a message on his phone in disappointment. Sally realized that he'd regret not serving a customer more than he'd regret the misery of cooking hungover. "Come on in. I've got a breakfast menu I could try out on you."

The hipster looked elated. "Oh-em-gee, can I hit up a couple of my blogger friends?"

"You're a blogger?" Sally led the man into the Fresca and motioned for him to sit wherever he pleased.

"Yeah." The man puffed his chest proudly while tapping away a new message on his phone. "I follow the *LA Weekly*, and I'm on Twitter at LocoRoccocoBanger." He slid into the same booth Sally had been sleeping in, regarding the ladle Sally had left behind with confusion but then just setting it on the table before returning to his phone.

"You work for the *LA Weekly*?" Sally asked with his throat choking the last two words up an octave in his panic.

The hipster adjusted his thick-framed glasses. "Me? No, I'm a bartender. I follow the *Weekly* and share and comment on a lot of their stuff."

Sally blinked skeptically, and the hipster remained fixed on his phone, muttering that three of his friends were coming by. Sally felt significantly more at ease cooking if it wasn't for a true critic. He began to head to the kitchen and pointed out over his shoulder. "The door's open."

As the kitchen door swung shut behind him, Sally heard the man muttering to himself about commenting on the article that a breakfast menu was being worked on.

CONTRACTUAL ASSURANCES

Sam tried to ignore that Felicia was in the men's room with him, and that he was standing there shirtless, and most of all that she didn't seem to care about any of those prior facts at all. She was on a tirade about some article for her section that had broken records for views and shares on social media in just the two hours since the morning's web edition had been updated.

Sam shook his head over the stained shirt he was running water over. "You shouldn't be changing the Newsletter last minute like that. Especially not with articles that haven't been proofed."

Felicia leaned her shoulder against the wall and crossed her arms. "I proofed it."

Sam paused at scrubbing his shirt. "We're supposed to have at least *two* people review every article. You know that."

Felicia rolled her eyes and lifted a hand in facetious confusion. "Here I thought that was reserved for the *prestige* of the print edition." Felicia brushed aside Sam's chastisement with a deft wave of her hand. "You should be *thanking* me for changing it. Have you seen the numbers?"

"I'm very happy for your section, Fel—"

"For the *website*, Sam. Seriously, almost everyone viewing it this morning shared it on Twitter. Calvin struck some perfect chord with the hipster weirdos that read our magazine."

"Fel, lots of people read our paper—"

"Yeah, but only the hipsters trying to be on the curve share it like this."

"You don't know—"

"Who else would want to share an article about a hidden gem of a restaurant being overshadowed and run out of business by the march of LA gentrification?" Felicia squared her hands on her hips.

Sam grimaced and resumed scrubbing his shirt in the sink bowl. "Beverly Hills housewives?"

Felicia read the sarcasm and proceeded over it. "Don't you think this is a writer we should be taking under our wing?"

"What about Matt Reade? His *Wicked* article was something."

Felicia weighed saying she remembered the article being Calvin's but instead went a different route. "Well, if you ask me, he's good, but he's not trying to do more than fill a portfolio."

"Oh?" Sam paused in wringing out the shirt to regard Felicia directly.

"He's good, but look at the article. He's not trying to establish a voice or gain a following. He just wants the byline to take wherever he goes next."

"If he *is* that good, shouldn't we be trying to keep him?"

"Here I thought loyalty should be valued."

Sam fought to mask his incredulity at Felicia making that remark, given her widely known personal history. "We weren't going to make the offer until next week, anyway. Maybe you're right that it's still a fair argument between the two. What do you want, then?"

"Obviously I want to groom Calvin, and I wanted it to be above board that I'll be working directly with him to try to help him succeed. Errol can have his little pet, Matthew."

Sam was fairly certain that he'd never before wanted Harry around to help as much as he did now. In the bathroom, being accosted by Felicia with no shirt on, he found himself asking what Harry would do. Instead, he could only rue the fact, quizzically, that he had spent years aggressively ignoring anything and everything having to do with Human Resources. That being the case, he conceded to at least get Felicia out of the bathroom. "Fine, I'll allow it for now. If only because it makes sense to at least offer you more steady support while not taking out of someone else's paid staff."

Felicia squealed and clapped. As she jumped at Sam to hug him, the door swung open. The other intern, Matt, had wandered in, and Felicia cocked an eyebrow at him. Before he could voice his surprise at the scene he'd come upon, she demanded, "What the hell are you wearing?"

Matt turned to the mirror. He saw himself in a dirty pair of faded overalls, a Trump 2016 T-shirt, and steel-toed boots before he yelped in terror and ran back out.

"You should be thanking *me*," Felicia tutted before leaving Sam in the bathroom.

THE FIRST STEP IS A DOOZY

There was light, the only thing they'd known since the conception of all things. The light of the Creator was brilliant, beautiful, glorious, and blinding. It shared its essence and beauty with them and in turn made them beautiful. They were the host, basking in the unending love and glory of the Creator. The more they praised and glorified the light, the more there seemed to be, which only made them worship more. That was their existence, that unending cycle of praise and glory of love and beauty.

Lucifer found the whole cycle boring. Somewhere in the space before time itself, Lucifer groused loudly that the whole thing didn't afford anyone a chance to have even the occasional drink in between the literally unending praise. When humanity was created, Aba was the one to ask why those lesser beings weren't praising Lucifer and all the rest of the heavenly host as their superiors. For the rebellion they stirred, they had been cast down.

When they careened into the pit and collected

themselves, Aba looked up into the dark void, trying to pull out even the tiniest sliver, or barest glow of the Creator's glory. In that moment, he felt a pang of regret for the rebellion and wondered if there might not be some way of undoing it and redeeming himself. The feeling had barely coalesced within him, but the mere fact it even could have is the very reason for what he did next.

"Helluva fall. Can you believe this place was just waiting here? It's like He knew we'd do that." Lucifer coolly surveyed the sulfurous depth to which they were exiled. Lucifer dusted himself off as he climbed to his feet and took a seat on a jutting rock overlooking the expanse of the pit.

Aba's face twisted into a scowl beside his master. Without question, Lucifer was his master since the only other being worthy of that title had rejected him. In the pit before them, the others who had been expelled were roiling. They gnashed their teeth in anguish at what they had lost. This was their punishment, to be left in a writhing mass of agony, rage, and fury while the Creator reveled in mastery of all things and creation.

Aba sprung to action with bloodcurdling roars and howls. With the corrupted sickle he had held through the fall from grace, he tore through the masses of demons and devils to violently place them in order. From a barbaric feral horde, he culled them to their first clans known as the Orders of Sins.

Those who convinced themselves they were superior without the light from which they had been cast away were the Pride. Those who fought and raged in fury at the light's rejection became the Wrath. Those who sought to take the place of whichever other demons they thought might somehow be closer to that light Aba made Envy.

Those whose lack of light propelled them to vile,

empty, and furious sexuality he set to the Lechery. Those who sought to horde material riches to account in futility for the infinite love they lacked became the Avarice. Those who could not move for lack of motivation without the Creator's love propelling them became Sloth.

Then there were the demons who were eating their feelings. They were the Gluttony. Obviously.

When Aba finished, he stalked back across the abyss to find his master. Lucifer was still perched on the jutting rock Aba had left him on. Aba knelt before his new lord, ignoring that Lucifer had somehow found a loop of string he was idly flipping and weaving over his fingers to make different patterns and shapes.

"My Lord, it is done. Your forces await." Aba knelt and the multitude knelt behind him.

Lucifer didn't look away from the mess of string wound over his fingers. "Got that out of your system?"

Aba didn't know what to say, but Lucifer hopped off the rock and waved for Aba to get up. "Come on, we've got the whole rest of the universe. Let's find something else to do."

Aba turned to regard the hordes. Knowing what Lucifer meant, he began to inform them of their purpose to corrupt the Creator's beloved, to go out with their vile natures and to spurn the hearts of men.

Lucifer had actually meant that he'd heard the humans had started fermenting crops to make ales and wines and felt a drink was a good way to pass some of the eternity they had. He figured Aba's interpretation wasn't a half-bad application of the invitation, though. "Might as well be productive, I guess," he conceded before proceeding to be completely unproductive in every way since then.

Aba put every being in Hell into order that day, and would later be responsible for overseeing the immortal strays whose stories had not been ended by the Creator, but who sought a place for their stories to continue eternally among the legions of Hell.

LEGALISM AND PROTECTIVE CLAUSES

Benny and the boys would normally have stopped at the restaurant to make fun of how pathetic Sally was, but once in awhile, in order to be the big bad Mafioso who could push around a sap like Sally, Benny needed to do the work of a big bad Mafioso. In this case, they needed a consigliere.

Benny needed the property as collateral for a loan that wouldn't raise eyebrows or alert Sally to his true ownership. That was the hope, and he didn't think it would be more than a lawyer taking ten minutes to point them to the right form for it and telling them where the owner's signature needed to end up without said owner needing to be present at the bank. They'd chosen the cheapest looking lawyers in the phone book, then gone with the one closest to where the three shared a house in South Hollywood off Pico.

They'd ended up on Jefferson in a dumpy little office in a strip mall that had a suspicious looking man with a graying beard offering them "fallet parkin'," so Benny had parked on the street three blocks away and asked the boys to double check their doors to make sure the car was secure.

The office had the kind of cheap, uncomfortable chairs that normally only the DMV knows to buy, and they were all chewed and torn. Many had burn marks or scrawled graffiti tags in permanent marker.

They had announced themselves to the receptionist,

who was sleeping on her hand while facing a small TV showing *The Price is Right*. When they repeated their arrival, she'd acknowledged and told them to take a seat without moving or opening her eyes. The sleepy atmosphere in the waiting area had promptly made Benny fall asleep on himself.

Benny was roused by a sharp set of jabs and slaps at his arm. Maury was bouncing like a toddler on Christmas and his eyes were electric. "Did you see him? Did you see?"

Benny smacked his lips tiredly. "Who? What?"

Claudio was snoring loudly on the other side of Benny, but Maury shook his hand with a stiff, pointed finger at the door that was shutting with a swish behind someone in a suit who had just left. "That was Trump!"

Benny scrunched his face in confusion. "Which one?"

"*The* Trump!"

"If that *was* him, good riddance."

"Mr. Anderson will see you now," the receptionist alerted them. When Benny sat up to look at her, she hadn't moved from her upright napping position.

Benny slapped Claudio in the chest to rouse him and led the trio into the office. The office they entered felt like it should be in a different zip code from the waiting room. It was expansive, lined with mahogany shelves with a shining ebony desk that swept fifteen feet across as a border wall between them and the lawyer.[17]

Craig Anderson had all the stereotypical lawyerisms about him. Sharp suit, wide grin with what seemed like several too many gleaming white teeth and a few too many sharp-looking canines at the corners of it. Benny

---

[17] The narrator apologizes for that simile but couldn't help it because of the possible Trump sighting in the prior scene.

was at ease if only because it felt like Craig was just the kind of weasel they needed.

"Gentlemen!" Craig flopped back into the cushy high-backed leather chair at the desk. The chair seemed to sigh gratefully as it welcomed him back into it, and he looked with raised, excited eyebrows at Benny.

Benny took a seat facing the attorney with his hand on his thighs. "I'm the boss of the operation."

Craig put a finger thoughtfully along his cheek and covered his mouth with the rest of his hand, waiting for Benny to proceed. With the windswept intensity of his visage and focus, Benny got the distinct feeling the man had a hyperactive attention disorder, or that he was on a significant amount of cocaine. "I've got a restaurant I need to take ownership of."

Craig chuckled affably. "Isn't that what the muscle is for?" Craig belted laughter, and to his obvious consternation, no one joined him. "Oh, come on. My receptionist had a read on you three the moment you came in, here." He held out his palm across the table to them with difficulty due to how wide the desk was. "Just pay me a buck each, and we'll have attorney-client privilege so we can cut to the chase."

"What's a buck get us?" Benny asked.

Craig groaned and dropped his head in theatrical exasperation. "Well, if you want to be precise about it: only ten seconds of my time based on my hourly rate. The point is if you're officially a paying client, I can protect whatever you tell me under that privilege."

Benny nodded and looked at his compatriots. Benny flitted through his leather wallet, Claudio tore open the Velcro wallet he kept on a chain in his back pocket, and Maury pulled out a balled mash of green bills he peeled one from. When each had produced a bill and put it in

Craig's hand, he sat back in a flash and had his hands steepled before his face. A glower shadowed his expression as he whispered for Benny to "proceed."

Benny was puzzled, first by the sudden change in demeanor then by the fact that the money seemed to have simply vanished in the lawyer's rushing movement back into his seat. "Okay, well, my boys and I are in the imports and sales business—"

"Cocaine or marijuana?"

"Cocaine," Benny answered uncertainly.

"Good, much better margins." Craig spun a finger in the air for Benny to continue.

"Anyway, we lost a shipment to a shithead holder. Stole fifteen kilos of pure from us, ruined the other twenty-five."

Craig looked at the ceiling with a slight squint as he mentally calculated. "So you're out close to a hundred K for the purchase, possibly double that if you'd cut and sold right."

Benny was taken aback. "Exactly."

"And you had to handle the kid so you need my help—"

"No, that's all fine. We've remunerated the kid who did it."

"Good word."

"What?"

"Remunerated," Craig clarified.

"What's that?" Maury asked.

"Remunerated," Craig repeated.

"The word. Remunerated. He says it's a good word," Benny said.

"What's it mean, though?" Maury asked.

"What? He thinks it's a good word," Benny said impatiently.

"It means paid back," Craig answered.

"What does?" Claudio asked, finally coming to attention from his sleepy reverie.

"Remunerated," Benny and Maury shouted at Claudio in unison.

Benny held his hands out and silenced the room, which made Craig snicker. "So, we're out two hundred that we needed to have in two weeks for an investment opportunity. We wanted to know if you could fix a way for us to set up a mortgage on my restaurant and to get the money out of escrow."

Craig cocked an eyebrow. "You need a banker, not a lawyer."

"The real estate isn't in my name."

Craig sneered. "Then it's not *your* restaurant."

Benny fumed at the impishness of Craig's retort and spoke through gritted teeth. "It's so it doesn't lead back to me if some fed starts looking at the books."

"So what about the money in the books? You don't have any put away?".

Benny didn't want to answer that, as it led right back to what Tessa had said ages ago about a cover business needing to actually do some kind of business to function as a proper cover, but he didn't want to admit that to the lawyer or to Tessa. "Some, but we need the two hundred still."

Craig made an ah'ing motion and narrowed his eyes knowingly at Benny, which the gangster found eerie. "So, when you say you need to access the money in escrow, you mean money that'll belong to the owner taking out the mortgage?"

"Bingo."

Craig leaned over the desk, clasping his hands. "Wouldn't it be easier if the restaurant were just *yours*, say by inheritance after a friend passes away, so you wouldn't have to worry about this loan nonsense?"

There was a stunned silence among the trio, and they all looked at one another. Claudio spoke first, his raspy voice hushed in amazement. "I see why you said we needed the lawyer, boss."

"You didn't need a lawyer, you needed to think like criminals. I'm only supposed to handle the paperwork, ideally. The counsel is gonna cost you extra."

IT'S A LITTLE ITALIAN JOINT, YOU'VE PROBABLY NEVER HEARD OF IT

Sally had tried, unsuccessfully, to rouse Tessa for ten minutes before finally giving up. Making breakfast for the one guy wouldn't be too difficult, but when he went back to the dining area to see if his guest had any dietary restrictions, he found the friends the hipster had mentioned were already there. A stocky girl swimming in a men's red flannel shirt and an emaciated-looking man with a shaved head and horn-rimmed spectacles had arrived.

Sally did his best not to stare and welcomed them. "If you're all in a rush to get to work," he checked his watch, which told him it was already after nine, "I can do something quick."

The girl looked incredulous and reached into her bag. "No, we're good, thanks." She opened a leather case to reveal an iPad with a keyboard built into the case.

Horn rims produced a MacBook Air. Blondie continued on his iPhone. Sally nodded and clapped his hands together and checked for dietary restrictions, of which there were none. "Well, give me about twenty minutes."

When he reentered the kitchen, he jumped in shock at Tessa standing with a grave look on her face and the unmistakable posture of a woman about to put a man in his place.[18] Tessa's arms were stiffly crossed and her posture slanted with one leg extended as she slightly chewed the inside of her cheek.

Sally collected himself and looked at her in confusion, mostly because she wore not a single drink from the night before. He was considering asking her what she'd done with the dozen or so of them, but she was quicker on the take. "What are you doing?"

"I'm getting ready to serve up breakfast?" He snatched his apron from the counter and moved to the sink to wash his hands.

"Sally, you know how Benny feels about customers." Tessa watched him gravely while following him to the sink where he was washing his hands.

"Yeah." He nodded slowly and went to the pantry to confirm what ingredients he had.

Tessa shuddered and added for good measure. "Far less how he feels about *hipsters*."

"Yeah." Sally gathered a half dozen eggs, cheese, and other sundries and moved to the counter with them.

"Sally, you have to send them away."

"Why?"

Tessa blinked. She couldn't tip her hand, she knew that. Sally had only a vague idea of how dangerous Benny was to him. Tessa knew full well because she had been hired to be the danger. Here she was trying to speak about something they both knew, but Sally didn't know

---

[18] If you're unfamiliar with this posture, it means you've never *noticed* it, not that you haven't experienced it.

how aware she was, nor did she want him to, so they weren't saying anything at all.

Sally didn't let the silence settle over them. He broke it by cracking eggs and beating them in a bowl. "Maybe you should go home."

"Giving me the day off because we're not opening?" Tessa tried with a saccharine, hopeful tone.

"No. I think you should just go home." Sally turned swiftly away from her, taking the mixing bowl to the stoves.

Tessa was taken aback by the comment, then taken aback even more by her being taken aback at all. "You don't want me to help?"

"I've got this." He poured the beaten eggs into a pan to begin slow cooking them.

Tessa bit her lower lip. "But what about last night?"

"I had fun." Sally started the next steps without looking at her.

"But—" Unsure what else to say, Tessa went quiet. They had spent the night joyfully planning what they'd dubbed "The Fresca's Last Stand," including menu items and looking up where to have flyers printed up to hand out around town. She'd come up with ideas just as enthusiastically as he had, so his reaction to her trepidation made sense to her. It was a betrayal. "But Benny," she opined, still anxious for her friend's safety.

"Benny'll get mad no matter what I do. I might as well enjoy serving customers if he's going to keep giving me shit every day anyway." Sally continued preparing the omelets and focused intently on the pan.

Tessa realized what she had mistook for exhaustion was actually rigid resolve. Sally was steeled and she knew he was going to cook. It mattered that much to him. She felt the phone buzz in her pocket and the fork in the road was clear before her. She could choose the phone and a self-important thug, or this man she admired who had real, true passion for something.

She grabbed her apron and joined him by his side, just as she did when taking lessons. "So, what's first?"

Sally looked at her, nonplussed, and she found herself a little disappointed he wasn't more surprised. "Well, I don't want to be a dick, and you can definitely help out in here in a minute, but can you go take drink orders?" She blinked impassively a few times, and he explained, "This isn't a cooking lesson. You're the head waitress. I'll handle the cooking."

Tessa nodded, racing out dutifully to the hipsters.

BRITCHES OF CONTRACT

Matt had locked himself in a vacant office in the Accounting wing. His enchantments weren't working properly so he couldn't just whisk himself around town like he usually would, not to mention the enchanting looks spell Gast had placed on him. He was currently secured in the office behind the desk in nothing but a leather speedo. The charm had reactivated and misfired yet again after he'd left the bathroom so he was on his Hell-sponsored phone calling Gast again.

"Yes?" Gast picked up, sounding harried.

"Hi, it's me, Matt?"

"I'm aware. The phone has caller ID. Do you need something?"

"Well, I'm having a bit of a problem." As much of a dilemma as his issue seemed, a Devil didn't seem like the kind of person to bother lightly, especially not one sounding as busy as Gast.

"Problem?" Gast said something indecipherable away from the mic. Matt guessed he was swearing. "What's your problem?"

"Well, that clothing charm?"

"Yeah?"

"It's making some interesting choices."

"*Interesting?*"

"Well, I'm in a leather speedo right now." Matt looked down to confirm and to adjust himself since it was pinching uncomfortably.

"Well, where are you?"

"Excuse me?"

"The charm is based on where you are. If you're at a BDSM poolside bar, that may just be appropriate."

"I'm in my office."

Gast cursed audibly this time. "Of course. When it rains it pours. Give me the rundown."

Gast listened and asked questions patiently of what had transpired around the office and saw the article Calvin had managed to get published on the *LA Weekly* website. "That shouldn't have gotten through," Gast bit his thumbnail nervously. "Eurydice was supposed to—" Then he recalled Eurydice had been told to stop and replace an article of *sound* journalistic merit. "Who's the editor for the section?"

"That food editor I told you about, the one always hitting on Calvin."

Gast threw his hands up. "Of course." He scanned the skyline outside of his office frantically, feeling trapped by the buildings looming high over his windows. While he still had no idea where Tie was, at least his client's smaller issue was easily managed. Getting something productive done sounded like a good idea. "I'll deal with that editor slipping articles in for him. That's likely why the charm is off. I'll get right on it."

"Gast, I—"

"Coat's on. I'm out the door." Gast hung up on Matt. As promised, he strode determinedly out his door and to the elevator. When he got in, the doors didn't shut. Instead, the lights in the office began to click off in slow succession towards him until the offices went from oppressive fluorescent lighting to the smoky blackness of the pit the Devils had been exiled to. A furious power was breaking down the illusion the Devils had constructed for themselves to leave Gast standing not in an elevator but a crag between the gnarled rocks of the pit.

Wreathed in flames, the pale face of Aba burst through the sulfurous darkness. Gast flattened against the gnarled rock wall behind him, choking for breath, eyes wide at the looming figure.

"You treasonous cur. What a fortunate cause that I bring before our Lord Lucifer to have prodded an incompetent and found an outright traitor in our midst!"

Flames began to burn around Gast's heels. He was too terrified to hop and dance away from the searing heat, instead cowering into it away from Aba's glowering countenance. In the flames, Aba's eyes looked obsidian, reflecting the red flames perfectly on the dark glassy surfaces. "Aba, I—"

"You dare tell me you have no idea where your evaluator is? By what treasonist act have you tried to save your worthless hide! I tell you this, Gast: you have until tomorrow. Find Tie, fix your broken deal, and hope that the least of your punishments is receiving banishment from that meat sack of yours!"

The flames roared for an instant and then recoiled instantly as Aba disappeared into the darkness of the pit.

Gast panted as the lights slowly clicked back on and the office manifested once more from the simultaneous reality of where the Devils truly were. From the cubicles and down the hall, heads of his colleagues were all fixed on him to see what the commotion Aba had caused was about.

Of the dozens looking at him, a Devil from Pride was the first to pull out his phone and hold it up. Gast heard the camera shutter sound of a photo being taken. Slowly, other Devils began to snort and chuckle and do the same. Gast quickly realized it was because he had soaked his pants.

Another Pride Devil jumped in front of the elevator before the doors could close, phone pointed at himself, taking a selfie video and getting Gast in the frame. The Devil bellowed, "Homies! I'm just out here at the office, grindin' you know how I do. Peep the awesome terror skills of my man, Aba Don, tho! Hashtag Devil Pee Pants!"

LIKE AND SHARE, PLS & THX

"Hi, everyone." Sally paused. He hadn't really scripted anything except for the meal he was planning to prepare, but he thought some autobiography might not hurt. "I'm Salvatore Degneri, and I'm here today in my kitchen of the—" He paused again, catching himself before saying the newly opened and opting instead for, "*soon* to be opening Via Fresca restaurant in Los Feliz."

He swallowed the words to steady himself. He hadn't liked the idea of confining himself to Italian cuisine, nor the name, but a free restaurant was too much to pass up. The owner, Benny, hadn't yet confirmed the opening date since their agreement the week before, but Sally knew it would cost Benny more to keep the place closed than it would to open it, so he was sure then that it would open soon.

"In the meantime, I'd like to start a little video blog. I guess a vlog? Is that really a word people say? Out loud? That's a silly word. Anyway, this is just a series of some recipes I'm hoping I can add to the menu here someday if we go beyond Italian cuisine."

"Are you really going to do that with your hands the whole time?"

Sally jumped and yelped. "Where'd you come from?"

Tessa didn't look up from the magazine she was perusing. "Outside."

He let out a shaky breath at the fright she'd given him. Benny had insisted Sally hire her as his waitress, and she usually never spoke in more than one word at a time. Those words for their three days to that point had been limited to: "hello" and "goodbye."

"What about my hands?" Sally examined them, forgetting the camera was still recording.

"You're holding them up like you're imitating Frankenstein." Tessa imitated him for the camera, which she was just barely in frame of over Sally's shoulders.

Sally realized he had indeed kept his hands in a position as if he had been holding a pair of mugs. He fumbled for an excuse and tried to aim it at the camera. "Well, this is the ready position for when you're at the stove. It keeps you safe and quick to respond to—"

"Yeah, sure, but maybe stop talking like cheesy parody of a news anchor."

"What?"

"Your voice. I guarantee it'll sound like you're shouting."

"How do you know?"

"Because you're not talking like you usually do. Drop the act."

"It's not an act. I'm trying to teach—"

"Just be yourself." She raised a challenging eyebrow that struck him silent.

Sally couldn't say why, but something caught in his throat with the simple earnestness of her statement. She flipped the magazine shut and came to his side. "Let's try it this way."

She muscled into frame beside Sally and smiled up at him. "How about a lesson, Chef?"

His throat was still tight, and he couldn't even swallow nervously. He'd certainly noticed how pretty the waitress Benny had insisted he hire was, but this was the first time since he'd shaken her hand to offer her the job she'd looked right into his eyes. For the three days thus far, she'd been feline in her disregard of him every day she'd come in and been told they weren't opening. "It's a good way to prepare people for some of Sally Degneri's genius when the Fresca opens."

Sally nodded dumbly, and she continued into the camera with natural poise. "Sally is the head chef at the Via Fresca, soon to open in Los Feliz, and today he's going to teach me, his head waitress, how to prepare one of his signature dishes."

"*Head* waitress?"

Tessa rolled her eyes impatiently. "Is there another waitress I'm reporting to?"

"Good point."

"Now come on. You're paying me to be here. Might as well use me for *some*thing."

Sally did his best to ignore the innuendo and began their first lesson. Since that day, Tessa had kept up with encouraging him to teach her more cooking. She had filmed all subsequent lessons in secret and posted them to his YouTube channel on his behalf. To her surprise, and thanks to their comfortable banter, they had garnered a couple thousand subscribers. Tessa had been fearful at first about the following being a liability when time came for her to pull the trigger.

She assured herself the video evidence of her investment in Sally opening the restaurant was a reliable cover for her innocence when that time came. She repeated it to herself more and more each time she uploaded a new video and smiled at more subscribers, and she ignored how much more like a lie it felt each time as well.

HELL PATENTS – COCOA BUTTER

Despite having no true gift for creation or imagination, the forces of Hell have been responsible for driving the ambition of man to invent a number of things over the ages. By way of trusts and other holdings, Hell does have rights to various patents in the human world through wards whose pride, envy, and greed were preyed upon to drive forward the machine of human progress in ways to benefit Hell's mission.

The factory line method of manufacture was created as a welcome byproduct of Avarice's work to maximize the returns of the soon to explode auto industry in the early twentieth century.

Wine and ale were entirely human inventions, but just about every other form of liquor on earth is the result of Devilish meddling to provide humans a wealth of options for liquors that the humans could use to ease their more sinful natures and inclinations to the surface. Tequila, especially, is the pride of Lechery and it's the liquor cited with the highest returns for that particular circle above any other. However, in the inventions being used for Hell's cause among humanity, only one was spurred by Hell for its own pleasure and selfish gain:

Cocoa butter.

As mentioned in prior notes and asides about Devils, is a highly pleasurable substance for the skin of Devils (just as much, if not more so, than for humans, who also delight in its properties as a moisturizer and lotion). However, the reason for this particular material is a simple one:

It's the closest earthly material in consistency, odor, and physical effect to Angels' poop.

Angel feces are rich in restorative properties and a highly useful material in Hell. Cocoa butter is the equivalent of an O'Doul's to a bottle of moonshine by comparison to the real deal's properties and effect. Because of the fall, Devils are highly sensitive to the effects of even the imitation, as they are to any imitation of form of the light and love they lost. As it is, Devils who were expelled yield brimstone and other noxious minerals and ores when defecating.

The effects of cocoa butter are superlative joy for a Devil. The closest a Devil comes to joy is either when fulfilling their deepest sinful natures or when coated in generous amounts of cocoa butter. The effect is something like a double dose of ecstasy, Hawaiian OG Kush, a pure mainline of heroin, and the euphoria of eating fried chicken after a month long vegan dieting paired with cayenne juice cleanses.

ROAD TRIP – PART 1

Lilith tore over the two lane highway through the desert with Tie cramped into a BMW coupe she'd found outside the casino. Tie was hunched over to fit his hulking frame in the compact vehicle with his knees jammed into his chest.

"You couldn't at least get a convertible?" He fidgeted to fit under the roof of the car.

"Of course I could have, but I don't want you too comfortable. We have things to discuss." Lilith was wearing large Tom Ford shades to protect against the sun's glare off the expanse of sand and rocks in every direction around them.

"I'm not going to attack you. We're on the same side. We have this figured out."

She didn't turn her eyes from the road. "Still, makes it easier to tell if you're hiding the truth if you're a bit more out of sorts."

Tie rolled his eyes into the roof of the car his face was mashed against. "You sound like Aba."

"Ugh, take that back. He just parrots from Lucifer. He doesn't actually understand a damn thing about how people work."

Tie swallowed his snide remark about her knowing that because she'd dated Aba, if only that one time. She was true to her word, though. She read the inarticulate noise of his for what it was. "Yes, I know Aba well *enough* to make the judgment. Leave it at that."

Tie grunted appreciatively. "Okay, well, if he doesn't get how the meat sacks-"

"Why's he Executive Director? I dunno, Tie. Maybe because his BFF is the head of Hell, and the underworld is as nepotistic as the Kardashians? Or maybe ask why if he *does* get it, then why isn't he a Vice President like the other Devils he himself put in their places?"

Tie struggled to flip his head under the roof to face Lilith so she could see him blink in appreciative pensivity at her remark.

"Exactly. Who really knows what goes through that frat boy Lucifer's head with anything he does, but Lucifer gave Aba the title and asked, 'You *sure* you want to be Director? I mean, you could just resign and we could chill.'"

"Never heard that before," Tie admitted.

"If Aba tells the story, he tweaks it to sound like a challenge. You know, Wrath and all that. Applauds Lucifer's genius at making his 'very title a source for my malevolent nature.'" She imitated his rasping growl in the final phrase and shook her head at the hypothetical (but admittedly spot on) Aba.

"Anyway, if I know Gast, he has a plan to deal with Aba, but I need to make sure my ward and her beau aren't collateral damage."

"Calvin and Karen?" Tie asked. Lilith nodded, fixing her gaze on the road ahead and tightening her grip on the wheel. Tie listened to the engine roaring. They were doing well over a hundred, and Lilith was weaving expertly between and around cars without hesitation. Even when some swerved in panic at her oncoming speed, she would foresee their swerves and be where she needed to be to avoid colliding with any other drivers.

"He *had* a plan." Tie sulked, averting his gaze once more.

"Had?" Lilith looked at the sad mound of Devil beside her.

"Well, yeah. He came up with it when we took that vacation back in the '80s. Was gonna tell you about it, but you were gone when we got back."

"And he never thought to let me know anyway? I could have helped still."

"Not like he had any idea where you were."

"I sent him an—" Lilith stopped herself and growled in frustration. "Of course. Let me guess, you two got heavy into the cocoa butter, didn't you?" Tie nodded as sheepishly as his head being mashed into the roof allowed. Lilith worked through it aloud for him. "So you two were riding the angel poop highway,[19] and Aba was probably monitoring any communications I sent."

"You didn't send Gast something about taking on Aba?" Tie asked in terror.

Lilith blew away his concern with one hand while her other casually steered them between a pair of cars as narrowly as parallel parking at a hundred fifteen miles per hour. "I just told him how to reach me if he needed or wanted anything."

"So why would—"

"Like I said: Aba doesn't understand the truth of half the stuff he spouts. That's a Devil through and through for you. He's a hell of a lot more envious than he is wrathful by nature. Hence why he's so protective of his status as Lucifer's pet. Lucifer tried to set him up with me, and he failed to keep me interested."

"So he—"

"Didn't take my shooting him down for a second date five decades in a row very well, no. Because he feels it reflected badly on Luce."

"So he—"

---

[19] Heaven, dear reader, is so full of happiness, that even something that would be an aggravation there- like stepping in poo of a member divine host- is an intensely joyous feeling anywhere else in the universe.

"Is probably targeting Gast out of lingering jealousy and anger, yes."

"So he—"

"Doesn't know Gast had some grand plan, he's just a petulant man-child of a devil, yes."

"So you—"

Lilith was plainly caught by surprise. "So *I*?"

"So you *were* going to try a long distance relationship with Gast?"

Lilith's breath caught in her chest, and she swerved into the shoulder and slammed the brakes. Tie hadn't thought it possible, but the force of the sudden stop ramming him into the dashboard and windshield hurt quite a bit. With a dense cloud of dust billowing outside and the smell of burnt rubber penetrating the car, Lilith asked, "Relationship?"

Tie groaned in pain behind his expression of "well, duh," which was an achievement for a hulking Mongol peeling himself from the dashboard and interior windshield of a compact luxury coupe.

Lilith adjusted her grip on the wheel, and Tie noticed it was with a certain amount of effort that she kept her eyes from glancing at him and to keep her voice steady. "Did *he* say that?" She betrayed herself, intentionally. Tie was sure of it, and she fixed her eyes on him behind her shades to read his reaction.

"If he didn't think you'd abandoned him for being just another boring Devil? Maybe he might've."

Lilith pouted at the news and took a deep breath. "Guess that means we really do need to get back." With a guttural roar of the tires spinning in the dirt of the shoulder, they were off again. Tie exhaled in relief. As the car swerved back into the traffic, it changed instantly to a Hummer, which Lilith was still swerving among the cars with the same precision as she had handled the smaller vehicle.

Tie settled more comfortably into the seat and thanked Lilith, to which she responded, "You earned it."

ON SALVATION

At the time of Christ, Hell was in transition from its clan-based oligarchy to a feudal estate monarchy. Lucifer was particularly enthused at all the great company coming in by the way of barbarian warriors, heathen pagans, and perverse Romans. Lucifer said the parties kept getting better and better. He was particularly enthused when Sodom was destroyed, commenting that: "Those Sodomites really bring the party to the next level."

Lucifer has never been much concerned with the opinion or well being of his retinue and the hordes cast down with him. This is why corporation-wide announcements have been rare from the CEO over the ages. One, in particular reveals much of the head of all the Underworld, however.

When The Creator sent Jesus to Earth, Lucifer is known to have done some work to impede this. Devils are all told an account of his interactions with Jesus are recorded in the meat sacks' Christian Bible. Lucifer cautions that the account severely undersells the actual panache and charisma in his pitch. No one in Hell has had the guts or wherewithal to point out that, regardless of how good his pitch to Jesus may have been, the scoreboard still showed a goose egg.

So, despite Lucifer's attempt at an honest day's devilry, Jesus was crucified, died, and stopped by the gates of Hell to pick up the keys. Jesus went back to the Creator, mentioning he'd see them all again at the end of Time.

Knowing that redemption for their sins was now just a matter of a stroke of faith for the human race, Lucifer issued this statement to his hordes on the matter:

"Just when the parties were getting good. Sorry bros."

BRUNCH SERVICES

Matt wasn't sure what else to do with himself. It wasn't as if he needed to work. That was his right and was supposed to be Gast's responsibility. He wasn't even sure what articles Gast would be working on for him. He'd made the deal so shortly after starting at the *LA Weekly*, he wasn't entirely sure how one went about "getting" articles to work on. Sure, there was the assignment meeting, but Calvin seemed to be finding articles to work on anyway even outside of that.

Case in point: this article Gast had let onto the website. Matt read it enviously for a fourth time on his phone while walking down Santa Monica Boulevard. Not knowing what else to do with himself, he had decided to go to a pub for some brunch and drinks. His enchantment had backfired again when he'd left the offices. He was now walking in a rainbow-striped halter top with the bottom half of a puffy cow costume for pants with a neon orange G-string plainly visible thanks to the generous waistline of the costume.

After the speedo the enchantment had stuck him with in the office, he was at least grateful for being more covered in the current outfit. He walked determinedly to the pub, hoping the enchantment might kick back on when he got there. Perhaps it was only misfiring in the office and the streets.

When he entered, however, he was disappointed to find the enchantment had dressed him in the "Trump-Pence '16" T-shirt and jeans once more. He groaned, knowing West Hollywood was the last place this outfit might fly in California. The enchantment was still bugging.

After he sat down, he noticed he was being actively ignored by the bartender who had noticed his t-shirt, but a portly man staggered up to the bar beside him. Matt wasn't sure how a man could be this drunk before ten in the morning, but he decided that for how he was feeling at that moment, it might be a reasonable goal to set for himself. The man reeked of cheap beer and stale cigarettes, and slapped Matt's back entirely too hard. "What's a young man like you doin' here thish early?"

Matt cleared his throat. "I'm just taking some time off. I'm a writer. We have flexible schedules."

The man narrowed his eyes. "A writer?"

Matt noticed the man was leaning back dangerously far on the stool to get a good survey of Matt and his outfit, lingering for a long while on Matt's t-shirt. "You doin' some kinda spy piece or somethin?"

"Spy piece? No, I work for the *LA Weekly*."

"So, yer really a Trump man!" The man clapped Matt happily on the back and cleared his throat, waving for the bartender. "Good! I thought all you writers were queers. Whash yer name?" The man slurred, patting at his chest and pulling a pack of Marlboros from his breast pocket. The bartender came over after rolling his eyes and admonished the man for attempting to smoke in the bar.

The man waved the bartender off and ordered his drinks. "A ghee n' tee, and whatever my friend wants, whash yer name?"

"Matt."

"What?"

"Matt."

"Yeah, I heard ya, Max what?"

"Reade."

"Max Read is drinkin' on my tab."

Matt sighed and tried to make himself as small as possible beside the man, but the bartender stared icily at him for his order. Matt requested a bottled beer to limit the bartender's opportunity to slip something poisonous into his drink.

When their drinks were served, the man swallowed half the highball in a single gulp. "You know what, Max, yer all right."

Matt, perplexed how the drunk had arrived at this opinion, said a low word of thanks and would have corrected him on his name, but the drunk man continued effusively. "Max, I know you got all these people out here sayin' yer a bigot, 'er a racist. Prob'ly sayin' yer full o' yerself but yer still fightin' on."

"I don't know."

"Hey, you keep up the good work. Max Read, good guys like you 'n' me? We'll make America great again." The man stood, slapped Matt's back once more, and walked out of the bar with the highball in hand.

Thoroughly perplexed, Matt considered whether or not he felt okay about drinking the beer bought by a man who hadn't even paid for it. Matt was lost in his thoughts to the point that he jumped when two pairs of hands slithered over his shoulders.

He recognized the pair of girls they belonged to instantly. "Natalie? Natalee?"

The girls cocked eyebrows in identical fashion, but Natalie tapped a finger to her lips in thought while Natalee looked to her for guidance. After a moment, it came to her, and Natalie snapped her fingers. "Matt Reade, right?"

"Yeah." He nodded, unsure when he'd actually met the girls despite the month they'd all been at the *Weekly* together. He'd barely earned any acknowledgment from them in his first week and hadn't been around the offices since he'd made the deal with Gast.

"I recognized you from your picture," Natalie said, more to Natalee to confirm with her friend.

Natalee's eyes were wide with concordance. "Oh my God, yeah, it's weird how that works."

"My picture?" He recalled the office picture on the board he'd tossed in the trash the day before. He hoped the enchantment hadn't backfired that much.

"It isn't backfiring that hard," Natalee assured.

"How did you know I was—"

"Same way you could, duh," Natalie explained.

"Wait, you have deals too?"

"Something like that," Natalee said before sipping on a yellow cocktail through a straw.

"Why aren't you at the office? Are your deals backfiring too?" Matt searched hopefully, but noticed quickly how well dressed they both were.

Natalee grimaced. "Ugh, what? No. We got fired from the *Weekly*."

"Yeah, by that bitch, Karen." Natalie's voice dripped with ire, and her visage melted to something less than its usual pretty countenance at mentioning Karen.

"Karen fired you? She's just an intern."

"No, she isn't!" the two girls snapped simultaneously. They took a breath together and silently agreed which of them should speak, so Natalie continued. "She got a job there." Matt recalled Gast had told him as much. It was why Gast had to go after Calvin that week.

"Yeah, so we get let go, and how weird is it we walk into our new jobs and find out, whoa, we were working with a guy who could've given *us* a hook up while he was there." Natalee punched Matt's shoulder.

"Against Karen?" The Nats nodded in unison, and he clarified, "But there was still only one fashion writer's position available."

"Whatever, like the Devil couldn't make them just love us both," Natalie argued. Matt had a hard time refuting it, even if his faith in Hell's abilities was based on very little actual product at the moment. For some reason, he still wanted the deal to be all his own, for him to be the special one— the only one Hell could hoist up. The thought clawed at him: if he was special, then why did he need the deal?

"Well, I dunno, maybe could have."

"Fine, enjoy it. We found back ups," Natalee dismissed Matt easily.

"Which is?" Matt wondered if the girls had made deals to become models. It might have explained their being at a bar so early.

"Vixens," Natalie answered with a coy smirk.

"Entry level, but it's something," Natalee added.

"Vixens?"

"Yeah, you guys who have deals with Devils and what not? We're the hot girls at the bar who ignore other guys and flock around you no matter how lame you are."

"Lame?"

Matt was preparing to refute the accusation by implication, but Natalee spoke up before he could. "Oh please, Hell gives you idiots clothes and does all the work for you."

"But it doesn't give you any charm." Natalie sipped her drink with raised eyebrows that dared him to argue.

Matt hesitated under her gaze. "That's...that's a matter of opinion."

Natalie snorted ungraciously. "I'm sure it isn't. How interesting can a guy who does nothing and has everything handed to him possibly be?"

Natalee's face contorted to an unflattering sneer. "You sound like Karen."

Natalie stirred her drink with her straw dejectedly. "Ugh, shut up."

"So, you're Vixens." Matt checked his watch, which had turned into a children's *Dora the Explorer* watch. "Awful early."

"Like I said, it's entry level. You work your way up to the fancier bars and times." Natalee surveyed the bar that was otherwise empty save the bartender.

"Like a waitress," Matt offered.

"We're not servants," the girls snapped in unison. Their faces were stony, and their voices carried an echo Matt found unsettling and inexplicable. Matt remained perfectly still until the girls relaxed again. "Besides, who's giving up *his* soul for someone *else's* dream?"

"Girls," a husky voice intoned from a table several feet away. Matt saw a gorgeous woman, middle-aged, red hair in a black dress just barely long enough to curve over her bottom on the seat. She was waving two fingers at the Nats, beckoning them over.

"We're employees. *You're* the slave because of how much you demand of the world, Matthew." Natalie's expression was both vacant yet pitiful.

Matt tried to puzzle out the meaning of their words but was interrupted by Natalee. "Also, the bartender is going to throw you out if you don't find a way to get a new outfit."

Matt looked down. His outfit had changed during his

lapse in focus into the leather speedo again. While the Nats sat with the perplexingly gorgeous woman at a table, Matt was chased out by the bartender swatting a newspaper at him as if he were a moth unable to find an open window.

ORGANIZATIONAL CHARTS

"Harry?" Felicia sang into his cubicle. Harry's cubicle was actually a four-seater space, but being the only person in Human Resources, the other adjacent departments had been willing to give him the run of all four desks for the sake of not having to share the space with him.

Harry was generally a man of jollity, unbridled amicability, and optimism. All of this came crashing down like the Hindenburg ablaze when he found himself in the same room as Felicia. Unbeknownst to Felicia, she was singularly responsible for half of the work Harry had managed since being slotted into the role of Human Resources Director.

New employee onboarding, payroll, insurance coverages—all of that gloriously fun bureaucracy and red tape added up to only as much as work as Felicia caused him with complaints, reports, memos, mediation sessions and settlement discussions for her attire, speech, actions, behaviors, and chronic fondlings.

Thus, dear reader, it was with a voice positively oozing with ire and derelict derision that Harry responded to her melodious call. "Felicia."

She smiled ignorantly and cooed at him. "I just talked to the big man, Sam, *our* boss, about the intern, Calvin?"

"Oh." Harry acknowledged her with no lack of plain disgust and wariness. He crossed his arms in stalwart readiness against her wiles.

"Well, I'd like the org chart updated and a memo sent to the staff that Calvin will, for the foreseeable future, be the Food section intern. I also need you to open a spot for a Food Staff Writer."

"Food. Staff. Writer." Harry repeated the three words with careful revulsion like dropping overstuffed, oozing sacks of trash into dumpsters.

Felicia nodded with a toothy grin. "I know you'll be responsible for all that fun paperwork and accounting stuff." Felicia rolled her eyes airily at the scope of it all. "I know we technically have a position for a Staff Writer in the Food section."

"We have room for *one* more Staff Writer," Harry corrected her sharply. "One."

"Well, I guess it'll be a Food staffer." Felicia reached into the cubicle and patted Harry's shoulder. "Thanks, Harry! You're an absolute doll!"

Felicia turned on her Donna Karan heels and was out of sight. Harry grimaced at the shoulder Felicia had rubbed and fumed at being told to do anything by her. What he hated most was that she was right: she did technically have clout to have at least one staff writer in her section reporting to her. Harry had used every turn of HR legalese and red tape to keep that fact hidden from her. The way he figured it, the harassment and complaints were only all the more likely if she had a direct subordinate.

Behind his disgust and fury, what actually hurt Harry was that it had been his own friend who'd signed off on it.

PRE-ORDER BONUSES NOT INCLUDED

Pitch rarely, if ever, manifested an office around his desk in the Avarice circle. Unlike Gast, he preferred to work in the open. Pitch was only as good as he was for two reasons: he let a hungry eye on his peers work motivate him, and the hunger from his ever-empty coffer drove him.

Pitch knew Gast was the same, even if Gast's coffer was a different sort of thing. Pitch didn't have time to puzzle over the effect of Lilith's departure because, against his will, an office manifested around him.

It was nothing fancy. It was erected only to providing privacy for him and his guest now sitting in the simple wooden chair on the other side of the desk.

"Pitch, always a pleasure," Aba said.

Pitch laced his hands together and maintained his composure. He considered proffering Aba the results of his audit with Gast from the day before but decided not to rush his hand. It could draw suspicion if Pitch were too quick on the draw with it. "Indeed. How can I help you, Aba?"

"I do believe in a number of ways." Aba's voice smoldered with a dark pleasure Pitch could easily guess at. Tie's going AWOL was knowledge around all the circles, as was Gast's encounter in the elevator with Aba. Photos had been sent to Pitch by more than a dozen other Devils already. "But first, something simple." Aba outstretched his alabaster arm and regarded it critically. "I'm tiring of this particular meat sack."

Pitch manifested the ledger of seized corpses from humans they had made deals with and flipped through the tabbed sections. Bodies already assigned to other Devils, those pending seizure, and those unassigned and available for a Devil seeking a new body or a Demon or Imp earning their Devil rank. When he pressed his finger to the tab of the third section and began to open it, Aba reached to stop him. "This one would be in the second section."

"I'm sorry, a body that's already been assigned?"

Aba sat back without a hint of answering Pitch's inquiry. He leered from his deep-set dark eyes in steady silent command for Pitch to proceed.

"You need an executive order to remand a body that is already assi—"

"And I am herewith using my executive power to—"

"Sir, do you have a signed mandate?"

"You—" Aba growled and swallowed back the vulgarities roiling in the gutter of his throat. "Write the mandate. I'll sign it, peon."

Pitch tried not to react to the last word. The temptation to laugh was too strong, and he had no idea how safe he necessarily was to enjoy this cloying game with the Executive Director, both because Pitch had no idea how far the Wrath Director's clout could carry to him in Avarice, nor did he know what kind of safety net Gast's plan could still provide (if Gast even still had a plan).

Politely, but not deferentially, Pitch spoke. "Sir, which of the executives should I send it to for signature?"

Aba's eyes shifted, taking a moment to comprehend Pitch's implication, and leaned forward quickly with both hands gripping the edge of Pitch's cherrywood desk. "*I* am an executive, you halfwit piece of—"

Pitch acknowledged Aba with a calm nod. "Executive *Director.*" Pitch was surprised at how successfully he'd managed to wipe any trace of cheekiness or insubordination from his tone, even achieving an undertone of contrition. "I'm sorry, sir, but Lucifer was quite clear after the reorg last century that he wanted only Vice Presidents representing executive-level mandates."

"Why would you presume to know what Lord Lucifer meant?" Aba's nails were clawing into the varnish and sinews of the desk's wood.

"I don't, sir. I have his memo on file from 1931." Pitch opened a drawer to manifest the record.

"And you don't think it's possible that our Lord Lucifer may have meant those with Executive titles rather than just Vice President titles?" Aba loomed over the desk with an audible snarl.

Pitch cleared his throat and read directly from the sheet of paper. "Bros, let's keep these kind of things limited to people with just VP titles, cool?"

Pitch waited for Aba's mouth to flap before he continued reading, cutting the Director off. "Like, those big orders. Mandates? Is that the word? Mandates? Chill, yeah, those. Let's leave those to just VPs. Nah, I'm good, I'm gonna peace out and chill. You VPs are the pros."

Aba fumed and for once his face actually betrayed a flush of red as he chewed the inside of his cheek at Pitch's recitation. Pitch concluded: "Yeah, *just* VPs. Aba? You good? We good? I'm gonna hit this dope ass party about to pop off in Austria if you wanna join."

Aba sat rigid. Pitch returned the memo to his desk then adopted a look of mild fear mingled with contrition. "If you're saying that you're certain Lord Lucifer made a mistake, then sir, I can-"

"No! Of course not! Lord Lucifer is infallible! How dare you suggest otherwise!"

"Well, sir, how do you want to handle this?" Pitch regarded the ledger he had opened as if he were stymied.

Aba exhaled liked a steam engine. "I don't need the

body to be remanded anyway. I simply want to ensure a body is given to me when it becomes available."

Pitch thumbed the ledger open. "That's no trouble at all. Your title does entitle you to automatic top position on a *wait*list if a body becomes available."

"Not if," Aba corrected Pitch pointedly, dropping a narrow index finger onto a specific name on the page. "*When.*"

Pitch looked at the name and furrowed his brow. "I'm sorry, sir, but Gast has no current plans or intention of abandoning his current body, so a pre-order—"

"Is where I want my name." Aba pressed his finger harder into the paper.

Pitch summoned his theatricality and gave the nonchalant shrug of a clerk whose jotting pointless notes should be of no concern to him. After all, what did he know about the battle between Gast and Aba? Far less the potential punishment of Gast losing his Devil rank and body as consequence of failing to outwit the Director?

With a few strokes of the pen, Aba's name was the first and only name on the pre-order list for Gast's body. "Should it become available for use, Gast's body will be your body." Pitch cleared his throat. "Any modifications you may want to the body will have to be made through Pride." Pitch stole a furtive glance at Aba. "Or Lechery, depending."

Aba's nose curled. "I'm sure it's in sufficient enough shape once I make manageable adjustments to the pomposities the current owner is so fond of."

"Pomposities." Pitch was unsure why he'd chosen that word to repeat, far less to say anything at all.

"Indeed, its current user is quite the uppity little gnat." Aba sat back with a conversational air, crossing his legs and looking repulsed by the topic but barreling forth all the same. "He's a flea that thinks because his host scratches that he has ascended to stand on equal footing with them."

"Have you ever heard the fable of the mouse and the lion?"

"Have you ever heard of keeping your mouth shut?" Pitch took as a soft no, and gestured for Aba to continue. "I've already seen the results of his audit, and it's as I assumed. He's a wolf howling at the moon, believing if he howls long enough and runs far enough he'll get his fangs in it. All that howling shows is the insurmountable distance between the moon's glory and the hound."

Pitch nodded in mild admiration at Aba's poeticism. Still though, he didn't want to tip his hand. He couldn't check on how much Aba knew of his involvement before Aba revealed he knew Gast had a plot at all. The signs were there: the evaluation, the audit, and now the pre-order, but Aba still wasn't baring his predator's fangs. If Pitch was reading Aba's posture and (admittedly verbose) tone correctly, Aba was genuinely enjoying a chat with a colleague.

"What better fun is there?" Aba asked.

Pitch contemplated Aba's inquiry. "Been a bit bored lately?"

"Ages and ages." Aba spoke with an almost theatrical melancholy. "All the ages of Hell. It's the same time and again: a young upstart, a rivalry, a battle, and then back to the grind."

"Repetitious, hm?"

"Yes." He nodded his bald head more vigorously as he considered the notion further. "I began wondering if it was a cycle of history that would repeat itself spiraling through and into eternity. I was about to give up."

Pitch gave a curious look at Aba, wondering if the Director really didn't get it. "Lord Lucifer might be glad for you to enjoy some more... personal time away from the hoi polloi of the offices?"

Aba turned up his nose at the notion. "I'm precisely where our Lord Lucifer wants and *needs* me."

Pitch put his hands up in surrender. It was a mystery to him how two beings could simultaneously love one another yet act so consistently in discord of that love actually bringing them together, but this is a phenomenon in the universe with Devils, Angels, and fourth graders alike.

Aba finally rose, clearly motivated by Pitch's inquiries to get back to work. "Notify me the moment that my pre-order becomes available to claim." Aba paused at the door and looked at Pitch curiously. "You know, *Pitch*, most Devils can never resist the temptation. We're all so bad at resisting temptation, after all. They *all* ask me how I did it."

"Did what?"

"Gave Hell its base order. Through all our evolutions and structures, the seven circles that have been transmuted through all our ages and facades. Every other Devil asks me how I did it."

Aba stood at the door, and Pitch could tell he was waiting to be asked. "I know how you did it. Through wrath and fury for Lord Lucifer. Word gets around." Pitch waved his hand through the last bit of it and turned back to another ledger of a Midwest dentist's obsession with his *Magic: the Gathering* card collection.

He didn't look up to see Aba's face set in dark disappointment. "Yes, that's how I did so for all the Devils, demonkind as a collective." His voice was so low in his throat it bubbled at Pitch in an oozing timbre. Pitch couldn't help but look up and notice the office was growing dim. The light from his desk lamp was fighting desperately to illuminate even the corner of his papers directly under it.

Aba emerged from the darkness to loom over Pitch's desk once more. "Devils do not ask how I sorted all demonkind." Pitch held his breath in the darkness. Aba's black eyes burned with points of brimstone at their cores. "They ask how I sorted *them*. They all ask how I know which sin they belonged to. Do you want to know? Should I tell you what I saw in you?"

Pitch shook his head. "No, I think I know well enough." Aba was stunned and wore his surprise plainly, even in the darkness. Pitch's easy response snuffed out the embers in his dark eyes. "I suppose it would be more fascinating to hear why you sorted Gast into Wrath. Keeping your enemies close type of thing?"

Aba shook his head. "No, Gast is unique."

Pitch finally felt himself honestly piqued. "How so?"

Aba fumed for a moment then blurted with a hint of confusion: "He applied."

With those words, Aba swept out of the room and was gone. A moment later, the office deconstructed, and Pitch was left at his desk with Aba nowhere in sight. All around him, Avarice Devils pretended not to be shooting furtive glances, so Pitch set himself back to work on his ledgers while thinking in panic that Gast had better have a good backup plan handy.

ROAD TRIP – PART 2

"License and registration?"

"Don't have them." Lilith smiled up through the

window.

"Ma'am?"

"I don't have them. Does it really matter in the grand scheme of things?" Tie groaned at Lilith's response.

"Ma'am, you were doing well over one hundred—"

"One twenty-two, yes." Lilith pointed at the gauge on the dashboard. "I saw it right here."

"And you don't have a license or registration? I'll have to ask you to get out of the car." The officer leaned down and glanced over Lilith's slender shoulder at Tie. "Sir, you too."

"Officer, you don't think that our speed indicated we were in something of a rush?"

"Ma'am."

"And that your stopping us is a serious impediment in that rush?"

"Get out of the car, ma'am." The officer backed away from the door and put his hand on the taser clipped to his belt.

Tie put his hand to his brow in aggravation. "Come on already. Stop playing with your food."

Lilith grinned and plopped her head onto her arms she had hung out over the car door. "Lovely of you to reach for the taser for me."

The officer barked: "Ma'am!"

"You're so quick to reach for the gun when you need to feel like a big man." She looked deep into the officer's eyes behind his sport shades.

The officer unclipped the taser. "You two! Out of the car! Now!"

The officer's partner came to his side and began shouting the same orders, and Lilith finally got out of the car. Tie watched disinterestedly from the passenger seat. Lilith climbed down from the high driver's seat of the

Hummer onto the sandy shoulder they had been pulled over into. Her step was graceful, and her poise that of a queen stepping down from her throne.

"You know, most people would think when you reach for your gun so readily in other instances it's because you're scared, perhaps of their skin color or the way they talk, but no." She spoke calmly, and the officer paused in approaching her with handcuffs. "It's not that you're afraid of them. You're afraid of yourself. You're not afraid of me because a gorgeous woman *should* make sense to you. You're *supposed* to want me."

Lilith gave a slow spin before him, but she finished it with a knowing narrow of her gaze. "You're afraid of wanting people your daddy beat you bloody for wanting. You're afraid of men because you were sent away by people you loved for wanting them. They scare you because you were told, taught, and punished into being scared of them."

The officer's partner stood still and looked in confusion at the exchange. "Gary?"

Officer Gary was flummoxed. "Shut up, Eddy, she doesn't know—"

"It's okay. I know it's my friend in the car you're really afraid of, and that you're really only afraid of him because you're afraid of yourself wanting him." Lilith stepped forward and put her hand on Gary's right hand over his taser. "I'm telling you it's not that you were wrong for those feelings still bubbling underneath. You didn't fail your father for feeling these things. You aren't failing him by being who you are."

Officer Gary was stupefied. He could barely bring himself to breathe the sweet scent of Lilith beside him. She looked sadly and sweetly into his eyes, her own overflowing with sympathy and pain for him. "*He* failed *you.*"

She pressed gently on his hand and lowered the taser back to his belt. Without a word, Officer Gary nodded dumbly to his partner and led the way back to their squad car. Officer Eddy stammered but no coherent words came out until he was back at the car with Gary, who had started weeping gratefully. "Gary, it's nothing to be ashamed of. We all kind of knew. We love you. I mean, you watch the Desperate Housewives religiously, for God's sake."

Lilith smiled proudly and climbed back into the Hummer. Tie checked his watch. "I thought we were in a rush?"

Lilith scowled like a school teacher. "Oh, shush. That was worth the delay. That poor man."

"You and your foofy open hearts philosophy."

Lilith pulled the car back onto the highway and pressed the accelerator to the floor. They had another hour to go. "You weren't there in the garden. God, the Creator, I mean, made *everyone*. All the different colors, cultures, and personalities representing aspects of the spectrum of light and love. All different kinds of people, humors, and sensibilities. You Devils do such a good job of dividing them by creating this mold they each believe they need to fit and use it to justify hatred of anything outside the mold."

Tie slouched in the passenger seat and looked out the window. "Pride in their own righteousness is the best way in every age to get a meat sack to wall themselves off to the Creator's light."

Lilith shook her head. "How right you are. Everyone gets so stuck on Adam and Eve, but I wish the story of Eden had recognized the people that led to the *other* races and cultures around the world the Creator made."

Tie chuckled. "'Adam and Eve, not Adam and Steve' is one of the funniest line one of the boys in Pride managed to get caught on up here."

"Yes, I recall." Lilith soured at the memory of hearing the line crafted in the Underworld, then being fed to so-called Christians to justify bigotry and hate. "Adam was such a nice, accepting, and loving man. How could he not be after having been so close to the Creator?"

"You say that like that meat sack was any different than us Devils. We remember the Creator and the light. That's why we hate the meat sacks."

"And what about all the humans since? The ones born without direct exposure to the Creator?" Lilith swerved the car in a wide arc all the way to the carpool lane then back out of it to the third lane to get around a pack of cruising commuters.

"We hate them because they can reach it if they just decide to. You know that."

"Because they can so easily obtain what you so terribly lost."

Tie only snarled in response and squirmed to twist his great bulk in the seat to turn away from her as if he were going to sleep. She shook her head at him and continued tearing her way down the highway; they were nearing the 134 freeway that they could take back into the heart of LA. As she swerved for the exit ramp, Tie muttered from over his shoulder, "Someone's awful forgiving of the guy she called a stuck up prude when I first met her."

Lilith huffed. "Oh, come on, it may have been the beginning of time, but even then there was more than just lights off, missionary, and sleep."

ASSIGNMENTS

"Miss Swanson-Thomas wants you." These were the first words that had greeted Calvin when he'd stepped off the elevator to the offices, delivered dispassionately by Lily from behind the receptionist's desk. He had turned them over with every deliberate step since hearing them.

On the one hand, his first response (to his surprise) was an internal, "Well, duh." Barely a moment later, the more anticipated anxiety began to wrap over him like a familiar, but no less uncomfortable, blanket.

Felicia intimidated him by sheer force of her *raison d'etre*, which Calvin could find no polite terms to summate. "Hedonist" seemed to be the best word he could use for it as he trudged down the hall to her office. What worried him most wasn't his inclination to describe her that way, but rather how amused he knew she would be to hear him use it.

He knocked twice lightly, and she called for him to come in. When he poked his head in, she smiled with predatory hunger. "Close the door behind you."

He nodded dutifully, not sure what else one did in a situation where they were clearly being commanded to create privacy for casual office sexual harassment. Although, Calvin corrected himself as the door clicked. He was supposed to be a willing party, so it wasn't so much harassment as sexual...coalition? confidance? collusion?

He shook the search for proper descriptive from his head and sat down facing her desk, at which she eyed him as a jungle cat sizing up the fawn approaching the pond for a sip. He began as casually as he could. "How's the article doing?"

He was surprised to see her actually address the

question with a focused, professional demeanor. "It's doing very well, which is a bit of an understatement."

Calvin was intrigued and leaned forward to peer at her monitor, which was on the administrative page for the *LA Weekly* website. Traffic, click throughs, and link shares could be tracked here by the editors. He did his best to ignore the dozen or so tabs behind it with the Pornhub icon.

Felicia pointed at the screen. "It's breaking records for views *and* shares, and it's only been up for *three* hours."

Calvin was stunned, and his head was burning with new fear. He'd just wanted something to give him a foothold against the Devil. It wasn't supposed to go viral. Now the flimsy article was more ammunition for the Devil to use against him. What few facts the article had, he'd pulled from the restaurant website about its menu and its owner, Chef Sally Degneri. Those tidbits were completely undone by the fiction he'd woven around them: that the restaurant was going out of business rather than never having opened.

"And it's good buzz?"

"Good? Great! All the hipsters in this town can't get enough of it. I think you hit really subtly on all the great hipster virtues: a small business, not well known, and anti-gentrification of a trendy area."

Calvin was stunned. He'd never seen Felicia speak so articulately about readership or, well, anything non-sexual. Suddenly, her choosing to remain at the *LA Weekly* despite being loaded made some sense. Maybe behind the sexual frustration was a person who was thoroughly passionate about writing.

"This article is the best thing I've had come into my box in the middle of the night." She looked again at the still-climbing numbers only briefly before her expression became demure once more. "But I think you could make it the second best thing to come in my box if you have even ten minutes to spread me over my desk like butter."

Calvin hadn't been drinking any water but still managed to choke as if he had been. Puzzling at the strangled feeling he was coughing out of his throat at just that moment, it gave him enough time in his panic to seize a solution to two problems at once. "I think a follow up might be worthwhile. Maybe a profile on the chef? Especially if it's getting so much buzz?"

Felicia looked only momentarily disappointed before she glanced at the numbers. "That would be great for next week's issue. We could even include your original review with it."

Calvin was relieved to see her turn her chair to her keyboard and begin typing but would swear that another button of her blouse had unlatched seemingly by sheer force of will to expose more of her cleavage.

Calvin stood quickly and was chagrined when she huskily commanded, "Come back as soon as you have the interview done. We can work on the draft together."

"I'll send you my first attempt," Calvin promised.

She shook her head and bit her bottom lip coyly. "No, I want you back here as soon as possible. We'll write it together. Every line and every stroke." She twisted sensually in her chair, and Calvin managed to choke on nothing again before ducking out of the office.

Karen had let him know she would be down the hall in what was now her official office next to Maggie's. He sped down the row of cubicles, averting his gaze from meeting the HR Director's as he walked with his head down into Karen's office and shut the door behind him.

"Hey! How'd it go?" Karen asked hopefully.

Calvin slumped into the chair and shook his head.

"Bad."

"She didn't—"

"No. Not yet, anyway. Although I don't think I'll be able to get another article past her without—"

"Oh God."

"Yeah. I don't even think I can get back in the *office* without her locking me in a room."

Karen giggled a little. "You're aware literally *any* other guy would be excited about that?"

"Yeah, except there isn't *any* other guy who gets to date you, and I'm terrified of her." Calvin shivered before he glanced over his shoulder warily.

"I don't blame you. She's more machine than woman now," Karen joked, imitating Alec Guinness from *Star Wars*.

"She was so preoccupied with whether or not she could that she didn't stop to think if she *should*," Calvin quipped back. Karen looked searchingly at him until Calvin's eyes went wide in surprise. "*Jurassic Park*. My God. Ian Malcolm played by the indomitable Jeff Goldblum."

"Sorry, I only ever saw the sequel, so I was pretty soured on ever going back to the originals."

"Bad call. The original's the only worthwhile one." Calvin smiled at the exchange, but his face shifted back to seriousness for the work at hand. "Okay, I've gotta find the chef of this ghost restaurant. Or try to, anyway."

"Try to?"

"Yeah, Felicia told me the article's blowing up online. So, now I've got a fake article going crazy that'll out me as a hack and ruin my career."

Karen pursed her lips. "Hate to say I told you so." She glanced at the screen and began reading something. "But I don't think I get to."

Calvin walked around to her side of the desk. "Why not?"

She pointed at a comment on the bottom of the screen. "This guy says he's at the restaurant and that the food is great."

Calvin stood back and put his hand over his mouth. "How about that?"

"My theory?" Calvin nodded for her to continue. "You wrote an article that was false *at the time* and got past the Devil."

"So it was false when it was being published and slipped under the Devil's radar."

"But became true when your writing sent customers their way and *made* them open!" Karen's voice rang with excitement and admiration. She was out of her seat with her arms around his neck and kissed his cheek exuberantly.

"Okay, so I *really* need to go talk to the chef."

"Why? It's not like the article's a sham anymore."

"Because the details are super flimsy, and I don't want him contradicting anything if someone else tries interviewing him."

"Now might be the time for you to try slipping a good article by too."

Calvin noticed her blushing and asked why. She gasped slightly in surprise at him breaking her reverie and admitted, "I saw Matt Reade this morning when I was coming in. You remember how slick you said he was dressed? That it was the Devil doing that for him, yeah?"

"Yeah, he said some part of his deal helps him be well dressed."

"Well, he was storming out like he was looking for a refund this morning. He was wearing a leather banana hammock and cowboy boots."

Belting laughter, Calvin tumbled out of Karen's office to head to the Via Fresca. As he had earlier, the fact that he was somehow unfettered with worry for the first time in many hours became itself a cause of concern for him.

He was astute to catch that.

THE WRONG SECTION

"If you're a PR guy looking for ad space, you're on the wrong side of the floor." Felicia didn't bother looking away from her monitor to offer the dismissal.

The man was too well dressed to be any kind of writer or editor. Only business types wore suits in Los Angeles, and very few even bothered putting on ties unless they were lawyers. Felicia never had much time for lawyers. They did their jobs for her, filled her accounts with divorce settlements, and she signed off on their invoices. They knew better than to make house calls, and any lawyer trying to bring a suit to her was still in the wrong place.

The man seated himself neatly on the chair facing her. His suit rested clean without an unflattering wrinkle or bunch in the fabric. In the summer heat, a three-piece suit sounded preposterous, but Felicia had to admit the man was making the thing work for him. His complexion was clear of any effect from the heat, his hair parted perfectly, and his black suit perfectly tailored. If he was a lawyer, she must be in very big trouble.

Gast offered a charming smile. "I assure you, I'm here on non-legal matters. I have some distressing news and need to communicate the resignation of the writer with whom you're currently engaged."

"Calvin?"

Gast nodded apologetically, and she huffed. "No, I'm sorry. I'm not engaged *enough* with him yet. I'll be needing at least a two week's notice on his resignation." She regarded Gast warily. "He didn't send you?"

"No, actually, I'm here to send you. You're going to tell him he's fired."

"Excuse me?"

"I'm actually working with another intern here. Calvin represents a danger to my client. I'm not trying to cause any stirs, so I'd like you to help me make this as...clean as possible." Gast tilted his head forward slightly to intone the gravitas of his instruction.

Felicia sat back, crossing her arms over her generous chest. "No, thanks."

Gast blinked. "Why does it matter to you?"

"Because it does. Matt's a little twerp. I'm fine with him being around, but I'm not firing my favorite toy just because some poofed-up nobody tells me to." Felicia sat back in resolute disaffection before she waved him off in dismissal. "There's the door. I hope it hits you on the way out."

Gast collected his resolve. "Madame, you don't seem to understand—"

"No, I understand perfectly. I can guarantee that it's *you* who doesn't understand that I don't have to do a single damn thing you tell me to." Felicia sneered and waved facetiously. "Buh bye."

Gast scowled. It had worked with others; he'd just show up and his charisma and demeanor would carry the right impression to at least open up a dialogue in his favor. This Felicia woman was not even giving him a crack in her armor for him to play it that way.

With great chagrin, he resolved to play it the way he knew Aba wouldn't expect him to. Gast slipped his spiritual form from his body like prying soiled undies off himself at the end of a long day. Liberated of his physical body, Gast roved through the air between them as a spirit. Settling on her shoulder with his empty body staring vacantly at her, he began to whisper and try to pry his way into her.

The first tendrils of his spiritual form had barely brushed against her psyche before a crack of lightning repelled him. Something had ousted him with such force that he was reeling. A third figure had joined them in the room. Even though he had been thrown back from Felicia by the force, she turned to face what should have been his invisible spirit form. Beside her stood the ever robe-clad figure of Aba Don.

Aba tutted and shook his head. "Gast, you should know better than to try to violate another Devil's deal in order to fulfill your own."

"I told you that you didn't understand." Felicia snickered at Gast impishly.

"My dear Felicia has had a long standing deal for us to help drown magnates in their downfalls and despair in exchange for wealth and her freedom to have her way with whoever, whenever she pleases." Aba's nose twitched ferociously before he continued. "Especially when it comes to coworkers on the job."

Gast tried to make sense of it all. How this deal had gone unnoticed by him, how Matt's deal had started malfunctioning. Finally, it made sense why Matt Reade was the deal Aba had chosen to challenge him on as opposed to any of the other deals Gast knew Aba found so much more distasteful.

Aba looked at Gast's empty body and grinned. "I'll be claiming this body now. I do believe there's a more worthy Devil waiting for it." Aba flashed a series of yellowing teeth in a broad grin. "That Devil being me, of course."

Felicia sat back and crossed her legs. "Happy to help, Aba."

"Lovely as always, my dear." With a snap of his finger, Aba vanished with Gast's vacant body.

Felicia turned back to her computer and clicked over to one of the pornography tabs she had open on her browser. "Now, little demon, run along. Unless you want to see things get weird for eleven o'clock on a Tuesday."

HELL & LONELINESS

Pitch felt the tug of energy in his ledger and opened his drawer. He pulled the book out and opened to the page with Gast's body. He saw it updating the body's assignment to Aba Don, the first on the waitlist for it.

Pitch slumped back in his chair and anxiously ran his hand through his fiery hair. Looking around at the endless rows of desks in every direction of Avarice around him, all he managed was a feeble, "I'll be damned." He lamented that he was alone in the sentiment.

AM I SAD BECAUSE I'M AT HAPPY HOUR, OR AM I AT HAPPY HOUR BECAUSE I'M SAD?

It should have felt like a celebration. Karen had finished her first month as an intern at the *LA Weekly*. The Fashion Editor, Maggie Smith, was a sweetheart and Karen loved working for her. Her colleagues, Natalee and Natalie, on the other hand...

"Woooooooo!" The Nats were cheering yet again for a round of shots guys they'd met at the bar had bought for them.

Karen was desultory at the end of the bar. Again and again, guys from the group that had glommed onto the Nats would peel off to try to engage Karen with the kind of cliché feint at sympathy she found even more cringe-inducing than their more blatant flirtations with the Nats.

"Not big on the noise and crowd? Yeah, me either," one had tried.

"Then why are you out with them?" she had responded and excused herself a moment later to retreat further down the bar.

Another had attempted, "Those guys are just celebrating a big day at work. I'm out with them to show solidarity, but I'm more of a quiet nights and theater kind of guy. You sure I can't buy you another round? Maybe we can find a more quiet place to talk."

Karen was finally at the very end of the bar, mostly out of sight, and was wondering why she hadn't left altogether. Maggie had stopped by and asked if she was okay. Karen nodded with her best smile and told Maggie that she was hit with some ideas for articles that she would come with in the morning. Since she had a little black notebook open with a pen in front of her, the lie held enough water for Maggie to smile appreciatively and say goodnight.

The black notebook had been a gift earlier that morning from one of the new interns who had started that week, Calvin Graves. She couldn't spot the other new intern, but Calvin was enjoying a lively conversation with Errol and another staff writer halfway down the bar between her and the Nats. She had tried joining that circle, but no sooner had she shifted beside them than another of the Nats' hangers on had found his way to her.

She was currently mortified that the moment Calvin had tried to engage her while she was beside him, one of the guys in a Marc Ecko t-shirt that was a size too small had just chosen to drape his arm over her presumptuously.

Karen scribbled in her book to herself: "What is it about guys that think they can manufacture intimacy through intimate-seeming gestures? Don't they know intimacy informs the gesture, not the other way around?"

On the first day they'd met, she was using her phone to write these kinds of notes to herself, but Calvin had suggested the value in using a dedicated notebook for it. Among the advantages he'd listed, one he hadn't foreseen was that it was much better at creating an isolating space for her since it looked more like serious work than typing on the phone.

She'd already filled several pages since that morning. She flipped back to reread some of the early notes, secretly hoping that Calvin might notice her using the gift in the corner and come by, but her writing looked blurry. She eyed the Long Island Iced Tea she was nursing. It was her third of the night, and normally one of them would mean bedtime for her.

She exhaled tiredly and glanced in Calvin's direction once more. He seemed ready for bed too by the way he was swaying and how grand his hand gestures were when he laughed and threw in a punchline to add to the peals of laughter of the group. Funny, she thought, that when booze had a person most awake and energetic was likely the best time for that person to go to bed.

"I love your book," a kind voice said beside her. "Much more elegant than using a phone like so many people do these days."

Karen turned to her left. Right against the wall in the dimmest corner of the bar was an impossibly gorgeous woman, even by Los Angeles standards. To say she was blonde like Karen was a disservice. Karen's hair was only like the sunshine it was so often compared to. This woman's hair was liquid sunset cascading around her pretty face and down her tan shoulders.

The woman wore a light summer dress with a modest black belt and strappy sandals. Karen looked at her book and back at the woman and deflected the compliment slightly. "It was a gift from a friend of mine."

"The boy over there?" The woman took a sip of her gin and tonic through her straw and nodded in Calvin's direction.

"How did you—"

"You glance at him between writing notes, and he's far from the loudest or most-" the woman shifted her gaze further down the bar to the boys surrounding the Nats, "- ostentatious of the men here."

"That's a kind word."

"The weak are the most deserving of kindness." The woman spoke with an intriguingly disinterested tone of pity.

"And when the weak are the most terrible?"

"Then they're judged by their sins, same as the strong." The woman took another sip.

Karen nodded and wondered if she should write this down, but it felt odd to do so in front of the subject she'd be writing about. The woman smiled. "Go ahead, write it down." Karen was surprised at how long she'd been weighing the thought. "It's quite an honor to be inspiring such weighted consideration. I'm sure your mind has already run leagues with follow-up notions and tangential ideas."

Karen didn't respond, but the woman took another sip then asked, "Clearly you're working with the paper." The woman nodded to the rest of the group. "But do you ever write your own stories?"

"No, I work in the Fashion section. I'm an intern."

"Well, I don't just mean for work. I mean in general. Do you let your voice speak out?" The woman tilted her chin at the book to explain her meaning.

Karen shifted nervously. She assumed it was the alcohol making her feel uncomfortably warm but knew that it was the unusually deep and intimate conversation she was having with a stranger whose demeanor and appearance were both unsettling in how at ease the woman was able to keep her. Karen thanked the woman and scribbled a note to herself about how the unease at feeling at ease must be a purely modern affectation. Had Calvin seen that note, he might have been less clueless about her affections in the weeks to come.

"So?" the woman asked sweetly.

Karen glanced at the note and fumbled for an answer. General excuses about having time to write but not being sure about sharing it or how to share it tumbled over themselves. "I sincerely hope you're not holding yourself back because you expect life to change. If so then why bother writing at all?"

The woman's question was filled with sadness. When Karen met her eyes, she was looking at Calvin again. It wasn't with the same sadness that she had spoken to Karen. Karen laughed and shook her head. "No, this is what I do."

The woman looked admiringly at Karen. "I love how that you say that so automatically."

Karen was puzzled. "I write. I love it. I love being around it. Everything else in my life, relationships, family, all that, it'll be built and developed around my passion."

The woman took another sip and lowered her glass with a slightly mischievous glance. "That's a very *masculine* stance." Karen was flummoxed and tried to find the resolve again to agree, but the woman spoke up first. "And it shouldn't be a *masculine* stance to take. That should be the *human* stance of a passionate person who cares about their job, regardless of their sex."

Karen nodded in appreciation of the woman's insight. She was about to introduce herself properly and ask the woman her name, but the woman continued first. "Like that old tripe about the woman who can *somehow* have it all. So demeaning by implication."

Karen's head was swimming. The Long Island Iced Teas were filling her mind with fog. "I pity the men."

"Pity?"

Karen nodded clumsily from the alcohol cloud around her head. The memory of the night would be hazy for her at best from this point on, but she continued with audible effort to articulate the sentiment. "I pity them. Really. Not empathize or sympathize. Pity. Look at what they think they need to be that keeps so many of them from being what they want to be." Karen swung an arm in a gallant gesture at the group of guys encircling the Nats before she drained the last of her glass.

Karen looked at Calvin again. "I think the best kind of person and relationship is one who shares what they are and what the other person is, and they share in making each other better and pushing each other to their passions."

A warm hand alighted over Karen's and pulled it away from her glass. "My dear, beautiful girl." The woman spoke with a warm, proud smile. "You are so, absolutely right."

Karen met the woman's sky blue eyes and felt momentarily sober. The moment quickly vanished because when she shifted in her seat even slightly, she felt her head and stomach swim and twist again. "But you're still waiting on him to come over here and ask you what you've got to say."

"Is that wrong?" Karen asked herself.

The woman laughed. "When someone has as much as you have to say? He should be coming over to hear what you've got to tell him." The woman finished her drink and motioned for Karen to follow her as she hopped off the stool. "Come on. I've got an idea to run by you."

"Really? I don't know your name, though." Karen still gathered her book and pen to follow the woman out.

"I'm Lilith. It's a pleasure to have met you, Karen." Karen sleepily followed Lilith from the bar. She was so entranced that she didn't bother to say goodnight to anyone else from the *Weekly* or notice that she hadn't ever told Lilith her own name. It's safe to assume that Lilith or no, Karen was unlikely to have ever noticed Matt Reade sulking in the corner near the door all night where he had been hoping to drum up the courage to approach Karen.

Matt ended up leaving dejectedly not long after. He wandered absently into The Bar where he'd meet Gast for the first time.

THE STEP AFTER NEXT

Karen wasn't getting much of her own work done that morning, the success of Calvin's article being one reason for it. The other reason was that she had sent a pair of articles to Maggie for review, which Maggie had said were both in print-worthy shape. Since she was spared the need to edit, she was left with time to try to worry over what Calvin's next steps should be.

Calvin had a good idea to go to the restaurant he'd inadvertently opened thanks to the hipsters who'd read his article online, but what next? What was the Devil going to do when he found out about Calvin's success? Was this success enough to throw the Devil's plans off course? Or was it just an annoyance that would bring down more fury on Calvin?

After all, he had been right to fear the article's popularity drawing too much attention to him. He might be able to wash it over that with a more legitimate follow up, but wouldn't that then put him at the mercy of the Devil's powers again? She was trying to scribble possible outcomes and what responses they could have ready for them in her black notebook, but nothing was coming to her. When she got the knock at her open office door and saw Lilith standing there, she was effervescent in her relief.

"Lilith! Thank God for you!"

"That's a first," Lilith quipped and walked in to hug Karen tightly. "How have things been since I dropped you off?"

Karen blushed and that was all Lilith needed as an answer before she motioned for Tie to come in from the hall. The hulking Devil had to stoop and turn slightly sideways to fit in the doorway, but he squeezed himself neatly into one of the chairs and nodded in greeting.

"This is Tie, one of my former associates."

Tie gave a polite salute from his brow with one of his large paws. Karen looked at Lilith. "Associates?"

"He's a Devil." Lilith shot Tie a stern look, warning him to keep quiet. He put his hands up in easy concession to the wordless command.

Karen felt strangled and staggered back into her seat in panic. "You were—" she tried to accuse Lilith who only nodded tiredly and sat Karen down to explain everything.

Lilith talked about Hell, the corporate order, Gast, Tie, and Aba Don. Then Lilith tied it all together. "That jealous little twat, Matt Reade. We'd have been back sooner, but had to hoof it to avoid passing through Hell until we were sure what was going on with Gast and Aba."

"So your friend, Gast—"

"*Boy*friend," Tie blurted.

"He's not my—"

"Boyfriend?" Karen asked in surprise.

Lilith put her hands up. "No, he's an ex-colleague."

"Ex-*boyfriend*," Tie teased again.

Lilith closed her eyes for a moment to collect herself. "Gast just *happened* to be working with Matt, and while I'm sure I could have resolved things for you and Calvin with ease if we only had Gast to contend with, Aba's involvement makes this a bit more dangerous."

"Because he's the head of Wrath, you said?" Karen asked.

"And Lucifer's BFF," Tie added.

Karen gave Lilith a curious look, but Lilith waved Tie off to press on. "That's not false, but it's neither here nor there at the moment. We need to find Gast, and the easiest way to do that might be finding Matt."

"Well, Matt went running out of here dressed in a leather banana hammock a couple hours ago. No idea where he went." Karen bit her thumbnail at being unable to provide better intel.

Tie started laughing uproariously. Lilith was more collected in her appraisal. "Sounds like his dress charm was fudged."

Karen nodded and shared her theory. "Yeah, because Calvin got an article—"

"Calvin's article alone wouldn't do it. Aba likely had that done to draw Gast into acting out as if the deal were failing." Lilith lightly tapped a finger on her chin.

Tie giggled in his seat and teased once more. "I wonder why Aba wants *Gast* to fail?" This time, Lilith's glare made Tie yelp in fright, and he stammered to cover himself. "Wrath and all that. He's an angry dude, right?"

Lilith shook her head and sighed in defeat. "Things may be further along than I'd wanted then. I think we *do* need to stop by the offices."

Karen's eyes went wide and she whispered, "You mean, Hell?"

"Depending on which manifestation of it you're visiting, it's not as bad as you think. Will you be okay without me?" Lilith placed a hand on Karen's shoulder and looked at her with patient care.

Karen considered it a moment and realized that the only threats from Hell were being aimed at Calvin in particular, so what else was there for her to worry about if Lilith was working on solving the problem? Karen nodded bravely, and Lilith bid her farewell.

It was on their way out that the sound of pornography coming from Felicia's office caught Lilith's attention. The resident of the office was clearly benefiting from certain protective enchantments from Hell. Lilith asked Tie, "Is this is another of Gast's deals?"

Tie shook his head as he followed her back to the garage. "I don't think so. Gast's more of a celebrity chaser. He took this deal as kind of an easy putt."

As they boarded the elevator, Lilith said, "Then I'm betting she's one of Aba's."

COMPLEMENTS OF THE CHEF

Calvin spent five minutes on the sidewalk outside the Fresca, not only because he was mystified by how busy it was, but because there was a throng of people waiting on the sidewalk for lunch already. Vintage dresses and flannel abounded. Calvin wondered if they were all writers or how they could afford the lunch break to stand and wait for what the harried hostess inside had told him would be an hour-long wait for a seat.

Calvin had tried asking if she was Sally, since she seemed to be the only person doing anything at all, but she had sped back into the kitchen before he could ask. He wasn't sure how interviews of chefs were normally done. Perhaps by appointment outside of service hours, but he found some comfort in being here sooner rather than later. He resolved to at least get a table and order a meal to introduce himself and explain his article.

Calvin had been tracking the comments and responses to the article since leaving the office. People were not only raving about the Italian cuisine but about the inventiveness of the chef. Commenters were posting that the chef was offering all kinds of "test" meals that weren't on the printed menu and had a preternatural sense of what his customers' pallets were.

Calvin was already worrying he'd stumbled onto another person with a deal with a Devil, and worried further how common a thing that actually was.[20] It was after he'd been outside for fifteen minutes that the hostess/waitress/chef appeared again in the doorway, apologizing to the throng. "Sorry, folks, we're out of

---

[20] Answer: more common than what you're guessing, but less common than what you would subsequently estimate.

food. We'll be open for dinner around five."

There was no audible reaction from the crowd, just the despondent tapping out of tweets on their phones, and a few who decided to post their reactions to Snapchat: "Here at the hot new restaurant, the Via Fresca. Yo, so lit that they completely ran out of food. But yo, the chef says they'll be back on for dinner, so your boy is gonna get back here for it."

Calvin was too busy stopping the woman from going back in. "Would it be alright if I joined you for the dinner prep?"

The woman looked confused, but her face lit up in hope. "Are you looking for a job?" She glanced at the dispersing crowd of hipsters and offered Calvin a smile of admiration.

"No. I'm, uh, a writer," Calvin explained.

She rolled her eyes. "Well go Tweet, Snap, or Yelp or whatever. We're very sorry, but we didn't expect this much rush off of *one* article in the *LA Weekly*."

"I'm the writer."

"From the *Weekly*?"

"Yeah." Calvin handed her the business card the office manager had printed for him. It was his only one since he was just an intern, and he was somewhat disappointed when she pocketed it as she ushered him in.

The restaurant was filled but every table had been served. There were a couple empty tables in the corner where she guided him and asked if he wanted wine, which he accepted graciously. He wasn't sure how to broach the topic of the article he'd written under, at best, hypothetical pretenses, but he was glad to see the crowd was genuine.

She sat at the table and regarded him eagerly. "So, how did you know about us?"

"I live in the neighborhood and looked you up. Your name pops up here and there online."

"The Fresca?"

"No, *your* name." Calvin meant the chef's name, Sally Degneri, but Tessa's face went pale until he proceeded to clarify. "You worked at two other restaurants before managing to open this one? You're a lot younger than the info online made me think you'd be." Calvin caught himself. "Or look a lot younger, at least." He took a generous sip of the wine, which she had introduced as a house white blend. It was superb, and he wished he had a better acumen for wine and food pairing but was sure it'd be perfect with a scampi.

"I'm not Sally." Tessa shared the revelation with evident relief. "My name is Tessa Hu." Tessa shot her hand out to make Calvin stop taking notes. "Please *don't* mention me in your article or whatever." Tessa locked eyes with Calvin until he nodded in timid agreement. With that, she sat back in relief and pointed a thumb over her shoulder. "Sally's in the kitchen. He's finishing up some cleaning, and he'll come out when the other guests leave."

There were only two tables of people left, and they were all on their phones, largely ignoring their plates which were devoid of food.

"So, you guys saw a small uptick in business since the article?"

"Small? We went from people only stopping to ask directions to running out of food. It's absurd."

Tessa reached into her pocket. Her phone was buzzing in her hand, and she bit her lip nervously. "I'll go get Sally."

Calvin was unfettered by her abrupt departure into the kitchen. The white wine was splendid, and in the time

Tessa was in the kitchen, the remaining guests had slowly risen and sauntered out.

Tessa hustled back out and bent over the table close to him. "Sally's coming out in a minute, but listen, he's..." She considered her words and resolved to be blunt. "He's really nervous. Like, yes, he's a great chef, maybe the best, but when it comes to talking about cooking? Or himself? Or anything? He gets stage fright. Like *crazy* stage fright. So just, please, don't do a hatchet job on him." Tessa squinted darkly. "Or else."

Calvin was mid-sip and coughed up into the wine glass. Tessa made the gesture of pointing her fingers at her eyes then at Calvin in turn to indicate she'd be watching him. She went back in the kitchen and left Calvin stunned.

Sally stumbled through the swinging kitchen door as if he had been given a hard shove through them. He offered a feeble smile, and Calvin was surprised to find Sally didn't look much older than himself. The chef sat down and gave a longing look at the bottle of wine Tessa had left out for Calvin, visibly pained that there wasn't a second glass.

"Tessa tells me you're the one who wrote the article?"

"Yes, and I—"

"Well, I've gotta say, thank you so much," Sally blubbered.

Calvin had been expecting more skepticism from Sally. Perhaps even suspicion of something crooked afoot he'd have to defend himself against. This man, weeping before him in gratitude, was a bit of a left hook. "Really, it's no problem. In fact, I wanted to write a follow up."

"A follow up?" Sally sniffed and pulled out a handkerchief from his pants pocket to blow his nose.

"Well, yeah. The article I wrote was relatively bare

bones, but I heard people talking about what you were doing here just this morning. Making up dishes on the fly? Guessing what your guests would like? A full cuisine version of omakase? It's unreal."

Sally shook his head and waved off Calvin's admiration. "It's nothing so fancy as that. We didn't have food for the full menu, so I was improvising,"

"One of the commenters said you recommended a meal based on what she ate last night?"

"Yeah, she had a really protein-heavy meal. So something light, sweet, and a little carby."

"And the gluten free biscuits and gravy?"

"That's just knowing your clientele in this day and age."

"But you're an Italian restaurant. It's really something."

Sally nodded and shrunk into himself a bit more.

"I'd really like to interview you, maybe see if today affects the restaurant menu moving forward?" Calvin waved his digital recorder to imply his request for permission. Sally's hand darted forward and gripped the wine bottle as he nodded nervously. It occurred to Calvin that he had slipped into his natural role as a reporter, rather than being there just to cover his ass against a Devil out to get him.

"So, how'd you get your start in cooking?"

"My mom and dad. I come from an Italian family." Sally sat back and curled around the bottle he was clutching like a baby against him, except for when he lifted it for large throaty gulps.

"So your family is why the restaurant is Italian?"

"Actually, that's my investor's doing."

"Investor?"

"Uh, yeah. I have a partner who owns the place, but,"

Sally took another gulp of the sweet wine. "Let's just say Italian isn't my first inclination."

"But your investor—"

Sally took such a painfully large swallow of the wine that he panted for air after he lowered the bottle. "Leave that out." He threw the bottle back once more then added: "Please."

"Okay... so why *didn't* you want an Italian restaurant at first?"

"Because this is America."

"I'm sorry, I don't follow."

"My parents are both Italian, and when my mom taught me to cook, she taught me how to cook everything. Not just Italian food, because she said America is great because so many different cultures come together and learn from each other, and that's especially true of cooking." Sally tipped the bottle upward again to chug. Calvin looked on in disbelief at the chef's desperate thirst for the wine, and then toward the kitchen to see if the waitress was filming it as some kind of prank.

Calvin cleared his throat when Sally lowered the bottle again. "Wow, and your dad?"

Sally opened his mouth to speak, but seemed to think better of it, taking another pull of the bottle. He sighed in satisfaction and finally addressed Calvin. "Said the same thing. He'd grown up... well, he grew up something of a stereotype of Italian American immigrants, so he told me the same thing: I don't have to be a stereotype, and if I want to be a chef, be whatever kind of chef I want. Be an *American* chef."

"Inspiring." Calvin sat back, putting his hand to his chin in admiration. "So, your versatility—"

"It's how my parents taught me to be." Sally looked at the near empty bottle forlornly and took a slower pull of the dwindling wine this time. "She taught me to be a good host, and ya gotta know how to make anyone comferble."

"I see." Calvin made note of the change in Sally's mood at the mention of his parents and wrote to himself to ask if they were still alive.

"Yeah, like a hipsher comes in, and they wanna eat fancy food wiv kale, I'll make it and make it'll taste good because that's what it's about. Good food making good people feel good." Sally lifted the bottle once more, this time with a reverence as if he were toasting someone before he chugged from it again.

"Okay, so what about dinner?"

"Dinner's good."

Calvin waited, but Sally didn't expand further, so Calvin guided the chef. "As in?"

Sally seemed to grasp Calvin's intent and looked abashed, at which he drained the bottle in response. Wiping his mouth with the back of his forearm, he took a deep breath to steel himself before he answered finally. "Well, it's a great meal, y'know? A lotta people like breakfasht, but I'm more a cuppa coffee and pastry kinda guy. Dinner'sh where real love and togetherness happens."

Calvin bobbed his eyebrows. Sally had finished the last of the wine in the bottle. "You gotta cute girl you wanna date? Are you gonna ask her to breakfast?"

"Good point."

"Maybe you ashk her to breakfasht *after* a good date." Sally shrugged slowly and as high as his shoulders could go. "I want to make the kind of dinners where good people have good times because of good food." Sally reached for the last of Calvin's wine in the glass and threw it back. The chef slumped back in his chair as if he has just finished running a race. Calvin had other questions but resolved to try them through Tessa. Interviewing Sally's waitress might be interesting to add since she was, so far, his only apparent help. Maybe the investor Sally mentioned would hire on someone else given this new success?

The front door swung open, and Sally threw his arms up. "Well, if it ishn't Benny!"

"What the hell is this circus?"

Sally answered as if it were obvious. "It's your reshtaurant. The Via Fresca."

Tessa came from the kitchen, and was startled to see Benny, Maury, and Claudio all standing at the entrance. She quickly stuffed her cell phone back into her pocket. "Damn right *my* restaurant. I been calling all morning and wondering what the hold up is, till Maury here keeps seeing some article about *my* restaurant all over the web."

Calvin would have pointed out that no one called it "the web" since the turn of the millennium, but Benny didn't strike Calvin as one who revelled much in discourse regarding semantics- to the contrary in fact. Calvin surmised this was the investor Sally had mentioned, but his apparent ire at the restaurant opening, especially to such fanfare, was baffling.

Maury, the largest of the trio by far, read from a tablet phone that looked like a modest biscuit in his large hands. "Yeah. Everyone's retweeting this article from the *LA Weekly*, saying the chef was freestyling meals for customers."

"What did I tell you about this restaurant?" Benny demanded with a reddening face, at which Sally shrugged and swayed dreamily in the chair across from Calvin. "I told you this restaurant don't open unless *I* say so."

"Well, I dunno, people showed up. I didn't write the

article." Sally said sleepily, then pointed at Calvin. "He did."

Benny stared down at Calvin and nodded, swaggering so close before him that Calvin was pinned in his seat between the mafioso and the wall. "That so? Where did you get off writing about *my* restaurant?"

Calvin considered that he could cite freedom of speech and press, but he felt sure that wouldn't fly in the face of the scary man who seemed to want his restaurant to remain closed for reasons Calvin was beginning to surmise.

"Hey, wait a minute, you said you were callin'?" Sally interrupted, clearly unaware of the looming danger of the room's mood through the blanket of alcohol he'd wrapped around his mind. "I didn't get any call." Benny froze, and Calvin saw something that looked a bit like fear on the large man's face. "I was in the kitchen by the phone the whole time. Phone didn't ring. If it bothered you, shoulda called. But you didn't call. Phone was right there on the wall. Phone didn't ring." Sally declared the fact firmly, albeit sloppily, and crossed his arms resolutely as a child would.

"Well, that's beside the point. I'm here now, and I'm telling you that you, writer boy, you're gonna do up a retraction and say the Fresca is on hiatus for a couple days." Benny slammed a hand on the table, making Calvin jump in his seat.

"Uh, why is it on hiatus, exactly?" Calvin immediately regretted letting the question slip.

Benny leaned to snarl right in Calvin's face. "Because we're reviewing the terms of the partnership."

Benny was suddenly pushed out of Calvin's immediate personal space and looked like a puppy that had mistakenly been trod on by its owner. Tessa had rushed over from the kitchen doorway and shoved Benny back from the table and had a finger up in his face. "Yeah, Sally, he was calling. He kept calling *me* and I kept ignoring it because guess what: I'd rather see this restaurant open than whatever this wannabe Tony Soprano wants to do with it."

Benny looked more hurt by Tessa's words than Calvin felt a mobster had a right to look by anyone's words. Sally turned clumsily in the chair, and it wobbled from his awkward positioning on it. "What's he callin' *you* for?"

Benny slapped his palm to his forehead then dragged his hand down his face in ire. "She's my hitman, you moron!"

"Hitman?" Calvin and Sally asked together, looking from Tessa to Benny in turn.

Tessa took a deep breath. "Nope, not anymore. Do your own dirty work."

Sally looked frightfully at Benny and realized he was within arm's reach and didn't wait to see if Benny was reaching for the blade in his pocket. Sally did an ungraceful flip of his legs over his head to roll backward out of the chair and onto the linoleum tiling next to Tessa.

Benny staggered back in shock at Sally's drunken acrobatics. Claudio and Maury joined in the yelling, but neither was sure what to do without orders from Benny.

Sally clambered into the kitchen, pulling Tessa along with him. Without much context, Calvin followed the pair, albeit with more grace than Sally had tumbled out of his chair. As they raced through the kitchen, Benny gave chase. As Calvin sprinted by the large sheet metal door of the walk-in fridge, Calvin instinctively pulled the door as hard as he could. The door whipped open and slammed into Benny's face.

Calvin scampered into the back alley where Tessa was pulling Sally towards a silver Mercedes Coupe parked back there. Over his shoulder, Calvin could hear Benny screaming, "You better run! Next time I see you, you'll be swimming in that hipster beer with that other hipster piece of shit!"

Tessa was arguing with Sally and opened the passenger door, forcing him to dive headfirst into the backseat. She ran around to the driver's side while shouting for Calvin to climb in. Calvin slammed the door just as Benny and his cronies scrambled out of the restaurant's backdoor. Benny was clutching his face in pain, still yelling, though it was inaudible through the shut car doors and windows.

Tessa dropped the clutch and tires squealed as they raced from the alley onto the avenue. Sally had flung himself headfirst into the space between the seatbacks and rear seating. He had been trying to right himself with significant difficulty in the backseat, made even more challenging with Tessa's aggressive driving. Finally, he seemed to admit defeat and groaned out from the floor in the back, "Just wake me up when Benny's ready to kill us."

FOOTSTEPS IN THE SAND

Matt had decided to wander further westward as his charm continued its backfiring, and by lunchtime found himself out on Santa Monica beach. On the promenade amid the tourists and minstrels he had been dressed in a red-dyed crocodile leather three-piece suit with matching top hat. When he reached the sand, he was dressed for winter dog sledding with snow boots.

Plodding along on the sand, he was startled when he

heard Gast's voice in the space around him. "Hey, kid. How's it going?"

"I'm dressed like an Eskimo in ninety-degree weather. How's it look?" Matt continued his trudge.

"I'm working on that charm for you. Should have all this sorted out soon. Hang in there."

"Oh yeah? What happened to me getting to spend my days sippin' on cocktails while you got me to the top? And why can't I see you? Where's your body? Don't tell me your body's doing the same thing my clothing is."

"About that—" It occurred to Gast just then that Matt may very well no longer be his ward. If the incident in the office had truly allowed Aba to demote him and seize his body, then Gast's contracts were all up for grabs as well.

"Yeah?" Matt challenged the invisible demon, spinning in the sand to try to raise fists in whatever direction he thought he'd heard Gast's voice coming from. "Well, maybe I think you're just a blowhard? You think I didn't read that contract? There's penalties if *you* fail to deliver."

Gast corrected Matt. "The penalties are for the *owner* of the contract failing to deliver."

With that, Gast swept away from the mortal plane and left Matt standing in full ski gear shouting at him on the sands of the Santa Monica beach. Tourists who saw the display were disappointed to see that the stories of Los Angeles' problems with the homeless were worse than they had heard.

NAKED LUNCH

"Where are you going, bud?" Harry popped up from the couch by the receptionist's desk where he'd been lying in wait as soon as he saw Sam approaching from the offices.

Sam only barely masked his chagrin at being pounced on by Harry. "Lunch. Come on," he urged in impatient acceptance of his fate

"Good, because we need to talk." Harry joined Sam at the elevators.

Sam looked at the portly director's grave expression and with surprise. Harry only ever got this way for one reason. "What did Felicia do now?"

"We need to talk *outside* of the building. It's about what *you* did."

"What *I* did?" Sam searched his mind as the elevator dinged its way to them floor by floor. "You mean letting Felicia take Calvin as her intern?"

Harry winced. "Damn it, Sam, why'd you say that on company property? Now I have to record your preemptive acknowledgement of potential wrongdoing as evidence of willful liability."

Harry shook his head and walked quickly onto the elevator, waving desperately for Sam to follow. When the doors shut behind him, Sam turned to Harry. "What responsibility? Sure, she's a sex-crazed cougar, but I only condoned their working together as his internship mentor."

Harry pinched his nose and clenched his eyes. "Damn it, Sam, more for the report."

"We're in the elevator!" Sam defended.

The doors opened on one of the lower floors, and people from one of the other businesses sharing the building boarded, making Sam shuffle closer to Harry at the back corner of the car. Harry whispered, "The *building* counts as company property." He shook his head and asked, "Where are you going to lunch? Wait until we get outside."

Sam felt his neck burn in embarrassment. If the first statement hadn't been incriminating enough regarding Felicia, surely he'd really stepped in it with the second one. He could see the spite and disappointment plainly on Harry's face.

The elevator stopped on the parking level, and they walked to Sam's car. Even when they had enough distance from the other workers in the building, Sam still whispered. "Listen, I get it. I know that she's a sexual harassment case waiting to happen, but as a," Sam struggled for a moment on the next word, "*friend,* do you really have to record any of the stuff I said in the elevator?"

Harry's eyes went wide, and he took in a panicked, rasping breath, holding it in before his eyes lost the electric fervor they had burst with. "Two things: first, willful negligence of a potential harassment case isn't just the kind of thing that gets you or me fired, it's the kind of thing that gives the plaintiff enough of a claim for damages that can shut down the *Weekly.* Secondly—" Harry wheeled on Sam, pinning the Editor-in-Chief against his driver's side door. "We're *still* on company property, you idiot!" Harry did an about face and stomped back to the elevator.

"Where are you going?" Sam called feebly after him.

Harry shouted back, "To write those reports!" This prompted Sam to lose all appetite for empanadas and margaritas alike. If this was as bad as it sounded, he resolved to take a couple swigs of something harder he kept hidden in his desk drawer.

CORPORATE REPRIMANDS AND SEIZURES

Gast was as cautious as possible moving around Hell's offices. When he found Pitch's desk, the office had already been manifested. It was an atypical move for Pitch, but one Gast appreciated. When he flit into the office, Pitch looked exhausted. "So much for the plan."

"I admit, I was a *little* slow on the draw and that's led to a minor setback."

"Yes, well, you were smart to booby trap your meat sack," Pitch admired. "Not sure how much time it's buying you. I heard from one of the Lust boys Aba tried altering your body with some tattoos and piercings and it kicked him out so hard that he's been inert since then."

"I wouldn't say *I* booby trapped it, per se, but yeah, it's a lucky thing finally."

Pitch gave a look of intrigue in Gast's formless direction and stroked the chin of his red beard. "Premature seizure, maybe? He's not a Vice President, so maybe he didn't have the clout to officially take the body from you, even if you did walk stupidly into his trap."

"Yeah, sure, let's go with that. Pitch, I need two things from you." Gast weighed the risks associated with what he was asking for and hedged his bets. "Or at least one of the two."

"It'd better be easy, because right now I'm barely on his list of suspected accomplices, and he's not going to take this body setback lightly on you or anyone he discovers is associated with keeping the body from him."

"Well, that's the first thing. I need my body back."

Pitch stared blankly into the space just beyond where Gast was manifested. There was a pause in which Pitch seemed stuck in time but then quickly threw his head back in incredulous laughter. "No way. I don't want my name anywhere on that seizure. You lost rights to it fair and square. The best I could do is delay Aba's claim to it with red tape and paperwork."

"That's something, I guess." Gast knew Pitch was right about it all, and he had no right to ask Pitch to put his neck on the line any more than that.

"You said two things, though?"

"Well, if you're doing the paperwork for my body to be transferred to Aba, I need you to also handle the transference paperwork for my contracts."

"I can do the same delay on those as well."

"Uh uh, other way around, those I need expedited."

Pitch narrowed his eyes. "Interesting play. Lucky for you, I'm no Sloth Devil."

"Also lucky for you, you have *other* allies willing to leave some fingerprints on the body seizure for your sake." Tie had entered the office and indecorously thrown Gast's vacant body from over his shoulder onto the chair.

Gast wasted no time. He was back in his body and smoothing out the suit that had been thoroughly ruffled and even torn in a couple places, but it felt good and safe to be back in his own skin. "How'd you—"

"Luckily, the Lechery Devils are easy as ever to bargain with." Lilith swept into the office behind Tie, golden hair shining through all layers of perception in the pit and Pitch's office, her smile confident and demure. Gast was stricken in his chair, sitting upright with eyes shocked open.

Tie snorted. "Told you ages ago: best thing about this body is how much fun the sex is."

Lilith rolled her eyes patiently. "Finally came in handy after a few hundred years of it barely fitting through doorways."

Gast was paralytic and his gaping gaze remained fixed

on Lilith in mingled panic and anxiety, so Lilith looked at Pitch. "Did you tell him everything yet?"

"Not a lot to tell. Just that Aba's not so much playing chess as he's a wild dog running in the street chasing cars."

Gast didn't respond to Pitch's intel, nor did his gaze waver from Lilith.

Lilith looked up at Tie. "Okay then, I think it's time we unified our fronts. Hopefully my ward's boyfriend has figured something out with that restaurant and Matt Reade's contract."

"Which Gast was just telling me to expedite transfer of to Aba."

"The Matt Reade contract?" Lilith double checked and Pitch confirmed it. He pulled the paperwork from his desk drawer to begin the transition of ownership. Lilith snapped her fingers and smiled admiringly at Gast, who still had not moved. Tie wondered if Gast hadn't again fled the body as a spirit. "Good thinking. That makes things much simpler if we play things to our advantage in proper order."

Lilith bid Pitch farewell and said they'd be back in touch soon. She ordered Tie and Gast to join her back at the *LA Weekly* offices, but Gast still didn't move. She stopped at the door and looked at him in concern. "Gast?"

"IT'S GREAT TO SEE YOU. YOU LOOK GOOD. I AM DOING GREAT," he blurted loudly.

TWO'S COMPANY

With no other idea of where to go, Calvin directed Tessa back to the *LA Weekly* office. While he agreed it would only be a safe haven for a brief period before Benny tracked it down, he trusted Karen to help them form a plan.

The car ride was tensely quiet save for Sally's occasional drunken outcries from the floor of the backseat. Calvin worried at how fatalistic the chef had become after his bottle of wine, and also at how difficult outrunning the mobsters would be when they eventually had his hangover to grapple with.

"Shoulda left me there! I had my swan song! The only, last, and greatest meal service of the Via Fresca! I should die a legend! Take me back and run! This ain't your hill to die on!"

Tessa remained quiet, taking Calvin's suggested directions to the *Weekly* office with only grave nods, and he communicated them in tepid notices of upcoming turns. When they arrived, Calvin led them down the hall to Karen's office, but Felicia called out to him from her own when she saw him passing by.

He entered with grim determination to begin excusing himself. "Felicia, I need to go talk with Karen. I went to do the interview and shit's hitting the fan in a big way."

Felicia shot a look of disciplinarian consternation from her desk and sat back with a raised eyebrow. "Excuse me? Calvin, do you understand that you are *my* intern? All our philandering aside, if you have an update on a story for *my* section, then as *my* intern you report to *me*."

Calvin was flabbergasted and couldn't argue the logic. Even though his being "her" intern was news to him, he still had bigger fish to fry. He started the verbal deluge to catch her up as quickly as possible. "I went by the restaurant and met the chef, but it turns out the restaurant is backed by a mobster, and the mobster isn't happy about the attention the place is getting, so he was going to ask his hitman...hitwoman? Assassin? Yes, he asked his assassin to kill the chef, but his assassin is a waitress who apparently *wants* to be a waitress so she quit—the assassin job, I mean.

"I guess one of those jobs pays really well because she drove us here in her Benz, but there's a mobster after us, so I need to figure out what to do next. I need to get to Karen's office to talk it over with all of them." Calvin checked mentally to confirm he had hit everything. When he was sure he had, he finally relaxed his tense shoulders and almost doubled over, heaving deep, panting breaths.

Felicia pushed herself back from the desk and stood slowly, then walked right up to Calvin. With a sudden ferocity, she swept the stationery and magazines from her desk. Gripping Calvin's shirt at the chest, she spun to lay on her back across the clear desk, and pulled Calvin forward face first into her cleavage. Moaning, she begged him loudly, "You sexy daredevil, you! Take me! Take me right here, right now!"

Calvin struggled for air as he flopped like a child pushed unexpectedly in the deep end of the pool. He eventually fought his face up for air. With titanic effort, he wiggled and twisted his way from between Felicia's thighs in which she had him in a vice grip with her ankles locked over his lower back. She managed to pull him forward onto her a couple more times with the hold so that he'd end up flopping onto her chest and stomach. It only made him fight his hips harder against her to try to free himself.

She vocalized her enjoyment loudly throughout. When Calvin finally won his way out with a spin, he fell into the wall, which prompted Felicia to sit up halfway to look down at him over her cleavage with a pout. Both looked at the door to the office that had been left ajar to see Sam

Dority standing there with a sickly pallor. "Fuck me."

Felicia rolled her eyes. "I'll pass. This one's enough trouble. Thanks, though." Sam fled to his office. Calvin scrambled out on all fours and raced the opposite way to Karen's. Felicia dropped her head back against the wood of her desk and swung one of her legs up to cross over the other, beating her fists against the desk on either side of herself while whining, "Fuck *meeeeeeee!*"

HITS AND OTHER JOBS

Benny and his boys got back to their apartment, and he slammed the door furiously behind himself after he had followed Claudio and Maury in. The boys watched from a safe distance as their boss paced, red with rage, in the corner of the room by the dining table.

"How much money did we give her?" Maury put a finger up to answer, and Claudio lowered it silently with a gentle hand and made a silent "shh" expression.

Benny bellowed to answer his own question. "THOUSANDS! And she has the nerve to turn tail and say she wants to be a waitress? A waitress! For a mook like Sally! What kind of assassin turns down the money we're paying, that we PAID, to bus slop from table to table?"

Benny growled and slammed a fist on the table, making both Claudio and Maury jump. Claudio edged his way closer to Benny with hands up cautiously like taming a bear. "Boss, there's gotta be some honor among thieves though, right? Maybe we can get the money back?"

"How? She's protectin' him. She won't let us get close!"

"Doesn't *she* have a boss? Remember at The Bar? She

asked that one old guy for permission to take our job on."

Maury confirmed with an eager nod. "Yeah! Maybe *that* guy can help? I'm sure it's no good for his bar if word gets out the killers there steal money and don't do their jobs."

Benny harrumphed. "You think it's like a taco stand? Leave a bad review and they lose business?"

Claudio and Maury looked at each other. Claudio spoke up in his raspy voice first. "Pretty much. Word gets around."

Benny mulled it over with his hands on his hips and eventually began to nod slowly. "Street cred's gotta be worth something." Benny cocked his head to motion for them to head back out.

Maury was on his phone as they climbed into Benny's car. "Actually, a bad Yelp review may be the way to go. Top review right now is: 'Five stars, killer bar!'"

PLANNING WITH A FATALIST

Calvin got to Karen's office out of breath and flushed. Karen resolved there was a better time to ask what had transpired with Felicia than right then. She had been introduced to the situation by Tessa, while Sally had slumped into the chair and interjected between each bit of the story with a despairing cry of how he was better off dead.

Karen hadn't explained too much of their side of it. She decided all that mattered was that Calvin had written an article and that they were all now targets of a gangster for it. The fact that the article may have also upset a Devil or two seemed an unnecessary additional concern for Tessa and Sally to be straddled with. The chef, she noted, was already having a rough time just dealing with the threat of the mobster. Adding Hell to the list wasn't going to accomplish anything.

When Calvin arrived, they all agreed they needed to find sanctuary and were filing back out, but Sally had settled into the chair and was reluctant to move.

Tessa tried to urge him. "Come on, Sal."

"No, you guys go. I don't want you suffering for my fuck up."

"Sal, we opened the restaurant together, we both ran that service."

Sally's face screwed as if he'd begin sobbing. "Naw, I fucked up by opening the restaurant with Benny's shady offer in the first place. Then I let his threats about my dad's history keep me quiet. I deserve this. You guys go."

Tessa knelt and grabbed Sally by both his shoulders to look him squarely in the eyes. "Sally, take it from the woman who was paid *handsomely* to kill you: you don't deserve to die."

Sally's expression darkened, and he turned away from her with a glower at her attempted encouragement. Karen came back in from the hall and stooped beside Tessa. "Sally? Listen, my boyfriend, Calvin, tells me you're an incredible chef. Unreal. Maybe you made a dumb mistake by making a deal with Benny, and then made more dumb mistakes letting Benny do everything he's done since. But Sally, nothing gets fixed for anyone if you make another dumb mistake and let that wannabe Ray Liotta just snuff you and your talent out."

Sally looked at Karen with melting resolve and his crossed arms sagged. Karen slapped his arm. "Come on. Do you really regret your mistakes? Then get up and help us fix this." Karen didn't wait; she joined Calvin in the hall, looking at him sternly. "Same goes for you."

Sally looked up at Tessa, and the assassin shrugged as if it were obvious. "That's why I reneged on the contract."

Tessa waved for Sally to follow Karen and Calvin, who had opted to take the long way around to the elevator so they could avoid Felicia's office. Sally called out after Tessa, "Why'd you take two whole months to quit, then?"

While waiting for the elevator, Karen summarized the problems at hand. "So, *you* have a mobster trying to kill you." She pointed first at Sally, then to Calvin. "And he wants to kill *you* also because the article you wrote is drawing unwanted attention to a restaurant he was trying to keep inoperable."

Tessa put a hand up nonchalantly. "I suppose he also wants to kill me for the whole not actually fulfilling my contract thing."

"Have you seen *The Whole Nine Yards*?" Karen asked.

Calvin got the group back on track, examining the morose chef in concern. "That begs the question: why does he need to *kill* you though? If the restaurant's his, he can just kick you out anytime."

Sally shook his head to try for some sobriety and clarity, and ruffled his hand through his dark hair. "It's supposed to be a front for him to clean up money from his work. Problem is, that work hit a snag this week because he lost a *lot* of his product."

"Lost?" Tessa asked.

"A hipster neighborhood kid he was paying to be a holder went and stole half his product, then ruined the rest. I might know too much for him to let me go."

Unfamiliar with the business practices of mob bosses and drug traffickers, Calvin raised his hand like a grade school student to ask a question. Sally was momentarily confused by the gesture and offered an unsure nod, indicating Calvin could ask his question. "He couldn't just get his money back from the hipster?"

Sally lowered his voice and glanced around the elevator waiting area for eavesdroppers. "Kid's dead. He put the product into some craft beer he brewed, lavender vanilla something or other."

Karen was baffled. "Cocaine in beer?"

"Coca Cola is made with the plant that makes cocaine." Calvin gave a timid shrug at the logic.

Sally slapped his palm to his forehead when Tessa chimed in with, "Doesn't sound half bad, actually."

Karen turned back to Sally with her face screwed at trying to make sense of Benny's plan. "Question still stands: he couldn't get the money from the beer? Or take a loan against his restaurant?"

The doors to the elevator slid open and the group found Lilith, Tie, and Gast all waiting in the car. "Darlings, we should talk."

Calvin looked at Karen, whose expression of relief was startling to him, then back at the gorgeous woman in the elevator who was flanked by a hulk and a slick-looking man in a disheveled suit. "Who're the suits?"

Karen skipped onto the elevator and Calvin followed her faithfully. Sally groaned and put his hand over his mouth in fearful consideration, surveying the new crew in the car. "Why am I getting a sinking feeling that there's a lot you guys didn't tell us?"

The man in the disheveled suit stepped forward beside the woman and held the door open with a hand. "I'm sure that's the right feeling."

Tie chuckled behind his companions. "Get in losers, we're going to church."

CALL YOUR PARENTS 3 – CALVIN & KAREN

After disembarking from the elevator, Tessa volunteered to drive one car, "but we need a second car," she suggested, eyeing the new additions to the crew warily, hoping none of them would end up in her Benz.

Karen turned to Calvin. "I can drive if you're a little stressed."

"First, that's an understatement, and second, I left my car in Los Feliz." Calvin pinched the bridge of his nose while he admonished himself. "I left it parked by a meter that already ran out. It's getting a ticket for sure. Probably towed considering I'm not picking it up, maybe ever."

Karen rubbed Calvin's shoulder consolingly and looked at the group in quick assessment. "Okay, Tessa and Sally, I'll take Calvin, Lilith?"

The lithe, gorgeous woman confirmed to Karen, "I'm with you of course."

Tessa did the math, she was taking one of the two remaining weirdos. Karen must have read Tessa's expression because their eyes met and remained fixed while Karen suggested the remaining assignments. "Tie? I drive an SUV so maybe better for you to come with me. Mr. Gast?" Gast looked affronted at the address only momentarily, but the dawning reality supplanted that with evident disappointment on his countenance when Karen instructed, "you can go with Tessa and Sally."

The groups split off to their respective cars, with Gast glancing over the roofs of all the cars in the lot at Lilith climbing into the driver's seat of Karen's black Lexus.

In the backseat with Lilith and Tie in the front, Calvin and Karen both decided it would be a good time to check in with their parents, while Gast helped Tessa and Sally find their way in her car.

Calvin's mother picked up almost immediately. He had, until hearing her cheerful voice, wanted to warn her about the danger he was in and let her know to be careful of anyone calling for his whereabouts in the coming days. However, a mother's sunny disposition is not something a son ever finds easy to dispel, no matter how dire his situation might be.

Calvin's mother: You're calling early. How's your day going, Cal?

Calvin: It's...it's good, Mom. It's good.

CM: Uh oh, you only repeat yourself when you've got something on your mind.

C: Yeah, it's this story I'm working on.

CM: Oh, the one on the Italian restaurant?

C: How did you—

CM: Linda sent it to me. She saw you were on the *LA Weekly* email. I didn't know you were a food reviewer.

C: Yeah, Mom, I was moonlighting. Just helping out wherever I can.

CM: Well, I'm sure they really appreciate it. Especially with your writing skills and your nose for a good story.

C: Yeah. I guess so.

CM: Is everything okay? Are you still bummed about the article thing from yesterday?

C: Oh. Yeah, a bit. I'm trying to work on something new for next week.

CM: Oh yeah?

C: Yeah.

CM: What is it?

C: A follow up story on the Italian restaurant and its owner.

CM: That sounds interesting. Is the owner really interesting?

C: Yeah, real interesting.

CM: Hopefully the story is a big hit.

C: That's the concern.

CM: Okay, honey. You have a good night.

Meanwhile, Karen's father was out of the house when she called. Her mother picked up and she tried to lean into the corner of the car against the window to create some sense of privacy for her conversation.

KM: Hi, honey! How's your day going? Did you father email you about our visit this weekend?

K: Uh, no, he mentioned it yesterday.

KM: Honey, is everything okay?

K: What? Yeah, of course.

KM: Well, you sound kind of quiet.

K: Oh yeah. I'm just in a car with some friends.

KM: Oh, well, you could have called later. Where are you headed?

K: I'm going to a...church service?

KM: Oh, that's nice. You found a church you like?

K: Giving one a try, for now at least.

KM: Okay, well, let us know how it goes. We'll see you Friday night. Your dad was supposed to email that he made a reservation for four at Nobu Sushi for Friday night.

K: Four o'clock? That's early.

KM: No, for four. Four people, sorry!

K: Four?

KM: Us, you and your boyfriend, your dad said? Calvin?

K: Sure, I'll ask him. He's kind of busy with a big project, but I'll mention it to him, okay?

KM: Okay, we can't wait to meet him, honey.

K: Yeah, sounds good. I've gotta go, I'm being rude, Mom.

KM: Okay, honey. You're the one that called. Have a good night!

SYMPATHY FOR A DEVIL

Gast had insisted on the backseat so he could lay on his back and put his thoughts together. He'd been constantly on the move for the last twenty-four hours and wanted the chance to take it all in.

Tessa knew the church Lilith wanted to take them to, so Gast's navigation wasn't needed. Meanwhile, the handsome but disheveled man monologued from the backseat as Sally had been doing before the stop in the office had sobered him up somewhat.

"Can you imagine that, though? Just appears out of the blue after thirty years. *Thirty years.*" Tessa pondered that Gast didn't look a day over thirty to begin with.

"Twenty years we work together, and then poof, she just walks right back in *with* my best friend, and of course things are way too crazy for us to catch up yet. I mean, I've got my boss trying to kill me and all, but still! Am I supposed to keep playing it cool? Or do I ask her what the deal was? I feel like I'm owed an explanation as to why she left. She just disappeared without a word and now she's back and we're right back in the same rhythm? Right back to work? And that's the scary part, we just slipped right back into our old tempos. Maybe it's not scary, though, maybe it's really cool. But it's scary how cool it is, you know?"

Gast continued dissecting his feelings to Lilith's departure, past, and return in the backseat until they were stuck in a traffic jam on the 5 freeway and Tessa interrupted him, "Dude, how *old* are you?"

Gast stopped mid-word. "Come again?"

"You keep saying *thirty* years ago this, and *twenty* years before that, but you don't look a day over thirty. But according to what you're saying, you're well over sixty."

"Wait, yeah, she's right." Sally spun halfway on his seat to look back at Gast. The seatbelt proved a difficulty, but with some effort he now had it going over his back so he could rest his chin on the seatback to look down at Gast. "You're *that* old?"

"Not at all. I'm several thousand years old."

"Come again?" Tessa squinted at Gast in the rearview mirror she adjusted to face him.

"You weren't kidding about being in the dark. I'm a Devil of the Order of Wrath."

Tessa and Sally both traded glances, and Tessa put on her turn signal. "Sally, how the hell did we end up with these kids? These psychos can't help us with Benny. We'll either end up dead or joining Scientology sticking with these clowns."

Gast took offense and sat up righteously. "Hey, the modern church of Scientology was *my* pet project. Damn thing was just a book club for loonies until I got hold of it."

"What?" Tessa demanded.

"Okay, here's the story you missed: I'm a Devil, and I had a deal with Calvin's rival at the *Weekly* that was going to make Calvin lose out on a job at the paper. To outsmart *me*, Cal wrote an article about *your* restaurant that he made up because my Muse wouldn't stop him from printing an article that was false. So, the article made it to print, and the rest you know."

"He made it all up?" Sally twisted back into his seat

with a sad slump, thinking of how many times he'd read Calvin's article after Tessa had found it. He'd been overjoyed to see his history and skills so respected after his months with Benny.

Tessa noted her friend's melancholy washing over him. She was glad she didn't keep any booze in the car but worried about the side arms she kept in the glove compartment and under the passenger seat for emergencies.

"As I understand it, yes. But while his intent at it being fiction got it past me, the fact that it carried a good amount of unintentional truth made it go viral." Gast slumped back into his own seat much as Sally had. "I bet on the wrong horse," Gast admonished himself but shrugged it off with the ease all Devils have at dismissing such self-deprecation. The last bit perked Sally up somewhat. "Ah, well. Not my ward anymore. Matt Reade is Aba Don's problem now."

Tessa glanced at Gast in the rearview. "Ward?"

"Industry term. It's what a Devil calls a human they have a deal with."

Sally looked over his shoulder. "You had a deal with Matt Reade for what?"

"To make him famous for his writing. By the way, insider tip for you two since you seem nice enough? If you ever make a deal with a Devil—which I don't advise, but just in case—always watch your prepositions. Some people make deals to be famous actors, but that doesn't mean they're famous *for* acting, just that they're actors who are famous for something or other. Dying while jerking off in a mosh pit, say."

"What do you make the deals in exchange *for*?" Tessa clarified Sally's question impatiently as she fought to change lanes and muttered curses under her breath.

Gast leaned forward between their shoulders. "Souls, obviously."

"What do you do with the souls?" Sally asked.

Gast pouted in consideration. "Keep 'em in Hell."

"Like, in storage?" Tessa was amused by the conversation if still mostly skeptical.

"Nah, for company."

"Is Hell lonely?" Sally asked.

"Loneliness *is* Hell, but no. Hell's chock full of demons. Overflowing, even. But you know what they say." Both faces from the front registered blankly to Gast's surprise, so he finished the thought with the adage: "Misery loves company."

"Demons hate Hell?" Tessa asked the sullen face by her shoulder.

"Everything hates Hell. It's a matter of working through pain to pass eternity."

Tessa looked over her shoulder at Gast while the traffic continued to lurch forward intermittently. "Okay, that's all very clever, but why should we believe some guy in a messed up suit with no horns or scales or—"

"I get this all the time. Humans and proof. No wonder Jesus had to feed thousands of people, and multiple times, no less." Gast rubbed his hands together and snapped his fingers. "Okay, you're a chef and wanna be the greatest there is? Guess what? I can sharpen your sense of smell."

The next moment, Sally was curling his nose in revulsion. "Oh God, I can smell- what is that? Gunpowder? Is there a gun in here?"

Tessa's face flushed red. "Two."

Sally looked in astonishment at Gast, who rolled his eyes and snapped his fingers again. "I'll limit it to really only being sharp in the kitchen when you're cooking or eating. This city will make you choke if your sense of smell is that sensitive, especially Hollywood. It's a wonder any dogs stick around this town."

"You just used Devil powers to give Sally super smelling powers?"

Gast narrowed his gaze again. "For you, I'll do a simple one: I'll improve your eyesight to make you an even better crack shot."

"My eyes are—" Tessa's pupils dilated instantly and she shouted, "Ow!" She put her arm over her eyes and shook her hand at the glove box. "Shades, shades!"

Sally fumbled to retrieve them and drawled out his disappointment when he found a small handgun in the compartment. "Aw, come on, really?" The sunglass case was under it, from which he extracted a pair of black Ray Bans for her.

"You had a slight stigmatism in the one eye. Yeah, it'll feel overwhelming at first because you're actually just not used to seeing that well, but your vision at night will be around that of a cat's. Again, useful for an assassin."

Sally laughed, sniffing the residual herbs and seasoning on his fingertips from his cooking that morning and able to pull out each one. "So, Hell just gives out superpowers?" Sally froze and his eyes went wide in terror. "Wait, we owe you our souls?"

"Those were demos. We'd need a full contract, and contracts usually come with other perks."

"Such as?" Tessa asked.

"We have certain demigods, a Muse, and other mythical creatures seeking refuge from their dying ages that help us perform the work our clients would otherwise do themselves. In the case of the writer, the Muse writes his articles. In the case of an athlete, certain demigods will lend their immortal strength and skill. Plus, there's the free clothes. Anyway, those are freebies. You don't owe me anything. Your souls are safe."

Gast spun on the seat to lay back again and shut his eyes while the traffic lurched forward. After only a moment, he sat back up to place his head right against Tessa's shoulder. "Although, the eyesight *should* be worth a woman's perspective on my little dilemma."

Tessa looked in despair at Sally who stifled his laughter while Gast started his ranting anew, not allowing a word in edgewise for the female perspective for which he had bargained anyway. "What do you think I should do? Do I play it cool or just wait a certain amount of time? It's been thirty years, but now I feel like if I bring it up as soon as we get there she knows I've been stewing over it, right?"

OPEN BAR

The bar was empty in the afternoon, which was good news for Benny and the boys. Only a middle-aged man, the one they hoped to find, was sitting at the bar with the day's copy of the *New York Times* open to the crossword puzzle and a pen being slowly chewed in the corner of his teeth. The puzzle was half-finished, and he didn't bother to look up when Benny leaned over the bar, obscuring the page in shadow with Claudio and Maury flanking him.

"I'm here about a contract."

The man didn't look up or take the pen out of his mouth, and spoke through his clenched teeth. "If you're looking for someone to work with, you'll have to talk to the patrons of The Bar. I'm just a bartender. I can get you a drink and not much else."

Benny guffawed. "You hear this act? This guy thinks I

don't know he's the don of this place. Like I don't know the assassins that come here aren't passing their contracts through him."

The man finally peered up from the page. "Excuse me?"

"I took a contract here three months ago, and you approved it." Benny pointed an accusatory finger in the man's face. "I saw the killer I hired confirm the job with you. Now that tramp's gone and reneged on that deal."

The man's eyes twitched angrily for a moment at Benny's use of the word "tramp," but his demeanor remained unfettered. "Did she?" The man behind the bar betrayed a smirk of pride.

"Yeah, so I want to know what insurance policy you have for your contracts because way I figure it, if one of your killers backs out on a deal, you're responsible." Benny placed his palms squarely on the bar and leaned over it so his face was inches from the man's. "Or else your whole operation gets exposed as a sham."

"How much was the contract for?"

"Hundred large," Claudio answered.

"How much did you pay up front?"

Maury looked perplexed. "Claudio just said, a hundred."

The man laughed. "You paid it all upfront?" He sat back down, scanning the crossword once more. "You all got hustled but good. What rube doesn't do half up front, half after?" The man chuckled and wrote in an answer in the bottom right section of the puzzle.

Benny snatched the paper out from under the man's pen. "Who're you calling a rube?"

The man didn't even move his pen from where it had been poised to answer number 54 down.[21] "Did I stutter?" The man began rolling up his sleeves as he got up from his stool. Only standing straight did Benny appreciate the man's bulk was not middle-aged flab but solid slabs of matured muscle. Despite the gray in the man's trim moustache, the stone set of his face showed plenty of strength and fury.

"You owe me the money that bitch stiffed me on. That or you owe me another killer."

"Oh, do I? And if I tell you that your shit luck is none of my concern, what then?"

"Then I do some killing myself and find another one of these bars where the killers actually take their jobs seriously."

The man blew a sharp whistle and the door to the kitchen opened. A couple of bus boys sauntered out, wiping their hands in dirty washrags. They glanced from Benny to the old man behind the bar and instantly dropped the rags to reveal each was carrying handguns aimed at Benny.

"So, I believe my next line is," the man put his hand around the back of Benny's neck and pulled their foreheads together, "your shit luck is none of *my* concern. Get out of my bar."

The man shoved Benny away, and Benny put his hands up and motioned for Claudio and Maury to do the same. The trio backed out of the bar with the guns trained on them the whole way until the door shut behind them. The boys from the assassin's guild that help run and manage the bar made the necessary arrangements to

---

[21] The clue for 54 Down on this puzzle is "A stackable cookie." The answer is "Oreo." Among the truths of the universe we have shared within this tale, another such constant of the world is thus: in the *New York Times* Crossword, if the clue is regarding a cookie, the answer is always Oreo.

guarantee Benny and his crew would not be allowed to even approach the entrance to the bar again.

They promised the boss an escort for the coming two weeks. The man told them to make the arrangements they felt appropriate although he was sure the escort was unnecessary. He had a phone call to make.

CALL YOUR PARENTS 4 - TESSA

In the car, Tessa's phone rang over the car speakers via Bluetooth, which she answered with a push of the button on the steering wheel. Sally pretended not to be overly intrigued that the caller ID on the dashboard display identified the caller as her "Daddy" and hoped that meant her father and not someone else.

Tessa was thankful Gast had paused his looping soliloquy when the phone started ringing. "Hi, Daddy."

"Hey, darlin'. Just checking in. Had an interesting afternoon here, thought I'd see how you're making out."

"Interesting? Are you okay?"

"Yeah, of course. I wanted to see how things were going with you and your chef?"

"It's going really good actually. I, uh, I think I'm going to keep on as his waitress."

"Oh?"

"Yeah, long story, but I really like working at the restaurant. He may teach me more cooking so I can be, like, an assistant chef too."

"That's an interesting turn. Run away from being a bartender to find out you want to be a chef?" Her father chuckled.

"Guess so," Tessa admitted appreciatively.

"Must be a hell of a chef."

Tessa cringed at her father's choice of words. "He really is. Are you sure everything's okay?"

"Well, that gentleman you took on the freelance work with?"

Sally sat upright urgently and mouthed: "Benny?"

Tessa nodded and ignored Sally's shock at her father's knowing anything about Benny or her contract. "He was in here just now. Not very happy with your choice of career."

"I figured he wouldn't be. I'll be okay, though. Benny's no trouble."

"Anyone who gets the drop and a well-aimed shot can be enough trouble, darlin'. Let me know if you want a couple of boys from the guild to help out. Never hurts to have a couple extra guns on deck."

Sally's swam from an ocean's depth of his confusion and astonishment, but Tessa answered her father calmly. "It's okay. I think we're plenty well stocked up over here. I'll call you later to check in, okay, Daddy?"

Her father said goodbye, and when the call disconnected, Sally demanded an explanation. "So not only are you an assassin, but did it just sound suspiciously like your *father* runs a hitman business? Or is 'Daddy' like a codename for an assassin's version of Charlie in the speaker box giving you your missions?"

Tessa spoke slowly to try to keep Sally at ease. "My dad doesn't run a hitman business." Sally relaxed slightly until she continued. "He's the LA regional director for the International Assassin's Guild."

"International Assassin's Guild?" Sally asked before looking back at Gast who had sat up once more, intrigued. "Do they offer stock options? Good health benefits? 401Ks?" Sally looked from the Assassin to the Devil in the car beside him, then shook his head in despair. "Why is the world full of so many conspiracies?"

"They're not conspiracies." Gast patted Sally's shoulder consolingly as Sally buried his face in the calm darkness behind his hands. "They're the inner workings of an unseen world that *happens* to be conspiring against you that you've only now become aware of."

MEDIATION

"So you *saw* them?" Harry asked again, for the fifth time, albeit this time with his emphasis on the third word.

Sam's forehead was against the edge of his desk, and all he could see were his own thighs, knees, and the edge of his seat between them. "Yes," he groaned.

"And what were they doing?"

Sam shut his eyes in despair. "She was trying to get him to…move on her, and he was most definitely fighting to get out of there."

"And you did what exactly to help?" Harry's eyes clenched in anger at the situation his friend had gotten them, and the whole paper, into.

Sam reran the memory once more, hoping that it somehow changed since his last interrogation by Harry, or that some new detail might emerge to redeem or at least excuse him. He agonized for a few moments in futility and finally admitted, "I said 'fuck me' and ran to find you."

"So you left her forcing herself on him?" Harry clarified from the small couch by Sam's door.

Sam sat up. "More so she was forcing him on *herself*." Harry's glare was sharp and hot, searing Sam into abashed apology instantly.

Harry fumed and with a deep breath collected himself.

"That's all you did? Nothing else to actually *help* him?"

"Well, he'd managed to wriggle free by the time I ran away, so it's not like he needed a lot of help," Sam flailed despairingly.

"Please don't repeat that when the lawyers get here," Harry commanded.

"Lawyers?" Sam jerked upright. Harry didn't bother saying anything in response. He only gave a disappointed look, which Sam swallowed in rueful acceptance. "So, on a scale of one to ten, how fucked are we?" Sam looked at Harry again, and the same expression awaited him. Sam groaned again, said, "Fuck me," and dropped his head back to the desk.

"I'd advise against saying that as well." Harry released a tired breath and walked to the window. "Although, we're not completely out of luck."

Sam was upright again, his eyes shining with hope. "How?"

"Well, if the kid didn't *want* to press charges. Sure, I have all this reported, but if he doesn't bring a case from it, then that's all there is to it."

"But how would we—"

Harry turned from the window to face Sam with a meaningful look. "We have something we could offer him."

"A job? A job where he'd be working with the woman who assaulted him?"

Harry was plainly flabbergasted and practically shouted. "You're keeping Felicia on?"

Sam's eyes glazed over momentarily, as if he were hearing something.[22] Finally he looked at Harry in

---

[22] A particularly enterprising Demon had been tasked by Aba to monitor the situation among the editors to ensure Calvin's

confident disbelief. "You're aware that she works for next to nothing? Why fire her when we could just dismiss the intern."

Harry was incredulous and looked around the room momentarily dumbstruck. When he looked back at Sam, the Editor was sitting confident in the solution he'd just proposed. "I heard a lot of buzz about Calvin's article that went online today."

"Yeah, it's the reason Felicia wanted him assigned to her in the first place." Sam bit his lip thinking over Harry's argument for Calvin, but his eyes glazed over once more before he shook his head. "One big article isn't enough, though. Not when Matt has had so many hits of his own. Calvin would need a *huge* follow up."

Harry's mouth flapped dumbly and he finally groaned in defeat. The Director trudged back to the couch, and flopped his chubby frame onto the cushions and rubbed the back of his neck and shoulders to relieve the tension while he thought over Sam's position, looking for a hole in it for Calvin and for an editorial position to finally reopen.

Sam clasped his hands over his desk and looked at Harry. "Harry, can you do me a favor?" Harry didn't speak, stunned at the earnestness of Sam's expression and gaze. Harry could only bow his head at Sam to continue. "I need Harry the friend, not Harry the HR Director."

Harry blew a daunted breath then nodded. "Sure, given the circumstances. Go ahead."

"So what if we let Calvin go? He's an *intern*. We're paying him stipends, so it wouldn't really be firing, would

---

termination. Aba's promise had been to relinquish his soon to be former body to the Demon as a promotion once he claimed Gast's body for his own.

it? We'd say his internship was up and it just isn't a fit, nudge nudge, best for you to find a better place for your talents and style. We could even make some calls. I know people at the *LA Times* and *LA Magazine*. They'd be lucky to have him."

Sam felt the plan made sense, and there was a logic to them as he spoke the words, but for some reason it wouldn't take hold and pained him to think this way, though he couldn't place why. He looked to Harry, the bureaucratic and officious Director of Human Resources to advocate the course of action he was suggesting as a clean and efficient path forward. If not that, he hoped his friend would tell him it was the right thing to do.

Harry did not comply in either regard. "We want *Calvin* here. More than we want Matt."

Sam slumped back and rocked in his desk chair. "That's how it goes in the biz, right?"

SAFE SPACES WITH UNSAFE PEOPLE

Llewyn was in the middle of what was looking like a record *Minesweeper* run. The Catholic church wasn't much for allowing games on their computers, and he'd been stuck with few options since his copy of *Diablo II* had been discovered and taken from him. One of the other Fathers poked his head in his office. "Llewyn, got a motley out in the hall for you."

"They asked for me?"

"They asked for a tour. Abbott said to send 'em your way." The other priest shut the door and continued on his way. Llewyn sighed and reached down to his ankles and pulled his pants back up before he paused the game.

He fumbled with the belt all the way to the door to his

office and walked out to the main atrium. He was surprised to see his brother's description was understated. Two goofy looking guys, a pair of very pretty women, and a veritable supermodel awaited him.

The two guys both looked fairly dorky, but all three of the women were gorgeous, and he was sure the Abbott hadn't gotten a look at them or the old lecher would have been out here before he'd ever give Llewyn the chance. "How can I help you, my children?"

The woman who looked most likely to be a supermodel adjusted her designer shades and smiled sweetly. Llewyn wondered if the smile she'd flashed at first had been at all flirtatious but abandoned the hope quickly. "My friends are theology students here for the tour of the seminary and the overnight for morning mass." Lilith gestured at the group, who smiled sheepishly at the random fib, which ultimately made it all the more convincing.

"Just your friends?"

Lilith smiled teasingly. "Yes, just *them*. I have some other work to see to."

Llewyn ah'ed with obvious disappointment and looked at the others. The other two women were both radiant in their own ways. The blonde girl shone with sweetness; the darker-haired woman had an enchanting sharpness to her. "Well, come this way," he ushered. "You're in time for dinner, and we have some cots we can set up for you."

Llewyn started to lead the group, but Lilith held Calvin back and told Llewyn he'd be along in a minute. "You know what to do?"

"I really don't see—"

"Calvin, trust me here. Writing is what you do. You love it. You're great at it. The Creator saw to all that. So, when all else doesn't make sense in this world, doing what you love with your God-given talent will *always* be a very viable course of action. We'll do our parts. Just schedule the email to send tomorrow morning and be ready."

Calvin took a deep breath and nodded despite his expression being plainly dubious. "Okay." Lilith was turning to the door, but he called after to her. "Hey, can I ask-"

"It was all her."

"How did you know I was going to—"

"Ask? You were bound to, but for the record, you can say that you didn't and knew all along." Lilith winked and added, "I didn't create feelings that weren't there or express anything she didn't quite have the courage to express."

Lilith had explained her indwelling of Karen for the past two months in the car ride over. Calvin could swear he saw what looked like admiration in Lilith's eyes as she offered the explanation to him. If nothing else, that proved to him that she really had been inside Karen. "Also worth noting is that the times you guys grew closer? Especially when you two finally sealed the deal? It was always all her."

Calvin admitted with a restrained smile that made his face flush. "I could kind of tell. Guess I was kind of intimidated by you and your... strength," he offered sheepishly.

"Couldn't be that. After all, you adore Karen. I think it might just be that I'm a bit more...forward than Karen is." With that comment, a smile, and a wave, Lilith was out the door in a sweeping scent of lavender and a rush of golden hair.

Calvin wandered into the church to try to find the

group. Outside the church, Lilith met with Tie and Gast to whom she doled out instructions. Gast was unusually quiet which, while surprising, she definitely appreciated for the time being. With proper luck, they'd have a literal eternity to sort out the last thirty years.

CALL YOUR FRIENDS – BENNY AND LLEWYN

Llewyn was back at his desk trying out *Spider Solitaire*. He was muttering curses to himself as he puzzled out how it was supposed to work, and swore again when he clicked the deck on the bottom right of the screen and it spewed a new row of cards over every column on the screen.

His phone rang and he answered it on speaker. "May the Lord be with you."[23]

Benny sounded frantic on the other end. "Llewyn, cut the shit, take me off speaker, and pull your pants up. I need your help."

Llewyn raised his eyebrows at Benny's tone and did as he was instructed. He pulled his pants up from around his ankles and awkwardly buckled his belt in his seat while he pinned the phone handset between his ear and shoulder. "Fire away, bud."

"That hitwoman—"

"Is that the right term?"

"What?"

"Hitwoman. It doesn't sound very PC." Llewyn waved

---

[23] Priests, it should be noted, are not required or instructed to answer the phone this way. McFadden took extra pains to appear more priestly than most in these ways since he was so much less priestly in other essential ways. For most priests without this concern, a polite hello is sufficient.

himself off. "Sorry, the church is trying to stay up on modern political correctness for outreach and all that."

"Right, well, the hitwoman—"

"It's just that, you don't call a cop a policeman or policewoman anymore, you call them *officer* to remove the gender and its implied importance." Llewyn rattled off the lesson as he fastened his belt and settled into the chair while still fidgeting slightly with the pants that weren't entirely comfortably affixed.

Benny growled in frustration. "Okay, fine, damn it, the *assassin*."

"That's better. It's the officer equivalent."

"Can I continue?"

"Please do. You were telling me how the assassin turned on you after two months working right next to Sally and how surprised and angry you are about her developing sympathy for the sad sack you've been kicking around."

"How did you—"

"Come on, Benny, how did you *not* see that coming?" Llewyn laughed unsympathetically at his friend's misfortune. "It was the plot of *The Whole Nine Yards*."

"We saw that together, didn't we?"

"Yeah. We rented it that night with the boys after shaking down that Salvadorian place." Llewyn shot a worried glance at his door in case someone had overheard him.

"Well, how was I supposed to know she'd actually want to be a waitress?"

Llewyn put his feet up on the desk. "Dunno. At least in the movie, Amanda Peet being a dental assistant made some sense. They make decent pay, especially at a private practice."

"Focus. I lost my assassin."

"That *is* a pickle." Llewyn leaned forward and spoke in a hushed tone. "So you're looking for a ringer?"

"Another one? No way, I'm already a hundred in the hole from that bitch hamstringing me, not to mention the money from that hipster shit and his beer. At least the boys got a hold of the beer. I'll admit, it's not half bad, but now the apartment's stuffed with a dozen boxes of 'Sweet Emotion' Beer."

"Go figure, a hipster who's a fan of Aerosmith."

"Feels like I killed the hipster equivalent of a panda," Benny said.

Llewyn began in a cautious tone, "Benny, you and I both know business is business, but I gotta tell ya: even if you're already in the hole, you *need* to have someone else's hands on this one. Or let this ship with the Greek pass. There'll always be another score."

"I haven't been caught yet. How's one alcoholic failure of a chef with no family or friends gonna bring me down?"

"It's not a matter of covering it up for the shitty cops who just want to close a case or call it 'cold' as quickly as possible." Llewyn gave a furtive look over both his shoulders despite there being nothing but bookcases over either of them. "You're dealing with ownership of prime real estate in Los Angeles that Sally inherited from his pops." Llewyn's voice lowered even further to a steamy hiss into the phone receiver as his heart began to pound. "The IRS could get involved."

"Look, I've got a guy on it. The restaurant and all the deeds are going to be in line. Once we knock off Sally, everything falls into place. If I have to cut a little off the top to give back to the tax man, it's all good. Although that's a racket I wish I could get in on."

"Taxes are the original extortion racket."

"Franco did always say that." Benny sounded wistful, to McFadden's surprise.

"You sure you're okay with this? I know you always had your..." McFadden searched for a word, "*issues* with Franco's philosophy and how he left the biz, but you're really good with doing his son like this?"

"His son is just another lazy mook. Gotta take Franco out of the equation because Franco took *himself* out of it twenty years ago."

"Sally always sounded like a nice kid."

"Just another stupid hipster foodie. His dad should've raised him tougher."

Llewyn recalled Franco always talking proudly of his son who was only five years old when Franco had retired from the gang. Franco had laundered his money and used it to buy some prime real estate. He'd told the gang proudly, his son could use the property to be whatever he wanted and chase real success. Llewyn was there when Franco, sloppy drunk, had showed pictures of his adolescent son, and how happy he was to get out of the game with that kind of success before it went too far.

Llewyn had never asked Benny about the car accident that had killed Franco and his wife at the end of last year. By that point, Llewyn had taken a page out of Franco's and was finishing up in seminary.

Now Benny was going to kill Sally and make the restaurant his.

"Listen, I gotta go figure out where to find Sally. Thanks for the chat. Helped cool me off and figure out my plan."

A fellow priest had knocked and poked his head in, waving for Llewyn. "That's good. I've got a few people to see to myself."

"A few?"

"Yeah, we've got visitors for the night. Theology students, which you think would have been on my schedule. Now I've probably gotta improvise a lecture or something."

"Which is hard since you don't know a thing about being a priest."

"Well, *in nomine patris, et filii, et spiritus sancti*, fuck off." Llewyn laughed good-naturedly and hung up the phone. He went to find his students, who he'd notice had less knowledge of Catholic priesthood than even he did.

He chalked it up to their being rather old-looking freshmen.

A LITTLE PARTY NEVER HURT NOBODY

Pitch was not much for getting out of his office to do his work. He liked the quiet desk job being a Devil of Avarice afforded him. Thankfully, his assignment as requested by Lilith didn't require him to go far.

As an infantryman, his body had been used to long marches and journeys. As a Devil, the body hardly ever found its way out of the Avarice circle. He made sure to point this out to Lilith as the height of his dedication to her, Gast, and Tie that he was doing so for the first time in nearly three decades, especially to visit the department he was currently standing on the precipice of, hand hesitating to knock and proceed.

Eurydice did not technically reside in Hell. As a Muse, she had never been banished there but could coexist in an accessible level of the complex while not actually being within the pit in any meaningful sense as the Devils are. Pitch took a deep breath at her door and steeled his resolve. After a couple light knocks, he poked his head into her office, finding her at a desk with her back to him, typing furiously and running her head down a line of a dozen monitors as she raced through the assignments Hell was constantly issuing to her.

Pitch stood in the doorway until she glanced over her shoulder at him. When she spotted him, the furious typing that had been nonstop for roughly a decade paused and her eyes swam dreamily. "Pitch!" she sang to him. Pitch's eyebrows went up at how the computer's notifications were already flashing furiously as more work piled up by the second that she was now completely ignoring. "Come in! How are you?"

Pitch cleared his throat and walked in. Eurydice kept one uncomfortable chair in her office by the door, and it was piled with papers that Pitch looked at unsurely for a moment before Eurydice huffed and snapped her fingers. They went up in flames and the chair was cleared for him. She snapped another finger and the chair became a much more inviting high-back armchair. Pitch smiled gratefully and took the seat.

"So? How are you?" she asked again with maniacally fixated attention. "I, uh, I haven't seen you since the Christmas party."[24]

Pitch considered it. "You mean the Christmas party back in '82? That's the last one I went to."

"Has it been that long? Wow, it feels like just last season." Eurydice cleared her throat uncomfortably and looked sideways to search her mind for another

---

[24] Hell's office does throw a "Christmas Party," but only because of the debauch and scandal all office Christmas parties elicit. No one in Hell except Eurydice actually celebrates Christmas, and she has been the sole participant in her office Secret Santa every year for the past century. She usually gifts herself new office supplies and wooly socks.

conversation starter. "Do you think you're going this year?"

Pitch looked pitifully at her then her computer. "Do you think you can?"

Eurydice looked over her shoulder and gasped. The emails and orders were piling up. She turned back to Pitch and tried an easygoing smile, waving dismissively at the computer with one hand while her other pulled her auburn hair braid over her shoulder and began nervously stroking her hair. "Of course I can. I just, uh, I usually pass on it if I can't count on seeing cool friends like you there."

"Well, I don't know if I'm that."

Eurydice's eyes burst open in panic, and she squeaked, "We're not friends?"

"Of course we are. I meant that I'm not what I consider cool, but thank you."

Eurydice took a deep breath in relief and twisted a little in her chair, running both hands alternately down her braid. "I think that's what makes you even cooler." She smiled at him, bit her lower lip lightly, and averted her gaze coyly with a bubbling giggle.

"Well, I'm sorry I can't make this more of a, uh, social visit," Pitch apologized and tilted his head toward the computer again. "I may have kept you so long that you'll miss the next fifty Christmas parties."

Eurydice huffed again and tried to chuckle, but this time it faltered anxiously in her throat as the computer began beeping in urgency for her attention. "It's fine. I can take a break anytime for *you*."

Pitch cleared his throat in indelicate surprise and looked around the room while absently ruminating about how Lilith might have given him this particular assignment just to see him uncomfortably navigate

Eurydice's affections. In retrospect, she'd had a not so subtle glint in her eye when she instructed him to "go get her, tiger."

Even if Lilith had said Pitch would make this part of the plan a sure thing, he couldn't argue that he knew well enough that Eurydice couldn't stand Gast or Tie after their antics at the aforementioned Christmas Party of 1982.

The two Devils had repeatedly suggested party games to try to throw Eurydice at Pitch— seven minutes in Heaven, spin the bottle, sex dice, porn or art, *Cards Against Humanity*—and in the process had gotten Pitch so drunk that he'd ended up streaking through the White House.[25] This was a large part of Pitch's insistence on staying behind his desk.

"Well, maybe we can discuss the Christmas party another time. For now, I just came to ask if you could do me a huge favor." Pitch swallowed nervously, recalling the phrasing Lilith had encouraged him to use. "I'd be in your debt in a big way if you could pull it off, so I didn't want to ask by email. Hence my being here in person."

Eurydice's eyes were alight, and she visibly swooned in her chair. "Anything. What can I do for you?"

Pitch tried not to recoil at the sweetness of the Muse and cleared his throat. "Well, Executive Director Aba Don recently seized all of Gast's contracts."

---

[25] The incident was never widely reported. A naked red-haired Frenchman was chased by several Secret Service Agents while shouting *"Zeut Allors!"* repeatedly. Pitch eventually did happen upon President Reagan in his private office, at which point he uttered, *"Quelle surprise,"* and promptly disappeared back to Hell. The only tape of the incident was stolen from White House security by Tie and has been played at every Underworld Christmas party since.

Eurydice's face went stony. "Did he? Good. Gast is such a jerk." She seemed to recall her company and corrected herself. "I know the two of you are friends. You're so sweet for putting up with a jerk like him."

Pitch marveled at Eurydice's logic. He made a note to recommend her for a job in Pride if she could do such mental acrobatics to salvage his character, but not even of a sliver of the same for his friends. "Well, since Aba took over that Matt Reade contract, it might be a good look for you to help Aba by running an article for Matt at the *LA Weekly*. I thought of it, and it'll probably make both of us look good to take that initiative."

Eurydice was practically melting in her seat and slid her desk chair closer to Pitch as she gushed, "You are the best. I can't believe we don't work together more. We should. You should *always* come down here with ideas like this. I'm sure you have *so* many. Wouldn't that be great if we were like, partners? Or maybe we should hang out and trade ideas outside of work more."

Pitch nodded stiffly at Eurydice's rambling and noticed the screens on her monitors were beginning to flash in red like a missile launch had been detected. "Okay, well, there was an incident at the Italian restaurant Calvin wrote about today? Maybe you could do an article on *that* for Matthew?" Eurydice resumed her effusive praise, but Pitch, feeling terrible for how much trouble just the five-minute diversion caused the Muse, immediately excused himself and ran out.

Eurydice swooned in her chair a moment after Pitch rushed out and turned back to her computer. She wrote the article for Matt and sent it up to the editors within seconds. Within a minute, she had calmed the terror of her computer and was back to normal. As she tilted herself back into work, she looked forward to taking a break later to call her mom and sisters and tell them that things were going great with her and the Devil she had a crush on, and that she was sure she had finally hit her stride with a good work-life balance.

DEMONIC RECONNAISSANCE

Tie had received his mission from Lilith and wasn't particularly pleased with it. It felt like too much subterfuge, and he had wanted a more active role. To be there with the smoking gun and a fancy one-liner like the humans always had the heroes say in their movies. A "yippee kay yay, mother fucker" wouldn't have gone unappreciated, but no, Lilith had said that was for the meat sacks and Gast.

Tie had found Benny and his group of weirdos, and was floating around listening in. Already he had some good info to bring back to Lilith: the ownership of the restaurant and the reason Benny wanted to kill Sally, but the brewery they had seized was another useful tidbit, as was their working with a lawyer.

Tie had briefly gone back to Lilith for instructions on what to do with the information. She said Tie's next job was finding the lawyer Benny had mentioned and doing some work on him. Benny didn't disappoint. He called the lawyer asking for details on selling beer, whether selling it privately or online required a liquor license.

Through the phone connection, and hearing the lawyer's voice, Tie managed to travel instantly to the lawyer's side into a palatial office that reminded him of Gast's preferred arrangement. He was sure that if Gast saw it, the Devil would casually shy away from matching it in the future, but first they had to ensure Gast would have an office in the future at all.

When Craig hung up the phone after the exchange with Benny about liquor sales, Tie whispered to Craig, "You know, you could probably get away with a billable hour for that call."

Craig's mind answered back instantly, "Duh. Of course."

Tie loved lawyers. If you made it about billable hours, it was always an easy way to get them going. "You could also find another billable hour in setting up the brewery as an LLC and back-dating its ownership to Benny as sole investor. It'd protect Benny from suspicion of selling a random kid's beer he has no legal ties to who's gone *missing*."

Craig grinned greedily. "Sounds like two, no, three hours to me, even if I can dupe up LLC papers in a jiff. I am such a good lawyer. Craig, you lawyer better than any other lawyer ever to lawyer."

Tie backed away, muttering, "Sure, guy. Enjoy that professional pride. I'll see you in the offices soon, I'm sure."

Tie returned to Hell to advise Gast and Lilith on this tidbit from his role in the plan. In an instant, Tie was back in Avarice with Gast and Pitch.

A CONTINUED SERIES OF FALLS FROM GRACE

Memory is a sensitive thing. Trauma, darkness, and age make it very organic. Many of the supposed Demons working in Hell now were once human. When Heaven had no place for them, Angels wound up in the pit as the first demons. Humans denied entry to Heaven- or those who don't ever actually die to gain that admission- can find their way to Hell just the same.

Like all the other demons suffering in the pit, they try to find their way through the seemingly never-ending course of time. Like the angels that fell from grace, many fallen humans join in the vengeful wrath of Hell against those who still remain on Earth who might achieve redemption and grace now beyond their reach.

If you are wondering, *Poltergeist* and the original *Paranormal Activity* movies are stunningly accurate representations of this as a result.

Many humans, because of the ages that pass, the trauma of their deaths, and anguish in their eternal sentencing will forget that they were ever human- especially if their physical bodies are claimed and used elsewhere in Hell.

In some cases, though, a person cannot forget because they cannot shed their bodies as mortals do in death. Perhaps they have been branded to remain in their body to forever be known as the first and original murderer. They might intentionally lose themselves in the work and existence of the pit because of their shame. Perhaps they might also take on a new name.

Cain had been sorted, as everyone else had, by Aba Don himself. Although unlike the other souls Aba had battled into order, Aba enlisted Cain into Wrath as a potentially useful ally or tool to have under his thumb. Cain had agreed to the assignment if he was allowed to change his name to reflect his new station.

INTER-CORPORATE SYNERGY

"So it looks like the paperwork is all there for Teddy. Doesn't take a whole lot on his end. He did the simple filing every year since he was eighteen."

Pitch clicked through some documents on his computer and acknowledged the information from the caller. "Thanks, Pete. Always good working with you." Pitch paused to listen. "Well, it's just as much you helping us. Love the synergy."

Pitch wrapped up the conversation and smiled at Gast and Tie, giving a confident nod that his end in the plan was in hand. Gast looked at Tie appreciatively. "Good job on the beer info."

"Isn't that the beer he said has cocaine in it? Pitch, old buddy, any chance your g-men could share some of the take with us?"

Pitch scribbled a note to himself. "I'll put another call into Pete, I'm sure they'll be willing to. Not like he's the DEA."

Gast was grim with focus on the task before him. "Okay, has Aba come to yet?"

Pitch shook his head. "Not as of sunrise. Your body packed quite the punch."

Gast lifted his jacket off the back of the chair and spun it over his shoulders. He grimaced at the state of his suit, torn and ratty. Pitch sighed sympathetically and snapped his fingers. Gast's tattered suit turned into a shark fin grey three-piece with a watch chain in the vest pocket and perfect white pocket square.

"What happened to keeping your finger prints off incriminating paperwork? Giving me a suit kind of flies in the face of that," Gast advised.

Pitch bobbed his head in momentary consideration.

"It'll be a good show, might as well have you well dressed for it."

"Any word from Lilith?" Gast asked both his compatriots.

Tie crossed his arms and leaned back against the wall. "She's waiting on her pet meat sack to finish his part. Says he was up all night."

Pitch cleared his throat and mumbled in a low voice, "I put the request in with Eurydice last night."

Gast betrayed a smirk at Pitch's discomfort but didn't chide the Devil just then. Gast hesitated, unsure how to proceed. Tie looked curiously at him, and Gast finally extended a hand to Tie at which the towering devil harrumphed. Tie coughed sheepishly before he muttered, "Don't tell Lilith I said this, but friends like you help me forget we're stuck in Hell."

The hulk enveloped Gast in a bear hug that thoroughly surprised Gast. When Tie released him, Gast shrugged at Pitch. "Only thing I've got left to lose is my body. Not like I've got much else, right?"

Pitch raised a skeptical eyebrow. "I think we both know that's false. Go get him."

Gast nodded and walked out of Pitch's office. Difficult as it was to say aloud, he did have one thing to look forward to: finally talking with Lilith about everything that had happened and was to come. It was a small thing, but it was a hope. In Hell, he mused, the smallest light of it shone pretty darn brightly.

As he reached the elevator, he kicked himself for using what Tie would call "the foofy sentimentality Lilith rambles on about."

He pressed the button for the executive level where Aba was recuperating in his office. "Sorry, buddy. I guess I'm not as good a Devil as you or Aba after all."

EDITORIAL DISCRIMINATION

Lilith sympathized with Gast's dislike for having to function as a spirit. As optional as a body was given the nature of their existences, she still found the lack of a body all too ephemeral. The privilege of physical interaction and presence is a valuable one to a person whose physical existence takes a certain force of will.

She'd found two editors in the *LA Weekly* offices when she'd arrived last night. They had camped out all night, drinking and lamenting their impending doom at the hands of Felicia and Calvin, but Sam was slowly working his way to justifying firing Calvin and giving Matt Reade the job. When Eurydice's article on the incident at the restaurant had arrived, the presiding demon had returned to Hell for his reward, seeing the job as done with the weak willed Editor in Chief. The article was a breakdown of how Calvin had been present for a local mobster's threats on the chef at the restaurant, and how that mobster had financed the Via Fresca. No article or communication had come from Calvin, and to Sam, that sealed the deal and Calvin's fate.

Lilith wasn't surprised at this; it was the easiest way to sweep a nasty problem under the rug to begin with. Not to mention the odds had been stacked against Calvin for the sake of both Aba's wards. Harry, for his part, had a steady misgiving about it and was advising the more sensible route of giving Calvin a job. Sam's refute, which became more valid as the night went on, was that Matt had gotten the article submitted within hours, but they hadn't see a peep from Calvin—never mind that Calvin had been manhandled by the Food Editor earlier that day.

"Well, that looks like the decision maker." Sam's head was killing him from the night of drinking, and he slid out of his chair and lay on the floor behind his desk when the morning light started coming through the windows exacerbating his hangover. Harry watched the drunken Editor on the ground from the couch with ire gnawing at him for Sam's cowardice.

"I already forwarded Matt's article to Errol telling him to run it as breaking news, ASAP. Who'd have thought the *LA Weekly* would ever scoop the *LA Times* with a juicy crime piece?"

"Let's exercise some caution here," Lilith spoke into Harry's ear, which the HR Director repeated verbatim. "If Calvin was there, it could mean he was working on something of his own."

Sam groaned from behind the desk. "And that we haven't heard from him *at all* since this happened? Harry, we needed a justification to quietly let Calvin go, and we got it. Now get me some Alka-Seltzer and water and drop it."

"I just think it's weird Calvin was there. There may be more going on. How did Matt know about any of this, anyway?" Lilith again succeeded in getting Harry to voice her counterargument word for word.

Sam groaned again from the floor, and Lilith could hear the Editor-in-Chief shuffling over the floor so that his head was visible to Harry from around the corner of his desk. "Fine! We'll see what Calvin has to say about it- if anything. Now, go! Alka-Seltzer!"

Harry rolled his eyes and got to his feet, muttering, "Lightweight."

UPPER HAND

Gast found Aba lolling unconscious in his chair, back in his original body. Gast was surprised to find Aba sitting in a more traditional executive office, though it was still dimly lit as Aba preferred. Gast spotted a mini bar in the corner and decided to at least have a drink before rousing the Devil.

With a glass of scotch in hand, Gast approached Aba and tried shaking his shoulder a few times, gently at first then with more vigor, but to no avail. Gast tossed back his scotch and went back to the bar for another glass. He returned with his scotch refreshed and a second glass full of tequila. He splashed the latter into Aba's face and walked around to the other side of the desk, taking a seat while he enjoyed the pleasant sip from his drink while the Executive Director sputtered through the liquor and finally woke up.

"You!" Aba wiped his face furiously. "What are you doing in that body! In *my* body!"

Gast took another sip and admired the scotch. It was a well-aged Glenfarclas, twenty-eight years. "You remember when we created Digital Rights Management to infuriate the meat sacks with their music, games, and movies? This body has protections on it like that."

Aba's face took on a hot complexion. His fingers dug into and tore through the leather arms of his chair. "Don't you dare talk down to me, you primeval pissant!"

"I'm aware the Bible isn't preferred summer reading down here, but come on, bud. You remember who I was, and you know what God put on my body to protect me."

Aba sat back, eyeing Gast warily. "The mark."

Gast took another sip and smacked his lips with theatrical nonchalance. "There you go. Turns out, it protects my body from being indwelt or possessed by spirits with less than savory intentions too. Go figure."

Aba's jaw was clenched so tightly Gast wondered if it could even be pried open with a crowbar. "You get to keep your body. So be it. Nothing you can do will restore your rank here." Aba summoned a ledger and checked it. "It looks like your *former* ward is about to have yet another article published, and when I was in the office yesterday, I took steps to have the seed planted to fire your little ally over *my* new ward."

"Oh, so you got the notice of the transfer of my contracts to you?" Gast drained the glass again and nodded in appreciation of it. Aba remained silent. "Good, because that's about to backfire."

"Have you forgotten the mobster who'll kill your supposed competition soon? All but removing any hope you have with that supposed gambit?" Aba leered with a sideways smirk.

Gast shook his head wearily and stood, causing Aba to spring to his feet in automatic defensive response. A saber had appeared in Aba's hand and Gast laughed at it dismissively, then moved back to the bar and refilled his scotch, speaking over his shoulder while he poured. "Put that thing away before you hurt yourself."

Aba eyed Gast suspiciously from across the room. "How do I know you're not lying about this mark of protection? I had your body, I saw no mark."

Gast took another sip of scotch and smacked his lips. "Because, I notice you're not using that sword to test it." Gast nodded at Aba's hand clutching his weapon, then made a wincing expression. "I know you had the body for a bit, but I guess the mark is somewhere you didn't think to look."

Gast saw the look of consideration on Aba's face. He

took a hearty draught of his scotch and raised his eyebrows impishly. "I'm sure the boys down in Lechery did, though." Aba's face contorted in disgust while Gast drained his scotch.

PROPER RESEARCH

Calvin cautiously walked into the office, which- he admitted to himself- was how he entered even when not under threat by mobsters or denizens of Hell. Lily Clark wasn't in the office yet, so there was no one to announce himself to. Most of the staff didn't arrive until nine, so he was an hour early and wondered why Lilith had been so adamant he arrive at this time.

He stood in the anteroom wondering if he should go into an office and stay out of sight or wait in reception to see when the editors arrived. Calvin was surprised when Harry came through from his wing carrying a large bottle of water and box of Alka-Seltzer. Calvin also noticed Harry was wearing the same clothes he had been in the day before, even if the portly HR Director looked no worse the wear.

"Harry, are any of the editors are in?"

Harry shot him an urgent look and motioned for Calvin to follow. "Tell me you have something on this Via Fresca thing."

"Well, I—"

"Because we got something in from Matt Reade last night on how it has mob ties," Harry said quickly as they reached the door to Sam's office.

"Yeah, I—"

"And how *you* were there when the mobster flipped his lid."

Harry's gaze bore a hole into Calvin, and Calvin managed only a sheepish nod. "Gotta chase the real story. I had research to do."

Harry looked Calvin up and down and motioned with his head for Calvin to proceed into Sam's office. Like Harry, the Editor-in-Chief was wearing the same clothes he had worn the day before, but unlike Harry, the Chief looked like he'd taken a long, blindfolded run through MacArthur Park. Sam was still on his back behind his desk. Harry cleared his throat and held up the water and Alka-Seltzer for the Editor to see. Sam slurred effusive thanks and clambered to his feet.

Sam gulped half the bottle of water down, gasping gratefully when he lowered it for air. By the looks of it, Sam was clearly suffering from the mother of all hangovers. Sam fumbled with the box of Alka-Seltzer, removed a package, fumbled more to open an individual packet of tablets, then fumbled a bit more to break up the tablets to fit into the narrow bottleneck. He resealed the bottle and began to shake it to speed up the dissolution process while he finally looked at Calvin. "Good, you're here. We need to talk."

Calvin took a self-affirming breath and sat down on the couch beside Harry, who was glowering disappointedly at Sam who was still sitting on the carpet against the end of the desk. "Good, I need to talk to *you*." Sam looked surprised at the pluck, and Calvin seized on the hesitation. "I have a story you need to read on the Via Fresca."

"We already have—"

"On the mobster?"

Sam paused. "Yes, how did you—"

"I was there with Matt. He went ahead and wrote the story as he saw it. I decided to do a little more digging and made some calls. I've got mine. I think it's a bit more robust." Calvin pulled out his phone and hit send on an email he had drafted before leaving the church that morning.

Sam looked from Calvin to Harry in confusion, and Calvin nodded for Sam to check his computer. Sam crawled around his desk on all fours to his chair and clumsily climbed up and toppled his aching body into the seat. Clearing his throat and blinking hard a few times at the screen, the Editor clicked around and began reading. "Corruption Cripples Genius Chef?"

"Give it a read," Calvin urged, noticing Harry lean forward in evident intrigue.

"Can you forward it to me as well?" Harry asked quietly. Calvin nodded and forwarded it to Harry, who pulled out his phone to read it also.

Sam had barely read past the headline and screwed his face in resolved dismissal. "We already have an article on—"

"Trust me, this article takes a different angle. I did a bit more homework to give the background of what we saw happen yesterday."

Calvin sat back and spread his arm over the back of the couch, showing that he had no intention of moving until Sam relented and read past the first sentence. When the editor did, his eyebrows instantly lifted. "Oh." Sam looked enticed for only a moment before squinting in visible discomfort at his stomach. The Chief shook the bottle again before twisted the cap off desperately for a huge gulp of the tonic. Catching his breath from it, Sam pleaded, "Harry, can you—"

"I'll go to the coffee shop and get your usual." Harry was already on his feet and at the door and turned to Calvin. "Can I get you anything?" Calvin looked mildly surprised, and Harry whispered, "Looks like you'll be here a while." Harry pointed with his thumb at Sam, who was hunched over his desk trash can taking deep breaths with his eyes closed.

COOKING THE BOOKS

When he saw even the stammering and consistently uneasy Calvin heading to his arena at the *LA Weekly* offices, Sally had found the courage—with some encouragement from Tessa—to head to his own battleground. Lilith had told him that morning to send Benny a message saying to meet back at the Fresca to settle things.

Tessa had offered to join him, but Sally wanted to be absolutely sure he followed Lilith's plan to the letter, and Lilith's plan had been for him to go alone. Lilith was sure if Benny saw Tessa there as well, his rage would surely boil over. She assured Sally, "You won't be alone, anyway."

Sally looked abashed and recalled that he hadn't been to church since his parents' funeral. "You mean God?"

Lilith stuck her tongue out and blew a raspberry to dismiss Sally's cheese. "What? No. God's got better things to be doing. Take care of your own mess. I've got someone else on the way."

Sally had arrived a few minutes early to the eight o'clock appointment and found a slender man with a neatly trimmed beard in a black suit waiting outside. He wondered if Angels liked blending in through inconspicuous attire. Sally introduced himself, and the man simply responded, "Ah, well, I'm here to meet with Benjamin O'Houlihan. Is he here?"

Sally furrowed his brow at the deflection and peered inside. "Not yet, but we can wait inside."

Sally ushered the man in. Once in the door, Sally turned on the lights, and the man asked politely, "May I sit?"

Sally nodded, and the man very neatly seated himself at the table closest to the door, setting his leather briefcase on the table. Sally watched the man curiously, wondering what sort of magic these supernatural compatriots had in store. Perhaps this was a special assassin from the guild.

"Would you like something to drink?" The man looked up at him without any reaction. "Sorry, I meant coffee, or tea, or maybe iced tea? I don't *have* iced tea, but I could brew some tea and put ice in it for you. I think we have juice, we're kind of low on stock." Sally recalled the day before had cleared most of the shelves.

The man shook his head and opened his briefcase. He pulled out a black three-ring binder without any label and set it on the table. Was that a spell book? Did Angels use magic books? Maybe modern sorcerers did? Do wizards use three-ring binders for spells? It would make sense from a durability and organizational standpoint, Sally thought. "Should I stay here and say a rosary or something? Is a rosary a thing you say?" Sally felt thoroughly unprepared for the situation.

"Uh, yes, it is, but that won't be necessary. The IRS is a government agency and does not show preference or deference to any religious order," the man said crisply.

"The IRS?"

The man nodded and flipped open his binder, running his index finger down a page he had marked with a blue tab in the hundreds of pages organized in the binder. "Yes, you're Salvatore Degneri? Owner of the property?

Your affairs are all in order. I did a cursory check this morning on the property and its back taxes just to be sure my visit couldn't be a two birds with one stone scenario."

"Owner of the property." Sally looked around the restaurant as if he had forgotten where he was, seeing the small building with new eyes, trying to puzzle out the information the man had.

"Yes, well, I'm here about the *companies* operating at this address. Your renters." The man grimaced, flipping to the first red tab in the binder. "The Via Fresca." He flipped to the second red tab just a couple pages past it. "And the Sweet Emotion Brewing Co."

"Sweet Emotion? Renters?" Sally walked to the auditor and asked to see the paperwork on the Fresca. The auditor flipped back, and Sally squinted at the page. After a few moments, he recognized it. It was the paperwork he had signed when Benny had approached him about opening the restaurant after the funeral. Elated with some good news after losing his parents, and not well versed in the legalese, he had signed the single-page agreement without much review, choosing to trust the former associate of his late father. "This is a lease agreement?"

"Well, yes." The auditor donned a pair of wire-framed spectacles. "It's your agreement to lease the space to Mr. O'Houlihan for a restaurant." The auditor gestured vaguely all around him. "It also states that, in exchange for being head chef, you forgo charging them any rent."

"But I thought that said Benny owns the restaurant?" Sally asked. "He was letting *me* use the space for free?"

The auditor looked baffled and leaned forward to pore over the document. "*No*, it says Benjamin owns the *Via Fresca* as an *LLC*. You agreed to rent the *property* to him at no cost in exchange for a position as his head chef." The auditor traced through the terms down to the bottom of the page. "It's very generous. But it does mean you have no taxable income to speak of." The auditor looked up from the page suspiciously at Sally. "That we *know* of."

Sally held his hands up. "Nope. I've reported everything I have."

The auditor nodded and flipped back to the earliest tab. "Well, that is true, all the taxes on your estate inheritance and property taxes since the property passed to you last year are paid up." The auditor squinted curiously for a moment but then shrugged officiously. "As of yesterday, at any rate. There was a wire transfer from a Las Vegas casino covering any delinquencies."

Sally suddenly understood. His father's accident, the days spent in the hospital until he'd finally passed, all Benny's supposed help sorting out his father's affairs. The property the restaurant occupied was his, and the revelation stunned him from his feet into the seat beside the auditor. Sally was considering going into the kitchen for a drink since he didn't think the IRS had any opinions on when was too early in the day to begin consuming.

Before he could, the door opened, and Benny walked in flanked by Maury and Claudio with a hungry glint in his eye that was immediately doused seeing the auditor at the table. The auditor stood and extended a hand courteously. "Benjamin O'Houlihan?"

Benny grimaced at the gesture. "Who the hell are you?"

The auditor looked to Sally, who nodded to confirm that it was Benny. The auditor spun his binder and set a hand solemnly on the page. "My name is Peter Mayweather, Special Auditor with the IRS. I'm here to discuss the taxes owed for corporate expenditures and earnings for the past three years."

Maury and Claudio exchanged looks behind Benny and mutually agreed to turn and walk out. Benny heard the door opening behind him and snapped, "Hey!"

Maury was in the street already, and Claudio gave a casual salute. "Sorry, boss. You know what they say. Death and taxes. We'll see you on the other side."

Benny was flummoxed, and the auditor continued. "It seems the Via Fresca, the business you've been operating out of this location is, well, stunningly unprofitable. Which makes it lucky that you're not being billed for rent." Peter noted the fact with a furtive wink at Sally.

Benny started to stammer refutations while looking from Peter to Sally to try to read how much the auditor had already revealed. "What the hell do you think you're doing here, you nerdy pencil pusher?"

Peter looked positively bored by Benny's bluster, which Sally found stunning. "Sir, I'm a company man. I've been with the IRS for twenty-three years. I can assure you nothing you say or call me will deter me."

Peter turned back to his binder and flipped to the rearmost tab. "It's your co-ownership of the Sweet Emotion Brewing Co. that raises the concerns I'm here about today."

Benny looked confused, and his jaw clenched tightly in what he thought this was about. "Listen, the stuff in those beers weren't my product. I had nothing—"

"Sir, I'm with the *IRS*, not the DEA. Your cocaine beer is not my concern. What *is* my concern is the past four years of income that have gone unreported."

"Four years?" Benny demanded stupidly.

"Yes, you're recognized as a co-owner of the company on its public filing. We'll be looking for Theodore as well." Peter turned his gaze from the page to Benny. "I assure you we *will* find him." Peter adjusted his glasses slightly and added with a more menacing tone, "*Wherever you may have put him.*"

"Whatever, send me the bill and get the hell out of here!" Benny commanded, his hand dug into the pocket Sally knew had his switchblade.

This should have been enough to push Benny over the edge. Benny had been slowly backing away as Peter continued down the filing, explaining the situation. Peter removed and folded his glasses. "In summation, you owe the IRS in the neighborhood of sixty thousand dollars in back taxes for earnings through Sweet Emotion Brewing Co., as well as a minimum of another seventy-five thousand dollars in accumulated fines and penalties. We'll have the precise amount pending a full audit."

That was all it took for Benny to snap to primal fight or flight mode. His eyes went wide with panic as he opted to the former and lashed out with the switchblade from his pocket. Sally fell backwards out of his chair in fright, screaming, "What the shit!"

This time, though, Benny's switchblade did not connect. The auditor dodged the blade with the kind of ennui normally seen of Kung Fu masters dealing with uppity beginners in movies. Peter avoided the slash, expertly grabbed Benny's arm, pulled him into a knee to the groin, then twisted and flipped Benny onto the tiled floor, where he kept Benny's arm twisted in an unnatural position that looked mere inches away from breaking.

Peter tutted. "*And* assaulting a federal officer. Mr. Degneri, when you collect yourself, I'd appreciate if you could call the police to assist in detention efforts."

EXECUTIVE MANAGEMENT

Gast wasn't entirely sure what to expect. Barring any snags in the plan, which Tie should have alerted him to, things should be close to settling back on Earth. Aba's robes remained the same rich silks they always were, but Gast saw it in his face. "What?"

The door to the office opened. What appeared to be a sandy haired, middle-aged man wearing a pink polo shirt, khaki shorts, and boat shoes carrying a Heineken walked in.

Aba dropped to one knee. "My Lord!"

"A-Don!" Lucifer bellowed, then turned towards Gast at the mini bar with his arms spread open. "G-Man!"

Gast raised his glass to Lucifer, who walked over to Aba's desk and hopped onto the edge where he chugged the beer then chucked the bottle into the fireplace where it shattered. Lucifer looked at Gast and snapped a finger in command. "G-Man, hook me up, bro." Gast knew what the Lord of all Darkness, the Prince of Lies, and Master of Evil would want to drink. Gast lobbed the bottle in a wide arc across the room that Lucifer caught easily. "Tequila! My man!"

"My Lord Lucifer. I'm dealing with a bit of insubordination, but it's nothing I need trouble you with. Gast seems to have found some way to disconnect me from my wards and contracts."

"Nah, bro," Lucifer assuaged while flipping a pair of Oakley shades from his nose onto the top of his head. "I cut you off."

Aba looked pained, and he failed to find any words but, "My Lord?"

"Dude, this one contract you have? Total shit show. That kid..." Lucifer snapped his fingers searchingly.

"Matt Reade?" Gast tried with a tenuous tone while shooting a clearly knowing glance at Aba.

Lucifer pointed to Gast gratefully. "Solid. Yes. That guy. Max Read. He's in Venice shouting in the streets that the newspaper he's supposed to be working at just fired him? Dude, that's gonna need some *serious* triage."

Aba steeled himself and looked resolutely at Lucifer. "I'll handle it just as soon as—"

"Dude, *chill*. Why are you sweating meat sacks still brah? They're finding their own way here. Screw this work, my dude. Leave that to bros like G-Man here." Lucifer slapped Aba's shoulder so hard, the Devil yelped. "I've been waiting for you to realize this game is never-ending for ages, man. I finally decided to pull the plug *for* you."

Aba was dumbfounded and looked at Gast in sputtering despair that the only thing he cared for—fighting in the name of his Lord and Master—was being taken away by that very master so that, "We can finally go kick it, bro!"

Aba relented to Lucifer leading him from his own office. Lucifer called out to Gast from the door. "Yo, G-Man, you've got the VP of Wrath job. My boy and I have a bar in Ibiza that is about to get *tore* up!"

Gast bowed a head gratefully. "An honor, but I actually have another person I'd like to recommend for—"

Lucifer dropped his sunglasses back to his nose. "Whatever, bro, sort it out with HR. L-Dog OUT!"

EDITORIAL MANAGEMENT

Sam finished reading and put his palms over his eyes. "How did you write this?"

Calvin looked confused, and Harry gestured for him to respond. "After the comments the mobster made yesterday about the guy he killed, I did some digging. Benjamin O'Houlihan is the registered owner of the Via Fresca, LLC, and also the owner of Sweet Emotion Brewing Co. Seems Sweet Emotion is pending investigation for tax evasion, but given Benny's comment about Toddy, he may have bigger worries than the IRS."

"No, trust me, the IRS is definitely the bigger concern," Sam said from behind his hands.

"Death and taxes," Harry concurred.

Calvin looked earnestly at the editor and continued. "I was tempted to just write up a story about a crazy incident, but there were too many threads worth pulling. I think it's a pretty interesting follow up feature about the genius chef and how LA stifles genius and creativity amid its seedy underbelly people ignore or just don't notice."

Sam sighed and blinked hard to try to focus his mind soberly and professionally. "When did this IRS investigation start? How long has it been going on?"

Calvin checked his watch. "If the auditor was on time? About a half hour at this point."

Sam looked up from behind his hands. "This is—"

"A breaking and developing story, yeah." Calvin met Sam's eyes patiently and saw, finally, something other than agony from a hangover in the Chief's gaze.

"That's some top-shelf reporting," Harry said with a meaningful look at Sam.

"Okay, Harry." Sam took a deep breath and a moment to steady his thoughts and stomach before he continued.

"Please draw up papers to release Felicia from her post. Office conduct and violation of conduct policy, yada yada, conduct." Sam waved a hand wearily. "If she tries to fight it again, we'll have Calvin share his side of it." Sam pointed at Calvin next. "Cal, how would you like a full-time staff writer position with the *LA Weekly*?"

Calvin looked from Harry to Sam in turn. His excitement at the turn of events was electric. As scared as he was that shaking hands and making it final might incur some demonic backlash, he still raced from the couch to shake Sam's hand. The motion of their hands seemed exacerbate the Editor's nausea, so Calvin also turned to Harry, sure he owed the HR Director some thanks as well, while Sam returned to his hunched position over the bin.

"Sam, while I'm drawing up the hiring and termination papers, I'll get on top of an employee reassignment as well." Sam looked confused, and Harry smiled. "There's finally an opening on the editorial staff for me."

SABBATICAL

Gast swept into Pitch's office, with a loud clap of his hands after which he rubbed them together energetically as if trying to make fire between them. Both Pitch and Tie sat in wide eyed suspense until Lilith stepped forward from the opposite end of the room to join Gast by his side, putting her hands over his.

"Gast?" Tie checked with raised eyebrows.

Gast spread his arms exuberantly, then put one over Lilith's shoulders and pulled her against him. "The one and only. Lil, you are a genius."

Lilith rolled her eyes but blushed nonetheless as she

nestled into the hug warmly. "Next you'll remind me that the sky is blue."

"Well." Pitch mused at something on his computer. "Looks like effective immediately, Aba is no longer on the Executive team. Lucifer has had him moved to Board Advisor."

"There's a Board of Directors?" Lilith checked.

"Lucifer is the only one on it." Gast confirmed.

"Guess Aba is advising him now." Tie added.

A buzz emanated from Gast's inside breast pocket. Gast extracted his phone and checked the alert. "Looks like I'm requested, per Lucifer, to submit paperwork for the promotion of the new Vice President."

Pitch sat back in admiration. "Look who won the war."

Tie clapped loudly with broad flaps of his arms. Pitch joined with more restrained light taps of his hands as a golf spectator would. Lilith stood where Gast had left her by the door, unmoving since Gast had shifted over to Pitch's side. His eyes met hers and Gast cleared his throat.

"Tie, ol' buddy."

Tie gripped the arms of his chair in terror. "Oh no. Don't you dare."

"Come on buddy, have a heart."

"Know your audience, Gast." Lilith suggested.

"Yeah, that's not the start of a good pitch to a Devil." Tie concurred.

"You know you're better cut out for this than,"

"No." Tie cut Gast off. "I *like* the Devilry and Demonwork. Upper management is for rubes." Tie sat back resolutely and crossed his arms like an indignant toddler. "I won't do it. I won't."

"Buddy, what is it you like about being a Devil?"

"I like the mayhem, and getting to run around with you, and getting to see meat sacks tear each other apart." Tie's face remained pouty and resolute.

Lilith approached him gently and knelt down. "Tie, you like seeing that huh?" The hulking Devil nodded warily. Pitch put his hand to his chin in fascination. "Well, you know how no other Devils are as good as you and Gast at making the meat sacks suffer?"

Tie looked pained. His head, seemingly against his own wishes, began to slowly bob up then down, until he committed to a full-fledged nod of agreement.

"Well, with you as Vice President, all Devils would answer to you in Wrath. You'd make them all better at their jobs." Lilith put her hand encouragingly on Tie's shoulder, and Pitch marveled at the hulking Devil's tightly knotted arms loosening, before he caught himself and steeled himself once more against her wiles.

"Nuh uh, you think I don't know what's happening? Gast is quitting. I know his deal. He's another immortal like you. He's trying to resign."

"Tie, you do realize I offered you the job before I tendered my resignation? I don't have anyone to submit my resignation *to* at the moment."

Tie looked thoughtful then huffed with his chin in the air at Gast. "Then I won't take the job and you can never resign."

"*Or*, you take the job and force Gast to just take a leave of absence. That way he can come back as a consultant if he ever needs the work." Lilith smiled up at Gast, which he bashfully averted his gaze from momentarily.

"That's a really good idea. That way, if I'm a consultant, you have an excuse to leave Hell to visit us without causing any stirs."

"*Us?*" Lilith stood up beside Gast as Tie watched them both in turn.

After a moment Tie's face twisted in revulsion and he waved his arms irritably to shoo them both. "Fine! Ugh, I wouldn't be able to stand those googly eyes down here anyway."

"Plus, this whole fiasco is sure to rile up the ranks a bit. You'll have some drama on your hands down here." Pitch added knowingly from behind his desk.

Tie's eyebrows twitched eagerly. "You're right. It'll be like the old days." Tie gave a final show of reluctance and finally he broke into a smile and relented. "Fine. I'll do it."

"Congrats!" Gast offered, but the end of the word was choked out as the giant Devil squeezed him in another bear hug.

When Gast was released he looked at Lilith and took her hands in his, enjoying the warmth running through his body from her touch, and the electricity tingling the back of his neck that made him want to race out right then and there with her.

"So, *us?*" She tilted her head toward him slightly.

"Yeah, you and me. Traveling and taking in the world together. I have a couple date ideas I think-"

"Whoa, slow down there. Let's not get carried away." Lilith stood back and crossed her arms daringly. Gast was flummoxed and blinked in disbelief. "You just lost your job. Let's get you into a stable situation, and we'll see about a first date."

Gast was flabbergasted. "*First* date?"

Lilith gave a stern look, as if it should be obvious. "It's been almost forty years. It's not like coming back to a movie on Netflix you stopped halfway through before you passed out."

"Lil, we're *thousands* of years old. Thirty years-"

"Is nothing compared to what's still to come."

He met her gaze and saw the hints of that wickedly wise smile he adored dance up the corners of her mouth. His chest swelled and he nodded before turning back to Tie and offering a casual salute with two fingers. "Okay Tie. It's been real. I'll submit the paperwork for your promotion. You handle the rest." Gast opened the door to the office for Lilith, and looked over his shoulder at Tie after she strolled out. "By the way, this makes us even for that little move with the chandelier and my table on Monday."

Tie shook his head in admiration of his friend and rival who he could just hear as the door closed chatting about somewhere to grab a drink to celebrate the resignation. Pitch pondered momentarily before turning in his seat to look up at Tie. "Since we're already making corporate moves, would a Vice President be able to approve an employee to hire interns for assistance with their duties?"

Tie chortled and gave a hard pat to Pitch's shoulder which made his face almost hit his desk. "What Devil needs an intern?"

"Not a Devil actually."

"That Imp with the arm coming out of his head?"

"I didn't mean him. He doesn't really need a hand." Both Devils laughed maliciously, slapping their knees in tandem. Pitch wiped a nonexistent tear from his eye. "I was thinking of someone else who helped us out."

RE-ORIENTATION DAY

Calvin had spent the morning after being offered the job waiting in Karen's office for her to arrive. It wasn't long after he'd sought the refuge that he'd heard the high pitched cackle of Felicia rolling down the hall. Calvin had been wary of her response to her termination being volatile, and the fact that it was laughter rather than outright rage was even more unsettling.

Laughter was eerie, but the next sound was outright terrifying. Calvin heard racing footsteps of Felicia speeding down the hall. Calvin saw her stop outside the office checking the cubicles first, then turning to the office and spotting him. Her eyes went wide with the thrill of her prey in sight. Calvin's breath caught in his chest and he froze, having nowhere he could possibly run, being cornered in the office.

The door to the room flew open and Felicia burst in. Calvin could hear Harry and Errol's voices calling after Felicia to come back, settle down and leave Calvin alone.

She paid their pleas no mind at all with her lunge at Calvin in the desk chair which toppled them both backwards onto the floor behind Karen's desk in a tangled heap of spinning chair legs and flailing limbs. Felicia grunted trying to plant her mouth on Calvin's and seemingly absorb his body into hers through writhing against him as he fought both her and the chair off.

Errol and Harry eventually came to Calvin's aid. The duo managed to get hands on Felicia's arms at the shoulders and, with great effort, heaved her up. Both looked in consternation at her. Errol expressed moral disgust. Harry, with old habits dying hard, was more officious and bureaucratic in his chastisement by citing employee handbook articles and California law on sexual harassment.

The two editors hauled Felicia out with her legs flying about in futility to try to get her toes into the carpet for a foothold. She shouted over her shoulder: "They can't stop us now! Facebook me!"

Calvin made a mental note to change his privacy settings on all of his social media accounts.[26] One leg tangled in the arm of the chair, the other in the base, Calvin fought to extricate himself, and looked over his knees to find Maggie, Lily and Karen all staring at him with red faces stifling laughter.

Lily had her phone out and Calvin heard the shutter sound of the camera taking a photo. Karen leaned jauntily against the door jamb and smirked down at the crumpled mass. She glanced at Lily over her shoulder. "Enjoy the photo, he's all mine."

Karen bent forward to offer her hand and help Calvin up. As she did he examined her carefully. "Lilith?"

"Nope. You're stuck with me."

Calvin's shoulders drooped in relief. "Best news I've heard in days."

He'd have kissed her if not for the audience right outside the office. He wondered if outsmarting a denizen of Hell wasn't sufficient reason for the breech of decorum, but Lily interrupted him before he could be so

---

[26] Calvin would update his Facebook, Twitter, Instagram, Snapchat, Google Hangouts and even his LinkedIn privacy settings that afternoon. However, a long forgotten Tumblr blog would be missed, which Felicia would visit in place of her estate holdings for her "nightly ritual." The Tumblr blog, being an outlet of yore for Calvin's fandom of the BBC's *Sherlock* and Marvel movies, would eventually lead Felicia to match her obsession with Calvin with an infatuation of Benedict Cumberbatch. For this though, who can blame her?

bold.

"Cal, Harry wants to see you in his office."

"Office, or cubicle?" Calvin was unsure if Felicia's termination meant her old office was Harry's.

Lily nodded in concordance. "He says cubicle. The office won't be his until the necessary paperwork is filed and logged regarding his transition of duties, title, and official assignment of the office," Lily waved a hand irritably at herself for reading through the length of H.R. jargon Harry had apparently clarified in the message to her. "His cubicle."

Calvin promised Karen he'd find her as soon as he was done. More so than earlier that week, he felt celebratory drinks were in order.

On the opposite end of the office, Calvin took the open chair in Harry's cubicle. He was another in a long line of Felicia's targets to sit there, but the first among them to be happy doing so. Calvin was wary still for one simple reason, the H.R. Director's immediate turn of the meeting with Sam to being transferred to Felicia's vacated post.

"Cal, while this is premature what with the paperwork still pending official processing, I'd like to welcome you to my section as our new staff writer." Harry extended a hand with a warm smile.

Calvin took it, but still sat stiffly upright. He wondered if he could determine what deal Harry had with a supernatural being. The Director looked at a pile of papers on the desk beside him wistfully. Harry was proud that after years in the purgatory of Human Resources, he had finally found his way back to the Shangri-La just a lateral office position away.

Of course, Calvin didn't know any of this, and after the past two days of the world revealing its previously unseen layers and unseen spaces of nefarious denizens (supernatural and ephemeral alike), he saw more fang in the glimmer of Harry's smirk than the soon-to-be editor could ever have intended.

"Well, Cal, I think we can at least have a quick chat about working together."

"Yes."

"I have my ideas as Editor for the section, but obviously I'm a few years out of the thick of the editing game, so I really want to hear your ideas, especially after the one-two punch you pulled off with those pieces on the Via Fresca."

"Of course."

"You found some pretty interesting angles in restaurant stories. I think there's something there. They're more than restaurants. They're the result of someone's passion and the owners and chefs bring their stories to the menu, so to speak."

"Agreed." Calvin's expression and tone remained flat despite Harry's increasingly conscious attempts to chuckle airily in vain attempts to get Calvin to relax. Harry finally looked taken aback at his soon-to-be protégé's reticence.

"Cal, listen, I know Felicia was a very laissez faire editor. If you want that kind of freedom to explore your voice and style, that's fine. I'm not trying to be a micromanager here. I'm only hoping we can work together on a voice here."

"Right."

"I was already excited to be getting back to the journalism side, but getting back to work alongside a writer with your moxie and drive is like a dream come true."

Harry's eyes dropped slightly and glazed over in a moment of self-reflection. Calvin was intrigued by the choice of words and finally lowered his guard in order to ask, "Get back?"

"I know, it feels like ages since I got sidetracked into Human Resources. I started out as a writer too. Guess I was so focused on protecting my job I didn't do a great job protecting my career."

"So, you had a job all these years in H.R. when you wanted to be a writer?"

"And now I have this chance." Harry clasped his hands in reverent gratitude. "It's thanks to you, of course. Not just the turn of events, but seeing you fight the good fight when Sam was about to go with Matt?" Harry sat back and offered a gale of admiring laughter. "Made me think *I've* still got some fight in me. I do still love the gig after all."

"You love writing and let yourself get sidetracked into H.R. for how long?"

"Eight years."

"Wow."

"Hey, it's *really* easy to make small excuses day after day until days add up to years. I finally got tired of making and taking excuses thanks to seeing a writer who refuses to make or take them himself." Harry leaned forward and patted Calvin's shoulder in paternal encouragement. "So, I'm excited to work *with* you and make a great section with you."

Calvin's shoulder felt tingly where Harry's hand had clapped him. Maybe Hell wasn't the only group out there with fire that could accomplish things after all. He'd have to let Lilith know she was right, but then again, he was sure she didn't need the validation from him.

"Well." Calvin searched his mind. "I think you're right about what you said."

Harry's brows raised and his eyes twinkled in bubbling

thrill. "Oh?"

"That our section should shift to being about the *restaurants* rather than just the food. What's the story that led to the menu? To the space itself? To the chef? Los Angeles is a diverse city, with so many of these stories."

Harry clapped his hands together eagerly. "Let's find them!"

"I'm on board, boss."

FAME MONSTER

"Sittin' on the dock o' the ba-aaaaa-ay!"

"Shut up!"

"I've been sittin' on the dock o' the ba-aaaay!"

"You're singing the wrong melody!"

"Yeah! That's a Lady Gaga!"

"Watchin' the ships roll in!"

"How dare you sully Gaga's heavenly melodies!" That was the last thing Matt heard before a volleyball biffed him right in the temple, sending him off the sea wall he had perched on to croon with a bottle of wine in a tightly wrapped paper bag. The bottle emptied most of its contents into the sand while Matt lay clutching it while wincing in pain with the laughter of the players he had been musically affronting fading away in the distance.

There was a light crunching of someone treading over the sand to where Matt was. Craig Anderson stood over him and grinned. "Sounds to me, friend, like you're having a rough day."

"You ever think you've got something guaranteed to go your way, only to find you're not only being screwed over, but also realize how dumb you are for thinking signing a deal with a Devil could do anything but ruin your life?"

"Contract dispute? You're lucky I found you then, kid." Craig pulled a business card out of his jacket pocket. With a flick of his fingers, he tossed the card onto Matt's chest. "It just so happens, that I have an opening in my case docket. A contract dispute could be fun. Especially if it's one for the little guy against some greedy magnate."

"Well, it's against a literal Devil."

Craig extended a hand which Matt took, and the sharply dressed lawyer pulled him up. Matt would have questioned what the attorney was doing on Santa Monica beach at midday in a three piece suit, but then again he was wearing a Russian ushanka, a full length wool duster and high heel combat boots. It was a startling change from the yellow duck inner tube and American flag g-string he'd had on before being knocked from his perch.

Craig didn't seem to notice the supernatural costume change, or if he did, made nothing of it. "Well, good news is when you've got the right guy on your side, you can fight fire with fire, even if that fire is *the devil.*"

Matt examined the card again and looked flatly at the lawyer. "Not *the* devil, *a* Devil. I signed a contract with one to be a famous writer and he stiffed me on the deal, then *another* devil- again, not *the* devil- took over the deal and told me things would work out. I just got an email saying I lost my job with the *LA Weekly,* and haven't heard from either devil since yesterday."

Craig exhaled forcibly, squinting at Matt and stuffing his hands in his pockets. "So, you literally signed a deal with a denizen of Hell?"

Matt rolled his eyes in ready exasperation. "Yes. I'm crazy. I'm some kind of vagrant just rambling mad." Matt waited for an insult, or for Craig to take off running in terror.

Instead the lawyer giggled. "Hey, a contract is a contract. Sounds like you've got a case to me."

Matt blinked thrice, stunned. "You're saying,"

"-I'll take on the case." Craig put his arm around Matt's heavily cloaked shoulder and began leading them toward a bar on the strand. "Might be a conflict of interest for a lawyer to take on a Devil, but we'll figure that out I guess. Come on, let's talk over some mai tais."

Matt trudged over the sand pulled by Craig's easy acceptance. "I like mai tais."

"Who doesn't? See, I knew you were a good kid. Shame how good kids like you are always being taken advantage of in this town. Cryin' shame. I tell ya."

INTERVIEWS ARE AWKWARD EVERYWHERE

"So, tell me girls. I understand this internship might just be a stepping stone on the way to where you want to go next, but I'd really like to know where you see that next step being. Tell me, where do you see yourselves in five or ten years?"

The computer and all its monitors were afire behind Eurydice. For a change, however, she was unconcerned with them. While her interviewees traded glances with one another, Eurydice allowed herself to reflectively swoon once more.

She had been visited by Pitch a second time in as many days when he came to deliver the good news. Tie, as the new Vice President of Wrath, had granted her the latitude to hire interns to assist in her work- by way of gratitude, Pitch had added with a wink.

She recalled how the buzzing and screeching alerts of requests from her computers had never sounded so melodious as when they were backdrop to his wink which she indulged replaying mentally several times while waiting for an answer from her applicants. Pitch had somehow even increased her joy with his departing remark: "Now that you'll have some free time, maybe you can enjoy an actual dinner out of the office once in awhile."

Enjoy! Dinner! Two spectacular words for the fantastic possibilities they carried spoken by her Pitch! She hoped with a cutesy wiggle in her chair and a sweet smile that he meant enjoying dinner with him. Or on him. Or of him. Whichever it was would be divine, but first the interview.

"Well, I guess we just want to get back into writing." Natalie replied finally.

Natalee nodded with wide eyed fervor. "Yes. We really appreciate everything Lucinda did for us in Lechery, but it's not for us."

Eurydice looked from one Nat to the other in turn, waiting for them to actually answer her question. She had been offered the referral of the plucky interns Lucinda was, "finding difficult to motivate." However, seeing the pair had experience in Fashion writing for the *LA Weekly*, Eurydice jumped at the opportunity to interview them for a transfer.

Neither girl aspired to answer Eurydice's actual question. She assured herself that it was a matter of humanity's natural tendency to look backward when they should be looking forward.[27] "Well, I'm glad to hear that you two are motivated to get back to writing, and are taking steps to get there."

---

[27] Just as much as it is humanity's tendency is to look forward when there are lessons to be learned by looking back.

The Nats both muttered barely audible agreements. Eurydice reminded herself that their most recent job had, quite literally, been hell. Neither deigned to speak, so Eurydice took the cue and continued. "What do you know about the position?"

The Nats regarded each other and communicated with the barest of eye movements. Eurydice admired it, since by appearance it might be fair to think that the two were twins. In fact, their resumes revealed that Natalie was from Michigan, Natalee a Beverly Hills native. They had met in their second year at USC rushing the same sorority.

Eurydice decided to take the reins and provide them some information. "I am Eurydice, one of the muses you may know from the pantheon of Greek *myth*." Eurydice punctuated the last word with air quotes. "My sisters and I are responsible for some of the greatest ages of art, poetry, and reason that human civilization has achieved. We worked passionately through the classical age, the rise of the Republic in Rome, to the Renaissance and age of enlightenment. As a Hell's Muse, I bring those talents for producing prose and written accounts of human history and action to service of Hell's deals with artists."

"Wait, so you're responsible for like, that painting of the lady on the seashell?"

"The Birth of Venus."

"Wait, that's her name? Is that where the planet gets its name?"

"No, she's named after the planet."

"That's not very flattering for her."

"She was a little chubby though."

"Yeah, but not *fat*."

"I'm sure a guy was responsible for painting that."

"Oh of course." Natalie concluded. The girls nodded

officiously at one another and looked back to Eurydice. To their surprise, Eurydice smiled warmly.

"The planet is named for *her*, girls. That was the work of one of my sisters. My work is more linguistic. Martin Luther's reform of the Catholic church?"

"Wait, the guy who rode on the back of the bus? That was about the Catholic church?"

"No silly, that was Rosa Parks. Remember? Outkast had a song about her."

"Oh, right. Okay, my bad. Sorry."

Eurydice giggled at the pair. "Anyway, I work here now, producing work for the people Hell has deals with, and I could really use a hand. I do want to help you both grow into future careers, but I'm also excited to help inspire you to what you want those next steps to be."

Eurydice beamed at the Nats and the pair traded pitiful looks, which betrayed their vulnerability finally. "That's the best promise we've heard."

"Yeah, not like our last job." Natalee rolled her eyes to correct herself. "Well, the *LA Weekly*, I mean. This girl we knew there, she was *so* sure of what she wanted to do and be."

"Yeah, Karen was like, unreal."

"And it made her work so hard."

"Yeah, I think we want that."

"It makes sense when you say it."

"We have to be inspired to want something."

"And starting with telling stories is a good place for us."

"We both love writing."

"*Love* it."

"I think working with Lucinda reminded us of that."

"Totally. We got hyped up on the rewards of hard work."

"When the right work is its own reward."

"You sound like a total dork."

"Shut up, so do you."

The girls devolved to giggles at one another. Eurydice admired them for a moment then glanced over her shoulder at the computer. With a shake of her head, she looked earnestly at the pair. "Well, it won't be easy, but since it's Hell sponsored, the pay and benefits will be good."

"Benefits? Oh my God, are we getting health coverage?"

Eurydice scoffed with a snort and wave of her hand. "Hell is one hundred percent Republican. Good luck. No, the pay will be good, and as for benefits, once you do figure out what you want next, I should be able to help you get there."

"Are you like, in a sorority network?"

"With your sisters?"

"What is the Muses sorority name? Alpha Omega?"

Eurydice shook her head and spoke quickly to interject on this building ramble of the Nats. "We actually just use the delta symbol. But, yes, you are right. My other sisters are in different lines of work around the world and in different dimensions, so we can help pretty effectively with wherever you eventually want to go."

The Nat's eyes' went wide in unison. Natalie clasped her hands together over her mouth, Natalee clapped them in quick succession at the thrill of such a breadth of possibilities. Eurydice stilled them with a single finger in the air. "You have to *earn* it first."

The girls bubbled eagerly to accept, which Eurydice agreed with and sent a message to a Sloth Imp in Human Resources to begin paperwork for the girls' to start.[28]

After hands had been shaken, Eurydice's eyes narrowed and she pointed at one keyboard, then another: "There's yours, and there's yours. Get to work. This interview taking this long means we'll already be working overtime. Since we went over, your next break time isn't for four hours. This counts as your lunch break."

THE MICE OF MEN

Maury and Claudio trudged down the elm shaded avenue of California boulevard in Pasadena. After the close brush with the T-Man, they were resolute that Los Angeles West of the 110 had some bad mojo they would do well to stay away from.

The two had fled to Toddy's apartment to sterilize the place of their fingerprints, and found a security box with a hundred thirty thousand dollars of cash. Toddy been telling the truth when he said the brewing business was a lucrative one. Claudio had quickly surmised that this only proved how screwed Benny was. If the kid was really making that kind of money, Benny owed the IRS a more than significant cut.

It hadn't stopped them from taking the metal box and its holdings. By Claudio's estimation, leaving it there wouldn't do Benny any good. Claudio now walked with the case under an arm while they continued aimlessly down the avenue.

When they happened on an empty storefront, Maury stopped and surveyed it. The store had been abandoned

---

[28] The Imp, being of Sloth, would get started on their hiring documents approximately a year later when the request would be sent by Eurydice for their resignation processing.

by a previous leasee and had a sign taped to the inside of the window advertising the number to call for interested renters. Claudio stopped walking and was about to ask Maury what the deal was when Maury muttered. "Used to be a pet shop."

Claudio looked. Behind the window were the telltale partitioned pens for puppies and kittens to be on display for passersby. Inside, Claudio could see a larger circular pen area he deduced was for people to play with potential new pets, past that inside were shelves and a cashier's desk. It wasn't hard to imagine the shelves lined with pet supplies or envision the rear where aquariums and fish were likely once on display.

"That's too bad. I'd love to see a lil' pup right now."

"A doggo would be bueno right now." Maury concurred sadly at the desolate space.

Claudio looked at the tin under his arm and snapped his fingers. "Hey, remember what Sally said about using a business to be a front?"

"Yeah, it's common sense."

Claudio extended his hand at the empty space. "Well, here you go! We've got the capital! Why don't we start up our own front and do it right?"

"You know who would know a lot about this?" Maury pulled out his phone and began typing out a message instantly with his meaty paws. "Llewyn."

Claudio was bouncing with excitement and envisioning the shop reopened for business. "Yes! He'd be perfect! He'd know how to get this cash put into the start up without attracting the wrong attention."

Maury hit send on the message and looked in the space beside Claudio. "Yeah. Plus, maybe instead of buying puppy mill dogs to sell, we can hook up with shelters to help animals get rescued."

"Rescue animals for sure. Poor strays."

"So we'll mostly need to buy the other merchandise and animals."

"Yeah, aquariums, fish, reptiles."

"Oh, can we get rabbits and hamsters?"

"Of course, buddy. And I'll even let you feed 'em and play with 'em all you want."

Maury's phone made a "wahoo!" sound indicating Llewyn had replied. Maury read the message and confirmed: "Llewyn's in!"

Claudio clapped Maury on the back then began typing in the number to call about renting out the space. "It's a great idea. Who wouldn't want to work with cute animals?"

"Yeah, he's fed up with the church it sounds like." Maury read out: "At least cleaning up after animals makes sense: they don't know any better. I'm in, he said."

"Yeah, this'll be great. The three of us'll run it and be our own bosses."

The pair began walking down the avenue again with a distinct bounce in their steps from the new idea. Maury checked his phone. "Llewyn says it'll make a great front, since he's never heard of mobsters using pet shops."

Maury and Claudio looked at each other when they stopped at the corner waiting for the light. Claudio averted his gaze and cleared his throat sheepishly. "I guess it *could* be a front, if we wanted it to be. Yeah. We'll have that option. In our back pockets at least."

"Yeah, down the line once it's up and running."

"Of course. For now we need to get it looking legit."

"Bingo. Let's take it one step at a time." Maury nudged Claudio with his elbow and winked. The light changed for the duo to cross the avenue, resuming their aimless stroll. Maury received another text message and was typing his response to Llewyn with his tongue poking out the corner of his mouth. "Sure hope Llewyn is okay with it just being a pet shop. You know, for a little while, anyway."

JUST DESSERTS

Calvin and Karen walked up the street to the restaurant with the large tomato sign, holding hands. "So, after a week like this, doesn't it feel like we can handle anything that comes our way?" Karen rested her head on Calvin's shoulder and smiled up at him as they walked.

Calvin considered it, agreeing with a hum at first, but then realized, "Karen, it's only Wednesday."

Karen stopped walking. "My God."

"I know." Calvin concurred and urged with a tilt of his head for them to continue.

They reached the Fresca and entered. Only one table was in use: the large table at the heart of the room, where two occupants were seated, Lilith and Gast. Karen and Calvin took seats opposite them, and both reporters noticed the body language between the two of them was significantly warmer than the day before. Lilith leaned slightly towards Gast, and even more so when she turned in the seat to the kitchen door that swung open. Gast, Calvin noticed, leaned slightly closer to her as well.

Sally and Tessa came giggling from the kitchen together and greeted the quartet excitedly. Both were carrying plates of food Sally had whipped up that afternoon once the IRS and cops had left with Benny and taken their statements from him.

Lilith had explained to Tessa after Sally left for the Fresca that she needed Sally to be in the dark about what would happen at the Fresca with the IRS and the police, and that the police presence was why Tessa needed to be out of sight. As an assassin, Tessa's lack of public records and government identification would have proven problematic.

The pair set the plates before the group and took seats opposite one another at the end of the table. Karen tried one of the stuffed mushrooms, and moaned as she chewed. She spoke ecstatically through the mouthful, "Oh my God, so lucky that this restaurant isn't going anywhere."

Sally bobbed his head nervously. "Actually, the Fresca *is* going out of business."

Karen turned to Lilith for confirmation since the plan had come with assurances that Calvin would end up with a job and Sally with his restaurant.

Tessa laughed and cuffed Sally affably. "You drama queen. He means the Fresca is closing because Benny is going to jail. Benny owned the Fresca as a company. The property itself is his, so he's opening his own restaurant in its place."

Sally chuckled proudly, while Calvin nodded in admiration. "Geez, this is some prime real estate. All I got was a staff writer position, even *though* an editorial position was open." Calvin shot a facetious look at Lilith but then shrugged and bobbed his hands like a scale weighing options. "Considering I'm alive and don't have Hell after me anymore? I'm happy with the results though."

Karen laughed along with Calvin and added the other victory to the list. "Not to mention the reign of the office succubus has ended."

Calvin spoke in the flat tone of traumatized relief. "Ding dong, the witch is dead."

"Which old witch?" Sally asked.

Tessa, Lilith and Karen all sang the refrain in unison. "The wicked witch!"

"You can thank one of our other friends for that. She had Hell's protection to keep whatever job she wants, so the only way we could get her to accept the termination and actually be kept out was because Pitch set her up with a gig more to her liking."

"Pitch?" Calvin asked.

Lilith leaned forward to inform Calvin, since Sally and Tessa had already heard about him. "Another Devil. Friend of ours from the Avarice circle. Pretty big deal. He's been offered the VP position to run Greed a few times. Always turns it down."

Gast chewed and swallowed a bite of garlic bread. "Says he needs to have something to aspire to so he can stay good at the Greed game."

"Sounds about right if I understand the Devil thing at all." Sally sat back with his arms crossed, enjoying the scene of newfound friends enjoying peace over food he'd made for them.

"What's the job Felicia took?" Karen asked.

"Pitch got her a position helping out our Muse, Eurydice." Gast replied.

Lilith nudged Gast with a mischievous smile. "Tell them about the Nats." When Gast looked at Lilith she scrunched her nose adorably and Gast chuckled.

"Those girls, Natalee and Nathalie? They took jobs as her interns but Eurydice forgot humans need to, you know, eat and sleep?" Gast reiterated the point by helping himself to another mouthful of food.

"So, you added Felicia to the team?" Calvin checked, while pouring himself a glass of the white blend he'd watched Sally drink the day before.

Gast winced and took his time choosing his words

carefully. "She's handling the more… erotic of the assignments, but yes. She's enjoying it from what I understand." There was a collective shudder between Karen and Calvin which Sally and Tessa shared a hearty laugh at.

Lilith elbowed Gast who paused from helping himself to more food and adopted a more serious demeanor. "There's still a problem, though."

Calvin looked around the table and counted off mentally: Benny, Felicia, his job, Hell. "Oh no, is that boss of yours coming after me? Will he possess me? Should I be wearing a cross?"

Gast put his hands up and made a gentle shushing sound to calm Calvin's mounting horror. When Calvin eased back into his seat, Gast explained. "No, it's Tie, the big guy?" Calvin nodded in confirmation that he remembered the giant Devil. He almost wanted to ask Gast how anyone could possibly forget the giant. "With Aba deposed, my buddy's the new Vice President of Wrath."

"Wow, congrats. Good news all around." Karen narrowed her gaze curiously. "I don't see the problem. He was adorable."

"I'll remember to tell him you said that." Gast winked teasingly at Karen. "Tie inherited Aba's seat and responsibilities. Among them is an outstanding contract with one Matthew Reade."

Calvin and Karen exchanged grave looks, and Calvin held his breath for a few tense seconds before he finally asked, "I don't have to give him my job, do I? Was this all to help you deal with *your* boss being an asshole?"

Lilith looked at Calvin with eyes full of patience and sympathy. "No Calvin, we don't want that, but we would like your help getting Matt back on track. He's got a lawyer helping him, and the contract is very clearly in default. We just need a recommendation to help him. As far away as you want him, but we would love an idea."

"An idea…" Calvin ruminated quietly, his eyes glazing over while he looked over the food filling the table. "Wait, your Muse can write *any* story, right?"

Gast nodded through a mouthful of hummus, swallowed, and then spoke. "If it actually happened or if you give us the idea, sure. She can deliver on commission, but she can't conceive from scratch." Gast leaned forward slowly with hungry intrigue twinkling in his eyes. "You have an idea?"

Calvin looked at Karen first, then back at Lilith and Gast. "Give him *this* story." Gast didn't catch the meaning at first. Calvin pointed at Sally, Tessa, Gast, Lilith and Karen all in turn."This whole thing. The restaurant, assassins, Devils, Lilith, Karen, Matt, me, you-give him this whole crazy escapade. Make him famous with *this* story." Calvin waved his hands in exasperation at the whole thing trying to shoo it all away like a bad stench to Gast's side of the table.

"I'll send word down to Tie." Gast grinned and extended a hand to Calvin. They shook then helped themselves to more food.

Karen looked at Gast in mild surprise. "So if Tie became the new VP, what about you?"

Gast looked at Lilith. Their eyes met and held each other's gaze as smiles crept up like blossoming flowers. They giggled together and bumped foreheads affectionately before Gast turned back to Karen. "I tendered my resignation."

"Devils can do that?" Tessa asked.

"Well, like Lilith, I never *died* either, and thus never really got *sent* to Hell. I just ended up there for something to do to pass the time until the end of time."

Calvin was unsure of what else to say but was sure that someone should say something. "So, you decided to move on from Devilry?"

"Yeah. Lilith coming back and this whole fiasco just proved that working for the sake of work is no way to approach eternity, so I'm going to find something more worthwhile to dedicate my talents to." He put his hand over hers. "With her."

"If you mean you're taking up golfing, it sounds like retirement," Sally quipped.

Lilith bobbed her head turning it over. "More like reality."

Calvin blew a heavy breath at the depth of the exchanges. "Sounds daunting either way."

Gast scooped a hearty amount of hummus into his mouth with a slice of pita bread. "That's eternity for you. It's a big thing. Good idea to find a worthwhile way to spend it."

Calvin laughed. "Finally, someone who understands my constant anxiety."

AT LAST

The Lounge sits on Selma Avenue, a relatively quiet thoroughfare right between the Hollywood and Sunset strips. It is small, compared to other evening spots in the neighborhood, barely a thousand square feet. It's all tables, lit only by the candlelight from the centerpieces which flicker over the washed red brick walls.

Adornments are minimal. A framed black and white photograph hangs over each table that most patrons barely notice in the dim which can change to depict scenes of times throughout history- even times before the human invention of the camera.

In a resplendent white tuxedo that shines even brighter than the focused spotlight should allow, Lucifer sits at a polished and gleaming black grand piano. His fingers dance over the keys in a little improvisational preamble to the first number of the night.

The tables are all filled, and the attendees are all silent, fixated on the stage. No one is sure why, or even entirely aware that it happens, but upon being seated for the night's entertainment, none speak- nor do they want to. They are fixated on the pianist shining at the head of the room. He is the sole focus, until his accompanist strolls onto the stage and hops onto the piano.

As if this were his cue, the lilting jazzy tune Lucifer had been caressing from the piano tightens and focuses. The first song of the night begins. Aba looks out at the meat sacks, reviling them and his place as entertainer to them. However, seeing his Lord Lucifer, enjoying their place as the focus and subject of the meat sacks' admiration for this moment, he resolves to continue and to perform as they agreed.

Lucifer had been favorable to Aba's suggestion of them opening their own lounge rather than wandering through the pig pens the meat sacks created. Lucifer had even allowed Aba to decorate the lounge in a way that he could feel comfortable.

Lucifer had only requested the spotlight for them on the stage, which Aba had not liked the sound of. Had he gotten his way, they'd have been swimming in the darkness like the rest of the attendees, the way Aba preferred having been for ages and eons. However, Aba admitted that Lucifer was right. The spotlight gave them both what they had wanted all those ages: they were the center of attention here.

The keys reached their cue, and Aba nodded gravely at Lucifer in acceptance of his new mission. The former head of Wrath among Hell's Fallen raised the microphone and, in a voice as silky as his usual tones were dour, he began to croon to the crowd, for the first night of many:

"At last, my love has come along, my lonely days are over, and life is like a song."

The End

ABOUT THE AUTHOR

Yennaedo Balloo lives in Los Angeles, CA where he crusades in vain to receive his due credit as the inventor of the semi-colon. He has authored another novel, *Beneath the Wood*, and is at work on more. He continues to be disappointed by the current administration's handling of the *Superman* film franchise, and looks forward to the day when science can prove that he doesn't actually exist.

Yennaedo blogs about writing and other musings at: optionalirony.com and tweets through @optional_irony

Made in the USA
San Bernardino, CA
29 June 2017